BOOK 3

DRIFTWOOD DREARY

LILLAH LAWSON

Midnight Tide
PUBLISHING

For Beth, Phillip Deville's biggest fan—after Stormy Spooner,
of course.

PROLOGUE

The little bell tinkled, and a girl walked in, probably no older than nineteen, huddled in a huge blue coat that seemed to dwarf her. It was a nineties relic, the coat; corduroy and slate-blue with an off-white fleece-lined hood that the woman at the booth, busily sweeping up hair, recognized immediately as a catalogue item from the original Delia's. The woman's best friend had once had that exact same coat, in the exact same color. She felt a pang at the memory, a pang that quickly turned to anger.

The girl approached the counter and hovered there. The hood that had covered her dark-brown hair slipped a little and exposed her face, which was far too beautiful and made-up for the type of client who came into a small-town salon, and for her to be wearing such a coat…

The woman swept the fresh-cut hair into a dustpan and sauntered over, forcing her cheeks into a bright smile, her customers-only smile. "Hi, welcome to the Curling Dervish. How can I help you today? Looking for a cut, a color, just a trim …?"

"None of the above," the girl said with an equally fake

smile. It didn't quite reach her eyes, and she stepped a little closer, lowering her voice just as a tad. "I'm here for … for the makeup."

"Oh! Great! Are you looking for a full makeover, a certain look for an event or …?" the woman responded, her voice a little louder than necessary. "I can do certain looks for events like prom, homecoming, weddings, photo shoots … some cosplay stuff. I'm just getting started, so I don't really have a portfolio, but if you tell me what you're looking for, I'm sure we can—"

"The other," the girl interrupted, her voice going lower still. It was actually irritating, the woman thought, the way she was trying to make herself disappear. Far more conspicuous than just being … you know, normal. "I just want to buy the …"

"I see," she responded brightly, cutting the girl off and reaching for a business card. "You want a tutorial!"

The girl's brow furrowed. "No, I—"

"Generally, with those, I give you a brief rundown on how to do a certain look yourself, and then you can buy any of the products you like at wholesale. Just tell me what type of event you're prepping for, and we'll go from there."

"Cinderella," the girl said, her voice little more than a whisper now.

"Excuse me?"

"Cinderella."

The woman slow blinked and put the business card back down. "Gotcha." She glanced around the shop, then said, "Follow me. Let's go sit down in the back and talk about your look." The girl was supposed to say *Cinderella's Ball,* but the woman could tell just from looking at her that the girl had forgotten most of the protocol either from nerves or outright terror, but it didn't really matter which. She was certain the girl was on the up and up, one of the sudden influx of clients she was getting by word of mouth. Despite her confidence in her abilities, the woman was surprised at how fast the word had traveled and how many people wanted her services. As much as she hated social media, she had to admit the cursed clock app had propelled her into the stratosphere. She smiled to herself, leading the way to the back room. She was finally getting somewhere. After all those years of scraping to get by, there was nowhere to go but up.

The girl was shaking under that heavy coat as the woman directed her to sit down beside the ancient hairdryer that only little old ladies asked for. Despite the girl's expertly applied face and striking physical beauty, she was shrinking into herself, as if trying her very best to become invisible. It wasn't unusual; many people, much older and much less innocent than her, started to get cold feet once they got back here.

"Okay. So. You're prepping for a Cinderella ball," the woman said, reaching into the locked shelf behind her for a small leather makeup case. "You'll want something a little dreamy, a little romantic, but still understated. Simple and elegant; just a little innocent. Sound about right?"

"Sure." The girl was staring down at her feet. She wasn't even looking at the products.

"What color is your gown?"

The girl seemed to dig into her memory to produce an answer. "It's pink," she said as she looked up, her voice getting a little stronger. "Rose pink."

"Oh, beautiful," the woman answered, rummaging in her case. "How about something pastel, soft, with a brown-black eyeliner to bring out your eyes and make that pink pop?" She met the girl's eyes, which wasn't easy, because she was downright shifty. "No doubt you want to knock your date's socks off, but we don't want to go too heavy. Is your guy the debonair Prince Charming type? Or more of a sly fox?"

"A little bit of both," the girl said, her cheeks flushing. "Depending on who he's with."

"Gotcha. So a look that's subtle but still dramatic. Just the perfect blend of soft romance that packs a punch where it counts." She produced a tiny palette and held it up triumphantly. "I've got just the thing you need. This palette has several pastel shades that go on super creamy and have just a hint of sparkle, but don't worry—it won't leave traces of glitter all over your cheeks; it stays put. You won't detect it anywhere else, you know what I mean?"

"Yes." The girl's eyes shone with tears.

"This'll be *so* gorgeous. Let me show you how to apply it, and then we'll wrap it up and get you out of here." The woman stood and turned the girl's chair around so she could see herself in the mirror. She leaned down close to her ear, close enough to touch, and whispered, "This look is going to be so totally killer."

"Totally," the girl whispered back, her eyes wide and bright.

Sloan opened the palette with a smile, a genuine one this time.

ONE

I'd imagined myself stuck in a hotel room plenty of times, on some high-up, swanky floor, ensconced in a plush bathrobe and holed up with Phillip Deville, rockstar of my dreams. My brain had gone crazy with scenarios over the years, long before I'd ever laid eyes on him in the flesh, much less reached out to touch that flesh.

However, not one of those times had I fantasized about *this*.

I was indeed holed up in a swanky hotel with Phillip Deville, high above ground level with a great view. And not only was I clad in nothing but the aforementioned bathrobe, but he was clad in one of his own, a fact that I found very distracting. Phillip's robe had clearly been made with a much smaller man in mind. The soft white terry cloth barely reached his knees, leaving his strong, muscular calves exposed, and his large arms were threatening to bust through the sleeves' seams, the luxurious material exposing more of his chest and shoulders than it wasn't. Even from my vantage point at the window, I could see a small patch of Phillip's black chest hair tufting out, a dark contrast against the flushed pink skin beneath. I caught myself licking my lips, LL Cool J style, and shook my head to clear it, admonishing myself for being such a horndog. Now wasn't the time to jump Phillip's bones. —I'd already done that plenty of times since we'd been here, and there were more important things to contend with. Much more important things. Life or death things.

But he just looked so *hot*.

I wished I could claim credit for Phillip's current state of undress and for the pink flush on his chest and face, but alas. It was more duress and upset than it was any type of carnal pleasure, much to my eternal regret.

It hadn't all been duress, though. My lover—Phillip Deville, *the* Phillip Deville–and I had been holed up at the hotel for a little over twenty-four hours, and so far, we hadn't emerged even for food, much less to take advantage of the amenities. I'd always loved a good hotel–even the cheap ones feel like a vacation– so it was killing me not to be able to try out the pool or order room service, but we couldn't allow any possible risk of being seen by the public. Besides, I told myself as I stared longingly at the menu and its fancy, over-priced cocktails, I'd already stayed here once and their room service wasn't *that* great.

That had been with my newfound friend Roberta, and things had been stressful then too. It felt like a lifetime ago, and yet, it had only been a week. Story of my life. So much had happened in the past three weeks that I felt like my own timeline was skewed and confusing, and the hits kept coming, yep, they kept on coming. I was losing my sanity piece by piece, so much so that I was internally singing shitty Smash Mouth songs while stealing covert eyefuls of my lover as he brooded.

I snuck one last greedy glance at Phillip's strong thighs as he sat perched on the bed, doing his best to pull the white robe across his lap so it gave him some semblance of modesty. He knew I was looking; Phillip knew (and heard) my every thought. I averted my eyes dutifully (though all I really wanted to do was rip the robe off him and run my tongue up and down those thighs), and asked him quietly, "Are you okay?"

"I'm fine," Phillip answered. As I turned to look at him, he smiled, a movement that was even more automatic, and completely perfunctory. The smile didn't reach his beautiful, wild green eyes at all, and he barely looked my way as he said it. Those eyes were unfocused, totally lost in thought, and more than a little worried. I hated seeing him like this.

"No, you're not," I said, moving from the window to sit by him on the bed. "You're anxious. Upset."

"A little, I guess," Phillip admitted, taking my hand in his larger one. "But let's not talk about my stuff now. Let's talk about your dad. After all, that's the more pressing, more important issue."

I started to argue but thought better of it. Phillip didn't like to dwell on his own problems; he'd rather help someone else solve theirs. While he was altruistic and genuinely liked to help people, I now knew Phillip Deville well enough to know that it was somewhat selfish on his part too. If he could focus on someone else's problems, he didn't have to deal with his own.

My beautiful, hulking rock star had been running from his own shadow ever since he accidentally made it too big and it overcame him.

Until now.

Now, it looked as though the roosters might finally be coming home to roost.

"I haven't heard anything else from Mama," I answered, enjoying the feel of my hand in his. I intertwined my fingers with his, applying gentle, firm pressure to his knuckles one by one. He sighed and closed his eyes. "I'm hoping she'll call me soon, but until then … I mean, it's not like I can go down there."

"Why not?"

"Phillip, we've been hiding in this hotel room for the past day, trying to avoid those assholes down there. How would you propose we get out of the hotel and on a flight to Florida—or even back to the house to get my truck—without being seen?"

"If you need to go, we'll go," Phillip said firmly, his dark-green eyes serious. "If they see us, they see us. I'm not going to let you sacrifice your needs—your family, your responsibilities—for me." One thing I'd learned very quickly about Phillip Deville, as I'd tried to keep him hidden these past few weeks, was that it was not in his nature to be hidden. That old rock star was still within him, dying for the limelight, no matter how much he tried to deny it. Cowering in a hotel room, hiding from reporters, was pretty much his worst nightmare.

"Well, if it comes to that, I could just go by myself—"

"No, I'm coming with you." Phillip's voice was firm. "I'm not letting you handle this alone like you did last time." His voice got softer, and he pulled me close. "I'm not losing you again."

"You didn't lose me the first time," I said, nuzzling into him, relishing a small moment of quiet to just breathe him in. He was still damp from a recent shower, still smelling of his usual musky sandalwood, but without the trace of cigarette smoke that always followed him. Bless his heart, he'd been trying to quit, and I loved him for it. He hadn't told me outright, but I'd seen the packs of Nicorette sticking out of his duffel bag, and I'd noticed the usual stale-smoke smell that came from his hands as he touched me was gone. And he had been touching me *a lot.* I thought back to before the shower, the activities that had left us sweaty and out of breath, and felt a pleasurable thrum start in my extremities.

Phillip had been worried, yes, but not too worried to not ravish me a few times since we'd been here, a fact for which I was very grateful…and very satisfied.

"Close enough," Phillip said, his voice low and crooning in my ear. "Close enough to know I don't want to go through it again. I love you."

"I love you too," I said, turning my head to face him. He planted a kiss gently on my lips, his mouth lingering for a moment on mine, then he nipped at my bottom lip with his sharp, white teeth. His arm drifted from my shoulder down the length of my robe, finding the tie that cinched around my waist with ease, pulling it, loosening it. I smiled against his mouth. *Finally.*

His kiss deepened, and I let my hand trail up his own robe, finding where it gapped near his leg, and inched my hand inward to touch his warm, damp skin. He let out a groan, and I squeezed his thigh as he kissed me harder, rougher…

The knock on the door was so quiet we almost didn't hear it in our mad frenzy. We stopped for a moment, both breathing hard, staring into each other's eyes, Phillip's expression a perfect marriage of annoyance and alarm, my own face no doubt mirroring his. Had we just imagined it? We'd been on edge for hours; it was certainly possible. Phillip's hand hovered over my waistline for a moment, suspended in the space just over my stomach, as though he was afraid to move, afraid to touch me. After another moment, he smiled and resumed his caress, his mouth inching closer to mine, ready to continue the blissful thing we'd started…

And then the knock came again. Louder and more insistent this time.

"Fuck."

It had started two days before. Phillip and I had been enjoying a brief moment of respite on Driftwood Beach, my favorite place, after the events of the week before, which had been hellish, to say the least. After everything Elvin had put us through, including Roberta, his own daughter, I couldn't believe any of us were still standing. Benny had come to and saved the day in more ways than one, and just in time. I was still struggling to understand the powers this goth amateur wrestler I'd only known for a couple of weeks had, which appeared to be even stronger than mine, but one thing was for sure: now that Elvin and Guthrie were both dead and we'd come through on the other side relatively unscathed, the ragtag group of young people I'd met at the Wolfden, especially Benny and Roberta, were family.

After the whole horrid ordeal, including a very brief but traumatic breakup, all we wanted to do was spend a few peaceful moments together alone, in front of the ocean we both found so calming. A quick moment of peace before picking up the pieces of our lives that had fallen spectacularly apart around us. We were lying there, enjoying the quiet, dreary solitude of the murky, solemn tide when we'd noticed a man standing some short distance away, leaning up against a tall, sturdy piece of driftwood. We'd immediately known him for what he was: a reporter, or journalist, or whatever they called themselves these days. A freelance content writer, perhaps. We'd run after the guy, who I recognized right off, fangirl that I am, as Dylan Quint from GOTHzine, a music publication that had recently rebranded from a print rock rag to an online content mill. We hadn't been able to catch him before he'd darted into a grove of trees and off down the road. We were still on the beach, me trying to catch my breath and Phillip cursing like a sailor, when a text from my mom pinged through.

My very estranged, by my choice, father's house had just

burned down, she informed me, and not only that, he was missing.

It was a lot of information to get in the span of five minutes. And we were still reeling from everything that had gone on before. I no longer knew what a full night's sleep was, and the constant visions and headaches plaguing me were driving me insane.

Phillip was surprised that I hadn't gone down to Panama City Beach right away to seek out my dad, but he just didn't understand. I hadn't spoken to my father more than once or twice a year since I was a teenager. While I was proud of him for getting clean and restarting his life after growing up watching him ingest every substance—and beverage—known to man for my entire childhood, the fact that he'd abandoned us still stuck in my craw. Especially considering he left us to shack up with a woman not much older than me. Daddy had abandoned me, leaving me with a drunken mess who could barely afford to keep food on our plates most of the time, and who barely knew I existed. Dad had gone on to get married and start a new life with his child bride, Dee, and their new baby—my half-sister, Shably (yes, like the wine; don't ask why a former drunk would do that to his kid. Thank god everyone called her Shay)—and only extended a lukewarm invite for me to join their lives once or twice on a year on holidays. So far, I had never accepted.

Phillip, whose family dynamic had been pretty wholesome from what I gathered, must think I was crazy, or heartless, or both, to not want to see my father. But he just *didn't* understand. He couldn't.

I'd go eventually if my dad wasn't found. But for now … well, I wanted to wait a little while longer. A day or two, maybe. To be with Phillip, just the two of us. He needed me, after all. And I needed him—needed to be alone with him. To make up for lost time.

To enjoy just being together before the inevitable happened —Phillip being outed.

Because how on earth would a 6'5" rock god with jet-black hair, wild green eyes, and a jawline that could cut glass possibly explain how he was absent for twenty-three years and then was just *back,* as handsome, youthful, and dynamic as ever, as though he hadn't aged a day? How could he explain his sudden re-emergence back into the world after being gone for so long, his fans having mourned his very publicized death? His funeral had been open to the public; his friends and bandmates had given interviews providing insight into his demise; fans still flocked to his grave on his birthday and on holidays to leave black roses and candles. What on earth would he say to such a devoted fanbase? How could he explain?

And yet, he would have to. Dylan Quint had seen him, and it was only a matter of time before he went public with what would assuredly be the most groundbreaking story to come out of the rock music world since 1994.

For Phillip, telling the truth—that he'd been brought back to life by a spell (twice, actually, if you wanted to get technical) and was now walking earthside in the same body (and at the same age) as he'd left it twenty-three years before was impossible. Nobody would believe it. And on the off chance that someone *did* believe it, it'd put us both—and our very motley crew of friends and associates—at major risk. Nobody could know how it happened or what powers I—and one other just like me—possessed. Nobody could ever know I was the one who brought Phillip back to life.

That knowledge that could mean death for me. It already almost had. More than once.

My hand still clutching Phillip's, I knew without a shadow of a doubt that he would never, ever give me up. He'd never tell the truth about how he'd come to be alive again. He'd carry that secret back to the grave with him. He'd climb in willingly, if that's what it took to protect me.

But as we stared at each other, silently reading each other's thoughts, listening to the third set of knocks sounding on the hotel-room door, we both knew good and well what we'd known since Driftwood Beach—the jig was up.

"What do we do?" I hissed, whipping myself off the bed and reaching for my clothes. I pulled on my Black Sabbath T-shirt and black jeans quickly and stepped into my black slip-on Chucks.

Phillip didn't answer me, instead cupping his hand over his mouth and calling out, "Who is it?"

"Room service," a muffled voice answered back. "I have a delivery of flowers for a…Ms. Spooner."

Phillip looked at me quizzically. I pulled my hair into a hurried ponytail and shook my head. "Only two people know I'm here, and neither one of them would send me flowers," I said.

"I'm going to answer it," Phillip replied in a fierce whisper, his face clouding over. I didn't have to ask why. He was fed up and ready to confront whatever—whoever—it was head on.

"Phillip, *no,*" I said, darting over and placing a hand on his chest to stop him. He could have easily overpowered me, but he didn't. He sunk back down instead, giving me a pleading look. "I'll get it. You're not even dressed. Just cover me, okay? Just…in case."

He nodded, displeased but resigned, and I walked over to the door, taking a deep breath. With so much happening all at once, there was no way of knowing whether the person on the other side of the door was friend or foe. Just a lowly room service lackey with a delivery, someone intent on doing me harm, or a snap-happy journalist hoping to break the music story of the decade? Might as well find out.

With another deep breath, I opened the door, doing my best to make myself seem imposing. A laughable prospect since I was barely 5'6" on a good day and had chicken arms. Only the low pulse of electricity in my fingers indicated that I had any kind of strength, and I flexed my hand instinctively, at the ready for whatever threat might come.

A man in the hotel's uniform, a burgundy blazer and dark slacks, stood there holding a bouquet of peonies. I looked at them in surprise. Peonies were my favorite flower, but not too many people knew that. My mom, Tess, possibly my (now former) best friend Sloan … certainly none of my new friends and not even Phillip. I took them reluctantly and thanked the bellboy, gingerly pulling the card from the plastic holder.

I sighed with relief as I opened the envelope and read the card. *"I'm so sorry about all this, honey. But it's going to be okay. I'm in town. We need to talk soon— can we meet? Love, Mama."*

That was sweet of her, I thought. I did feel better to know my mother was here in Savannah, keeping an eye on us. It was the least she could do after years of lies and drunken neglect, but I'd take it.

I looked up at the room service guy, who was standing there expectantly. "Oh, sorry," I said, digging in my pocket for some bills. I'd stayed at a nice hotel maybe two times before, and things like tipping the bellboy were totally off my radar. "Oh damn, I don't have any cash…"

"I've got it." Phillip appeared behind me, still clad in his white robe, and produced a twenty-dollar bill. "Thanks, man," he said, then pushed past me to shut the door. He took the flowers from me and read the card, his brow furrowing.

"You should have let me handle it," I said to him sternly. "What if that bellboy recognized you?"

"He was too busy eyeing the money in my hand to look at me," Phillip said with a shrug. "I was getting nervous watching you standing there. Somebody could've snatched you right out of the doorway."

Phillip had wanted to go home immediately—as in, back to my house in Brunswick—but I'd talked him out of it. My little singlewide off in the woods wasn't going to provide him—or me—with any kind of protection or privacy. If this journalist or photographer or social media coordinator or whatever he was calling himself had managed to find us on a deserted, isolated stretch of beach the next town over, he obviously knew where I lived. I'd suggested we book a hotel, which might be more inconspicuous, not to mention cushy. We deserved a little luxury after all we'd been through. I was relieved when he agreed, not realizing how badly I'd needed some time away to decompress. Though between our diligent moves to keep ourselves hidden and the developing situation with my father, Phillip had been unable to relax.

"Why are you still so freaked?" I asked. "Anyone – or anything – that was after me is long gone. If anything, you're more at risk than I am!"

"Force of habit, I guess," he said with another shrug. "After all you've been through…" He gestured at the flowers. "You never know."

"They're from my *mother*," I argued.

"I know," Phillip said, digging in his bag to produce a black T-shirt and dark jeans. I smiled despite myself. He wore the same uniform pretty much every day. And today we were matching—dark, inconspicuous partners in crime. "But Stormy, look, if that Dylan guy knows I'm here, it's not like we can make him unsee it. If he was able to track me to some random beach on a random Tuesday, he can track me anywhere. Which means anyone can track—and hurt—*you*. I'm not going to run for the rest of my life just to avoid a camera. Not when there's more important stuff going on."

"Phillip—"

"I'm just saying, Stormy, that eventually he – or somebody else – will catch up with me." Phillip pulled his jeans up over his long, muscular legs and buttoned them. I grabbed a pair of black socks from his bag and threw them at him. "Thanks. I'm just thinking…we've got to be prepared. Rather than figuring out ways to hide, I need to figure out what I'm going to say – how I'm going to explain – when the news breaks. How best to spin all this in a way that protects you."

"It's going to be everywhere," I said with a shudder as he reached for his black combat boots. " You're going to be famous all over again."

"Maybe not," Phillip said calmly, sitting down and lacing up his boots. "It's been over twenty years. Fame is a fickle thing. When I died, I was in my prime, the band was in their heyday … now it's like … well, I'm old now. Or I should be, anyway. People have moved on. We're not the 'it' thing anymore, if we ever were." He looked at me and smiled sadly. "And it's not like I was ever Axl Rose. I'm not a superstar. Maybe I'll be able to fly under the radar more than you think."

"Oh, you sweet summer child," I, sitting down on his lap. He pulled me close. "Are you kidding? Just look at you. You're like a vampire come to life, and that's very much the 'in' thing right now. All the angsty teens are rediscovering old rockstars from the eighties and nineties. There are whole fan groups on Instagram dedicated to the lead singer of Ratt, for the love of hell, so it stands to reason they're deep diving into Phillip Deville too." I booped him on the nose. "You're the perfect poster child in every way. The death of the autotune era, all the cool kids are rediscovering rock music and falling in love with hot, sexy lead singers all over again, and here's a real, bona fide rock god from the alternative era, in the flesh, literally back from the dead? What could be more perfect?" I gave him a sloppy kiss on the lips. "You're about to be huge. You're gonna be the next Vampire Lestat."

"Don't call me a vampire," Phillip said with a laugh, grazing my neck with his teeth. "Unless you want to get bit."

"I mean, I'm happy to take one for the team." I giggled and nuzzled into him.

"I probably shouldn't," Phillip murmured into my neck, his breath making my skin prickle deliciously. "Being vegan and all, you're probably B12 deficient as it is."

"Wow, it's so hot when you talk to me about vitamins."

Phillip pulled back, still laughing. "If I recall, all hell broke loose for ol' Lestat"—I grinned at the way he pronounced it correctly, *Les-dot*—"didn't he have to pretty much fight a whole crew of undeads at some big show? And he unleashed some ancient evil that had been buried in two immobile vampires for centuries? A lot of people got killed for his stupid ego."

"Of course you've read Anne Rice," I said, rolling my eyes, but I was beaming. "Of course you have."

"I've read all five books," he boasted. "The last one was killer."

"Five?" I laughed. "I think we're up to like, thirteen books now."

"What? Are you serious?" Phillip scratched his chin thoughtfully. "I wish bookstores delivered. I need to catch up on those."

"Oh, you sweet, sexy, dusty old relic." I chuckled, making a mental note to buy him the damn books on Amazon. He was simply too cute.

I started to tell him about Anne Rice's public retirement from all things vampire and her big comeback, but then my phone pinged. I grabbed it from the nightstand and settled into Phillip's shoulder. The text was from Roberta.

Are you guys good?

Yes, I typed back. *Still holed up in here. Just got a delivery of flowers that almost gave me a coronary, but they were from Mama. I think Phillip is about to crack, though. He's going stir crazy in here.* I bit my lip, then typed, *How are you guys? Benny? Lee?*

While I was waiting for her response, Phillip got up from the bed and poured us both a fresh cup of coffee from the tiny two-cup pot on the small bar that doubled as a kitchenette. It wasn't great coffee —likely some generic brand repackaged with the hotel's logo—but I accepted the paper cup from him gratefully and took a long sip, ignoring the immediate dry, sandpaper feeling of my tongue from the hot liquid that scorched it. The levity from the moment before had dissipated, the way it always did when we heard from anyone. It was always bad news, it seemed, and we'd become accustomed to the dread that came along with the chiming of a cellphone.

We're okay. Ish. Lee is taking care of Benny. He won't let me do anything.

I responded with a grim smile. *Sounds about right. Taking care of everyone but himself, I'm sure.*

Yep. Same old Lee. As I began to type, another text pinged through. *I'm actually with your mom, Stormy. She said she didn't send you any flowers.*

I frowned at the phone, then looked up, dreading having to tell Phillip. The look on his face as he stood by the counter told me he'd already figured it out. He'd pulled it from me, as usual. We'd been joined by that magical tether—which I found wonderful most of the time, but occasionally was annoyed by —that allowed him to hear my thoughts and sense my feelings ever since I'd brought him back. Combine that with his super-human strength, ability to heal from mortal wounds, and odd habit of sensing things before they happened, and my undead boyfriend was basically a superhero.

I stood up and grabbed the little card and read it again. A bunch of platitudes about how it was all going to be okay, and then a request to meet. If it wasn't my mother, then who had sent me the flowers, and why?

"Probably that Dylan guy or some other journalist trying to get us to come out of the hotel," Phillip said from behind me, and I jumped. I hadn't even heard him. He wrapped his arms around my waist.

I sighed, leaning into his shoulder. "Fucking assholes. But you know, Phillip, I think you might be right. Let's just get it over with."

"I think so too."

I tapped out another text to Roberta and hit "send" before I could stop myself: *I guess we can't hide forever. Want to meet for lunch tomorrow?*

She responded immediately. *I was just going to ask you the same. We need to talk, and texting is no good. Lunch it is.*

I groaned. Roberta had dropped so many bombshells on me in the past several days. If she "needed to talk," that meant she had more of them, and I wasn't sure I could handle any more. As much as I loved Roberta, and I really did—the dark-haired vixen I'd once gleefully described as my ex-husband's "mistress" among other, worse (and definitely sexist) monikers— was fast becoming one of my best friends. But she seemed to attract trouble as much as I did, if not more so.

Despite my dread at having another talk in which I'd likely be flatlined with forgotten memories of past trauma or be roped into some hairbrained scheme against an evil villain, I felt a pang of excitement at the thought of seeing Roberta, even though it'd only been a couple of days. We'd become such fast friends, and we had so much in common. It was nice, having somebody like that to talk to, to laugh and vent with, who you knew had your back, who wasn't interested in a friendship based on competition. I hadn't realized as I'd sat alone in my trailer so often after my divorce just how alone I was. How lonely I had become. It had crept in so slowly, so quietly, that it had almost overtaken me before I'd realized what was happening.

Sloan, my former best friend, had been my closest confidante and partner in crime from middle school up until very recently. I'd been too blind to see how harmful, how co-dependent it had been. I don't think Sloan herself had even realized how toxic our friendship was until it had all come to a head. I'd been totally blindsided when she'd betrayed me, and truth be told, I was still reeling a little. To discover that someone you thought was your "person"—your best friend, soulmate, BFF, whatever you want to call it—actually hates you and has for a long time, and not only that, but they've been planning to do you harm with a whole host of people who hate you too... well, it takes a toll. When I'd finally been able to confront her at Elvin's, after she'd conspired with him to kidnap Lee and try to kill Benny, it had literally come to blows. Both the emotional *and* physical kind. I'd never forget the hatred on her face, and even after I'd quite literally knocked her on her ass, I still felt so much anger and bitterness toward her. Our friendship was over, for good. I could never, ever forget what she'd done to me, the years she'd spent gaslighting me, manipulating me, and trying to hurt the people I loved. And why? Because of a little jealousy over a magic I'd never asked for? A power that had brought me nothing but pain?

Even with all the drama that came with Roberta, I knew that she had nothing but good intentions toward me. I could feel it brimming out of her like an aura, and it was an awesome feeling; nice to know I had a friend who had no agenda, who didn't want to compete with me or try to knock me down a peg. With Roberta, what you saw was what you got.

Hit you up in the morning to make plans, I typed, then added, *Love you.* I hit send, slid my phone into my back pocket, and turned around to face Phillip.

"Have you talked to Jason and Ollie?" I asked him, leaning forward to plant a quick kiss on his jaw. Jason Langley and Nate "Ollie" Green were the two remaining members of the Bloomer Demons, Phillip's old band, the cult favorite that had thrust him into fame. The drummer, Kim Rzeznick, had passed away shortly after Phillip's death. I knew that Phillip must be thinking of his band mates, as well as his family and his ex-wife Barb, in light of being discovered. All the implications … what it would mean for the people whose lives had been so impacted already. It was a lot.

"I texted Jason this morning," Phillip replied, rolling his eyes.

"I assume that eyeroll means someone didn't react the way you wanted?"

"They're excited," Phillip said after a pause. "Of course they are. Neither of *them* have to explain how and why I'm back. They're thinking tours and albums and money. As if the band could ever get back together. What a stupid fucking idea."

Phillip's mouth was saying one thing, but his face was saying another. He wasn't a very good liar, for whatever many other talents he possessed. A tremor of alarm went through me, but I kept my mouth shut and gave him a tight hug. He was so much taller than me that I had to stand on tiptoe to wrap my arms around his neck. I pulled his head down to mine and gave him a peck on the lips. "They won't do anything you don't want them to. You know that. They're like your brothers." The unspoken words lay between us. Phillip had actual brothers. Blood family, relations that I knew, even if Phillip didn't, were still very much living and had no idea their world was about to be turned upside down. So far, the only people from Phillip's old life who knew he was alive were his band mates and his ex-wife Barb, who he had briefly seen and talked to a week ago. I was still dealing with my feelings of envy and jealousy over *that*. I knew that the thought of seeing and talking to his family again filled him with equal parts dread and excitement.

"I know," he said into my neck, his lips warm and soft against my skin. "They're good guys."

"And you're a good guy too," I said, facing him again, smiling as I looked into his eyes. "Whatever you decide, I'm behind you.

"I love you," he said, and I kissed him again, ignoring the dread that had started up in my belly.

"We're in this together, Deville," I whispered as I pulled away, touching his stubbly chin with my finger. "For better or worse."

"That's what I'm afraid of," he said with a sad smile, his eyes far away. "That it's going to get much, much worse before it gets better."

"Naturally," I said in a bright voice, making devil horns with my fingers. "The lives of a rock star and a witch are never dull." I trailed a kiss from his collarbone to his chin, enjoying the pleasant shudder that went through him. I looped my fingers with his and pulled him toward the bed. "But for now, it's late. Bedtime."

"As you wish," my prince answered.

Two

The flames shot out the windows and onto the roof. They were a deep, dull red, not the bright-orange flames normally associated with a house fire. It was as though the house itself was angry, consuming itself in its own rage.

I stood, helpless, tears drying on my cheeks as I watched, my feet stuck to the spot, the sand beneath unfamiliarly light; soft, so unlike the damp, dark sand I was used to. At home on Jekyll, the sand was almost gray, a match to the always ominous sky and the bleached, dreary bones of the trees on Driftwood Beach. At nearby Tybee Island, sand mixed with dirt and silt from the mouth of the Savannah River, turning the beach into a mottled, dirty state of perpetual dampness. Here, the sand was soft and pale; welcoming. I stared straight ahead, watching as the house transformed into cinders, cinders that were drifting upward from the burning beams, flying off into the inky black night like upside down snowflakes.

I blindly reached out beside me, feeling for Phillip's hand, craving its warmth and safety, but it wasn't there. I pawed at the air, reaching out to my other side, hoping for Phillip, or Roberta, or even my mother—anyone who could offer me *comfort—but I was alone. Completely, terrifyingly alone. Again.*

I tried again to move my legs, to make myself run into the night, away from this place, to flee the sight of so much melting heat. But I was stuck to the spot, rooted there, a tree growing out of an unlikely home. I'd been bound twice in my life—once by Lydia, and again by Elvin—and this felt both different and the same. The heat seemed trapped inside my own body, melting my bones down to liquid, the pain an all-consuming thing that was both inside and outside of me, a black hole that used to be my heart. Now, darkness.

I opened my mouth and began to scream. The name I screamed out was one I hadn't uttered in a very long time. Not since I was a child. All that pain, that loneliness, that sadness, that bitterness, that fear came out of me in a flood, like flowing lava, like pulsing blood, in one loudly screamed word—

"Daddy!"

The hand that shook my shoulder was rough but warm. I felt its heat through my thin T-shirt as I sat straight up in bed, my eyes open wide, trying to throw it off me before I got burned.

"Stormy!"

"No, it's burning!" I tried to shrug myself out of whatever was holding me down, the heat dangerously close to my skin.

"Stormy, it's okay," Phillip said from beside me, pulling me into his arms before I fully knew where I was. I blinked a few times, still seeing dull red flames behind my eyelids. I leaned into Phillip's strong chest, allowing him to hold me, though I was covered with a sheen of sticky sweat and it couldn't be very pleasant for him. "You're not burning."

"I...I..." I faltered, mentally back on the beach, the lick of the flames still fresh in my mind. I shuddered. "I was having a nightmare."

"I know, honey." Something about the term of endearment

made me want to hide, to nuzzle further into his shoulder. "It's okay. You're okay. It was just a dream." Phillip's voice was tender, so why did it make me feel so sad? I felt like a little kid, lost and alone, scared and confused.

I rubbed at my eyes, picking the sleep from them, and took a shaky breath. "It was a bad one."

"I heard you call out," Phillip murmured. "Hell, everybody on this floor probably heard it. You were calling for your daddy." I had to smile at the way he pronounced it—*Deddy*—just like my Southern drawl, which was no small feat for him with his Boston accent, thick as chow-dah. "You must be so worried about him."

"I guess I am," I admitted, pulling back to look at him, feeling exposed and embarrassed.

"Stormy, it's okay to admit that," Phillip said, sitting up and flicking on the bedside lamp. His eyes were bleary, but his expression was serious. "It's okay to admit that you love your father."

"I know."

"Do you?"

I sighed; Phillip knew me too well, and he was always in my damn head. Chills ran up my arms, and I rubbed at them absently, swallowing. "It's weird. I haven't wanted much to do with him since he left us. And then once he got remarried, I *really* didn't. I've been wanting to go no-contact forever, and the only reason I didn't is because I guess I…I just couldn't bear the thought of *completely* cutting him off, especially since I have a sister now…" I bit my lip. "And now that I know he's in danger, it's like…I can't stop thinking about it. I can't stop thinking about him."

"Of course you can't," Phillip said tenderly, rubbing my shoulder. "Anyone would be worried in your situation. It's complicated, but you're a good, caring person." He gave me a squeeze. "Remind me what your stepmother told the authorities?"

I only knew bits and pieces of what my mother had been able to glean from the police officer who had called her. We couldn't figure out why he'd phoned her in the first place, since they'd divorced over a decade ago and my dad had remarried. They hadn't talked in years. They didn't even live in the same state! Not to mention my stepmom Dee had turned up after the fire with my stepsister in her arms, rattled but safe. "She said that she and Shably had gone to her parents for a family weekend, and that my dad had said he was going to visit a friend in Pensacola. A guy's weekend or something. They were going to fish and go sing karaoke—good ol' boy shit. So unless he changed his mind and went home, none of them were in the house."

"I assume they've tried calling this friend in Pensacola?" Phillip asked.

"No answer, and nobody home when they sent a deputy out. But if they're gone on a fishing trip, that tracks. They might be out on the water with no cell service. It's just that—"

"The entire went up in flames, so who knows what they'll find in the wreckage," Phillip finished for me.

I thought back to the frantic voicemail from my mother, how beside herself she'd sounded. *"Your dad's house burned to the ground, Stormy! And he's missing!"* I hadn't heard her so scared in, well, ever. For someone who had said many times over the years that she hoped my dad would die and rot in hell, her voice sure had been cloaked with tears. Now that I was on the other side of my own divorce, I could understand my mother a lot better. It was indeed possible to hate someone who had utterly betrayed you and love them at the same time.

Phillip gave my hand a squeeze, feeling my emotions. "I hate to ask this, but"—he looked at me, his face dark— "just in the interest of dotting all the T's and crossing all the I's..." He smiled grimly. "Would your stepmother have any reason to hurt your father? Maybe some other woman…?"

"I don't know," I answered honestly. I'd told Phillip my dad had been unfaithful to my mom, hence the question. "But I really don't think so. For starters, she's this tiny little thing not much older than me, and she's sweeter than divinity; she wouldn't hurt a fly. She's one of those syrupy sweet country girls; you can imagine." Phillip nodded. "And Daddy's been playing the family man for several years now." I thought for a moment. "But the old him? You wouldn't have to hunt for a reason to hurt that guy."

"I wonder if he might've fallen off the wagon," Phillip mused. "Got in with some bad people from his past, pissed the wrong person off."

"I don't know." I bit at a fingernail. "All I know is that I shouldn't care, but I do. I'm worried, Phillip. Really worried."

"That's all there is to it, then," he said firmly, pulling me close. "We can't just sit here doing nothing. We need to go down there." His voice took on a note of finality. "And that's just what we're going to do."

"But—"

"We're going," he said in a tone that brokered no argument.

"What about the fuckers outside?" I demanded.

"I'll deal with them." I leaned back to look at him again. His face was set in a hard line of resolve. "Let's face it, Stormy. They've spotted me, and they know it's me. I can try to hide and wait it out, and they might take off, but they'll be back. I'll say something to try and fob them off, and hopefully they'll…" He stroked his chin thoughtfully. "Hopefully they'll leave me alone after that."

While it was true that Phillip, even in his heyday, had never been *super* famous—not a legend or infamous rock star whose reputation preceded him, like Bowie or Axl Rose—he had been well known enough to be considered famous. His band, the Bloomer Demons, had enjoyed a cult following among the grunge, alternative, and goth kids who enjoyed the dark, dreary, and slightly scary aesthetic of the music combined with the sexy and dangerous persona of their front man. Phillip had easily been the band's most popular member, and when he was alive (the first time), he was never without a throng of groupies and wannabe rocker kids vying for his attention. He'd enjoyed that persona to the fullest, he'd told me. And when he'd died, he'd only solidified his own legacy. He'd never be on par with David Bowie, but he was included in the annals of history alongside all the other rock boys who had met their demise too soon, often tragically. Phillip was underestimating just how beloved he was and how excited his fans would be to find out he was alive. To say nothing of the *story* it would make. Even those who weren't Bloomer Demons or Phillip Deville fans would get swept up in a scandalous, juicy tale like his—a rock star supposedly dead for over twenty-three years suddenly emerging in a random, rural Georgia town, no worse for wear and seemingly unaged?

They were going to have a field day.

Phillip Deville would be more famous than ever. And he could deny it, but I'd seen the look on his face, in his eyes, when he'd talked about the band getting back together. A part of him wanted it.

I wasn't sure that was something *I* wanted, though. But did I have a choice?

"Let's wait a little while longer on Florida," I begged. "Let me see if we hear anything from my stepmom tomorrow. If not, we'll talk about going down there later."

"You're afraid to go," he countered, looking at me with knowing eyes. "You're afraid you're going to see him. What about that scares you, Stormy?"

"Don't go psychoanalyzing me, Deville," I said grumpily.

"Of course I'm nervous, of course I'm scared. After everything that's happened! You just worry about you and let me worry about me."

"Yes, boss," he said. He gave me a sweet smile to let me know he wasn't ruffled by my outburst. "I certainly do have enough to worry about with my own drama. That's for sure."

"So what will you do then?" I asked, finally calm enough to sink back into the pillows. I pulled the duvet over myself and gestured for Phillip to join me. "Just go down and greet 'em?"

He grinned, nuzzling me under the covers. "Hardly. I figured I'd call up GOTHzine and offer them an exclusive if they call off their shitty reporter and tell him to stop lurking in the hotel lobby."

"Exclusive or no," I pointed out, "they'll want a picture. And they're going to ask a lot of questions."

"And I'll feed them a few lines and be done with it."

"You make it sound so easy," I said, lying back, my arms behind my head. "As if we haven't been trying to avoid this very thing since you came back."

"Yeah, well," he replied, getting back out of bed. He stood up and walked over to the balcony window, staring out. "There's so much traffic. You always hear of Savannah being this sleepy, Antebellum old thing full of moss and wisteria and from a time gone by. But it's as bustling as Boston, even in the middle of the night."

"We're right downtown," I said. "So it just seems that way."

"It'll be a good backdrop, this place," Phillip mused, still staring out the window. "Downtown Savannah is very quaint. I love the trees."

I laughed. "Don't you dare touch one. They're covered in chiggers!"

"I don't know what a chigger is, and I don't want to know."

Phillip laughed, turning back to face me. Then his face turned pensive. "First thing in the morning, I'm going to make a phone call or send an email or whatever it is I need to do. Go ahead and get it over with. That is, if it's okay with you." I bit my lip. "I'd like to have your blessing first. I want to make sure you're okay with it—with being in the spotlight, however fleeting—before I proceed."

I wanted to argue with him that I suspected it wouldn't be fleeting at all. Nor would it be as easy or painless as he thought it would. Phillip simply didn't understand the time we lived in. Gone were the days of calling up a reporter and giving a straightforward statement or meeting for coffee and a quick interview where you signed off on the questions and left with your image fully in your control. These days, celebrities had to hire entire teams to manage their "brand," a feat that required round-the-clock monitoring and availability to deliver a statement, a rebuttal, or a well-timed tweet or Instagram post to offset anything that might leak. Everything was cultivated to the point that it was hard to know what was real, if anything. With everyone on the planet connected via multiple apps, it was impossible for anyone with a modicum of celebrity to keep a low profile. Your every move could end up on Twitter or Facebook, pictures splashed over Instagram, videos uploaded to TikTok, and your every intention analyzed and picked apart on reddit. And it wasn't just the media spurring it on anymore. Journalists, reporters, and influencers all used social media to garner likes and views and engagement. The more salacious and interesting a story, the more they stuck with it. They would wring Phillip's particular story out for all it was worth until there wasn't a drop left. Even if it never blew up and he was able to fly somewhat under the radar, which was unlikely…even then… the attention would be too much to bear.

And there was no way in hell he'd be able to keep me a

secret. When you were famous and you looked like Phillip Deville, people *would* ask if you had a girlfriend. And Phillip wouldn't be able to lie, not convincingly. They'd be picking apart my entire life, pulling up old tweets and pictures, before the day was out.

Phillip just didn't understand.

But how could I explain? It was his life, after all. He'd come to this decision of his own free will, and who was I to tell him he had to stay hidden?

I could choose to stay out of the limelight myself, of course. But to what end? It would mean having to stay away from Phillip. Likely breaking up. That was something I'd already tried, and it had been miserable. A few days without him and I'd been inconsolable, missing him so much that my longing had become a chasm of pain and despair. I didn't want to do that again, not even if it meant sacrificing my privacy and anonymity.

Phillip simply meant too much to me. He was worth it.

"Come to bed," I said, patting the pillow beside me. "You'll need your beauty sleep if you're going to make that important phone call in the morning."

Phillip smiled and moved away from the window, sliding into bed beside me. He reached his arms out, and I entered them happily, sighing as I snuggled against his broad chest. He placed a kiss on my temple, then raised my chin with a finger so I was facing him.

"Can you sleep?" he asked in a soft voice.

"Yes," I lied, though I knew I wouldn't be falling asleep any time soon, not after that dream. My entire body felt jumpy with nerves, and my heart thudded fast in my chest.

"Liar," Phillip said, pulling the thoughts from my head. He leaned down and kissed me tenderly on the mouth, a sweet, nurturing kiss that soon turned into something more passionate. He placed his hand behind my head and brought me closer as I moaned against his lips, wanting to be devoured. His breath was hot and sweet, tasting of the toothpaste he'd used just before bed. "Maybe I can help tire you out."

"Maybe you can," I whispered, reaching down to touch his taut stomach, my fingers trailing from his belly button over to his hips, down his thighs, and back up between his legs, waiting for the inevitable catch of his breath and involuntary shudder that always made me weak. I kissed him again, inching myself closer to him, not able to get close enough. No matter how close we were, it always felt like I wanted to be closer, deeper, as if I could actually get into his skin and inhabit him for a while.

"You're so weird." Phillip laughed against my mouth and grazed my lower lip with his teeth, making me growl. "Should I be worried that you want to wear my skin?"

"Are you afraid of me, Phillip Deville?" I nibbled at his earlobe with my teeth.

"Should I be? Considering what part of me you're currently holding?" Phillip's laughter was like music. I applied some pressure, and his laugh was replaced by a gasp.

"Alright, that's it. You're not playing fair." Phillip flipped me over onto my back, his hard body suddenly on top of mine, and bared his teeth. "You don't scare me, witch."

"Oh yeah? Then prove it." I smirked.

And he did.

Three

I stepped into the elevator after Phillip, standing in front of him in the small, cramped space, as though I could somehow protect him. With him standing at 6'5" barefoot, it was a fat chance I'd be able to shield him from anything with my barely average stature. I jabbed at the button for the ground floor, and as the doors shut, I turned to him with a hopeful smile. "It'll be nice to go out to a fancy restaurant," I said brightly. "We haven't gotten to do anything like that since, well, ever. Remember that steak you ordered the day after we met? I thought you were going to recreate that scene from *When Harry Met Sally* and have an orgasm right there at the table!"

"I think I did, to be honest," he said with a grin, reaching over to ruffle my hair. "No offense to your vegan sensibilities, but I'm pretty sure that steak was in my top three life moments, both the last one and this most recent one."

I grinned. "And what are the first two? Life moments, I mean."

"Wouldn't you like to know." Phillip's eyes twinkled, and he brushed the side of my face. I craned my head up toward his, and he leaned into me, his sensual mouth pursed for a kiss.

The whoosh of the elevator doors rudely interrupted us as we settled on the third floor. A man clad in modern business attire—a blazer, dark-blue skinny jeans, and very pointed, very shiny black shoes—stepped into the elevator, a smallish brief-case tucked under one arm. "Morning," he said, not looking at either of us directly to see us nod in acknowledgement. I thought he looked kind of familiar but quickly dismissed it. There were plenty of hipster tech-bros all over Savannah who looked like carbon cutouts of this guy. I turned back to Phillip as the man settled in one corner of the elevator, giving us as much privacy as possible. I took the opportunity to inch myself up and give Phillip a quick peck on his jawline. He kissed me back, but his body was a little tense. Being in a cramped space with a stranger was apt to make him feel apprehensive.

My phone buzzed in my jacket pocket, and I slid it out, hitting the unlock button and reading the message. It was from Mom. *I've booked a table for four,* it said. *I'm already here. Just outside smoking a cigarette, but I can go in and order drinks for everyone if you're close by.*

I tapped out a quick response, smiling. It had been years since I'd eaten at the swanky Italian eatery, but Phillip would love the place. Not only was the food absolute carb-heavy nirvana from what I remembered, but the atmosphere, with its tongue-in-cheek mafioso vibes and dark, dimly lit décor, would make him feel right at home, to say nothing of the infamous filet mignon or the always flowing red wine. I figured Phillip and I deserved a little indulgence. *We're in the elevator on the way down. Give us ten minutes, tops,* I typed quickly. The restaurant was only two blocks from our hotel. "Uber?" I asked him.

"It's only a short distance, right?" he replied. "The air is crisp, and it's so pretty outside. Let's walk. I'd like to see some of historic Savannah; I've always wanted to do that with you."

The rest of the sentiment hung unspoken between us: *let's do this now while we still can.*

I smiled. "You got it. Even though you haven't known me long enough to have 'always wanted to' do anything with me." I had to admit that a walk along the beautiful cobblestones of historic Savannah with my love, the sun shining down on our faces and a cool breeze in our hair, sounded like a slice of heaven.

As the elevator neared the ground floor, I slid my phone back in my pocket and faced the doors, hoping that it wouldn't be crowded. I had already mapped out the fastest course from the elevator to the outer doors to keep us from being seen or having to interact with people. Despite what Phillip had said about coming clean, I was secretly hoping for a few more blissful days—or even hours—of privacy with him. I'd been so relieved when he'd rolled over in bed that morning and told me he was going to wait until after lunch to make his phone calls. It was just a few short hours, but I'd take what I could get.

I was trying so hard not to be resentful, but God, every time we had so much as a moment of peace, or thought we did, something else came up. It was never ending. I couldn't help but feel bitter about it. When would it just be *our* time?

Some thoughts were beginning to form, though…thoughts that contradicted how I'd been feeling all this time. I didn't know why; maybe it was being in beautiful Savannah, or the gleam Phillip got in his eye when he talked about the past, but I wondered…maybe it wouldn't be so bad? Maybe Phillip was right, and he'd just be a blip, a fun little story that would make a BuzzFeed or PopSugar headline and trend on Twitter for a couple of hours before disappearing, and then we could go back to our lives. In our world of constant BREAKING NEWS and new trending topics every five minutes, Phillip could quite literally be a flash in the pan. Better yet, maybe the reporter we'd seen had already packed up and left. I'd seen a headline earlier on Facebook that there was a sex scandal with some lead singer from a Nu Metal band who had harassed dozens of women, many of whom had already bravely spoken out about their harrowing experiences. Then a video had leaked with some pretty damning, undeniable proof of his depraved nature. Pretty soon, internet sleuths all over social media (because let's face it, the Venn diagram of metal/alt rock fans and true crime junkies is a complete circle) had dug up all sorts of information on Colt Leather, information that might prove the singer was more than just a garden variety harasser; he'd also harbored some pretty heavy serial-killer fantasies. Worse, there were multiple women missing in or around his hometown. With stories like that to deep-dive into, why would anybody be interested in a Phillip Deville lookalike in podunk South Georgia?

I convinced myself it'd be okay and was thinking ahead to the luscious lemon and hazelnut pasta dish I planned to order —I'd checked the menu online to ensure they had vegan options—as the doors to the elevator whooshed open. Then three things happened so fast that neither Phillip nor I had any time to react.

First, the man on the other side of the elevator reached into his briefcase and pulled out a huge iPhone with an attached ring light and what looked to be a fancy, miniature micro-phone. He swiped the phone open and held it out to Phillip, so close that the phone actually brushed Phillip's cheek and made him jump.

At the same time, we could see two other men through the elevator's open doors, flanking either side. One held a large, professional looking camera. He turned, maneuvering to get around me since I was blocking his clear shots of Phillip. The other man I recognized from GOTHzine—Dylan Quint—the man we'd chased on the beach. He held out an iPhone as well, its tape recorder app open and recording. As he inched closer, the man in the elevator with us leaned forward and hit the "stall" button, forcing the doors to stay open. We'd been ambushed. And we were trapped.

I inadvertently glanced past the chaos in the elevator to the hotel's whirling, circular door to see a woman standing there in a long, elegant black coat. I caught her eye for the smallest of seconds and she smiled, her lips impossibly shiny in the bright light of the hotel lobby, her long, sleek blonde hair pulled back in a French braid. She wrapped her coat around her slim frame and stepped through the spinning door and out into the night air.

I shook my head to clear it, certain I'd just hallucinated. It couldn't have been her, could it?

"Mr. Deville, could we have just a moment of your time?" the man in the elevator was saying as he pressed the phone toward Phillip's face. I decided to forget the woman for now and turned to Phillip, putting my hands on his shoulders, moving to pull him out of the elevator and away from the man. I had no idea how we'd get past the two photographers standing just outside the doors, though. And even if we did, all three of them were already recording. "Is it really you, Phillip Deville? Can you tell us where you've been all these years? Why did your family and bandmates tell your fans you were dead? Were they in on it? Why did you decide to come out of hiding after all this time? Now that you have, do you plan to release any new music?"

I kept pulling on Phillip, but he was stuck to the spot. It was like one of Lydia's holding spells, but he wasn't hexed; he was just stunned. And from his body language and the cacophony of angry emotions coming off him, he was only seconds from erupting in total fury. I knew the look on his face —it was one I'd seen in more than one interview toward the end of the Bloomer Demons' peak when all the reporters had gotten too invasive, too tactless with their insensitive questions. Phillip always handled those with a charming combination of evasiveness and good old-fashioned snark, but occasionally, they'd get one over on him, one that would stun him momentarily. He'd have that look on his face that he had now, like a deer caught in the headlights, but one willing to fight you tooth and nail to get out of your car's path. Even if it meant mowing that car down and taking out everybody in it. To someone who didn't know him well, it was a calm, almost introspective look, but I knew better.

"You are Phillip Deville, right?" the reporter was asking, his phone close enough to Phillip's face to graze his skin. My fingers, still on Phillip's shoulders, began to tingle.

"Who are *you*?" Phillip asked suddenly, seemingly taking no notice of my hands on his shoulders or that I was still trying to pull him out of the elevator. It was futile, like trying to pull a furious bull toward a water hole. He wasn't moving. "And why are you accosting me on an elevator?"

"Kevin Ramford, VICE," the man said in a practiced, perfunctory tone, then he pushed the phone even closer to Phillip; had he wanted to, Phillip could have stuck his tongue out and licked it. "Can you tell us about your life these past twenty-three years? Your fans are dying to know where you've been."

"Oh, are they dying?" Phillip responded, his mouth curling into a slow, sinister smile. *Uh oh.*

"Mr. Deville, you have to know that your fans, those who have loved and mourned you for over two decades, are eager to know how you've suddenly reappeared after being—as we thought, anyway—dead all these years," the man said, his tone giving off a hint of exasperation, but it felt like pretense. He was performing for an audience, the crowd of narrative-starved, faceless consumers on the internet, frothing for the latest livestream or hot take. "Don't you owe it to those fans to tell them what happened and why you allowed them to think you were dead for twenty-three years?" He smiled, then pressed the phone harder into Phillip's face. "Don't you think you owe them an apology?"

It was as though all the air in the elevator was suddenly sucked out. Things were deadly silent for a moment, and then Phillip Deville *growled*, a low rumble coming from deep in his chest like he was a feral feline ready to devour its prey and suck the meat off its bones.

The man, Kevin, shrunk back to the elevator's wall, one hand bracing behind him, his eyes wide. He seemed scared, as he should be, but the excitement in his eyes was hard to miss. This was going to go viral. I could almost hear his inner monologue, and my hands were absolutely buzzing with rage.

I had to diffuse the situation.

I turned to Dylan Quint, the reporter outside the elevator doors. "I thought you worked for GOTHzine," I said to him stupidly. "But he said he's with VICE."

Dylan Quint's face was very pale beneath his dark, bushy beard. "Yeah, huh…VICE bought out GOTHzine last year. It's a subsidiary now."

"Oh. I should have known." I shook my head. "What gives, Dylan? Why would you guys think it's okay to ambush us like this?"

"Well, you haven't come down in two days. We didn't know when we'd get another chance," Kevin said, even though I hadn't been talking to him. He held the phone out to Phillip again, but he had enough good sense to keep it a little further away this time. His hand shook a little, which gave me great satisfaction.

As I stared at him, I realized why Kevin Ramford seemed familiar. Just a few short days ago, when I'd been staying here with Roberta, I'd run smack into a man in the lobby. The papers in his briefcase had gone flying, and I'd been so embarrassed, gushing apologies as I'd tried to hastily help him organize everything. He'd been understanding and told me not to worry about it, and before I'd had a chance to apologize further, he'd disappeared. Now I knew why he'd been so gracious—he'd been tailing me.

I'd brought Phillip to this very hotel, thinking we'd be able to lay low. Instead, I'd led him straight into an ambush. Kevin Ramford was peppering Phillip with more questions, but I didn't register them. I was too busy feeling guilt roll around in my belly, making me queasy.

"Are you aware that I'm standing in an elevator?" Phillip asked calmly. "You're harassing me and distressing my companion and filming us without our consent. Is this really what you want to do?"

Every word had been polite and firm, but the threat underneath was loud and clear. Kevin took another step back and gave us a dazzling, professional smile. "Of course, Mr. Deville. My apologies. Let's step out of the elevator and talk somewhere more comfortable." He gestured with an outstretched arm for us to exit.

But as we stepped out of the elevator, the heavy doors finally sliding shut behind us, that safe haven now gone, Phillip whirled back on the reporter. "Actually," he snarled, his eyes flashing, "I'm late for a lunch, thanks to you. We're leaving."

"But you said—"

Phillip advanced on Kevin, stopping inches from his face. "Back *off*, dude," he hissed.

Dylan Quint stepped forward and touched Kevin on the shoulder. "Dude. Back off the guy. Give him some space."

With a sigh of resigned exasperation, Kevin stepped back and turned off his phone. Then he reluctantly shut off the ring light and stared at us. "Fine. I'm done."

Phillip smiled. "Looks like your colleague has more sense than you do." He looked at Dylan Quint. "Though I'm still pissed at you for spying on us at the beach. Give me your card, and when I'm ready to chat, I'll consider giving you a call."

Dylan Quint's face brightened. "If you would, Mr. Deville, that would be great. And sooner, rather than later, preferably—"

"You don't call the shots, buddy." Phillip's arm hovered in mid-air, and for a moment, I thought he was going to punch them both, but he was only reaching to take the slightly sweaty looking card from Kevin's trembling hand. "I'll call, and I'll even give you an exclusive." Dylan Quint's eyes widened. "But on two conditions: one, when I fuckin' feel like it, and two, you delete ALL the footage, and I mean all—videos, photos, audio, and whatever else you have. If you leak even one gigabyte of the shit you took today, the deal's off. And I'll fucking sue you into oblivion, to boot."

"Yes. Of course," Dylan answered eagerly. "You got it; everything's deleted. We won't post anything until we hear from you. Do you think you'll be calling this evening, or—"

"I said when I fuckin' feel like it," Phillip snapped, putting a hand on the small of my back. "And don't think about getting my exclusive and then leaking all that shit after the fact, either. When I show up for the interview, I'll have something in writing for you to sign. Deal?"

"Yes, okay," Dylan agreed readily. Kevin Ramford and the cameraman stood there dejectedly, as though they'd been cut out of a deal. I supposed, in a way, they had.

Phillip steered me forward, and we exited the building without more disruption, though we could feel the eyes of everyone in the foyer—guests, staff, and reporters—on us as we left. Their gazes burned into my back like a brand. I had no doubt that the footage they'd gotten, even though Phillip had refused to answer any questions, would've been plastered all over social media and TV before the hour was up if Phillip hadn't cut that deal. Every part of my body quivered with relief. We'd come so very close.

But so had they. I wondered if Kevin Ramford and Dylan Quint realized how close they'd come to being dismembered in an elevator. They were damn lucky that Phillip—and me, for that matter, since I could still feel the almost-painful, frenzied buzzing in my fingers—had spared them.

"You wouldn't have hurt them," Phillip said, in my head as always, putting a protective arm around me and pulling me close as we resumed walking. "As for me, well…we'll just say I didn't want a murder charge on top of everything else." He laughed. "Let's get you that hazelnut pasta thing. You've been fantasizing about it so hard that it's stuck in *my* head."

I giggled, but my brain was awhirl. My hands buzzed, and I pressed my fingers so hard against my palm the nails cut into my skin. Phillip might be certain I wouldn't have hurt those men, but I wasn't so sure.

I had been looking forward to this dinner, but as we slid into the booth in the dimly lit Italian restaurant to see Roberta and my mother sitting across from us, their faces dour, I knew it wasn't going to be a night of socializing.

As glad as I was to see Roberta, my skin prickled at the sight of her. My newfound friend, normally bubbly in the worst of circumstances, looked truly harrowed today. "What's going on?" I asked as the waitress placed our menus on the table.

Burt waved a finger as if to say "hush," ignoring my curious look. We ordered our drinks—red wine and a glass of water for Roberta, Phillip, and me, and my mother primly ordered a Shirley Temple, the first time I'd seen someone order one in the wild—and waited for the waitress to retreat. Phillip's hand on my leg was a welcome and warm presence, and he gave me a gentle squeeze. After the incident in the hotel foyer, we were both on edge.

As soon as the waitress was gone, Burt immediately asked, "Ready to go on vacation again?"

"I wasn't aware I'd ever gone on one," I said with a dry laugh, trying to ignore the feeling of dread creeping up my chest. "You're counting the Wolfden as a vacation spot?"

Burt chuckled. "Everybody sends their regards, by the way," she said with a brief smile. "Jamie and Nikolai especially; they're all so appreciative of what you guys did for us with Elvin. Rescuing Benny and Lydia and Renee. They haven't called because they were giving you guys some time to enjoy being alone together." I smiled at her. "But I'm supposed to tell you that the Wolfden is your home— *both* you guys— and they want you back just as soon as your little legs can carry you there."

"That's really sweet," I said, flushed with pleasure. I had loved the Wolfden, the little trailer and RV community just outside of Hinesville, from the moment Roberta first brought me there. I'd met some great people whom I'd formed friendships with. Of course, it turned out those people were all friends of mine in childhood, hence the instant connection I felt with them, and as my memories had started to return, I'd realized just how close-knit a group we all were. The thought of going back there, among people who I shared such a history and kindship with after being so lonely for so long…well, I could think of much worse prospects.

"What do you say?" I nudged Phillip with an elbow. "Should we get a trailer and hitch it at the Wolfden?"

"I'd be just fine with that," Phillip responded easily.

"You'd live in a trailer in dry, dusty South Georgia?" I asked incredulously. "A rich and famous rock star like you?"

"In a heartbeat," he said with a smile. "Why wouldn't I? As long as I've got you, I'm happy. Plus, I like it here."

It appeared I wasn't the only one who felt a genuine kinship with the Wolfden. I leaned forward and kissed Phillip on the lips, beaming.

"Ugh, y'all are gross," Burt said, smiling. Then her dour face was back. "We'll work out the logistics of the big move later, though. I wasn't kidding about the vacation, Stormy. We need to get down to Florida. Quick."

I sighed, tracing circles of condensation on the table. "Right. This is about my dad, I assume…?"

"Yes," Roberta said. "We've had … some news." She turned to my mom, biting her lip. "Laureen, did you want to…?"

"What is it?' I demanded, my mouth going dry.

Mom looked down at her lap for a moment, a gesture I'd come to associate with her now-sober state. It seemed she did that when she was gathering courage to talk about something difficult. She looked up at me, her face pale. "Stormy, honey… they've…they've found a body."

"What? Who has?" I asked though I already knew.

Her face was ashen. "It was in the wreckage at your father's house."

"Is it Daddy?" I gripped the table, hard enough for my knuckles to go white. Phillip's arm was around me in a flash.

"We don't know," Mom said. A wave of relief crashed over me, followed by a smaller wave of hope, hope that it could be somebody, anybody else. "They can't, um, they can't identify the remains…they were too burned…it's going to take a few days. You know, DNA testing and all…" She took a long gulp of her Shirley Temple, seemingly unable to continue. I was so distracted I'd never even seen the drinks arrive.

"What else do we know?" Phillip asked Roberta, his arm around me tight, holding me up, which was a good thing, because I felt so woozy I thought I might faint dead away right there at the table.

"Pretty much nothing," Roberta answered. "We only know about the body because Dee called Laureen and asked you guys to come."

"That's interesting," Phillip said. His voice had gone all business, and I loved him for it. I could barely think straight. "That the current wife would call the ex-wife and ask something like that. You'd think she'd let the police do it."

"From what I, um, what I gather, the police aren't being much help," Mama replied, her voice wavering, as though she were fighting back tears. "I was surprised she called me too, but I'm glad she did. The police are investigating, but they aren't looking at this as anything but an accident, a run-of-the-mill house fire. They don't seem to think it was arson. Dee suspects otherwise. She thinks someone set the fire deliberately. She's scared whoever did it might come for her and the little one. And she wants us down there for when they identify the body." Mama reached forward and touched my hand. "So if it *is* Chad"—her voice broke—"we'll be there to find out."

"I guess that's kind of Dee," I said because I didn't know what else to say.

"Yes," Mama said. It appeared she didn't either.

"So when should we head out?" Roberta asked softly.

"When did I say I was going?" I asked, sitting up.

"What?" Mama looked at me in surprise. "Honey, I know all this has been hard, but he's your father. We can't just stay here and do nothing."

"Why not?" I asked. "Let the police identify the body, and once we know, we know. If it's not him, we can determine that something is up, and cross that bridge when we come to it. But if it is him, well…" I shrugged, briefly looking down at my water glass. "We can move on."

"Stormy!" Mama's voice was a breathless, shocked whisper.

"This has been really hard on her, Laureen," Burt explained, though her dark brown eyes gave away her disappointment in me. "It's no wonder she doesn't want to get involved, is it?"

"She's been really obtuse about going down there for days," Phillip said, and I cut him a dirty look. "She knows she's the key to all this…this madness."

"Yeah, and I'm sick of it." My voice came out sullen and angry. "And you can *all* stop talking about me as if I'm not here. I *am* sick of it, all of it. Every time one stupid obstacle is out of the way, here comes another. Y'all expect me to just wave my magical fingers—which I still don't even know how to properly do, by the way—and make all the big, bad problems just disappear, and nobody understands that I *don't want to!*"

"I do understand," Roberta said, reaching across the table and putting her hand over mine. "It's bullshit, Stormy. We all know that, and we know you want to go back to your life. Of course you do! But we can't just stand by while your father is missing. It might be related to everything else that's happened…You won't be going in alone; you have all of us at the Wolfden, and Phillip, and your mom, too—all of us backing you. And we won't ever let you go in alone. Not ever again. I promise." Her eyes were pleading with me.

"Are you offering to form a coven with me?" I asked with a slow, silly smile.

She looked surprised. "Haven't we done that already?" She squeezed my hand. "Why else would I be here, offering to help you find your father?"

Tears sprang to my eyes. Not wanting to appear emotional, I busied myself with grabbing a breadstick from the basket the waitress sat down on our table. As she took our orders—I ordered the decadent lemon hazelnut pasta I'd been dreaming about, Burt ordered eggplant parmigiana, and both Phillip and my mother ordered steaks—I was grateful for the moment it gave me to gather my thoughts, to control my feelings, and to decide what to do.

I'd only been down to see my father, Dee, and Shably once since he'd moved to Panama City Beach. It hadn't been for his lack of trying. He'd called to invite me to pretty much every holiday since I'd been married to Tess. So had Mom, if I was giving credit where it was due, though she'd always been drunken and slurring as she made grand promises about the meals she'd cook and what a good time we'd have. Tess' father was long dead, and his mother had no real interest in him after she remarried and moved to Oregon, so he had missed the family dynamic and had gotten along famously with my mother. He'd never found her drunken rambling or chaotic life to be a real bother, despite my constant embarrassment. He'd had a slightly more aloof, cool relationship with my father, but he'd genuinely liked him too.

"We all had shitty childhoods. You can get over it and be an adult, or you can wear it as armor the rest of your life," Tess had said once, cracking open a Natty Light. "Ain't no question, if you ask me."

It was one of many things Tess had said to me over the years that, while technically right, had been an asshole thing to say.

I could make amends with my mom. As a kid, she'd neglected me, but I'd always known she loved me. And after Daddy left, we'd tried to patch our relationship, even *before* she'd quit drinking. Now, knowing that she'd gotten sober and seeing her put everything into helping Roberta and me, I was certain she'd never given up on her devotion to me. She'd just been sick, that was all.

Daddy, though, was another story. He'd shown little

interest in me from the very beginning. I had no memories of him teaching me to ride a bike, or taking me fishing, or watching morning cartoons with bowls of cereal in our laps. He had not accompanied me to father-daughter dances or taken me out for ice cream. The only real memories I had were of him sitting on our worn couch, watching football or wrestling. Many a night, I'd sat watching WWF or WCW, all the wrestlers I'd come to know as pseudo-celebrities: Sting, Hulk Hogan, Ric Flair, Macho Man Randy Savage. I'd watched, pretending not to realize it was all a "work," and even as a kid, I had given those guys credit for the sheer amount of choreography and artistry that went into faking such a sport. But it hadn't really been my thing, at least not at first. I'd done it for my dad. So we would have something to share.

Dad loved his wrestling. Those were really the only outings he'd ever taken Mama and me on, wrestling at the flea market. Which, incidentally, was where I'd first seen Benny, a memory I had only recently uncovered. But even those excursions were few and far between.

Most of the time, he had been parked in the living room, blitzed, zoning out as if the TV were a spaceship that might suck him from the atmosphere. The few times he did leave, he'd stay gone for hours or even days at a time. I found out in adulthood that he'd been out on benders, cheating on my mother with anything that moved. She'd told me recently that he'd even had a woman on the side who lived right under our noses in the same trailer park as us.

Daddy had very little interest in his daughter, but that was almost welcome, considering how he treated my mother. He'd looked at her like she was a fly buzzing around his head that he couldn't wait to swat out of existence. He'd verbally abused her for my entire childhood, calling her awful names, telling her she was ugly, she was fat, she stunk, that her drinking would put her in an early grave. He told her she'd lost her looks and that no other man would ever want her. And I'd been there to hear it all. Just my father, staring into the TV as though he could will himself into it, casually hurling abuse at my mother. That had been my normal.

Folks were always coming over in those days – usually some ne'er-do-well who looked worse for wear, unwashed and rude, sitting on our couch, waiting as my father doled out whatever they were buying in little knock-off brand plastic baggies. Elvin was one of those people. His dealings with my father birthed the arrangement that caused my entire undoing. Everything, including whatever I was now—a witch, I supposed—and everything that had happened, then and now, ,my meeting Phillip; all of it was orchestrated by some long-ago arrangement that my father had made with Elvin. All to get cheaper weed. All to feed a high that never seemed to satisfy him, to try and escape from a life of his own creation.

I never knew whether Daddy had invited me down so many times because he was genuinely contrite and wanted to make amends for my childhood, or if he just wanted to show off his new life—his pretty, much-younger trophy wife and his beautiful baby daughter who was everything I'd never been. Simply so he could play pretend at a family life that we'd never had. Neither option appealed to me. I wasn't interested in making amends. If Daddy felt bad about the way he'd treated Mom and me, that was his business. Let him work it out with a therapist or live with the guilt; I owed him nothing. And if he just wanted to show off and play the big family man to feed his own ego, well, I obviously wasn't on board.

I was a grown woman now, and I'd seen my share of heartbreak. I'd made many mistakes, all of them born from the trauma I'd experienced as a kid. I just wanted to move on; why was that so hard? Why did my past keep trying to drag me back?

I realized everyone was staring at me. I'd been sitting

there, lost I thought, holding my food in mid-air for who knows how long. I dipped the crunchy breadstick into a dish of olive oil sprinkled with fresh basil and nibbled on the end. Pure heaven, but I felt like hell. "I hate this," I said finally, chewing. "I just fucking hate it. You know?"

"I know." Roberta's expression was sympathetic.

She did know. Burt's own father was much worse. I sighed.

Her soft brown eyes were kind and full of empathy, probably more than I deserved. I was being a total brat. "Once it's all over, it will be well and truly over forever, Stormy," she assured me. "We just have to like, get these last few ducks in a row. I know it. I feel it. And then we can go back to our life at the Wolfden. All of us. I promise."

"Are you sure that's a promise you can keep?" I asked.

She nodded. "There aren't many people I would swear to, but I'm swearing it to you right now. We're going to end this shitty, terrible situation once and for all. Close the chapter on our shitty childhoods. Finito. So what do you say? Are you on board?"

I stared at her for a moment, Phillip's warm, strong arm a constant presence around my shoulder, buoying me. God, I loved him so much. I thought for a moment, still chewing.

"Let's say we go down," I said, Roberta's shoulders dropping in relief. "What are we going to do? The local police are investigating his disappearance and the fire, and even if Dee thinks they're doing a subpar job, we can't just take over. How are we realistically going to help?"

"I figured we'd talk to the locals first," Roberta explained. "Benny knows a couple of people who live in Panama City just over the bridge from the beach. We can connect with them, start asking around, see if anyone knows of your dad, knows of any of the stuff he was involved in. We'll keep our eyes and ears open. Just hang around and…see." She swallowed, then continued. "While we wait for them to identify…the body."

I took a sip of my wine and, with my other hand under the table, squeezed Phillip's. He squeezed it back immediately, making me feel better. "So what are the chances that ol' Uncle Elvin has something to do with this?"

Roberta looked at me strangely. "My dad's dead, Stormy."

"I know," I said, staring right back at her. "But dead people don't always stay dead. This lunk of meat right here is your proof." I nudged Phillip's sturdy frame with my shoulder and blew him a kiss. He responded by flipping me off before breaking a breadstick in half and shoveling it into his mouth. "God, you're classy." Now that I'd stopped fighting everyone and agreed to go to PCB, I felt much, much lighter. Funny, that.

"I watched as they buried him," Roberta said in a low voice. She clearly didn't want to talk about it, and I didn't blame her. Her feelings for her father were very complicated, and she'd been through so much worse than I had, and only a few short days ago. I'd never get the image of Roberta, tied up on a dirty couch, her face streaked with tears, out of my head. "I made sure. Damn sure. He was in that casket when it was lowered into the ground. And I stayed to watch the dirt get dumped in. So unless some graverobber came and dug him back up, Elvin is gone. For good."

"Okay," I said quickly. "I'm sorry. I didn't mean to upset you."

Roberta waved that away, taking a sip of her own wine, appearing thoughtful. "But you know…Elvin and Guthrie weren't the only 'bad guys,' Stormy. We're talking almost twenty years of their dealings. They had associates all over the place. Guys like Shank and Tess who were on Guthrie's payroll. Thugs, basically. Who's to say one of them hasn't cropped back up and is trying to exact a little revenge?"

"But what purpose would that serve?" I asked. "It seems

like with both Guthrie and Elvin being gone, they'd just scatter."

"No," Roberta said. "When you cut down a weed, another one just grows to take its place."

As she said the words, a person in the back of the restaurant, loitering in the hall near the bathrooms, caught my eye. He was tall and thin, almost underweight, with a shock of greasy, burgundy hair falling down over one eye and large gauges in his ears. He looked out of place in his Hawaiian shirt and cargo pants. He was looking intently at me, but when he noticed me looking back, he darted into the men's bathroom. I stared at the closing door for a moment, then shook it off. I was seeing spooks everywhere, and likely, it all meant nothing.

"But *why*?" I asked Roberta, turning back to the conversation. "Why here; why now? Why would an outsider care about Guthrie and Elvin? I mean, magic is kind of a niche interest. Not your everyday mob stake."

"It's not just about the magic, honey," Mama spoke up, her voice quiet. She was holding onto her Shirley Temple glass so tightly it looked as though it might shatter in her hand. "It's never been just about that."

"What?" This was news to me. "What do you mean?"

"Elvin and Guthrie loved magic shit, sure," Roberta explained. "As fanatical as they were, that was just their private hobby; it wasn't their *business*. Their 'organization,' if you wanna call it that…" Roberta sounded matter-of-fact. "…it's always been about drugs."

"Oh." Of course. I'd never even thought of it, but it was the logical explanation, one that I should have put together a long time ago. Elvin's whole preoccupation with my magic had been mainly just about him and his own weird, kooky obsessions. But the business that he and Guthrie—and Lee and Shank and Tess and Sloan and everyone else in between—had been in was just normal, run-of-the-mill drugs. Had I really been so arrogant to assume it was all about me, about some dumb magic? For god's sake, I had known all along that Guthrie was originally Phillip's dealer—that's how they'd met in the first place. "Well, I feel dumb."

"Oh, give yourself a break," Roberta said. "You've barely had time to think. There's still a lot to fill you in on. Twenty years' worth, give or take." She crunched on another breadstick. "We can talk more on the trip. Since y'all are going?" Her large brown eyes were full of empathy and hope, but a fiery determination burned there too. This trip was about more than just helping me. It was Roberta's way of exacting justice, of making things right. For all of us.

I sighed.

I looked at Phillip. His face gave nothing away, but a familiar flash of his eyes and another quick squeeze under the table told me all I needed to know. He was leaving it up to me, but he wanted to go. Phillip Deville would never, ever, opt out of such an opportunity.

Out of the corner of my eye, I saw the waitress making her way back to our table, her tray loaded with our meals. My stomach rumbled painfully. "Maybe I'm just saying this because I want to shovel that pasta in my face and stop talking about this shit," I said with a dry chuckle. "And I'm sure I'll regret it later, but…fuck it. We're in." I turned to Phillip with a goofy smile. "I guess we're going to Florida?"

"I love the beach." Phillip shrugged, holding up his hand to make the devil sign beloved by metalheads everywhere. Then, with a sly grin, he let his thumb pop out, wiggling his hand to make a hang ten, laughing uproariously at my grimace.

Four

I emerged from the hotel bathroom in a cloud of steam, the cold air from the AC hitting me like a slap in the face. I'd spent too long in the shower—I was going to make Phillip late—but I couldn't get over the amazing water pressure.

That and I was just plain old stalling. I loved my little trailer and would never feel anything but at home there, and I was used to roughing it—happy to, most of the time. But being pampered with room service, high thread-count sheets, a mini bar, and an amazing bathroom with two showerheads and a jacuzzi tub had me feeling all kinds of precious. Maybe the hotel in Florida would be similarly nice, I hoped as I ran my fingers through my freshly dried hair, teasing it. Oh, who was I kidding. It would be a dive.

The truth was, I wasn't ready to leave this cocoon with Phillip and head back out into the real world where shit always seemed to be coated in fifteen layers of stress and secrecy, and where I was always either on the run or running after someone, constantly prying open secret after secret only to find more awfulness buried within like my own personal set of torturous

Russian nesting dolls. At least here, time had stopped for a moment and I could breathe.

But outside these cushy hotel walls, life carried on, from my missing father and the mysterious circumstances surrounding his disappearance to the likely curious and cheerful buzz of fans as they woke up tomorrow to news breaking that cult-status rock star Phillip Deville had been found alive, well, and bumming around the beaches of Florida. I could hide in here forever, but I couldn't stop the forces at play from bursting their way in. Might as well face the music while I had some semblance of control.

"You're still primping?" I stood in the doorway and laughed, regarding Phillip, who was seated in front of the hotel vanity, squinting into the mirror. "Save some of that makeup for me. I do need a turn, you know." He'd been preening in front of that mirror since before I'd gotten in the shower. I surveyed him; there was no need for all that fussing because he looked damn good. His hair, starting to grow out, was tousled with a little pomade, giving him a shiny, sexy bedhead that was undeniably hot. He'd let his facial hair grow just past a five-o-clock shadow, and I was surprised to see a thread or two of gray on his chin. Like most men, it gave him a debonair sort of worldliness that only made him all the more sexy. I walked over to him, noticing on closer inspection that he'd used a swish or two of my eyeliner under his eyes, just enough to smudge and give a slept-in, grunge look. It was very nineties, but it worked. Lord, did it work.

Phillip Deville had always, always been hot as fire, if my decades-long fandom was any indication. But with a scruffy beard, threaded with strands of silver foxiness, slicked-back hair, and smudgy, smokey eyes? My mouth actually watered.

Phillip had already dressed in the new black shirt and jeans he'd bought earlier at the local mall, and laced up his black leather boots, the bottoms of his jeans rolled up over them. The fitted black blazer I recognized from the day when I'd almost murdered him from jealousy upon finding out he was meeting his ex-wife for dinner hung on the chair, freshly dry-cleaned and ready to slip on. Phillip looked so damn good. He turned to me with a sly look, and as he did, I caught a whiff of his delectable cologne, hints of musk and ocean water enveloping my senses.

"They aren't going to be able to smell you through their phones, you know," I teased him, and he pulled me down into his lap, grinning.

"I know," he murmured into my ear. "I did that for you."

"Mmmm, I'm grateful," I murmured back, snuggling into his neck. His skin was warm and clean, and I wanted nothing more than to drag him over to the bed and bite him on his scruffy chin. "You smell amazing."

"So do you," he growled, and I purred into his neck. If we were quick…

But no, we had somewhere to be. I couldn't keep stalling, not even for the sexiest of reasons.

"Go ahead and do your makeup," Phillip said, seeming to come to the same conclusion, reluctantly standing up and giving me the chair. "I'm as ready as I'm going to be."

"Are you nervous?" I asked, settling into the chair and reaching for my concealer. I dabbed a little more than usual under my sleep-deprived eyes and blended it with my foam brush, patting it gently over my puffy skin. I glanced in the mirror at Phillip standing behind me. His face was pinched with nerves, but he shook his head.

"Yes and no," he admitted. "Dealing with the media is the same as it's ever been, I guess, so I'm not so much nervous about the interview itself. It's more…the fans that I'm worried about."

"You think they'll be upset?" I blended a neutral

eyeshadow over my brow, then swiped a hint of red in the corner of each lid.

"I don't know," he answered. "I hope not."

"Well," I said, hoping my hand would stop trembling long enough to apply my liquid liner straight, "I guess we'll know soon enough. I think…I think it's going to go okay."

"You're probably right," Phillip said, but when I searched for his eyes in the mirror, he was looking off into the distance, his face full of uncertainty.

I sat on a bench directly in front of the statue, sitting slightly to the left so I could peer around and see Phillip and the reporter, Dylan Quint, sitting on a bench across from me. I couldn't hear much of them speaking with the large expanse between us, but if I craned my ear to the left, I could just barely make out Phillip's voice.

He had chosen this little park because he said it seemed peaceful. Obviously, Phillip wasn't as up on his Savannah history as I was. But he was right; the beautiful green foliage, sweetly placed benches, and tourists milling around looking at statues of James Oglethorpe and John Wesley were rather quaint. On any other day, I'd be cackling with laughter at the irony of this goth-metal rock king choosing such a goofy, downright wholesome locale for an interview, but I was too nervous to laugh at Phillip today. What was going to happen once my lover threw the gauntlet down and revealed himself to the world?

We were lucky it hadn't happened already. By some divine miracle, the guys who had ambushed us by the elevators the night before had, so far, refrained from releasing their footage. Before Phillip would even sit down, he'd presented Dylan

Quint with a piece of paper he'd drafted, explicitly banning them from releasing the footage and pictures under threat of legal action, and Dylan had signed it quickly.

But they hadn't kept totally quiet. I'd managed a covert Instagram search while in the bathroom earlier and had seen that #PhillipDeville was trending. News had definitely "broken" that he'd been spotted, and a few diehard fans were speculating wildly about that, but so far, there was no official word from Dylan Quint, Kevin Ramford, or anyone else. It was all just rumors for now. I'd seen a couple of theories, including one very far-fetched kidnapping plot that involved the British royal family that had me laughing uncontrollably, but for the most part, the news had not broken on any major news outlets. Yet.

It wouldn't surprise me at all if Dylan Quint had leaked a teaser from some anon account just to gain a little traction ahead of time. I figured that by dinnertime today, the news would be circulating among the Who's Who of media conglomerates. Which was why this interview was so important. Phillip had one shot to get his narrative out there before one could be created. He might not quite understand, but I certainly did, as someone who lived in this world and had never left it—you become the story before the story becomes you.

I thought back to that scene in the foyer and felt a chill. The way the journalists had confronted us so easily, how they'd caught us off guard. How I'd stupidly led Phillip to the hotel like a lamb to slaughter. Phillip had handled the situation in a relatively chill way, but it still bothered me how easily the man had stepped onto the elevator and how calmly and confidently he'd turned to us and demanded that Phillip speak. As though we owed them something, as though we had no right to privacy at all. Thankfully, Dylan Quint or someone at

Vice/GOTHzine had had the good sense to tell Kevin Ramford to keep his ass at home today.

While following celebrities and influencers and political figures on social media and seeing how one fluke could become a viral sensation was entertaining, how the concept of "fame" had changed so drastically even from the early aughts. It was one thing to live through those changes and see them play out in everyday life. But it was another thing entirely to suddenly be *living* it.

I knew my life was about to change in a very, very big way. I'd undergone some pretty major changes already. And while it should seem that learning I was a witch—with actual powers and all that entailed—and that there was an entire past's worth of experiences and memories that had been wiped clean would be the biggest transition I had to go through…I couldn't help the sense that this, this thing with Phillip, would be even *bigger.*

This threat—or promise?—of newfound fame, combined with my new, very uncertain life as a witch at the forefront of a coven I hadn't even known existed two weeks ago, was all very stressful and very hard to wrap my head around. But there was something else too. Something that had been nagging at my consciousness, popping up in my dreams, making it hard for me to sleep. Something I hadn't allowed myself to fully think about yet. But I couldn't keep the thought contained forever.

The woman I'd seen standing near the front of the hotel, wearing a sleek black coat and dressed to the nines like she was a rich woman headed to a cocktail party, the woman whose face had worn perfectly applied, elegant makeup; all dramatic eyes and impeccable foundation, but bare lips shiny with ChapStick…

Phillip had been too distracted by the elevator ambush and hadn't noticed her.

But I had.

I hadn't said anything to anyone yet. Why I was keeping it quiet, I didn't quite know, but I thought it might have something to do with the fact that I missed her. And I was ashamed to admit it.

What I did know, though, I knew without a shadow of a doubt—the elegant, beautiful woman standing in the doorway, watching us as we dodged cameras in our faces, trying to navigate a situation out of our control, her face lighting up in a dazzling smile, had been Sloan.

Whatever nerves Phillip had had back at the hotel seemed to have dissipated. He sat with perfect posture, one long leg slightly positioned over the other, his black boots propped against the foot of the bench, his large hands clasped in front of him and resting lightly in his lap. The wind moved his black hair, whipping some of his shiny locks in front of his face, where they fell just below his brow and over one eye. Phillip pushed it gingerly to the side with one long, graceful finger, and as he did, the reporter snapped a picture.

That's the money shot, I thought to myself. *Might as well pack it in now.*

Jesus, he was handsome. Sometimes I'd look at him and my breath would catch, in awe of the fact that Phillip Deville was alive and hearty and strong and *oh so beautiful* and somehow, despite everything, *mine.* As he sat there, graceful and hulking at the same time, his black hair a sharp contrast to his bright, striking eyes, I found it hard to breathe. Phillip was so laid-backand yet sophisticated, effortlessly cool and sexy. It just came naturally to him. Phillip Deville lived and breathed rock god; he didn't even have to try. As if on cue, he extended one arm and casually busied himself with adjusting the sleeve of his black jacket, effortlessly sexy, almost as though he'd heard me.

"Let's start with the obvious," Dylan Quint was saying as I snapped back down to earth. "Obviously—because we're sitting here talking to you—you're not dead. Can you explain, Mr. Deville, where you've been for the past twenty-three, almost twenty-four, years?"

"Of course," Phillip answered in a measured tone, an easy smile on his face, as though it were the most natural question in the world. "I've been everywhere. Like the Johnny Cash song?" He waited for the reporter to smile, and when he only got a puzzled look, he went on. "I lived in Boston for a while, traveled some, then I moved here to South Georgia not too long ago."

"Well, what I mean, Mr. Deville…more specifically…what have you been *doing* all these years?"

Phillip shrugged. "I was just living. Laying low. I wasn't deliberately trying to hide." Phillip lied smoothly, brushing his hair out of his eyes again. He leered a little, the sunlight catching his bright white teeth. It was the wolfish grin I'd come to know and love. The rock star grin, the grin that made Phillip. Another money shot.

"How did you stay hidden for so long?" Quint pushed. "You're a recognizable figure. It seems like someone would have spotted you, unless you were making some concerted effort to like…"

"To disappear?" Phillip chuckled deep in his throat. "And they did, from time to time," he answered evenly. "Recognize me, I mean. I suppose people just assumed I was a lookalike or something and went on their way." His eyes twinkled with mirth. "People can convince themselves of anything if they want to believe it hard enough."

"Can you explain how the whole thing started? Why you

faked your death?" Dylan Quint asked, sitting forward eagerly. I could almost read his mind through his body language. He was flashing forward to the awards, the promotions, the recognition he might get for this interview.

"I didn't fake my death," Phillip clarified. "People thought I had died, and I just…let them think it. I never corrected them."

I covered my mouth to hide my surprise. Phillip hadn't thought this answer through. There was a death certificate. The internet sleuths, the amateur reporters, they'd go looking and they'd find it. All it would take was a membership to one of those genealogy websites and someone would find every single public record available. Phillip simply didn't realize just *how* accessible these things were now.. But how would he explain *that* away once people started digging?

"But allowing people to think you had passed away?" the reporter pressed. "Isn't that unfair?"

"I suppose it is, in hindsight," Phillip replied. "I wasn't exactly in my right mind at the time."

"Can you take us through those moments?" Dylan Quint asked. "Your last moments, as it were, or what the public at large *thought* were your last moments?"

"Sure," Phillip said patiently. "I did indeed overdose; those reports were true. I had quite a hefty drug problem, you understand. After that last time—and I did legally die for a few seconds— everyone in my life, my family, friends, my band, they all came together and staged an intervention. They told me they couldn't let me slowly kill myself.

"And I knew they were right. I was headed down a very dark path, and I wasn't going to make it if I didn't make some big changes." Phillip paused for a moment, likely remembering his very real past, and my heart hurt for him. "However, I knew as long as I continued with the band—continued as a rock star, if you will—that I wouldn't be able to kick the habit.

Unfortunately, for me, as with so many others in my profession, sex, drugs, and rock 'n' roll do indeed go hand in hand. It wasn't possible for me to get clean and turn my life around so long as I was famous."

"So you decided to leave public life?"

"Yes," Phillip answered. "It was a split-second decision but not one that I made rashly. I'd been thinking about leaving the business for a very long time. The overdose was just...the straw that broke the camel's back."

"That's understandable. But why not just...retire? Make an announcement that you're done with showbiz and quietly fade into the night?" Quint asked.

Phillip nodded. "I could have done that, yes. But as you well know, being in the profession that you're in, just announcing that you're leaving music isn't a foolproof way of getting your privacy. You see actors and musicians doing that sort of thing from time to time, announcing they're quitting the biz or whatever, but it always takes months, sometimes even years, to completely leave the public consciousness. The paparazzi still follow them. The gossip mill still makes money off them. They get harassed online. They're hounded for interviews or tell-all books. It doesn't end just because you decide you're done."

"You were afraid the public wouldn't let you go?"

"Perhaps," Phillip said thoughtfully, stroking his chin. "Or perhaps I was more afraid I'd use the public—and my fans—as an excuse not to ever let go *myself*, even though I knew I needed to."

"I see." Quint nodded, appearing thoughtful. Now it was a smile I was hiding behind my hand. Phillip Deville could charm the pants off anyone.

Phillip paused, then went on. "And in my case, there were unique circumstances that led up to my decision, that made it possible. You see, news leaked about my overdose almost immediately. The word was out before my family had even arrived at the ER. And someone leaked to the press that I'd died." He shook his head. "Even though I'd been revived, everyone in the media thought I was a goner. And they ran with the story. When I came to in that hospital room, and all my family and friends were there staging that intervention… well, all my fans had already heard from Kurt Loder"—his lip turned up at the mention of the MTV veejay, who he hated—"that I was dead. They already thought I was gone."

"So you just…"

"So I just…decided to let them think it," Phillip finished for him. "It seemed like the best decision at the time. It'd give me some time to decompress, to get clean, to decide what to do. Celeb death hoaxes were already a thing…I figured if I changed my mind and popped up a few days later, like, 'surprise, I'm not dead,' it wouldn't be a huge deal; people would understand. But as the days went on and I started rehab, I realized I didn't want to come out of hiding. I didn't want to come back. I wanted to stay gone." Phillip's face was deeply sincere and a little sad. "There was such a freedom in it. For the first time in years, I felt like I belonged to nobody but myself, and I wasn't ready to give that up."

I felt a pang listening to him. He might be lying about the details, but the feelings he was expressing were very real. A current of worry ran through me. What if getting back into this very public life was a mistake? One that would harm not only Phillip, but me as well?

"So you disappeared," Quint prompted, the charmed look gone from his angular, bearded face, replaced with an expression of almost irritation. I wondered if he had been into the Bloomer Demons, way back when. "Leaving your fans to mourn. And did you indeed stay clean and get well during that time?"

"I did," Phillip said. "I haven't touched a single drug in over twenty years."

"Mr. Deville, you never did say definitively what you've been doing all this time. You mentioned some travel. Did you get married again? Have any children? How have you made money?"

Quint was getting too personal. That look returned to Phillip's his face, the homicidal deer in the headlights look. But Phillip took a deep breath and answered. "I don't know what to tell you. I laid low. I lived off my estate for a long while and did a few odd jobs to make money when I needed it. Nothing terribly fancy or that needs going into detail." He shifted and crossed his legs, sighing. "And no, I never did remarry or have any children, but…well, I do have someone special in my life, and let's just say I'm very much looking forward to the future in that regard."

He didn't look my way—I knew he didn't want to draw any attention to me lest Quint decide to focus on me, even temporarily—but I could feel his inner gaze warming me, lighting me up with a glow. I could feel his love, his intention, and it made my heart start to thump fast and hard. I stared at Phillip, watching the way his strong jaw moved as he spoke, the way his long, inky eyelashes tickled his cheek as he closed his eyes to carefully curate his answers. He was so beautiful it hurt.

Marriage and kids? I hadn't even thought about it. Not once. I hadn't had the chance. But evidently, Phillip had.

Oh, boy…

I tucked those thoughts away, intent on concentrating on the interview, but the idea poked at my brain like a Q-tip in the ear, tickling ever so lightly, distracting me. What would it look like—what would it feel like—what would it *be* like—to be married to Phillip Deville? To tour with him, meet his family, set up a home with him, possibly have his children…?

Stormy Deville…

I didn't have any real feelings on changing my name. The only reason I'd taken Tess' was because I didn't feel any strong tie to my parents, my father especially. I didn't know how many people even knew my maiden name was Bradley; I wasn't sure Phillip even did before the news of Charles 'Chad' Bradley's house burning down and him being missing had taken over our lives. At the time, changing my name to Spooner had felt like I was purging my past, a thought that was laughable now. Could I shake off Stormy Spooner for good and become someone else? Stormy Deville did have a nice ring to it.

I shook off the thoughts again and focused on paying attention, avoiding the flashes of heat in my head that were undoubtedly coming from Phillip. He wasn't looking at me, but he was *thinking* at me, and inside my head, he was laughing. His chin rested on his closed fist, a gesture of both attentiveness and slight annoyance. His body language said he was getting bored of this interview, and he was pretty much done, whether Dylan Quint was or not.

"Is there anything you'd like to say to your fans? The fans who mourned you, attended your memorial, bought your posthumous album, who have visited your grave every year since? The fans who have admired and loved you, even in your absence?" Lord, Quint was laying it on thick. He seemed to be taking this betrayal quite personally for an impartial rock journalist.

"My fans," Phillip said in a dulcet tone, as though butter wouldn't melt on his tongue. "I assume most of those fans have spent the past twenty-three years focusing on much more important things than little old me." He threw back his head and laughed, his sharp, white teeth glinting in the sunlight. Then he stroked his salt-and-pepper jaw and smiled a megawatt smile, another money shot for the coffers. I felt a pulse of heat low in my belly, a pulse that his fans would no doubt feel too once this interview went live. Good Lord, Deville…

"Of course, though," Phillip said, his grin still firmly in place. Behind the grin, though, his eyes were sad. Only I knew the truth—the hidden pain that he still felt. This was hard for him. Spinning tales, pretending that he'd been alive all this time, that he'd been quietly experiencing life when the truth was, he'd actually missed the past twenty years, and had had no time to make up for all the regrets of his past life. "I'd like to say thank you to the fans. Thank you for your love and support, and for listening to my music all this time. It does my heart good—truly—to know that people still find my work meaningful, that it resonates with them. I'm very touched that they've kept my memory alive all these years. And I hope my story—either version—can be a cautionary tale about how *not* to handle things, and that those fans who struggle with addiction or mental health problems seek out help. There's no shame in that." Phillip clasped his hands in his lap and leaned forward. "That's it. That's all. Just thanks."

"And I suppose there's just one more question, the one that everyone will be wondering," Dylan Quint said as Phillip stood up to go.

"What question is that?" Phillip asked. "I think I've answered all the big ones. The sound bites."

"Oh, there's just one more big one, Mr. Deville," Dylan Quint answered.

"Shoot."

"Is there new music on the horizon?"

I expected a flippant denial, or possibly a deflection, since Phillip had told me he and the guys hadn't ironed out details. From what he'd said, his former bandmates were interested in a reunion for the financial possibilities, but he'd acted like he wasn't sure, telling me he'd only agree to something if I was on board.

But Phillip did not seem surprised by the question, nor was he offended by it. In fact, he stopped laughing, his eyes taking on a little sparkle. He leaned forward, almost conspiratorially. "Well…as you know, the Bloomer Demons can never reform with the original lineup." His face fell a little. "Since Kim is gone."

"And Kim Rzeznick is really gone?" the reporter asked. Phillip flinched almost imperceptibly. "Really, truly? Nothing faked?"

"He's really, truly gone," Phillip said, his face darkening. "God rest his soul. And I told you, I didn't fake—"

"So no current plans for a reunion or any new music?" Quint interjected, and in a way, I was thankful for his rudeness. I didn't want Phillip to feel sad, thinking about Kim. And I didn't like where this interview was headed, not at all.

"I didn't say that," Phillip said slyly, and my breath caught. "I am, after all, a musician. Whatever form that artistic expression takes…well, we'll just have to wait and see. I can say that I've been writing some music lately…and I wouldn't mind having the chance to perform it. We'll just have to see how things go and if it's something the fans might be interested in." He smiled. "I guess the answer is 'stay tuned.'"

"Well, that's certainly very exciting," Dylan Quint said, barreling forward. "I know another question that fans have is about your ex-wife, Barb. Have you had any contact—"

"I believe you said that was your last question," Phillip said, his voice turning on a dime from sly and lighthearted to curt and dry. "And I think it was a good note to leave things on. I won't be answering any more questions today."

"But Mr. Deville, the fans want—"

"I think the fans will respect my privacy and hers," Phillip said, extending his hand to shake Dylan Quint's. "And so should you."

Dylan Quint had the good sense to stop it there; he extended his own arm, skinny and limp next to Phillip's strong, muscular one, and shook his hand. He clicked his phone off and slid it into his jeans' pocket, his face a mixture of excitement and disappointment. He'd clearly wanted to get more, but what he *had* gotten was a gracious plenty. It would be viral in no time.

I took my cue to get up from the bench and walk over to Phillip, as eager as he was to get out of here and back to the hotel. Some of what Phillip had said had alarms bells ringing, and other things had me warm with pleasure. I extended my own hand and shook Quint's, figuring I may as well cultivate a good relationship with the reporter; if things went the way I thought they would, we'd likely be seeing him again.

"Sorry about yesterday," Quint said to me as I pulled my hand back. "That ambush was unprofessional."

"Yeah, it was," I answered. "But it's all forgotten now. Just see that you uphold that contract you signed."

"Are you his manager?" Dylan asked, watching as I put the signed piece of paper in my bag. "I thought you were just the girlfriend."

I bristled. "*Just the girlfriend?* Is this 1950? Are you high? Jeez."

Phillip put an arm around me and gave me a goofy smile. He could tell I was upset, and about more than just the disrespectful, sexist camera guy. "So that wraps it up," he said, a curt nod and a straightening of his shoulders doing the talking for him.

"If you're certain you won't answer any more questions, then yes," Dylan said, extending his hand to shake Phillip's again, this time off camera. Phillip obliged. "We got enough pictures and stuff for the article and a few extra for our Twitter and Instagram." Despite Phillip's obvious irritation, the reporter was beaming; he looked positively thrilled to have gotten the story. I didn't like the guy, but I could hardly blame him. Breaking a story like this was the opportunity of a lifetime. "We'll probably put up a teaser, the big 'breaking news' announcement, on social media in a couple hours or so? The hour after lunch is always good for the most activity and clicks. Then late tomorrow morning we'll post the whole interview. That work for you?"

"I guess," Phillip said with a shrug. He still didn't quite understand, or have any interest in, social media.

"We've already sent payment to the address you gave us," the reporter said, and rattled off an email address that took me by surprise. It was the one linked to my payment app. I had totally forgotten that Phillip had insisted on being paid for the interview.

Phillip nodded. "Good. Well, I guess that's it, then. Thanks for your time."

"Were you a Bloomer Demons fan?" I asked Dylan Quint on impulse. He looked surprised. "You were, weren't you?"

"The biggest," he said after a pause, then smiled. "I used to visit Phillip's grave every year. I guess that's weird now."

"How did you find Phillip?" I asked. "How did you know to come here?"

"I'm afraid I can't say. I have to protect my source," Dylan Quint said after another uncomfortable pause, then extended his hand to shake mine again. We'd all shaken hands so many times it was beginning to get awkward. "It was nice meeting you both. And Phillip—Mr. Deville—I'm really glad you're alive. I really was a huge fan of yours. Still am."

"Thanks," Phillip said.

Dylan Quint moved to leave, then turned around and said, "Prepare for the onslaught, Mr. Deville. When the story breaks, it's going to be everywhere. I mean, rock stars faking their deaths is a tale as old as time—Tupac, Elvis, Jim Morrison—but you're the first who ever came *back*. It's going to be wild for a while. Paparazzi, crazed fans, the whole nine. You might want to lay low somewhere for a while."

"We intend to," Phillip said with a grim smile. "Somewhere you'll never find us, god willing."

I hoped and prayed he was right, but as we walked down the cobblestone street back toward the hotel, I couldn't help but think that Panama City Beach, Mecca of spring breakers everywhere, was probably the *last* place in the world we should be going.

FIVE

"So are we going to talk about it?"

I had my back turned to Phillip, hastily packing my duffel bag. I was glad to be going home briefly before heading out on the road so I could re-up on clothing and take a minute to pet Blinken and my newly adopted kitty, Nod. I'd already made arrangements with Lee, who had agreed to come check on them and feed them while I was away. I felt sorry for them, Blinken especially. Over the past few weeks, I'd barely been home, and I knew they were feeling neglected. I only hoped Blinken wouldn't scratch Lee's eyes out since the last time he'd seen him had been under different—and scarier, at least for Blinken—circumstances.

I sighed. "Talk about what?" I asked, even though I knew very well what he was referring to.

"I know you must have thoughts," Phillip said, coming up behind me and putting his arms around my shoulders. "About everything I said in the interview. Some things more than others."

"I mean, sure," I said, leaning into him. It was impossible not to melt whenever he touched me, even when I was annoyed. His skin touched mine, and I lost all resolve. "I definitely have thoughts…but I'm not sure they matter at this point. It sounds like you've already made up your mind."

"Honey, please don't be like that," Phillip said, squeezing me tighter, his mouth near my ear. "A lot of what I said, about making new music and stuff, I was just saying to…I don't know, heighten the suspense. To make the interview sound good. I knew he'd ask, and I didn't want to just outright say I had no plans."

"Why not?" I asked, turning to face him. "If that's the truth, why should you have any issue saying it?"

Phillip looked uncomfortable, his eyes cutting to the side.

I poked him in the chest. "Because you *do* have plans," I said accusingly. "You *are* planning to make a comeback."

"I wouldn't call it that…"

"*Don't call it a comeback?*'" I laughed, and he looked at me, confused. "Phillip, if you're wanting to get back into the music thing, to reform the band… just say that. It isn't like I wouldn't understand. I know music is your passion, and I know now that you're back in touch with Jason and Nate…"

"We haven't discussed anything concrete, really," Phillip said quickly. "I just wrote a few songs, got a few melodies down, when you and I were apart. And it made me realize how much I missed the whole thing. Honestly, the guys are into it for the money, but I don't even know if they've been practicing. It's been so long, so much has changed…" He sighed. "And without Kim…Look, I don't even know what the future holds. I'm just…we're just…thinking about things. That's all." He put his hands on my shoulders and looked deep into my eyes. "I'd never do anything that would cause you harm or make you unhappy. We're a team." His eyes bored into mine. "If you're not comfortable with it, say the word, and it'll never happen."

"Well, I suppose you're lucky that I'm literally the world's biggest Bloomer Demons fan," I said with a dry chuckle. "So it isn't very likely I would say no. And you knew that going in, which is why you felt so comfortable telling Dylan Quint to 'stay tuned.'"

"You're right. I'm sorry," he said, peering at me. He brushed a tendril of hair from my forehead, his touch warm. "I mean it, Stormy. Whatever I said in that interview, it all changes if you say so. I won't do *anything* to jeopardize your safety, your mental health, or what you and I have. You're the most important thing in the world to me. And you always will be."

I looked deep into his dark-green eyes. I could tell he was sincere. How had I gotten so lucky? "You're the most important thing to me too."

"I know," Phillip said, smiling back, his eyes soft. "I'm grateful for that every day. I love you."

"I love you too."

He met me for a kiss, his lips tender and sweet. When he pulled away, I cupped his stubbly cheek. "I'd never ask you not to make music," I promised. "We'll figure it out. Whatever you decide—with the band, without—we'll work it out, okay?"

"Only if you're sure."

"I'm sure," I said. "I love you. I want you to be happy."

Phillip's arms crushed me to him. "I want you to be happy too."

"I am," I said, pressing my head to his chest, feeling his heartbeat thumping steadily. "I'll be even happier when all this is over. Do you think we'll ever be able to just sit down and relax?"

"God, I hope so."

God, it was good to see Lee. I pitched forward and wrapped him in a clumsy hug, his white-blond hair tickling my temple as he bear-hugged me back. In such a short time, Lee and I had gone from strangers, to enemies, to almost-lovers, and now we had settled into an almost sibling-like friendship that I'd come to value deeply. It was probably circumstance, the two of us being thrown into stressful, high-trauma situations together that had bonded us, but I'd take it. I hoped the friendship would stick since I just adored Lee Courtenay. I pulled back and gave him a wide smile. "You're sure a sight for sore eyes."

"You act like I didn't just see you two days ago," Lee said, his freckled cheeks turning up with laughter. The light, purplish bruise fading on one of those cheeks was a sad reminder of the latest ordeal we'd all been through, but beyond that, he didn't look any worse for wear. In fact, he looked healthy—and happy. The smile on his lips was genuine. It might have been the happiest I'd ever seen him.

"Well, that may be true, but the last time we all saw each other, things were a bit tense," I retorted, cuffing him on the arm. "You can't blame me for being a little on edge."

"I'm safe," Lee said softly, putting a hand on my shoulder. "We all are. That's all that matters." His light-blue eyes were filled with kind concern. "And you're going to find your dad safe and sound too. I just know it."

"Sure we can't lend a hand?" I turned to see Benny—all muscular limbs—emerging from Lee's car, clad in his usual black denim shorts and cut-up T-shirt. As he came up the porch steps to embrace me with a friendly hug of his own, I couldn't help but think how good *he* looked too. His eyes were bright and he looked happier than I'd ever seen him as well; in fact, I wasn't sure I'd ever seen an actual grin on his face until now. Benny was often decked out in various levels of goth makeup and clothes, so seeing him au naturale like this was a bit of a novelty. His own black hair—thicker and with more threads of auburn than Phillip's but around the same length—was pulled back in a mini-ponytail, and he wasn't wearing his signature contacts, so I could see his soft brown eyes in all their natural glory. They made a nice contrast to the smattering of freckles across his tanned cheeks. It tickled me that both he and Lee were freckled; I imagined them giving each other freckly butterfly kisses, an image that filled me with warm giggles and would likely make them both glower with annoyance if they knew.

As I stepped back, Benny's eyes met Lee's, the two taking an eyeful of each other, and they flushed simultaneously. I looked at Phillip and grinned. Just watching them stand together on my porch, feeling the chemistry they had with each other, it was undeniable—they were soulmates, and without each other, both were totally lost. It did my heart good to watch as Benny casually wrapped an arm around Lee's shoulders, pulling him close, and leaned down to place a sloppy kiss on Lee's temple. The way they instinctively leaned into each other reminded me of Phillip and me.

I hated to break up the moment. I'd rather stand there watching the two of them and their obvious happiness forever, but Phillip and I had to get going. "To answer your question, the biggest favor you can do for me is just watch my cats," I said, "And keep an eye on the place in general, if you don't mind. I doubt anyone will come around but…well, it's me. You never know."

"We'll keep it all safe and sound," Lee assured me. "Scout's honor. I won't let anyone, or anything, come into this place. And I'll give the cats more love than they can handle. Anything else you want seen to?"

I shrugged. "The last person I trusted with watching the place was Sloan, and she failed miserably, so the bar is set pretty low. All I ask is that you give the fur babies some kibble and water and maybe a chin scritch now and then. Make sure nobody is robbing me of all my valuables." I laughed. "Not that I have any."

"Have you heard from her?" Lee asked. "Sloan?"

"No," I answered, deciding whether I wanted to tell them I'd seen Sloan in the hotel lobby the day before. My first instinct was to sit on it until I made heads or tails of what I'd seen; what if it wasn't her, and I was having delusions that were related to my own anxieties? But after all the conflicts I'd had with Phillip recently over us keeping things from each other, I knew I had to tell them. We couldn't all help each other if we were keeping secrets. Besides, what if Sloan showed up here? Better to have Lee and Benny on high alert. "I haven't heard from her. But I did…I feel like I might have seen her yesterday." I quickly filled the three of them in on what I'd seen—a woman fitting Sloan's description, lingering in the doorway, dressed to the nines, as the journalists had tried to ambush Phillip.

Phillip's face was thoughtful. "Why would she have been there, do you think?"

"I don't know," I answered honestly. "Just to be nosy, maybe? I wouldn't put it past her. I can imagine she's curious about what's going on, what happened to us after we left Elvin's compound."

"You should have told me right away," Phillip said, but he didn't look angry, only curious.

"When we left her, she was pretty much the worst for wear," Lee mused. "She must have hightailed it to Savannah as soon as we left. How did she recover and get into town so fast?"

"Not much to recover from, really," I said, absently touching my cheek where Sloan had scratched me with her nails. It was healing quickly, thanks to some Neosporin and a few zaps from Benny's magic hands. I'd managed to cover it up with concealer—a really great concealer that Sloan herself had recommended to me years ago, in fact—but I could still feel it. Occasionally, it seemed to ping, like a reminder. Just a faint itch, a little burn, to make sure I didn't forget. A reminder of what had gone down between my former best friend and me. "I just zapped her one good time or two. I didn't do her any serious, lasting harm. I imagine she just drove home, or took an Uber. How she found us at the hotel, though, I don't know."

"Could she have any help?" Benny asked. "Who's still around among Guthrie and Elvin's associates?"

"Um…Shank, maybe?" I said, shuddering involuntarily at the henchman's name. That was the only word I could think of when I thought of Shank: *henchman.* "I'm sure there are others, but he's the only one I actually *know.* Unless Lydia or Renee…" I looked at Lee uneasily, hating to even bring up the possibility that his mother and aunt might be involved. I wanted so desperately to trust them, but I couldn't quite bring myself to, not fully.

He shook his head. "No. Aunt Renee has been holed up at my father's old place, and she's pretty traumatized. Grieving and everything … she's barely gotten out of bed. And Mom, well, she was on the first bus back to Boston yesterday morning." His freckles stood out against the paleness of his cheeks. "And besides, neither of them would help *her.* My mother especially, not after Sloan was dating my dad. They're on our side, Stormy, I swear. If they weren't before, they definitely are now after all they've been through."

Phillip grabbed at my hand. "What about Tess?" he asked softly.

I started to shake my head, to protest. I couldn't believe my ex-husband, even with as many mistakes as he'd made over the years, could do anything to hurt me. But … a part of me wondered.

Because I'd believed the same thing about Sloan too.

I bit my lip. "I'd like to think he wouldn't be involved, but … well fuck, I just don't know anymore." To my horror, tears pricked against my eyelids. "I don't know who I can trust. I suppose he's just as much a possibility as anyone else."

"I'm sorry, Stormy," Benny said, his eyes flickering with empathy. "I know it's hard."

"Oh, just ignore me," I said stupidly, wiping at my eyes, trying for a laugh. "It's been a long couple weeks. I'm overwhelmed and full of theatrics. I'll be fine."

"You've been through hell," Lee said. "You raised the dead, got kidnapped, raised the dead again, went through a breakup, recovered a bunch of lost memories, reconciled with your mom, discovered your powers, your cat got catnapped, then your friend went missing, a dead body turned up in the marsh, and then you found out your best friend betrayed you." He listed the events off on his hand, tapping them together as he ran out of fingers. "Now your dad's missing. I think you're allowed to feel sorry for yourself for a second. That's a *lot,* Stormy. A lot for like, a few years. To have all that happen within a few weeks…well, it's no wonder you're half insane."

"Who said I'm half insane?" I asked, laughing, wiping at my eyes again.

"We all are," Benny said with a grin. "The Wolfden, home for the wayward, hopeless, and insane."

"Save me a room." I chuckled. "Sounds like my kinda place."

"You'll have to call ahead to Nikolai or Jamie to reserve one," Benny replied. "Clara's been so fucking extra recently, I need a few days' break."

I opened my mouth to ask about that—I'd been having some weird feelings about Clara myself lately—but decided against it. I had enough on my plate, goddamit. Clara, a female amateur wrestler and Benny's ex (who still apparently had a major thing for him despite him having moved on to Lee), was by far my least favorite of the Wolfden's members and the only person who gave me pause when it came to trusting the group implicitly. I kept remembering the showdown she and I had had outside of Jamie's trailer, just after Benny had been shot and his body taken. Clara didn't know me, and I got that she might not trust me right off the bat. But I sensed it was more than plain old distrust driving her. It didn't help matters that she gave me an eat-shit look every time we were in a room together.

So far, I'd ignored Clara, and I intended to keep doing so, but I wasn't prepared to put up with her shit, either. She might be able to wipe the floor with me, strong and powerful as she was, but I had my own built-in self-defense mechanism, and I'd use it if I had to.

Lee turned to Benny and gave him a peck on the cheek. "You guys are welcome to stay here and chill; anything at the house is yours," I said, knowing all too well what it felt like to need privacy and alone time. "You might need to do a food shop, though. I haven't been home enough to stock up on supplies. There's a bottle of red on top of the fridge. Just make yourselves at home."

"I appreciate it. It'll be nice to have a respite, just the two of us," Benny said, and Lee smiled. "Just the two of us, alone, for more than a second."

"I get that," I said, turning to Phillip with a smile. "We felt the same way, holed up at that hotel for two days. Though I think ol' Rockstar here was chomping at the bit to give that interview and get back in the spotlight."

Phillip's face colored. "It wasn't exactly like that—" he started huffily, but I stopped him with a finger under his chin.

"It's okay, Phillip. You can admit you like the fame." I gave him a tickle until his lips curled up in a smile. "Who wouldn't? And after all, that's why I first fell in love with you."

"And here I was thinking it was because of my body." Phillip grinned.

"Believe me," Lee said, opening my screen door and heading into the trailer, "it was that too. He laughed and waved his hand in a *shoo* motion "Now you two get the fuck out of here already. Love ya, bye." He and Benny went inside and slammed the door, their laughter sounding from inside.

Six

I breathed in the salty sea air and placed my hands on my hips, looking around, surveying the long stretch of light, sandy beach and the turquoise water, so clean you could see the fish from yards away. I was more excited to step onto the white sand of Panama City Beach than I thought I'd be. I'd grown up right next door to both St. Simons Island and Jekyll Island and was just an hour and some change from Tybee Island, so the appeal should've been lost on me, but somehow, it wasn't.

"What do you say?" Phillip asked, placing an arm around my waist. His skin was warm and clammy; the Florida sky was overcast with a hint of sun peeking through, the air surprisingly humid. "Should we take a quick dip?"

I turned to him and smiled. Normally, I'd be all business, but the water looked so inviting, so clean and refreshing. We didn't have to meet Dee for over an hour, and Roberta and Mama were settling in at their motel room. "Let's do it," I said, and he grinned, grabbing my hand and pulling me toward the water.

The spray lapping at my ankles felt warm and salty-soft as it hit my skin. I squealed with laughter as Phillip picked me up and pulled me into the sea with him, only stopping when the water was at his chest level and almost over my head. He cradled me in his arms and we floated, seemingly weightless. The only thing I could feel were his strong arms holding me tight.

I gave a mock kick and wrestled myself free. "I *can* swim, you know, Deville."

"Let's see, then." He laughed, splashing me, rivulets of water running down his bare chest. "Give me your best doggy paddle."

"Nope." And with that, I disappeared under the water, swimming a few yards away and doubling back, grabbing ahold of his black swim trunks from underwater and giving them a tug. When I came up for air, he was gasping with laughter and embarrassment.

"Don't do that! I thought you were a shark!"

"That was the idea," I said with a giggle, treading water around him. "Though all you had to do was look down. It's not like back at home where the sea is mixed with a million tons of mud and slime."

"Hey, don't knock my favorite beach," Phillip said, pushing up his legs and floating on his back. Still treading water, I watched him. His black hair was slick and wet and plastered on his forehead, his eyes closed, his long eyelashes inky against his pale skin. He was beautiful, as always. For the millionth time, I thought to myself, *How did I get so lucky?*

"The question is," he answered, not opening his eyes, his face still turned to the sun, "How did *I* get so lucky?"

"Get out of my head," I said automatically, happily.

"The only thing that would make me luckier," he continued, spitting a stream of ocean water up into the air, "Was if you had taken off my trunks when you were down there."

"Pig!" I splashed around a little, feeling warm to the bone with contentment. If only we could stay here forever, just floating in the sea, lazing on the beach, letting the sun and sand claim us until dark. If only we had no adult responsibilities and could just *be*. Maybe one day.

Phillip turned his head and looked at me. "It'll happen, sweetie," he said softly, the water lapping at his cheek. "I promise."

"I'll hold you to that," I said.

Phillip glided one arm across the water between us and it came to rest on my shoulder. He flicked a bead of water at me and grinned. "You won't have to."

I sat there and gaped. I didn't want to get out of the car.

There was nothing left of the house. Nothing but cinders, ash, and the cloying, dank smell of smoke that I thought I'd never get out of my nostrils. Acrid and decaying, it was nothing like the pleasant, waxy smokiness of a lit candle or even a hearty bonfire; this was altogether different. The smell of burning and melting wood, rot, and entire rooms having died by fire; the smell of utter destruction.

"I can't bear the thought that he might have been in there," I said in a small voice, and Phillip grabbed my hand. I glanced in the side mirror. Roberta was holding her hand over her nose in the backseat. "Even though I hated him at times, I just can't."

"I'm so sorry," Phillip said from the driver's seat, for once not leaning forward take me in his arms. He seemed to sense that I needed space, and I was eternally grateful for how well he knew me, how deeply he understood my needs.

"I only came here once," I continued, my eyes fixed on a spot in the middle of the ruined home. It was a pile of jagged, burnt wood and cinders now, but if I recalled correctly, that middle room had been the baby's room. My half-sister Shay, who would now be almost out of her toddler years. When I'd visited, she'd still been an infant in diapers. I'd put her to bed one night, crooning a lullaby I'd remembered from my own childhood. "Lullaby Looly." It was one of the very few poignant memories I had of this family, this family that I'd rejected. It hadn't been for Daddy's lack of trying, but I just couldn't do it. I couldn't get past my own childhood to take part in a new family. The one Christmas visit I'd given him had been all I could give, and the thought that it might have been the last hit me in the chest like a punch.

"At least you know your sister is okay," Roberta said, seeming to read my mind. "I know you must be eager to see her." Then, to my surprise, she lifted her voice and sang, *"The gods bless thee and keep thee from cruel annoy, sing lullaby looley."*

"How do you know that song?" I asked, looking at her sharply.

She shrugged. "My dad used to sing it to me when I was little."

I looked down at the floorboard. "Of course. That's probably where I learned it too." I unbuckled my seatbelt forcefully, not sure what else to do with my sudden angry energy, sending the metal clasp flying into the window with a loud *thunk*. "FUCK!"

Phillip extended his hand, on offer but not forced. After a moment, I took it, and he laced his fingers through mine. "Do you want to get out, have a look around?" he asked.

"No," I answered, then sighed. "But I guess I'd better." I wrenched the door handle and got out of the car, my extremities feeling heavy as lead. The smell was much worse outside; it smelled like smoky death. Knowing that someone had died in this fire, even if it turned out it wasn't my dad, was a hard pill to swallow. It made looking at the smoldering heap even harder. To know this had been someone's final resting place and that their death had likely not been a quick or painless one.

"What time is Dee supposed to be here?" Roberta asked, putting an arm around my shoulders and walking in step with me as I shuffled up the walkway.

"Any minute," I said, grateful for her presence beside me. Phillip walked around to the back of the house, or what was left of it. "She's been staying with a friend. They're going to watch Shay, and Mom is going to pick her up and bring her here."

"Is that gonna be weird for you?" Roberta asked. "The two of them together?"

"Very weird," I said with a dry laugh. "But probably weirder for them than for me. You remember the old Laureen. She would have scratched Dee's eyes out as soon as look at her. But I guess now that—that they think—" I found myself unable to finish the sentence, and Roberta wrapped her arm tighter around me.

"Hey, we don't know yet. Not for sure," she said reassuringly. "I wish we'd hear something. I feel like it's been long enough for them to have run the DNA."

"Yeah, what about that?" I asked, looking at her. "It doesn't make sense. It's been two days since the fire, and they still haven't identified the body? They still haven't located Dad's friend he was supposed to be fishing with? Maybe Dee's right—they're either stalling or just completely incompetent." I bit my lip. "I don't know much about how these kinds of investigations work, but I was under the impression they could identify bodies in, like, a matter of hours. It seems like they'd have multiple officers and branches working on this and yet ... we haven't heard from anyone." I wrapped my jacket around myself even though I wasn't cold. The humidity was thick in the air, and residual heat came off the burned relic that had once been my dad's house. Still, I was chilled to the bone. "I can't help but feel … something's … wrong. Beyond the obvious."

Roberta sighed. "I feel it too." She gave me a nudge, and we both looked to the corner of the yard where Phillip was crouched down, attempting to peer into what was once a crawl space. He dug at the dirt with his long fingers, then pulled his hand back as if he'd been stung. As I suspected, the house was still hot in places. "Looks like your boyfriend does as well." She gave me a sisterly punch in the arm and a bright smile. "We'll get to the bottom of this, Stormy, I promise."

"That's just it, though," I grumbled. "*Is* there a bottom? Because I'm beginning to think there isn't."

"You're starting to burn, hon. We should probably head back to the motel."

"Mmm." I rolled over from my back to my stomach on the donut-shaped beach blanket and threw my arms over my head. I didn't care if I burned. I just wanted to bliss out for a while.

Mama had delivered Dee to the charred remains of the house she had shared with my dad shortly after my conversation with Roberta, and things had been … tense, to say the least.

At least the two of them were getting along. If "getting along" meant Mama trying her best to be warm and comforting to Dee but slightly failing, her own awkwardness getting in her way, and Dee doing her own best to showcase her politeness and intelligence and only succeeding in making herself seem a little desperate. They were trying, and I had to appreciate that, but the whole thing had been terrible. There'd been a forced conversation between the three of us (Phillip and Roberta had kept their distance to give us privacy) as we stood there among the smoke and ashes, trying to avoid the elephant in the room that nobody wanted to talk about, but all three of us were thinking: was it Daddy who had burned up in there?

According to Dee, the police had been deeply unhelpful, avoidant even. They had conducted a half-assed search, coordinated with the Pensacola police, to see whether Daddy was staying with his friend Arnold, but after going to his house and finding him not there, they'd pretty much given up. "I'm afraid to even go down to the PD again, they're so rude to me," Dee had said with a sniff. "They act like I'm *bothering* them. Like I'm being a nuisance. And you tell me—haven't they had more than enough time to identify the body?"

"I don't know, Dee," Mama answered, a worried expression on her face. "But I tend to think they could have—should have—been done by now."

"I just need to know whether my husband is alive or dead!" Dee had collapsed into tears, both Mama and I trying to comfort her, ignoring the turmoil in our own hearts. Dee made it about twenty minutes before the smell of the smoke and the sight of her ruined house had been too much for her, and she'd wanted to leave. There was nothing for Phillip, Roberta, and me to do but go back to the motel for the night and try to get some rest.

I'd tossed and turned all night, the smell of acrid smoke lingering in my nostrils, waking up every few minutes to the phantom sound of my cellphone ringing, hoping it was the police or Dee with information, only to find that nobody was calling. Finally, at five a.m., I'd gotten up and tiptoed out of the motel room. There was nowhere to go, not in the wee hours, so I'd just sat in the cab of the truck, staring out at a lone seagull in the parking lot picking at an old, crumpled bag of Bugles.

On a whim, I'd opened my laptop and started writing. I needed a distraction, and it felt good to type mindlessly, to get words out on a screen. Pretty soon, my hands were flying across the keyboard, and after an hour, I looked out the window to see the sun had risen, the seagull had long ago finished the bag of Bugles and flown off, and Phillip was standing outside the motel door, wrapped in a robe, staring at me curiously. I'd given him a little wave and shut the laptop, saving my writing before I did. Somehow, , I'd managed to write an entire article about Phillip Deville and what it was like to be the ultimate fangirl-turned-rock-star girlfriend.

It was a good article, too, I thought as I dug my toes downward into the warm sand. Good enough that I might even think about pitching it somewhere. I'd have to let Phillip read it first, get his permission since he was the subject matter, but I figured he'd be okay with it. Playful and funny, it put him in a very good light without giving away *too* much personal information.

I'd done a little scrolling before we'd come out to the beach while waiting for Phillip to come back from the convenience store next door with sunscreen and Gatorade. From what I could see, the livestream had done really well, with several hundred thousand views, and the accompanying article with a transcript of the interview was still being shared all over Twitter, Instagram, and Facebook. There were a few kids doing TikToks having "conversations" about the interview. And #PhillipDeville had been a trending topic on Twitter since *yesterday.*

Given that Phillip was very in-demand right now, if I wanted to flex my writing skills (and make a little money in the bargain) now was the exact time to put it out into the world.

Phillip had said absolutely nothing about his interview or its reception since we'd been in Panama City Beach. He had been completely focused on Daddy's disappearance and making sure I was getting through this okay. It touched me deeply that he cared so much about me and my family, a family he barely knew. So much so that he'd be willing to put his own life and career on the back burner to care for me first. I was flattered but not at all surprised. Phillip was a good guy—the *best* guy.

I'd told him all of this as we'd walked to the beach and started setting up our towels. "That's great," he'd said, and asked me if I wanted him to put on my sunscreen, to which I'd happily obliged. Any excuse to have that man's hands all over my back and shoulders ... or anywhere else, for that matter.

We'd been lying on the sand, getting sun and gazing out at the water—the surfers riding the waves, families frolicking in the surf, and people playing frisbee and volleyball a few yards away—for at least two hours now, and I didn't want to go back to the motel. We hadn't heard from anyone today, and I was jumping out of my skin with nerves and anxiety. Sitting in the motel room staring at the dingy walls was not my idea of an afternoon well spent.

"I'm sure we can think of something to occupy your time."

I rolled over, pushing up my sunglasses and giving Phillip a mock glare. "If you don't get out of my damn *head* ... "

"Well, if you're not ready to leave yet," he said, ignoring me, "I'll go take a quick dip. You good?"

"I'm good," I said, laying back onto the towel and throwing my arms over my head to block the sun. If only I could stop my cacophony of thoughts enough to actually relax, to get some rest ... even if I didn't actually sleep, just having five minutes of silence would be enough ...

"Stormy. Stormy, honey, wake up."

"Huh?" I rolled over, wincing at the tight pain in my shoulders that I recognized immediately as a sunburn. "What?"

Phillip stood over me, his black hair falling around his face. He leaned down and offered me his hand. "You fell asleep," he said, closing his fingers around mine and pulling me to a sitting position. "I hate to wake you, but you're burning. You need to get out of the sun."

"I know, I feel it," I said with a groan, letting him pull me all the way up to my feet. I slipped my feet into my black sandals and gingerly pulled my cut-up Joy Division tank top over my head, wincing again as it touched my tender skin. "I should have listened to you before."

"I'm glad you got some sleep at least," he said, leaning over to brush sand off my legs. "We have some news."

"Daddy?" I said, stopping in my tracks, staring at Phillip with wide eyes.

He frowned. "Er, no. I shouldn't have phrased it like that. I heard from Roberta."

"And?"

"She tried to get in touch with Benny's friends, you know, the guys who live down this way they thought might know your dad? They won't talk to her. Keep hanging up the phone every time she calls." Phillip grinned. "Benny sure does know some upstanding people."

"Okay ..." I stared at him in confusion. "What does this ..."

"Benny and Lee are on their way down," Phillip said, shaking the sand out of my beach towel and rolling it up. He tucked it under one arm. "Benny's going to go visit the guys himself, and Lee wants to help too."

"But what about—"

Phillip gave me a salty, sandy kiss on the mouth. "Don't forget your phone. It's laying there in the sand."

I leaned down and grabbed my phone, brushing the sand off the screen, and smiled as it lit up with a text message from Lee.

"Blinken and Nod are in tip-top shape, have been fed all the treats, and Jamie is coming over to take the next shift of

catsitting duty. So don't you worry your pretty little head about it. See you tonight."

This was probably a recipe for disaster.

The little dive beach bar—hilariously monikered The Naughty Clam—was already full to capacity with what I assumed were a combination of locals and tourists. And judging from the sound of the place, everybody was evidently three drinks in already. Between the loud satellite radio dialed up to eleven and blaring Iron Maiden, the rowdy banter, the clink of beer mugs and shot glasses, and the occasional *crack* as someone hit a ball on the pool table, I could barely hear Phillip as he pulled me close to croon, "Should we get a table?"

"Is there even one free?" I asked. He scanned the room, pointing to an unoccupied corner over by the bathrooms. I gestured to everyone, and we all hurried to grab the table before someone else did. Benny, to the surprise of nobody, made a beeline for a free pool table and started chalking up the cue. Lee took a long swig of his beer, then sat it on the table, hitting me with a dazzling smile. "Would you mind making sure nobody roofies me?" he asked, and I nodded, sidling into the booth beside Phillip as Lee meandered over to the pool table to join Benny. I noticed with a smirk that he grabbed a handful of Benny's ass as he walked around and grabbed his own pool cue. Roberta crammed in beside me, and on the other side of us, Mom and Dee sat awkwardly side by side, their bodies stiff.. They were like two totally separate entities, sitting together, neither acknowledging the other. Weird, but better than the alternative, which was a catfight. The *old* Mom would have already been clutching a fistful of hair.

What a strange little crew we were, all of us here together, in Panama City Beach of all places, and for such a strange reason. Though it really shouldn't seem strange, not after all we'd been through. I watched Benny and Lee exchanging shit-talk at the pool table, the sexual chemistry between them evident even from yards away; it was so thick you could cut it like beer foam. Phillip was a warm, sensual presence beside me, his muscular leg against mine, the scratchy denim of his black jeans enough to send a little thrill through me as it touched my bare leg. And Roberta, scanning the drink menu as though it had something exotic and different to offer and not just the usual boring list of domestic and draft beers and cheap wine, all marked up considerably. I felt a wave of love and gratitude wash over me for all of them, all who had come here to help me, to support me, to be with me.

For the first time in a long time, possibly forever, I felt like I had a family.

"Are you okay?" I asked Mom. Being here, worrying about my dad while having to navigate the awkwardness with his new wife, technically her replacement, and trying to support me through all this, must be hard enough on her. But here she was sitting in a bar, when I knew good and well she was clinging by her fingernails to her sobriety. "Lee wasn't thinking when he suggested this place. Phillip and I can go somewhere else with you, maybe to get a bite to eat? I saw a wing place around the corner. We could grab some munchie dinner?"

Mom smiled at that. One of my few happy memories from growing up was Munchie Dinner. Most Friday nights—there was the odd one when Mom didn't remember, or when she hadn't had the money to run to Walmart—we'd load up on junk food for our supper. We'd each settle on the couch with a huge plate filled high with chicken tenders, mozzarella sticks, pizza rolls, onion rings, and funnily enough, carrot sticks.

Mama had always insisted that there we have at least one vegetable present. Of course, we'd both drowned those little healthy matchsticks in ranch, negating all the health out of them, but it was a fond memory, especially now that I didn't eat most of that stuff anymore. Vegan ranch just didn't quite hit the same.

"I'm fine, honey," Mama said with a reassuring smile, but I could see the sadness behind her eyes, and a little anxiety too. She gripped her purse handle tightly. "Besides, what's a rabbit like you going to eat at a wing hut?"

Phillip snorted beside me, and I elbowed him in the side. "I'm sure they have French fries or something."

"Deep fried in lard," Mom said. "I got that lecture years ago. Honey, I'm fine. I promise. You look like you got burned today. Your shoulders are slap pink."

I touched at my shoulder absently, aware that she was changing the subject on purpose. "Yeah, a little. They don't hurt that bad, though. Phillip put aloe on them for me." I blushed, my face likely going pink to match my shoulders. Phillip had indeed put aloe all over my sunburned shoulders, but he hadn't stopped there, insisting on putting lotion all over my back, then my legs, then my thighs … culminating in an accidental game of slip-and-slide that had seen me slide right off the bed and onto the floor, Phillip tumbling right after me.

Not that we'd let that stop us, though. The floor had turned out to be the *perfect* location for the activities we'd gotten up to next.

Phillip pinched my leg, and I reached over and pinched his back, taking a long sip of my drink as I recovered from my thoughts. If Mama noticed the vibe between us, she was politely pretending to ignore it.

"I'll go get us all drinks," Roberta said, slapping her hands on the table, her disgusted expression making it very clear that she'd noticed our display. "Laureen, you want a Coke?"

"Sprite, actually," Mom answered. "The last thing I need is caffeine."

"Me too," Dee said, cutting her eyes to Mom briefly, then looking away awkwardly. "I don't think I can bear to drink. My nerves are shot." Mama looked momentarily pleased to have a fellow dry buddy, and I was surprised to see her reach over and give Dee's hand a conciliatory pat.

"And you two lovebirds?"

I cut my eyes to Mama, still reluctant, but she nodded. "It's fine. Order what you want. I'm going to be fine."

"Okay, well … I guess I'll just have a, um, a Jack and Coke."

"Same," Phillip acquiesced.

"Two Sprites, two Jack and Cokes. And a frozen mango margarita the size of my head for me," Roberta said with fake cheerfulness. "They always have the best boozy slush drinks at the beach."

"She says that like she didn't just come from the beach." I laughed as she sauntered away and laughed harder as I saw her flip me the bird from behind her back as she approached the bar.

"Bless her heart," Mama said, her eyes on Roberta's retreating form. "She's trying so hard to hide it, but she's a mess."

I swallowed. She was right; Roberta was barely holding it together. As soon as we figured all this out with Daddy, I vowed to myself, I needed to sit down with her and talk, see if I couldn't help in some way. Everything that had happened was taking a huge toll on her, and she was taking too much on herself, helping me. She needed my support too.

I looked over to Benny and Lee, the two of them leaned up against the pool table, Benny's arm around Lee's waist. Lee was showing Benny something on his phone, and the two of them were laughing.

I tensed involuntarily as two men approached my friends. They were dressed in good old boy clothes—Carhart jackets, ball caps, and dirty, ripped jeans and work boots—and figured them for locals, definitely not tourists. They had the *at-home-here* swagger that made that evident, even if they hadn't been dressed like two dudes just off work. One of the guys grabbed a free pool cue, and while I couldn't hear him over the loudness of the bar, I could make out what he said by reading his lips: "Game?"

Lee leaned in closer to Benny and cocked his head to the side, asking him without words if he wanted to play. Benny nodded, and the two of them shared a look that could only be described as *scorching*. I beamed, proud of Lee. I thought back to the conversation we'd had that night in Jamie's room, how upset he'd been at the mistakes he'd made, how much he worried that he'd fucked things up with Benny forever because he hadn't been able to come out, to confess publicly that he and Benny were together. Now, it seemed that they'd turned a corner.

The four of them shook hands, introduced themselves, and resumed shooting pool.

Dee was scrolling through her phone. She'd been checking it for updates every ten seconds since we'd been here. She must be out of her mind frantic. I'd never really liked her, mainly out of a sense of loyalty to Mom, but I sure did feel sorry for her. Her husband, the father of her child, missing, possibly dead. Her house gone up in flames. I couldn't imagine what she was going through. She looked up, noticing Lee and Benny. "Those two are cute. I should tell them we have a PRIDE parade here now."

I smiled, bemused. Dee was from an even smaller town than I was and had led a pretty sheltered life. She probably did think that PRIDE was the height of progressiveness. I didn't begrudge her. She meant well.

"Chad and I went once," Dee continued as Roberta approached the table, arms weighed down with all our drinks. I jumped up to help her.

"Chad went to a PRIDE parade?" Mom asked incredulously as I placed her Sprite in front of her. She took a sip, her face a picture of disbelief. "That doesn't sound like the man I married."

"Well, it's the man *I* married," Dee said, her voice a little high. "We had a great time. He even bought one of those little rainbow flags—"

"I'm just saying, that doesn't sound like Chad's thing—" Mama continued, oblivious to the fact that she'd upset Dee.

"It sounds like he's become more open minded. That's great," I jumped in, hoping to diffuse the situation before it began. Though the picture in my head was likely the exact same one in Mama's—my drunken father screaming belligerently at the TV when we'd inadvertently watched an old rerun of *Golden Girls* in which Blanche finds out her brother is gay. That lovely family TV night had ended with Dad throwing his full PBR can at the TV, beer pooling all over the carpet and Mama and me grabbing towels from the bathroom to mop it up. Rather than helping us, Daddy had slammed out of the house and driven off, presumably to go to the bar where no queer content threatened to ruin his good time.

He never acted like that when he was drunk, and often, he didn't even remember when he was sober, but like Mama, it was hard for me to forget. And equally hard to accept that he was so different now.

"I agree. I'm glad Chad changed," Mama said, the tiny straw still in the corner of her mouth. She kept sipping, her drink more than half gone already. "I didn't mean anything by it, Dee. I'm glad that he's a better husband to you than he was to me. Genuinely, I am."

"Look, I know things weren't great between you two," Dee

said, two blotches of color appearing on her cheeks. "He told me plenty. But he's *missing,* Laureen. He's missing, and he might be dead. Do you not understand?"

Mama sat up straight, slamming her drink down on the table. Her own face was red now. I knew that look. The hive had been kicked over, and the queen bee was about to come out. "I do understand, Dee. I do understand that Chad is missing and tensions are high and we're all worried. But it would be nice if you could acknowledge that this is extremely hard for Stormy and me for more reasons than just the obvious. All this stress … uncertainty … it takes a toll. Brings up old memories, old trauma. It's very hard to just let all that go because Chad might be—" She stopped herself short, her face a thundercloud. "None of the pain he caused goes away just because he's missing."

"But it's not the time. Or the place," Dee said hotly. "Not without Chad here to defend himself."

"*Defend himself?* " Mama parroted with a harsh laugh. "As though he could."

However much they'd been avoiding eye contact with each other when we'd arrived, they were definitely looking each other dead in the eye now. Dee had her hand curled so tightly around her glass, I wasn't 100 percent certain she wasn't about to fling it into Mama's face. And my mother looked about four seconds away from stabbing Dee in the neck with her straw. I looked down into my Jack and Coke, suddenly no longer in the mood for it, or food, or anything else.

"Guys …" Roberta said in a small voice. I could only see her eyebrows; the rest of her face was thoroughly tucked into her large frozen mango monstrosity. "Y'all."

But it was too late. Dee had already flung herself out of the booth, sloshing Sprite all over the table, her face beet red. "If you think I'm going to sit here for one second and—"

"If you can't handle the truth of what I'm saying—"

"Ladies," Phillip tried to interject, mopping at the table with a napkin. "I think it would be best for everybody if we let cooler heads prevail. Why don't we step outside for a cigarette?" I shot him a glare—both he and Mama had quit, last I checked. He looked back at me, his eyebrows raised, and I could feel his thoughts. *One problem at a time, okay?* He patted the square box of nicotine gum in the pocket of his black T-shirt and my shoulders relaxed.

"Why did you even come down here, anyway?" Dee demanded. "Stormy is the one I wanted here; she would've called you with updates. There was no need for you. You're not Chad's wife anymore."

"I came here for my daughter!" Mama spat. "To offer her support. She didn't want to come! Do you think it's easy for her, coming down here after years of almost no contact, to possibly identify her dad's dead body?" I bit my lip. The truth was, I hadn't had contact with Mama regularly for just as many years, and her glossing over that to make herself out to be some kind of saint didn't really jive with me, despite the fact that I agreed with a lot of what she'd said. I felt my own blood pressure rise.

"Now, look," I cut in, trying to keep the angry edge from my voice. "Y'all both need to cut it the fuck out right now. I don't want to be in the middle of this shit. I have my own shit to deal with without the two of you acting like middle school mean girls!" I was shouting now, my attempt to remain calm forgotten. My fingers were tingling like mad, and I shook them in front of me, trying to get rid of the almost painful sensation in my fingertips. "SHUT UP! CUT IT THE FUCK OUT! JESUS CHRIST!"

Mama and Dee both went quiet immediately, Mama's face still red, Dee sniffling and trying to hold back tears. Phillip and Roberta both stared at me, their eyes wide.

"Stormy." I looked over. Lee was standing at the table, pool cue in his hand, looking at me with huge eyes.

"What?" I asked irritably.

"Um. Everyone in the bar is listening to you," he said in a low voice, cutting his eyes to the left. "Watching you."

"Well, they should learn to mind their own business," I said pissily, still angry, even though I knew I'd gone too far.

"We should get out of here," Lee said, his voice still low. "Now."

"What?" I asked. "Why?" But as I said the words, my eyes fell to the table just across from the jukebox. I could feel the heat of Phillip's gaze as he noticed it too. Both Mama and Dee had the good sense to stay silent. Roberta's margarita now almost reached her hairline. We'd all seen them at the same time.

There was a young couple sitting together in a booth, the type of pair you'd see at any bar on a date, except … the girl was brazenly, happily filming the scene my family had just caused in public with her smartphone. And from the excited and frenzied look on her face, she had every intention of sharing the footage.

"Fuck," said Phillip in a low voice behind me. *"Fuck."*

The silence in the car was deafening. I sat wedged between Roberta and Phillip in the backseat, the two of them staring out the window, lost in their own thoughts. Lee, in the front passenger seat, had his hand on Benny's knee as he drove, but gone was the playful mood from earlier. None of us had spoken more than two words since we'd left The Naughty Clam, our half-full drinks shedding condensation onto the table we'd abandoned.

Phillip was obviously worried about the young woman who had filmed us. He and Roberta had rushed over to their table to ask her to stop filming, which she had, but not before shoving her phone into her oversized purse with an expression that made it crystal clear she wouldn't be deleting anything. Not wanting to cause a further scene, they'd left it alone. We knew there was no chance of that happening, and any kerfuffle Phillip got involved in would only end up making more of a spectacle. But he wasn't happy about it, which was evident in the look of fury still etched on his full lips as he stared through the glass.. With his "comeback" so new, a link to a missing persons and possible arson case, combined with a huge, messy family fight in a dive bar, was the last thing Phillip needed or wanted. Guilt rolled uneasily in my belly. I'd made an already fraught situation so much worse with my angry outburst, and he couldn't even be visibly angry about it front of me because my dad was missing.

Roberta sighed beside me. She hadn't spoken more than two words since the big fight, choosing to instead suck back her margarita like it was her job, then flouncing out to the car in a silent huff. I felt guilty about putting her through all of this too. She'd insisted on coming down here to help me, to offer me support, but Mama had been right—it was taking a toll on her already weighed-down shoulders.

I wondered whether being around my family made her think about her brother. She must miss him, especially in light of everything that had happened with her dad and Guthrie. She didn't have much family, and I knew from experience that had to hurt. Even being around the dysfunction of *my* family probably seemed better to her than having no family at all. It must be painful, to feel so alone. I put an arm around her shoulders and gave her a friendly squeeze, and she turned briefly, her profile giving away the slightest of smiles, but then she turned back to the window, her face hidden again in shadow.

As for Lee and Benny, I could sense what was going on between them. They couldn't wait to be alone, to get their hands on each other. I could feel their love for each other, burning big and bright in my mind and heart. It left an aura I could almost see, a bright orange-red, and when I closed my eyes, it made me smile.

I reached over and grabbed Phillip's hand. Despite his moody expression, he clasped mine back immediately, a movement that had become second nature to us both. I rested my head on his shoulder and sent him a silent message, one I knew he would hear without me having to say a word.

I love you.

"I love you too," he said out loud, the only words that had been spoken since we'd all gotten in the car. I smiled.

I'm sorry.

No need.

Up front, Benny rummaged with his right hand through a giant CD book—the leather-bound kind with a zipper and little plastic sleeves, the likes of which I hadn't seen since at least 2002. "Music?"

"Please," I said eagerly, chuckling as I watched him drive with one arm and rummage for CDs with the other. "Anybody ever tell you about Apple Music? Or Spotify? Or cable radio, for goddess' sake?"

"I don't have time for any of that shit," Benny answered good-naturedly as he extracted a CD from the sleeve. "My CDs have been serving me just fine since I first bought 'em, and until they crap out on me, I'm good." He slid the CD into the deck, and I watched it disappear into the car's console as Benny turned the volume up.

The sweet, slow synth of Duran Duran's "Chauffer" swirled through the speakers, starting off quiet and then swelling through the car like the crest of a wave. "I figured you were a metalhead like the rest of us," I said with a laugh, surprised but not displeased at his song choice. I remembered the video for this song, a black-and-white artistic confection that had shades of S&M and put in mind things I'd like to do to Phillip.

"I am," Benny answered, looking back to fix me with a smirk. "What's more metal than Duran Fucking Duran?"

"Seriously." Roberta snorted.

"Don't you dare disrespect Simon Fucking Le Bon."

"He's right," Phillip said beside me, the corners of his mouth turning up in a grin for the first time since we'd left the bar. "Super underrated band. Like, they were popular, but everyone assumed they had no depth. They had some killer tunes. I assume still do? They haven't …?"

Sometimes I forgot that Phillip had been on ice for twenty-three years and didn't always know the current ins and outs of the music industry, the state of bands he'd once loved, or how to use a cellphone, for that matter. I grinned and caressed his fingers with my own. "All alive and accounted for, and if I recall correctly, still making music." I raised his hand to mine and placed a kiss on his palm. "You want to invite them on tour?"

He smiled. "Maybe. Le Bon still married to that model?"

"Yasmin." Benny nodded. "Yup."

"She was hot."

"Yup."

"I thought you were into dudes," I said, punching Benny in the shoulder with my free hand. "Traitor."

"I am." Benny laughed. "Mostly. Hot is hot, though."

All the tension had left the car, and the mood was much more lighthearted now, almost carefree. I leaned back into Phillip, letting the song carry me into a tentative kind of peace. Benny had certain—very big —powers, but it seemed he had another one too—the power to disarm people who were tense and hurting, and to bring people together over a common, shared love of something as simple as a song or a shared memory. I could now see how he'd formed the Wolfden seemingly out of thin air, getting such a wayward, motley crew of people together to become a family that would die for each other. He just had that sort of way about him. He was a natural leader, the type of guy who everyone loved, rallied around, and followed. He was a pied piper. He was a muse.

"You have that power, too, Stormy," Benny said, his eyes on the road. His hand, curled into Lee's as it sat on his lap, mirrored my hand with Phillip's. I thought of yin and yang, black and white. "We're twins, in a way."

"Look," I said, my voice playful, but I put a little edge in it. "If you swinging dicks don't get out of my head and *stay out,* I'll make sure the next thoughts I have are scandalous enough to put you both in a coma."

Neither of them said anything, but Phillip's laughter appeared in my head, fast as lightning.

Then bring on the coma, baby.

Before Benny had pulled fully into the motel parking lot, I could see that something wasn't right. It was too lit up and had too many cars. As he inched toward one of the few parking spaces left, he muttered "Shit" under his breath.

The motel parking lot was completely full, save for a couple spots at the very end by the dumpsters. As Benny drove slowly to claim one of those spaces, I surveyed the scene, grateful for Benny's tinted windows. Phillip said nothing, but his hand clasped in mine was holding it tight enough to hurt my fingers.

The parking lot was covered up with people. Most of them just standing around or milling about, waiting.

Waiting for Phillip.

The kid at The Naughty Clam had worked fast.

In fact, it dawned on me as I peered out the window, there he was, standing over by the handicapped spaces. I also recognized Kevin Ramford, the shunned reporter who'd tried to ambush Phillip back in the hotel in Savannah. How had he gotten here so fast, I wondered, then realized that they must have already figured out Phillip was here. So much for staying under the radar. I identified one or two possible journalists whose faces seemed familiar. Alongside these faces, there were quite a few folks who must be fans—surprisingly, a large number of them seemed to be young women, and a lot of them underaged, from the looks of it. I watched them with a mixture of envy and awe, taking in their clothes—upscale takes on the "vintage" or "grunge" look we'd worn in the nineties; not quite right but a reasonably close facsimile—their impeccable makeup, and shining, youthful hair, and felt a pang of insecurity. I'd been a rock fangirl once, full of youth and promise, and I, too, had been obsessed with Phillip Deville. Now I was just a thirtysomething whose youth was fading, fast. These girls were fucking gorgeous.

Yeah, but you actually got *the guy, you idiot,* I told myself, biting off my negative thoughts. *You literally got Phillip Deville, the man they're here to see. He's yours.*

I knew he was inside my head, no matter what I'd said a few moments ago. Normally, a remark like that would have him touching me with warmth, acknowledgement. A small, sensual smile or a flick of the eyes to let me know he'd heard me and that he loved me. But Phillip wasn't paying me any attention. He was too focused on the scene outside. He stared out the window, his face dark.

"No chance of me getting to the motel room unseen, I guess," he said, his voice dripping with steel, and Lee turned in his seat to look at us.

"I wonder who tipped them all off," he said, meeting my eyes, his freckles standing out against his pale cheeks. "It couldn't have been that one rando with the phone. I could see him managing to follow us here, but he wouldn't have had time to let all these other folks know. How on earth did they find you?"

"Whoever it was, they're an asshole," Phillip thundered, his voice loud and angry in the small SUV. "But I guess it doesn't fucking matter now."

"If you don't feel like talking, you can just say 'no comment' and push right through them," Roberta offered. "Just walk straight inside, and they'll have no choice but to leave."

"He can try that, but you know they're going to swarm him the moment he steps out of the car," I said. The only reason they hadn't already descended upon us was because they probably didn't recognize Benny's vehicle. "And don't underestimate how long they'll be willing to wait outside the door to our room. Half of them probably brought sleeping bags."

"I can turn around and leave?" Benny suggested, turning to Phillip. "You guys can stay in our room with me and Lee for tonight."

Phillip considered this for a moment. "No," he said finally, taking a deep breath and squaring his shoulders. "I've played this game a million times. Doesn't matter how long you avoid them, they'll just keep waiting. You change locations, they'll follow. Better to face the music now and get it over with." He gave me an apologetic look. "I'm sorry, Stormy."

"Don't apologize to me," I said, raising his hand to my mouth and kissing his knuckles. "This isn't your fault."

"Yes, it is," he said. "I'm the one who decided to make a comeback. And at the worst possible time. I'm so sorry. I'm going to make it up to you somehow. Starting with this." And with that, he threw open the door and stepped out, all 6'5" of his long, lean body emerging from the car like the rock god that he was.

A literal roar of female voices came from the other side of the parking lot, along with the stamping of feet as fans and reporters ran over to our parked vehicle parked. I gaped at Roberta. "It's like the fucking Beatles on Ed Sullivan."

She grinned back at me, her eyes wide. "Let's jump out and make a break for your room before they notice us."

"Too late," Benny said, and a moment later, a fist was pounding on the glass, a face pressed up against my window. All I could make out of the girl's smooshed features were freckles that seemed magnified as they scrunched against the glass. "I fucking hate you!" she yelled at me, holding her hand up to the car and flipping me the bird. "I hate your guts!"

I swallowed and managed a small wave and a friendly smile. "Hi!" I called back in a cheery voice. I turned to Roberta with a shaky laugh. "I guess they figured out he has a girlfriend," I said with a shrug.

Benny and Lee were laughing in the front. "She can't see you, anyway," Lee reassured me. "She just knows you're back there."

I caught a flash of burgundy hair and what looked like black leather, and then the person disappeared into the crowd. I craned my neck, scanning, but it was just a bunch of reporters and groupies.

"Welcome to the jungle, baby," Roberta said, nudging me in the side. "You're gonna dieeeeeeeee."

When the girl, who undoubtedly would've fought me for the title of *Phillip's Biggest Fan,* had finished shouting expletives at us and moved back from the car, I stepped out, pushing through the throng of people who had already descended on Phillip, taking my place by his side. Roberta, Benny, and Lee also emerged from the car, hanging back a little, going relatively unnoticed. I couldn't help but see how comfortable, how at ease Phillip looked, standing there amongst the crowd, head and shoulders taller than all of us, his dark hair shining in the glow of the streetlamps, a slightly mischievous smile on his face.

"Look, guys," he said, his voice booming out over the crowd, which fell silent immediately. "I'm just here to grab a bed for the night. We're here on private family business, and I'd really appreciate if you'd all clear out so we can have some privacy. Okay?" He didn't wait for anyone to answer, but instead nodded as though he'd been given an affirmation. "Thanks." I figured that was it and moved for him to take my arm and walk back to the motel together. But Phillip paused, his expression turning serious, then spoke again.

"My girlfriend Stormy's father is missing. He hasn't been seen since a suspected case of arson burned his house to the ground two days ago. Chad Bradley has another daughter and a wife, too, and they all love him and want to know what happened to him. The police are being less than cooperative so far." He swallowed and went on, his voice booming out over the crowd. "Instead of focusing on me and my boring activities at a motel, maybe some of you journalists in the crowd could look into Chad Bradley's disappearance."

My mouth gaped open as I stared at Phillip.

"And that's all I have to say. I appreciate everyone giving us our privacy." And with that, Phillip took my arm and steered me toward the motel.

"Jesus, you could have warned me," I whispered hotly to him as we walked.

"I thought I'd take advantage of the attention," he said sheepishly, shooting me a quick look. "I thought—"

"Wait!" a voice cut through, interrupting Phillip. I recognized that voice. I turned and groaned audibly as Dee stepped out from her car, which was parked just across from ours, her blond ponytail bobbing behind her as she stepped forward. "I can clarify about Stormy's father!"

To her credit, she'd momentarily gotten everyone to stop looking at Phillip and me. We should have run for it, rushing into our motel room and slamming and locking the door, but I was stuck to the concrete, unable to move.

"You have information about Stormy's father and the missing person's case?" a woman asked. She was holding out a little silver mini-microphone like the kind I'd seen on TikTok videos, attached to her phone, which she was using to film. "And who are you?"

"I'm Stormy's stepmother, Deidre Bradley," she said smoothly, and I realized as the ring light hit her face that she'd reapplied her makeup since the bar. My hands involuntarily curled into fists. She had prepared for this. I doubted she'd been the one to tip them off, but she'd obviously anticipated this scene and had planned to use it to her advantage. It was no different than what Phillip had done, but for some reason, it made me mad.

If I hadn't been so angry, I would have given her credit for how smart it was.

"What Phillip said is true. Stormy's father, Chad Bradley, my husband, is missing," Dee said, her face composed, only one tiny forehead wrinkle giving away her worry. "It was our home, the one we shared together with our young daughter, that burned down. Police can't rule out arson, but as of right now, we don't know." She paused, dabbing at an eye with a tissue. When she looked back up, her face was full of fierce resolve. "My husband Chad had planned to go away this past weekend for a fishing trip with an old friend, and we're hoping he's just out of cellphone range and has no idea what's going on. But the police found a body at our home, a body that has yet to be identified." A gasp went through the crowd, and Dee paused for a moment, fishing in the pocket of her fitted white blazer to pull out a flyer, one of the ones they'd had down at the precinct. In the picture, my father looked distinguished, with his graying hair slicked back and his aviator glasses hiding his bright blue eyes. His mouth was relaxed, an easy smile plastered across his face, a smile I didn't really recognize. Dad's smiles had been few and far between when I was a kid, and half the time, it was a cruel, mocking kind of smile, the kind brought on by a very dirty (and often problematic) joke, or from mocking my mother. This was the smile of a nice, kind man who didn't have much stake in anything serious, someone who was happy go-lucky, friendly, and kind. The collar of his white polo shirt made a sharp contrast against his tanned skin, and he had a great many more wrinkles than he'd had when I was a kid, likely a result of living right on the beach, but also from a life well-lived.

To my horror, I felt tears spring to my eyes, but thankfully, nobody was looking at me. Phillip held me tight.

Dee went on. "This is Chad. It's the most recent picture we have of him, and he'll likely be wearing an outfit similar to this one. He lives in those polos. He loves his golf." She smiled, her straight, white teeth—she'd had those fixed and whitened since the last time I'd been down for the holidays—gleaming under the lights. "If anyone has seen my husband or thinks they might know something about his disappearance, please call the Panama City Beach police department on their tip line ASAP and let them know everything you can. They have no leads, and I'm desperate. We're relying on you to help us find my husband." Her voice shook a little, and she wiped at her eye again. "Please. If you know anything, call them. Or you can call me directly. I'll pass out cards with my number." I blanched; that was way out of protocol and would likely piss off the cops.

Also, she hadn't really said anything about me. I was a footnote. She'd used Phillip to get her little press conference and then acted like I barely existed. Jealousy and hurt raced through my veins even though I didn't want to be that small, that pathetic. There were more important things to worry about. But I couldn't help it.

"I'm going to the room now," I said to Phillip in a low voice, trying to swallow back my tears. "I can't be here for this. It's too much."

"Let's get you out of here," he started, but I'd already shrugged off his arm and made a beeline for the motel, leaving him behind. Behind me, I could hear Lee, of all people, asking the crowd to step back, to give us all some room. I could barely make out his calm, careful voice over the screeching young girls who hadn't been deterred from their obsession by my stepmom's weird hijack.

"Please, everyone, Mr. Deville is just trying to get to his room. This is no time for more questions, obviously." I was impressed by how deftly Lee was handling it, but I didn't turn around. I had to get away from the throng, all the peering eyes, the fake concern, and Dee's plea for sympathy, which had no doubt been genuine but still stung. I had to get away from it all, right now; even my own friends, who were huddled together staring at me sadly from Benny's car, and even from Phillip, who had dumped me right in the thick of a clusterfuck, as he'd said in his own words, at the exact wrong time.

SEVEN

"Fuck!" I paced back and forth in the small room, ready to crawl right out of my own skin. I pressed my hands to my face. I couldn't stop wiggling my fingers, the electricity in them buzzing and tingling. "How could she *do* that?"

"You can hardly blame her," Phillip said evenly, sitting on the bed, unlacing his black combat boots. "I mean, I basically did the same thing. Free publicity; maybe the cops will take her seriously now."

"I get that, but—" I stopped, exasperated, then resumed pacing. How could Phillip be taking his damn shoes off so casually at a time like this? Not even the sight of his tight abdomen and the downy black hair that ran from his navel down below the waistband of his jeans as he shrugged out of them could distract me from the upset I felt. "But to just take over—"

"It's the best thing that could have happened, probably," Phillip said, walking over and placing his hands on my shoulders. He looked deep into my eyes, his hands pressing down to stop me from trembling. "It took the focus off us for a minute so we could get inside, and we didn't have to answer a bunch of asinine questions."

"Yeah, but now your—your—your *brand* is going to be associated with this, this …" I trailed off, collapsing in a fit of tears. I shrugged Phillip's hands off and slumped on the bed, distraught.

"My brand?" Phillip sat down beside me and tried to take my arm, but I shrugged him off again. "Please, never refer to my 'brand' again. I'm not some … some product. This is my life. And yours. I refuse to let either of us be reduced to something so shallow."

"You can't seriously tell me you didn't realize that your music, your persona, is a fucking commodity," I said, my voice coming out nastier than I meant it to. I furiously wiped at my face, wishing he wouldn't see me cry. I didn't want him to feel sorry for me, to try and comfort me. I just needed to feel this right now, to let my emotions wash over me and dissipate. Or else drown.

"Stormy, this isn't what you're *actually* upset about, is it?" Phillip asked. "It's okay to admit that you're worried."

"Don't tell me how to feel," I shot back, but the wind was already leaving my sails. "Maybe I just need … I don't know. Some time to think."

"I'll leave you alone," Phillip said softly, then he kissed his index finger and pressed it to my lips. He grabbed for his pants and moved to put them on again.

He'd never be able to leave the room, not with that mob outside. He was stuck here. I opened my mouth to tell him that, but before I had the chance, my phone started buzzing in my pocket.

I pulled it out, looking at the screen, which was blurry through my tears. With a sigh, I hit the green button and held it up to my ear. "Mama. Hey. Don't worry, we're fine. We got into the room before—"

"Stormy," Mama interrupted. "I have someone here who needs to speak to you."

My brow furrowed as I heard the phone being passed to someone else, then a male clearing his throat. The next sound I heard was a voice I hadn't heard in a long, long time. A voice that, the moment it spoke, caused my heart to stop and my breath to catch in my throat.

"Stormy Fiona Spooner," Daddy said on the other end of the phone, his voice that of a man blissfully unaware, who hasn't a clue what all has gone on in his absence, "What is this I hear about you dating a famous rock star?"

God Bless Phillip Deville.

I owed him a thousand personal apologies for all the times I'd called him a shitty liar. He'd pulled out the most epic lie of all.

I still wasn't quite sure how he'd managed to convince an entire parking lot full of reporters, journalists, influencers, and fans, but with one simple phone call to The Naughty Clam, he'd managed to clear the entire crowd out in less than half an hour.

"Hi," he'd said in a dulcet voice, twirling the landline cord around his long finger. "My name is Phillip Deville. Yes, Phillip Deville of the Bloomer Demons. I was there earlier having a pleasant drink with some friends, and I was wondering if you might like a little impromptu entertainment this evening?" I'd gaped at him in confusion, and he'd winked at me. "My fans have figured out I'm in town, and I thought I might play a little set at a local hotspot, and your bar immediately came to mind. What would you think about me playing tonight? You would? Oh, great." I'd shaken my head in disbelief, watching him spin the tale. "Excellent. I can't wait. An hour or so? Perfect. Spread the word; this is going to be a great show." He'd hung up the phone, leering at me, pleased with himself. I hadn't been convinced his little ruse would work, or that the bar would even believe it was the real Phillip Deville. But much to my shock, within a couple of minutes, an audible buzz had started among the throng outside, and slowly but surely, we began to see the beaming headlights of all the cars and trucks as they pulled out of the parking lot, presumably headed toward The Naughty Clam.

"You can't do that to them," I'd said, feeling guilty, Phillip grabbing for a fresh black shirt from his bag. "We caused that scene earlier, and now we're tricking them into thinking you're playing a show?"

"One thing at a time," Phillip said, tying his laces. "I had to get them cleared quick so I could get you to your dad. I'll figure the rest out later."

Bless him. He'd really done it. And now we were jumping into my truck and pulling out of an empty parking lot, heading just two streets over to the motel where my mother and Roberta were staying, to see my father.

I hadn't had a chance to ask many questions, because as soon as I'd heard his voice on the phone, I'd also heard Dee rushing into the room. Through her screaming and crying and peppering Daddy with questions, I couldn't make heads or tails of what I was hearing. After a few moments of ear-shattering sobs and reassurances on the other end of the line, Roberta had picked up and said, "Just get over here," and hung up.

My stomach was in knots as we pulled into yet another motel parking lot, Phillip deftly maneuvering the steering wheel with one arm, the other one wrapped tightly around me.

"I'm so glad he's okay," he said softly, glancing at me. He

pulled into the parking space next to Roberta's SUV and turned off the truck. He turned to me and asked, "Are you ready to go in?"

"No," I said, taking a deep, shaky breath. "And yes."

"He's alive," Phillip said, looking into my eyes, giving me a little jostle of reassurance. "He didn't burn up in any fire, he wasn't hurt. He's *okay*. He's alive. That's all that matters, Stormy. The rest … the rest we can work out. Together."

"I know," I said. He was right, but it was so damn hard to swallow for some reason.

"Literally and figuratively, huh?" He chuckled, then opened the truck door. "I know, I know, get out of your head, yadda, yadda, yadda." He came around to my side of the truck and opened the door for me, offering his arm. "Let's go see Chad Bradley. He's got a lot of splainin' to do."

All I could do was stand there and stare at him. I'd never admit it out loud, but in my heart, I had already assumed my father was dead. I had already begun to let him go—what little of him I had clung to—bit by bit. It was a weird sensation, looking at someone you'd already begun to grieve for.

I took stock of him, sizing him up, buying time as I watched Daddy wrap a thin arm around my mother awkwardly, the two of them hugging with their lower bodies far apart from each other, as though they might accidently copulate by osmosis. On the other side of the room, Dee sat, naked envy and sheer relief vying for the most real estate on her face. On any other day, I might have giggled.

Over my mom's shoulder, Daddy was looking at me. He was much thinner than I remembered. After he'd left Mom and gotten "clean," or at least some semblance of pretense of clean, he'd filled out and gained a good bit of weight. Mainly around the jowls and in the belly, the same areas most middle-aged men fill out. His hair, once a reddish gold he'd worn clipped in a pseudo-mullet much longer than the trend had allowed for, had slowly begun to go salt and pepper. I'd noticed how much he was filling out and watched as the silver strands slowly took over the red every time he'd text me a picture of himself, Dee, and Shay, or whenever they'd send me a Christmas card. I'd come to think of Daddy in my mind as a graying, stocky man who was on the other side of middle age.

The man standing here now was thin as a rail, as thin as I remembered from my childhood, if not more so. Gone were the slight jowls and beer gut. He was a rake, his chin and cheeks almost gaunt and angular. His hair was cut short, and there wasn't a single red-gold strand to be found. He'd gone completely gray, his hair almost white in places. A heavy five o'clock shadow branched out from his chin and cheeks, and he ran a hand over the stubble as he regarded me with eyes that were way too full of laughter considering what we'd all been through. He stood awkwardly, his free arm splayed out by his side, as though he were trying very hard to be serious and stoic when all he really wanted to do was break out in dance.

"Daddy," I said finally, taking one step forward. My legs felt like lead. Now that he was standing here in front of me and the initial shock and denial were wearing off, I began to feel something like relief. "You're okay."

"I'm okay," he said, nodding, his face lighting up. He also took one step forward, then we both sort of teetered there, a yard or so of space between us that felt as vast as the universe. I was aware of Phillip standing behind me, a comfortable and safe presence. Roberta was there too, and Mom, and Dee. But all of them had faded away.

"I …" I began, but then my phone started to buzz. I pushed my hand in my pocket and silenced it, then took another step forward. "It's good to—"

My phone immediately buzzed again. I pulled it out, frowning, and moved to silence it a second time.

"It's good to see you, darlin'," Daddy said, bridging the gap between us and pulling me into a bear hug. "It's been too damn long. Ain't you a sight for sore eyes."

I hovered there for a minute, afraid to touch him, just tapping him on the back with one hand, not sure how to do this. We hadn't hugged since, when? I was an adolescent? I didn't even know. "I … we all … thought you were …"

"You thought I was meant for the extra-crispy bucket," he said with a laugh, and pulled back to look at me, his hands on my shoulders. "Shoot, darlin', I'm sorry. I didn't mean to give everybody a fright. I was off fishin' with my buddy Arnold, and neither one of us even thought to check our phones until we was two miles down the road from his house." His eyes danced as he looked me over, his mustache twitching a little as his lips moved. "When I turned the damn thing on and saw all the messages and calls I missed, I about had a stroke."

"I bet," I said, my voice wavering a little. No, no, no, I would not cry. Not in front of him, and Phillip, and everyone. I couldn't. "Your, um … I'm sorry about your house."

"You and me both." He grinned, and that was when I realized this weird happy-go-lucky thing was all an act. He was rattled as fuck, but he was trying to put on a brave face for all of us. His mustache wasn't twitching from mirth; he was trembling. "But hey, me and Dee have insurance, and it's right good insurance, ain't it, Dee? We'll be aight." I had to smile at the way he said *aight,* just like he had since I was a kid.

"Did they tell you they—that they found a body?"

He was still clutching me by the shoulders, and his grip on me tightened, though the smile hadn't left his face. "Yeah, they did," he said, shaking his head absently. "I can't make heads or tails of it."

"Why did you come here?" I asked. "To Mama's hotel?"

"Well, I went back home, but there was no home to go to," he answered, and I felt stupid for asking. "I called Dee, but she didn't answer." That must have been the precise moment Dee was playing for the cameras because there was no way, with the way she'd been checking her phone earlier, that she would've failed to take his call. "And I had a bunch of texts from your mom, so I figured it'd be a safe bet to call her. Just so happened she picked up and told me that you all were nearby. So I hightailed it over here."

"I'm glad," I said, my voice still shaking. Damn it, Stormy, *stop it.* But I couldn't contain it any longer. The dam burst, and the tears started coming out like a flood. Before I could stop myself, I pitched forward and landed in Daddy's arms. They went around me automatically and held me tight, one arm cradling my head against his shoulder, just like he'd done when I was very little. "I'm so glad you're okay. I'm so glad you're alive. I thought—"

"Shhh, darlin'," he said into my hair, letting me cry. "Shhh. I'm right here."

I wanted to just stand there for a minute and be held, to actually enjoy this moment I'd let myself have, but of course my stupid phone began buzzing again. It must be important; whoever it was had called me four times in the span of two minutes. Reluctantly, I pulled away from Daddy and slid the phone out of my pocket, peering at the screen. "It's an unknown number," I said, and moved to put the phone away.

"You might want to answer it, hon," Daddy said, and his face suddenly looked very, very old and very tired.

I looked down at the phone again and sighed. Every cell in my being pushing against it, I touched the green button and held the phone up to my ear. "Hello?"

"Hello, is this Stormy Spooner?"

"Yes, it is." My heart had begun to pound.

"The wife of James Tess Spooner?"

I stopped breathing. I reached an arm out blindly to clutch someone, anyone, for support. I found Phillip's hand. "Ex-wife. But yes, that's me."

"Mrs. Spooner, I'm calling from the Panama City Beach police department. Can you possibly come down to the station? We know you're here in town."

Phillip was the only thing holding me up. "Can you tell me what this is about?"

"Well …" There was muttering on the other end of the line. "I hate to do this over the phone, Mrs. Spooner, but … well, I'm afraid that you're next of kin."

"And you're calling me because …" I was stalling. I already knew what they were going to say.

"Mrs. Spooner, I regret to inform you that James Tess Spooner is dead."

"Oh." I could hear an ocean in my ears. A dull roar that was becoming louder and louder and louder still.

The voice continued. "I apologize for your loss, Mrs. Spooner. As you're the next of kin, we need you to come on down to the station and identify the body."

"I don't imagine there's much left to identify," I said absurdly, and to my horror, I started to laugh. "He died in the fire, didn't he? He was the one in my dad's house?"

"I'd rather we not discuss anything further until you've arrived at the station, Mrs. Spooner," the voice insisted. "Can someone drive you?"

Then Phillip was catching the phone in mid-air because I'd dropped it. Then *I* was dropping too, dropping onto the motel's cheap, thin carpet, screaming like a banshee and scratching at my face as my my two befuddled parents and an ashen-faced Roberta tried to quiet me, to comfort me.

But there was no comfort to be found.

Tess was dead. Tess was dead. Tess was dead.

Just before I passed out, I heard Phillip's calm but pained voice say, "I'll bring her right down, officer. We're on the way."

Eight

I woke up freezing, despite my pajamas, several layers of blankets, and Phillip's warm arms around me. The knowledge came soaring back before I even opened my eyes.

Tess. My first love. My husband. Gone.

He had hurt me immeasurably over the past couple years, especially in the past few weeks, given his involvement with Guthrie and Elvin, to say nothing of the cheating, his drug use, and all the other little betrayals. But he had been my husband. We'd known each other since we were kids, had been through all sorts of things together. Before things had gone belly up, he had been there for me through a lot of dark times, had known my secrets, my hopes and dreams, and had even shared some of them with me.

It had been Tess who talked me into applying for a job at the library. He'd heard me complain about not wanting to be a cashier at Kroger for the rest of my life. He was one of the few people who had known my secret aspirations to be a writer, and it had been a stroke of genius on his part when he'd come home one day, cracked open a beer, and told me he'd seen a HELP WANTED ad at the library.

"But I'm not qualified," I'd protested. I'd been frying up onion rings to go with our veggie burgers for dinner. That was another thing about Tess—he was a carnivore through and through, but he'd happily eat vegan whenever I was around, which was most of the time. He'd never been the type to tease me or make me feel bad for my dietary restrictions or anything else. "Don't you need a degree to be a librarian?"

"I dunno, darlin'," he'd said, tipping back his beer and coming over to give me a sloppy kiss on the cheek. "All I know is that the sign's been up for over a week now, and I know you're smart as hell. You read a lot, more than anybody I know. And I reckon you'd be as qualified as anybody else, degree or not. I think ou'd be good at the job. What's the harm in puttin' in your application?"

And so I had. And just as Tess had predicted, I'd gotten the job. Jean, my boss, and I had gotten along like a house on fire in the interview, and she'd hired me on the spot as her assistant/receptionist. I'd been working there for two years now, and she'd already given me a promotion to assistant manager, though it was more a title than anything.

My job ... I'd barely been in over the last few weeks, and who knew if I even had one at this point. I'd had a brief conversation with Jean a few days ago. I'd told her that a family emergency had come up and I needed to take a leave of absence. While she'd told me to take all the time I needed, something in her tone told me she'd had her fill of my shenanigans lately, and that once we were back face to face, there would be consequences. I wouldn't be surprised to find that she was interviewing candidates in my absence, and I honestly couldn't blame her if she was.

I couldn't muster up the energy to care. It seemed no matter how I tried, no matter how much I fought against it, tried to chase down all the loose ends that seemed to be unraveling before me, the worse things got. No sooner than I'd discovered my father was alive, Tess was gone. When would it just *stop?*

Apparently, the answer was never.

Why the *fuck* had Tess been in my father's house? And who had started the fire? Who had killed him, and why?

The thoughts swirling in my head combined with the deep, deep pain I felt in my heart made me dizzy, even though I was lying in bed. Reluctantly, I pried my eyes open, unsurprised to see Phillip staring at me with concern from the other side of the pillow. He reached across me to the nightstand and produced a tissue, handing it to me. He watched me quietly as I dabbed at my eyes, removing the crusted vestiges of sleep and all the tears I'd cried the night before.

Phillip cupped the side of my face. "I'm so sorry, honey," he said softly, his eyes boring into mine. They held all the same pain that he no doubt saw within mine; he mirrored me. I was touched. The one time he'd met Tess, my ex had made a pretty bad impression. But Phillip had been married and divorced himself; he knew how I must feel, no matter what type of person Tess had been in life.

"Will you help me sit up?" My voice came out a croak. Phillip hooked his arm under my left and gently pulled me up to a sitting position. Out in the parking lot—perhaps from a car radio or someone's Bluetooth speakers near the pool—I could hear the faint hum of Dio's "Holy Diver." I had the sudden, totally inappropriate urge to laugh.

Tess had loved that song. So many times, we'd be working on some house project—painting the kitchen cabinets or repairing the damned broken board in the living room—and we'd fight over the radio. I always wanted to play my records —Bloomer Demons, of course, or Alice in Chains or Bauhaus —while he was more fond of the classic metal and hair metal of the late eighties and early nineties. Dio, Judas Priest, Motley Crue, Lemmy. Tess had unabashedly loved "Holy Diver," and

I'd loudly (and half-jokingly) complained every time he'd play that song. Hearing it now, I put my head in my hands.

"I'm going to get you some coffee," Phillip murmured, and got up from the bed. I pulled the sheets tighter around me, as if I could absorb the warmth Phillip had just left behind. I felt so cold.

"Thanks."

He busied himself with the one-cup hotel coffee pot, pouring in the water, tearing open the little envelope of coffee, extracting a filter. My stomach rumbled painfully; I hadn't eaten dinner the night before. After leaving the police station, I'd been so upset that all I wanted to do was go back to the motel and bury my head under all the pillows, which was exactly what I had done. Phillip had gone over to The Naughty Clam for a bit, not playing a show but placating some of the fans by signing a few autographs and taking a few selfies, leaving me to cry it out and process it on my own. Had I not been so insane with grief, I would have had quite a lot to say about that and been wildly curious to see what the internet had to say about his impromptu appearance, but right now, I just couldn't care. After he'd gotten back from the bar, he'd come to bed and wrapped his arms around me, making sure I knew he was there, but we hadn't really spoken. I found I didn't have any words.

The moment I'd walked in the door at the police department, Phillip on one side escorting me and Mama on the other with Roberta trailing close behind, I'd known it was going to be a bad scene. For some inexplicable reason, the cop at the reception desk had congratulated Mama and me on my father being found. He probably meant well, but the whole thing was weird; he was oddly proud of it, as though he'd discovered him in some secret hiding place, when my father had just driven home from his friend's house of his own accord. "I bet you're glad to have your daddy back," the cop had said to me with a smile brighter than I'd thought necessary under the circumstances.

I hadn't said much in reply; what was there to say? When the cop had finished signing me in, he'd been noticeably colder. "You can't bring all of them in with you," he'd said, pushing a VISITOR sticker over to me.

Dutifully, I'd pulled off the backing and stuck it on my shirt. "Let's go get this over with."

An officer led me down a little corridor with a sticky linoleum floor that smelled strongly of Pine-Sol, the old-fashioned kind that reeked of cedar and lemons, and through an unmarked door. A blast of cold air hit me, whipping my hair back. I'd instinctively wrapped my arms around myself, and a woman had said, "Sorry, we have to keep it cold in here."

I nodded. I knew why. The male cop had passed me over to the female cop then; names were exchanged, but I didn't remember them. The female cop had been nicer, but she was clipped and professional, too; this was just a job for her. We'd talked for a minute, she'd explained some things, but it was all a blur. All I really remembered was the moment she'd removed the sheet and I saw Tess' body.

He hadn't been as badly burned as I'd expected. The cop pulled the sheet down to his torso, and I took him in, feeling oddly calm and quiet as I did so. His dark hair had grown out long, longer than I'd ever seen it, and his boyish face was unmarked except for one small patch of mottled skin on his left cheek. I stared at him, taking in one last look of the lips I'd kissed so many times, the silly little goatee he'd always refused to shave, the pierced right ear with the skull stud in it, the small snake tattoo over his heart. It had once been an "S" for Stormy Spooner. After our divorce, he'd gone and had it touched up to make it into a snake, something he made sure to show me afterward. I'd been so upset by that, but now it all seemed so ridiculous. I had loved him once, loved him fiercely, and he had loved me. That was all that mattered now that he was gone.

I'd nodded to the cop, and she'd put the sheet back over Tess' face as left the room without another word, walking straight to the car in silence.

Now, I watched as Phillip poured coffee in a paper cup and stirred in two sugars. "Sorry, no creamer, at least not any that's vegan," he said apologetically as he handed the hot cup to me. He sat down beside me on the bed and put an arm around me as I took a long, scalding sip. "I know it's probably the last thing you feel like right now, but you need food. What can I get you to eat?"

"Anything but burgers and onion rings," I said, and promptly burst into tears.

"This is delicious, Dee, thanks," I said as my stepmother piled another mountain of mashed potatoes on my plate. We were at her parents' house, where Daddy, Dee, and Shay would be staying indefinitely. Dee's parents spent half the time in Michigan, where they were originally from, and half the time in Florida. Right now, they were up north, so it was just us.

"And 100 percent plant-based," she said with a proud grin, taking her seat and pouring out a glass of wine. "I looked up some recipes on the Food Network website. Plant-based is all the rage now."

"So I've noticed," I said with a smile, spearing off a piece of my Beyond burger and taking a bite. To Dee's credit, she'd managed to whip up a pretty decent vegan version of Salisbury steak, mashed potatoes, and squash casserole that could have fooled even the most culinary-inclined granny.

"Phillip said you needed comfort food." She looked over at

Daddy and gave him a wistful look. "I thought we all could, honestly."

"Good call," Daddy said, digging into his potatoes. "So what do you use in these here taters if you don't use milk and butter?"

"Well, you use plant-based butter—"

"Aka margarine," Phillip muttered, grinning at me, and I kicked him under the table.

"—and whatever plant-milk you like. The recipe I saw called for oat milk, but that stuff just tastes like oatmeal to me. So I used almond milk. It's good, right, Stormy?"

"It really is." I crammed a mouthful of potatoes in my mouth and closed my eyes. It actually *was* delicious, however much Phillip might tease, and I was grateful for a warm, home-cooked meal. I was finally starting to feel somewhat sane again. Barely.

"Okay, we've got our hands all washed!" Roberta appeared holding Shably, who held out her hands over her head excitedly, as if to say *see?* I smiled at my little sister, surprised at just how much she'd grown since the last time I'd seen her. That Christmas, she'd still been very much a baby. Now, she was practically ready for pre-K. Her little tufts of dishwater hair had grown into long, shiny strands, held back with a pretty lavender headband, and her long legs were encased in Princess Elsa leggings. She was going to be tall, from the looks of it; probably taller than me.

"I sit by Sis," she declared in her little voice, and Roberta grinned, bouncing her in her arms.

"You want to sit by Sis? Okay, you can have my seat. We'll switch." She moved Shay's booster chair to the seat on the other side of me and deposited my baby sister into it. "You'll have to ask big sister Stormy if she'll help you cut your steak."

"You mean her 'fake,'" Phillip said and snorted.

"I apologize, everyone," I said, placing my hands on the

table and giving them a look of contrition. "For my boyfriend's endless and unfunny dad jokes."

"I thought it was funny," Daddy said, and popped open the tab on his PBR. I frowned slightly, and he caught my look. "Don't worry, mon petit baybee"—his faux-French accent was butchered and ridiculous—" I have two a week. Dee rations them. You can ask her."

Phillip raised an eyebrow at his term of endearment. Dad chuckled and explained.

"She was obsessed with that skunk from Looney Tunes when she was a little gal," he said with a grin. "Pepe Le Pew-Pew or whatever he was."

"Pepe Le Pew." I grimaced, feeling my cheeks flush with embarrassment. Phillip's mouth was already turning up at the corners; he loved it. "I was little and didn't know any better. I just thought he was cute with that little hop."

"Little skunk always chasing the girl cat," my father said, laughing. "Stormy couldn't get enough of it. She had all them stuffed animals, socks, posters ... and her little friend always liked that other character, that—"

"So only two a week, huh?" I cut in with a wink, my cheeks still burning.

"It's true," Dee said brightly, spearing a piece of broccoli with her fork. "Some weeks, he doesn't even drink them both."

"You want one, hoss?" Daddy asked Phillip, and I almost laughed out loud as Phillip nodded and sat up a little straighter in his chair. *Hoss, really?* I caught Roberta's eye, and she placed her hand over her mouth to hide her laughter. It appeared that even the coolest of rock stars felt nervous around their girlfriend's fathers. Phillip looked downright proud to be opening the shitty beer my father handed him.

"Too bad Laureen couldn't make it," Daddy said, reaching for the rolls. "This is a nice meal, with nice company. She ought to be here."

"She said she was tired," I explained, leaning over to help Shay cut her Beyond burger into small cubes, laughing as she used her hands to pop them in her mouth, ignoring her fork. "Here, use this, little sis. You just washed your hands, remember?"

"She's probably avoiding me," Dee said, taking a sip of wine. "We … well, we didn't exactly have words, but things were a little tense," she rushed to explain. "We were both so stressed, Chad, and worried about you. I imagine all this has taken a toll on her."

"And seeing you sitting here drinking probably wouldn't help," I said before I could stop myself. I shook my head; I didn't want to be a jerk tonight. It wouldn't help anyone. "I mean, just because she hasn't been sober that long."

"Drinkin' was always your mama's game more than mine," Daddy said, and passed the basket of rolls to me. I waved them away, and he pushed them further toward me. "You better eat, young lady. Keep up your strength. You might be grown, but I'm still your daddy. Now take you a roll."

I dutifully complied, then ripped the roll in half and put it on Shay's plate, giving her a conspiratorial wink. She immediately crammed the entire roll piece in her mouth with her grubby fingers and kicked at the chair legs happily, her shoes *thunking* against the wood.

I resumed eating, keenly aware that everyone around the table was dodging the subject of Tess. I knew they all probably wanted to know how it had gone—if they'd told me anything, if they'd asked me any questions, how his body had looked, if there was any information. I could hardly blame them for wanting to know. After all, Daddy's house was gone, and Tess had been found inside. The thing that nobody would say out loud was that plenty of signs pointed to Tess having started the fire in the first place.

But I had nothing to tell them. The police hadn't given me

any information, had asked no questions, and had given me no indication that they were even working on the case, though I knew they had to be. I was as in the dark as everyone else. And even if I had had some information, I wasn't sure I could talk about what I'd seen under that sheet. It was too hard. Too painful.

Feeling everyone's eyes on me, I managed to say, "They didn't tell me anything. I'm sorry."

"I'm sure we'll hear from them tomorrow," Dee said, tearing a roll with her teeth, momentarily feral. "And if they don't, well, I'll just call another press conference of my own."

Phillip opened his mouth to no doubt voice his feelings about *that,* but I beat him to the punch, not wanting another fight between family. I used the one weapon I had in my arsenal, guaranteed to distract and co-opt any tense moment. And it'd be revenge on my dad for spilling about Pepe Le Pew. "Shay, I noticed your leggings have Princess Elsa on them," I said brightly, taking a too-large sip of my wine. "I bet you love the movie *Frozen,* huh."

I tensed up the moment my father found me on the back patio scrolling through my phone. I'd been avoiding being alone with him all evening and had begun to think I might get away from the house without having to talk to him when he'd offered to put Shably to bed. But then Phillip, ever the gentleman, had insisted on helping Dee with the dishes, and I hadn't been able to make my getaway.

"You and me need to have a pow wow," Daddy said, sitting down beside me on the porch swing.

"You shouldn't say pow wow," I said, my voice coming

out more cross than I intended. "It's disrespectful to Native culture."

"Oh. Well, I didn't realize," Daddy said, looking at me thoughtfully. In his right hand, he held another beer. "I won't say it no more."

"What did you want to talk about?" As if I didn't know.

"This has all been hard on you," Daddy said, reaching his arm around and giving me a stiff hug. I wanted to move closer, to lean into him, but I couldn't do it. I was too anxious. I just sat there instead, letting him hug me but giving nothing back in return. "The house fire, Tess …"

"This is just the latest," I said bitterly, pushing against the floor with my feet, making the swing go faster. "My life has been a series of heartbreaks for a long time now. Which you'd know if you'd been around."

"I'm sorry, sweet pea." Daddy sighed. "I've made a lot of mistakes. I know that. I have a lot to make up for, and I'd like to start by talking things out, getting everything off our chests."

"And if I don't want to?"

Daddy looked at me and said nothing, only stared at me, his bushy eyebrows raised on his tan face.

I continued. "It's been a lot. I just don't think I have it in me right now, Daddy. Honestly, I just want to go home."

"But there's things I need to tell you, things about the fire, about Tess, that—"

"I *can't.*" I shot up from the swing, sending it flying back into the screen. "Not now, okay? Just not now. I can't." Before Daddy could protest or say another word, I opened the sliding glass door and ran into the kitchen where Phillip was washing dishes, Dee drying beside him, the two of them laughing at some shared joke.

"Phillip. Let's go. Now."

"Sure thing. I've got just a couple more plates—"

"*Now,*" I said forcefully. "I want to go home now."
I didn't have to tell him a third time.

"I promise I'll be right back," I assured Phillip, ignoring the look of almost-hurt on his face as I gently shut the hotel door behind me, patting my pocket to make sure I had the plastic key. Hopefully, he'd be asleep by the time I got back, not because I didn't want to spend time with him but because I knew how tired he was. He'd spent all day holding me up, being my rock, and he might not let on, but I knew it had taken a toll on him. I wasn't the only one who wasn't sleeping, and we had to spend a lot of time on the road tomorrow. Spending all day absorbing my emotions and trying to keep me strong while dealing with both my parents, my stepmom, and energetic, demanding Shably—not to mention Roberta, who was hovering around like a mother hen—was a lot. Then there was that awful scene with my father after dinner that kept playing through my head. He'd tried to talk to me, to explain, to apologize, and I'd shot him down and literally fled the house before he could. Why did I have to go and act like that?

I was glad Benny and Lee had already headed back to Georgia, and I was even gladder I was leaving tomorrow morning. When Phillip had offered to stay on longer so I could spend some more time with my dad, I'd practically fallen over myself to convince him not to book another night. He meant well —his relationship with his own family before his death had been much better, so he just didn't understand—but I was more than ready to go back. I was desperate to get back to my life. Just the idea of doing something small and mundane like changing Blinken's litter or frying some okra made me want to cry with yearning.

The moment my feet hit the beach and I felt the cool, gritty sand beneath my feet, I could feel my body letting go of some of its tension, and I sighed with grateful relief. It was almost completely dark, but there was still a hint of light left, just enough to make out the empty lifeguard stand a few yards away and what looked to be a family hanging out at the very end of the long, huge wharf. I could barely make out a bright red jacket and matching ballcap on one of the figures. It looked like they might be pushing a baby carriage or perhaps one of those carts for carrying luggage. Likely they were looking for grazing sharks or hammerheads, both of which were frequently seen in Panama City Beach.

Living near the ocean my whole life, I'd seen my share of annoying tourists, drunken, destructive spring breakers, and curmudgeonly retirees, but I'd always loved seeing the families. They were always so heartwarming. Mom and dad, usually holding hands all lovey-dovey, full of the excitement and exhilaration of finally getting some time away from the grind. Their kids' excitement, who were usually happy with just a pool float and an overly air-conditioned hotel room. Something about going on vacation as a kid with your family was an experience that couldn't be topped. Every time I saw a happy family at the beach—mom, dad and the 2.5 kids—it made me feel warm and fuzzy inside.

I blew a silent, invisible kiss to the unknown family, thankful for what they'd unknowingly given me, and made my way down to the water, dutifully rolling up my pant legs to my ankles and letting the warm spray wash over my feet. It left a sheen of salt on my skin as it receded, one that wasn't entirely unpleasant. It felt cleansing and reminded me of the salt bath Phillip and I had taken together the day after we'd met. We'd been cramped in my little bathtub, his breath warm and sensual on the back of my neck as we'd lain there in the salty water that lapped over our skin. Time had seemed to stop, and we'd been half panting with lust by the time we'd gotten out. That had been the beginning of a courtship that had turned into the love affair we had now.

I felt a momentary pang of regret that I hadn't let him come with me. Swimming together in the ocean at dusk was pretty romantic and, well, hot. The memories of that salt bath were starting to take over, and I felt a warm, electric sensation in my belly. I was wasting a very good opportunity.

I decided I'd go fetch Phillip in just a few minutes and make it all up to him after I'd had a moment to myself. Right now, I just needed—not wanted, but needed—to be alone.

I waded further into the water, letting it caress my knees. It wet my pantlegs, but I paid it no heed. It didn't matter now … so many things didn't matter.

I returned to the room fifteen minutes later, ready to grab Phillip by the arm and drag him into the warm spray with me to frolic by the moonlight, feeling rejuvenated and whole again, ready to share that feeling with him.

But he lay huddled under the covers, his soft black hair over one eye, fast asleep.

NINE

"There's so much I don't understand," I said. "So much I still don't know, that I don't remember, that I don't get. And it seems like there's never time to just sit down and make someone tell me everything. And even if I had the time, who would I ask?"

"Roberta," Phillip said thoughtfully, running the guitar strap through his long fingers. "She's the obvious one, and I suppose your mother could fill in the blanks. Maybe Lee or Benny too."

"But it's getting all of them in a room together when we're not all fighting forces of evil or trying to locate a missing person that has proved to be the trial," I said, aware that my voice was verging on whiny. I looked at him curiously. "Don't you think it's kind of goofy to put that strap on your bass?"

"Why?" he asked, looking at me with a surprised expression.

"Because you bought it at Guitar Center," I explained, scratching Blinken under the chin. He wriggled in my arms, wanting free. I'd been forcing a lot of love on both him and

Nod since we'd returned, and they were sick of me. "It's commercially made fan merch, basically. And you're going to put it on your bass and play a show. It'll just look … I dunno, basic." I placed Blinken down on the carpet, and he sauntered off, tail swishing.

Phillip shrugged, his face bemused as he set to hooking the strap onto the bass. He looped the strap over and connected it via the little leather-bound holes on the ends. "I actually thought that was the appeal. It's funny, you know, and very unassuming. I figured the fans might get a kick out of it."

We'd been back from Panama City Beach for three days, three blessed, uneventful days. For three days, I had done no magic, had hunted no missing people, had not smelled even the faintest whiff of danger or mystery. All Phillip and I had done was hang around the house. We'd cooked and eaten some decadent meals, had loved on the cats, listened to music, caught up on some TV, and stayed up for hours talking. Much to my happiness, we'd done much of it naked in bed.

I now knew that my lover not only made a mean vegan spaghetti, which I discovered in Boston, but that he could seriously *rock* a batch of lemon-blueberry muffins, and that he poured one mean gin martini. Both of which were sitting on my coffee table right now, just waiting to be enjoyed.

I reached for the muffin first. "There's nothing unassuming about coming back from the dead and playing a huge rock reunion show," I said, peeling back the paper on my muffin. I sounded judgy, because I was. It was hard to stop being nasty when I felt like this. "I mean, is there any possible way you could show off more?"

Phillip looked at me, his brows furrowed together. We'd been round and round the conversation over the past three days, and we always seemed to come back to square one.

I shouldn't have been surprised when Phillip told me the

first night we were back that he and the rest of the guys in the band were thinking about playing a reunion show. I had known it was coming; he'd pretty much told me it was. From the way the interview had gone off without a hitch, to the reporters and fans camped outside our hotel room in PCB, to the impromptu signing he'd done at The Naughty Clam (once I'd gotten over the initial shock of Tess' passing, I'd learned it had been a much bigger event than Phillip had initially let on; he'd signed hundreds of autographs and gotten himself trending for the second time in a week), it was obvious that Phillip was planning a comeback.

We'd been in bed, me lying in the crook of his shoulder, both of us naked under the soft, clean sheets, when he'd twirled a strand of my hair around his finger and said, "How would you feel about a Bloomer Demons reunion?"

"You've already had one," I'd answered, but then it hit what he was really asking me. "You mean like a show?"

"Just a little one," Phillip said, still twirling my hair. His voice had the quality of someone trying to hide their excitement, going a little too hard for nonchalant. "Just the one show. Would you be okay with it?"

I'd told him yes automatically, and he'd pulled me into his arms and done things that had made me forget about my feelings, at least for the time being. And every time he'd asked me since, I'd parroted the same answer. And yet, he knew how I really felt, which was *why* he kept asking me over and over. He knew it, and I knew it, but neither one of us wanted to be the one to say it.

"Do you not want me to play the show?" Phillip asked yet again. His voice was casual, and he was looking down at the guitar, tuning the strings, but I could feel his anxiety.

"I didn't say that," I said evenly, biting into the muffin, the turbinado sugar crunching satisfyingly under my tongue. "I've told you several times—"

"I know I keep asking, but I feel like you're not being honest," Phillip said, finally looking up at me. "Stormy, do you not want me to play the show?" His eyes met mine. "Tell me the truth."

I sighed, sitting the rest of the muffin down and picking up the martini. "If I said I didn't, would you cancel?" I thought of the implications. They hadn't issued tickets yet, but there was already a date. Plans were being set in motion—the venue was being booked, the promotional staff had been hired, and Phillip, Jason, and Ollie were trying to hire a drummer to take Kim's place. They'd started hinting at it on social media. Jason had created an all-new social media presence for the band, and combined with all Phillip's latest publicity, it meant that their followers were growing by the hour, and it would be very hard to take it back now. The inevitable, instantaneous backlash that would happen on social media. All those fans disappointed. His furious bandmates. The dream of playing music again, this experience he'd been looking forward to ever since he'd sat for that interview, gone in an instant.

"Yes," he answered, looking back down to the bass. He plucked the G string and tightened it. "Without question."

"But why?"

"As if you have to ask." Phillip plucked the second string and smiled in satisfaction; that one was still in tune. "You're more important to me, Stormy, than literally anything else. That includes the band, the music, all of it. If you asked me to cancel, I'd cancel."

I sighed, feeling guilty. "And that's precisely why I'd never ask you not to play the show."

He tuned the third string, then peered at me. "But you don't want me to play."

"No, it's not that," I answered honestly. "I'm your biggest fucking fan, Phillip, remember? Nobody is more excited than I am to see you guys play. If you think that just because I know you now and that you and I ..." His eyes flashed, and I felt my cheeks get hot, my extremities start to tingle. They always did when he looked at me like that. "... If anything, it's made me even more of a crazed fan. I can't wait to see you guys up there. I always wanted to see Bloomer Demons live, and now I can. The fact that all my friends will be there, and all those fans ... that just makes it even better." I felt a little thrill in my belly as I said it. I *was* really excited. "If anything, I guess I'm just annoyed that you didn't tell me about it until after you guys had already decided, but ..." That wasn't entirely true. He'd been keeping me in the loop, but I'd been so distracted that I hadn't taken it seriously. I'd just kept hoping things would die back down. I had only my own denial to blame. "But I know that's not really your fault, either."

"Then what's the problem?" Phillip asked. "What's got you all tied up?"

I sighed. Phillip knew when I was lying. It was better to tell him the truth than play this song and dance that was so beneath us. "I guess I'm just a little afraid. You know that exciting, exhilarating feeling you get when you ride a really scary roller coaster for the first time, or the first time you drive by yourself, or the first time you get on an airplane or whatever?" I swallowed. "That bundle of nerves in your stomach that feels good but also feels terrifying?"

"Sure."

"It's like that, but ... bigger, I guess."

"What are you afraid of?"

"I'm afraid that after the show, you guys will blow up and be huge again, and you'll go on tour and cut an album and you'll never be here. You'll just leave me here, alone, with all this shit to deal with, and our relationship will fizzle out and that'll be the end of us!" My words came out in a flood, and I felt deeply embarrassed as soon as I'd said them. I clapped my hand over my mouth in a childlike gesture.

Phillip was smiling. "Do you really think, after everything, that I'd let that happen?"

"Some things you can't control," I said. "Haven't we learned that well and good?"

"We have," he agreed putting down the bass and walking over to me. He took my hands in his own, which were large and callused from all the practicing he'd been doing. "But there are plenty of things I can control. That *we* can."

I opened my mouth to protest, but his lips crushed mine before I had a chance to say anything. I kissed him back, giving myself over to the moment, letting his warmth, his strength, take me over. It felt nice to give into it. A part of me felt more than a small thrill at the thought of him being bigger than life again, a legit rock star, like he'd been in his heyday— with *me* on his arm.

Phillip pulled away from the kiss, his mouth curling up at the corners. "You on my arm, yes, that's exactly what I want. So what do you think?" he asked, his lips still inches from mine. "Wanna be my manager?"

I looked at him curiously. "I'm not remotely qualified. Besides, I have a job."

"About that." Phillip winked at me. "Are you honestly planning on going back? Like for real? Because I think you've only worked two days at that library the entire time we've been together. And you've been back home for three days and haven't even called your boss."

"I was waiting until Monday. And it hasn't been *that* long," I said defensively. "And I do love my job …" I really did love working at the library. But Phillip had a point. With the way things had been going for us, and likely would continue to go, going back to a regular nine-to-five schedule was going to be tricky. Jean had been holding my job for me, and had been really understanding and empathetic thus far, but she wasn't going to put up with my flakiness forever. And all that aside, the job didn't pay me enough. Not enough to support myself, two cats, and contribute to all the meals and booze that my 6'5" hunk of lovin' required to sustain himself, though at the rate he was going, he was going to be flush with plenty of money for the foreseeable future.

"I can take care of myself," he said, and I pulled him close, planting another kiss on his lips. His breath held the faint scent of Listerine, the old-fashioned brown kind.

"I'll think about the library thing," I said in a soft voice, letting my lips graze his, enjoying the feel of his mouth. "But Phillip … I can't be your manager. I wouldn't have a clue where to begin. And as much as I love the idea of controlling the Bloomer Demons, I think being so close to the situation, so close to you … well, it might get complicated. A conflict of interest, you know? I'm not sure it'd be a good idea." I smirked. "I don't want to be the Sharon to your Ozzy."

"You're a lot cooler than her," he remarked. "So if you quit the library, what do you want to do?"

"Honestly?" I looked him square in the eye, straightening my shoulders. "There *is* something I've always wanted to do, but I've never been brave enough to give it a try. I wonder if maybe now's my chance."

"What's that?" Phillip's face perked up with interest. "Tell me."

I swallowed, suddenly feeling shy. "Well … I've kind of always wanted to be a writer."

"Like books? Phillip said with a smile.

"Maybe, somewhere down the line," I answered. "But, mainly … I think I'd like to write about music. You know, like a rock journalist. An interviewer, like the guy who writes for GOTHZINE and who interviewed you." I smiled, embarrassed. "I think … I actually think I'd be good at that. Like, I know music, and I can string words together pretty well."

"You could absolutely do that," Phillip said assuredly, and

pushed a tendril of hair behind my ear. He was grinning from ear to ear; he looked proud. "I can't wait to see what you come up with. Have you thought about how to start?"

"A music blog," I said a little too quickly, revealing that I had indeed already thought about it. "I actually, um … well, I wrote an article I thought about pitching, just sort of introducing myself, and introducing *you*—nothing too in detail, just a quirky little thing I thought might be fun." I was talking too fast from equal parts excitement and worry that he'd be put off by the idea. "I won't pitch it unless you give me the green light, though. I know you'll want to read it first."

"Don't need to," Phillip said to my surprise. "I'll read it when it's published. Pitch it where you want; I trust you."

I was deeply touched. I swallowed, a large lump in my throat. I might as well tell him my whole idea. "I thought if it was well-received, then I might … chronicle our time on the road. Write about the tour. It'll serve as a road diary for you guys, help promote you and everything, and maybe getting your fans' eyes on it will sort of propel me into the scene? Maybe someone will notice my work?" I shrugged. "I don't know, maybe it's stupid. If you feel like it's exploitative—"

"Stormy," Phillip cut in gruffly. "I just asked you to be my manager. To literally handle all the decisions for my band. Do you think I'd mind if you write some blog posts and articles about the band?" He grinned, pushing his large hand through his black hair. "In fact, I can't think of anyone I'd rather have writing about me. You'll put me in the best possible light."

I laughed and gave him a shove. "I plan to be unbiased, Phillip Deville."

"Impossible. You love me too much."

He was right about that. "You know who would make a great manager," I said, the thought suddenly occurring to me. "Lee."

Phillip furrowed his brow. "Lee Courtenay? What makes

you think that? He doesn't even have a background in that sort of thing, does he?"

"Well, more than I do," I countered. "He managed his dad's affairs for a while there, and I think we both know Guthrie wasn't exactly an easy person to work for. Besides, he totally handled that crowd outside the motel room the other night. If he hadn't stepped in, you would've been trapped in that spectacle for god knows how long."

"I think our getaway was down to your stepmom and her shenanigans," Phillip argued. "And it was just weeks ago that the guy kidnapped you, so I mean …"

"A lot of things have happened since then," I pointed out. "If we dwell on each individual one, we'll never get out of the maze."

"Maybe," Phillip said. "I like him, I do, but I don't trust him like you do."

"Just think it over," I said. "Whatever you decide, I'll support you."

"I'll think about it," Phillip said thoughtfully. Then he reached forward and grabbed at me, his hands going under my shirt and tickling my stomach. "Right now, though, there's a certain music writer I plan to ravish and manipulate into giving my next album a rave review."

I sighed, immediately warming to his touch. My blood started to heat up as he pressed his soft lips to mine, and I moved to caress his face, my fingers tangling in his shaggy black hair. It was always so soft, so fine.

The kiss deepened, and I moved my fingers to the back of his neck when there was a knock at the door. Phillip groaned against my mouth. "One of your Wolfden kin?" he asked, pulling away with a mock grimace.

"Not likely," I said, peeling myself off the couch and heading toward the door. "I think they've seen enough of us lately. Besides, I told them all to leave us the hell alone for a few days." I put a hand on the deadbolt, then hesitated, calling out, "Who's there?"

"Larry and Curly. We're looking for Moe," a male voice said from the porch.

I grinned and threw open the door. Jason and Ollie, Phillip's bandmates, stood in the doorway. Jason had his guitar case slung over a shoulder, and Ollie had a six-pack of Yuengling in one hand and a six-pack of Jack and Coke, the kind in a can, in the other. He held both out to me with a leer. "Can we come in?"

"Hey!" Phillip yelled, jumping up from the couch. "You fuckers didn't tell me you were coming to Georgia! You could've called, you dicks!"

"Where's the fun in that?" Jason asked, clapping Phillip on the back. "We wanted to surprise you."

"Yeah, we figured since you agreed to do our big reunion show in Boston, the least we could do is fly down to Georgia for rehearsals," Ollie said as I took the drinks from his hands and moved into the kitchen. I smiled as I opened the fridge and shuffled things around to make room. I loved seeing Phillip with his bandmates. These guys were basically his family. They might not be blood, but they'd known him since they were all teenagers, and they loved him like a brother. I began to feel a small thread of excitement at the prospect of their reunion. To see the Bloomer Demons again after all this time … after years of assuming that would never, ever happen … well, it was going to be magic.

Seeing Ollie and Jason standing in my living room had shaken off my trepidation and worry. I grabbed a can of Jack and Coke, popped the tab, and stood in the doorway of the kitchen, watching the guys. Phillip had already grabbed a pen and a pad of paper and was busy writing out a setlist as Jason tuned his guitar. Ollie was drumming the coffee table with his hands. I grinned, taking a swig of my drink. They were already in full band mode, and it hadn't even been five minutes. Like no time had ever passed.

And just like that, Stormy Spooner, Bloomer Demons fangirl #1, was back.

Ten

I grabbed my gin and tonic off the bar and pressed a handful of dollar bills into the tip jar, giving the bartender a friendly nod as I jumped off the stool and headed toward the front of the venue. There was no standing room left anywhere, not even in the aisles. It took me a good ten minutes to wedge my way through the crowd to the front, where I had to hoist my legs over and push myself into the VIP area. I felt a pang of guilt when I looked back at the throng of people pushing and jostling against each other, craning their necks to see the stage. I'd been that girl way too many times over the years. How many shows had I been to where there had barely been standing room, with some guy breathing hot, sweaty beer breath on the back of my neck, pressing his groin into my thigh accidentally on purpose?

As I turned to scan the crowd, I caught the eye of a woman about my age or a little younger with glittery blue devil horns poking out of her jet-black bob. She couldn't be taller than five feet on a good day. She was standing behind an absolute giraffe of a guy; he had to be almost Phillip's height at least, and his thick-heeled Doc Martens made him even taller. The young woman was trying to inch her way to either side to get a good vantage point, but neither the drunk couple making out on her left or the group of teen girls taking selfies on her right were willing to part with even an inch of space. I felt for her; she wasn't going to be able to see shit.

Despite all those old memories of shitty, beer-soaked jack-asses and chaotic crowds, I wouldn't have traded my time as a music junkie, traveling to shows and catching tours all over the place, for the world. Every single mosh pit gone awry, every single spilled beer, every single disgusting come-on from a metalhead with more piercings than he had sense, were worth it.

It had been years—close to five, in fact—since I'd been to a show of any kind. And I had to admit, despite my misgivings and my overall dour mood, I was thrilled to be here.

I was finally—*finally*—going to see the Bloomer Demons! My most *favorite* band of all time! Live!

I still could scarcely believe that Phillip and the guys had pulled things together in three weeks' time. The guys showing up to our house for impromptu rehearsals, and planning had turned out to be a godsend, as Phillip had bitten off more than he could chew, assuming they could handle it all over Skype and the phone (he still didn't quite get modern technology, but he was trying). They'd rented space in an old, abandoned pool hall on the outskirts of Brunswick, and I'd had a blast watching them rehearse. I'd invited Roberta, Nikolai, and the rest of the guys to join us a few times, and we'd had a couple impromptu parties there, us with drinks, just watching the guys play. It had occurred to me that this new life—band rehearsals, late-night games of pool, drinks with the motley crew—was the exact type of Southern-friend, downhome fun that Tess would have loved. He'd always tried to get me out more when we'd been together, but I'd been such a homebody. I felt a pang of regret that I was now living the life he'd always tried to have with me. I wondered if the pain I felt at his death would ever fade.

It wasn't like I had still been in love with him. Far from it. But every time I remembered him, a fresh, searing pain filled my belly. That was something I had to live with, something I would never be able to get over.

But I didn't want to think about Tess tonight. I looked around the venue, taking in the décor and the layout, loving how opulent and dark it was. Black curtains graced the stage, and the walls had vintage movie posters from the silent-film era interspersed with old cymbals, drumsticks, and faces of guitars from instruments and musicians of time long gone. . This was the perfect place for the band's reunion show. Lee had gotten every detail perfect.

I did feel a teensy bit smug over my suggestion that the Bloomer Demons take Lee on as their manager, which had turned out to be a real nugget of wisdom so far. In those three short weeks, Lee had done so much wheeling and dealing that he'd managed to book a two-show reunion—one tonight, and one two days from now, both at the same venue—several print-magazine articles, including a front-page spread on *Rolling Stone,* and had brokered a deal with Spotify for both the band's backlog, plus a forthcoming new album. Studio time had already been scheduled for next month. I was seriously impressed with all that Lee had managed to do, and I knew Phillip was even more so.

I was so happy that I didn't even mind being back in Boston. The last time I'd left Phillip Deville's hometown, running away in the middle of the night while Phillip showered, I'd sworn to myself that I'd never come back. It held too many memories—being held captive in an old, abandoned farmhouse, being beaten and drugged by Shank, ending up in the hospital, and running from the cops were among the things I'd experienced during those few days. Then there was being followed by Lee, Roberta, and my ex-husband Tess … to say nothing of how Lydia Courtenay had literally bewitched me after we'd gone to her for help.

But here I was…Phillip and I had driven up the night before in my old truck, Jason and Ollie in the rented tour van behind us, retracing the steps of our first trip together. But this trip had been much more cheerful, much more exciting. We'd gabbed the whole way about the show and our plans for the next few months. We had even stopped at the same diner where Phillip had sat smirking as I wolfed down French fries and black coffee, back when we were first falling in love. I had to admit, it was only right to have the Bloomer Demons reunion show, the big comeback, in Boston, the town where they'd once practiced in Phillip's family garage. Their home. And hell, I'd gotten three long, cushy weeks of respite right in the cozy confines of my own trailer, so I felt well-rested and ready to party.

And party we would. The show was going to be epic, and the after-party would be even *more* epic. We'd hang backstage for a while, where the booze would be flowing, and then a select few people would be invited back to Jason's place (formerly Phillip's family home, which Jason now owned) to celebrate. Then I'd spend a night with my lover in his old teenage bed. The last time we'd been there, we'd done quite a few things that still gave me a thrill when I thought about them. Tonight, I planned to put those old thrills to shame and make some new thrills.

I took a long swig of my gin and tonic and made my way to my seat, which was right in the front row. Phillip had come through for me. Damn right he had. After all the concessions I'd made for him to be here, I deserved to be sitting right on the stage! Thankfully, he agreed with me, and had made sure that me and all my "people," as he called them, would be right up front where he could see us.

The row was empty, save for Nikolai, one of several of the Wolfden's members who had joined me at this show. He sat with his legs crossed and his arms folded in his lap, as though he were sitting calmly on a school bus. I sat down beside him and nudged his arm. He turned to me with a sweet but slightly guarded smile. When Phillip had handed him and Jamie their front-row tickets, he'd actually turned pink with embarrassment. After getting to know everyone at the Wolfden, I'd come to realize that Nikolai was used to being the man behind the scenes, the window dressing that quietly got things done without garnering much attention. I wanted him to know that I saw him. And that I appreciated him.

"Get you a drink?" I yelled to him over the roar of the crowd. "You look bored. I can't believe that, man. You're at a Bloomer Demons show!"

"I'm not bored!" he yelled back, his face brightening a little. "I was just waiting for the rest of you guys to get here!" He gestured to my drink and shook his head. "Jamie's drinking tonight, so I'm DD. Nothing for me." I smiled; the friendship between Jamie and Nikolai was so wholesome it was like something from a Disney movie.

"You guys can ride home with us on the bus," I offered. "I'm buyin'." I was in a celebratory mood, and I couldn't stand to see Nikolai sit there without a drink in hand. It was downright desolate.

He shook his head again, and I noticed a look come across his face; one of discomfort or perhaps embarrassment. Then I realized. "Oh. You don't drink. I'm sorry. I didn't mean to—"

"it's okay," he called back. "You didn't know!" He patted the leg of his jeans to reveal a Dr. Pepper bottle stashed there, and I had to laugh. Nikolai was wearing JNCOs; real, authentic, actual vintage JNCOs from the nineties with the huge pockets, embroidered logo patch, and wide enough to fit four legs comfortably. They were even fraying at the bottom.

"Please tell me you've had those since high school," I said, and he laughed and nodded.

"Middle school, actually. Hey, I'm not *that* old," he called back with a grin, and something about the look on his face stopped me momentarily. Something about the way his blue eyes lit up in his face, the way they crinkled in the corners, seemed familiar. A strange sensation went through my body, something akin to déjà vu or just very tangible nostalgia. I had the urge to reach out and touch him—not in a sexual way, or even in a romantic sense—but to just grab his arm and hold it, to give him a squeeze, to put an arm around him.

I swallowed, collecting myself, and pulled myself out of the weirdness. That sort of thing was happening more and more lately, and I needed to learn to control it. So many of my friends felt new to me, but they weren't new, not really. I was still recovering memories, and sometimes, they seemed to get jumbled in my head. I'd remember how I knew Nikolai sooner or later. For now, it didn't matter.

"They're great! I wish I still had my pair!" I yelled back at him, and settled in my chair, quickly checking my phone for the time. The show was set to start in about twelve minutes. I wondered where Roberta, Jamie, Lee, Benny, Mom, and Clara were; likely parking their cars. I hoped Roberta had followed my instructions on how to find the parking deck rather than circling Beach Road for two hours trying to find free parking near enough to walk.

I hadn't really wanted to invite Clara, but she was part of the Wolfden's inner circle, and to exclude her would have added to the weird, grudgy standoff she and I seemed to have going on. Neither of us had said a cross word to the other, not since the tense exchange we'd had when Benny got shot, but there was a lingering whiff of bitterness in the air. As a woman who had once been a petty teenage girl, I knew we were going to have to duke it out eventually. Whether that was an *actual* physical fight or just a battle of words, I didn't know, but I hoped it was the latter. Clara was an actual wrestler who was built like a tank and could break me in half.

I looked at my phone again. They were cutting it close. At this rate, they'd barely have time to get their tickets checked and stamped, and make their way to the front row before the show started, never mind getting drinks. I texted Roberta. *Where are you at, bitch? Show's starting in like ten minutes.*

Her text came through right away. *Just parked. Circled the block about eight times before Benny finally stopped bitching and parked in the deck. Walking up to the venue now. Be there in five.*

Hurry up, I texted back, grinning because I'd been right.

I don't care if I miss the opening band, she responded. *As long as I don't miss Bloomer Demons' big opening. Oh, by the way, your mom isn't coming. She called me a little while ago and said she's got a bad headache. She's resting in the motel room. She said to tell you sorry and she'll catch the next one.*

I pushed my phone back in my pocket and frowned, disappointed. I hadn't realized how excited I was for my mom to come and see Phillip play until I knew she wouldn't be here. She knew how important this was to me, and to Phillip ... couldn't she have made an effort? She'd driven all the way to Boston from Georgia only to back out at the last minute? What was that?

A small voice inside my head spoke up in a nasty voice, an old voice from my past, one that I remembered well. *She doesn't care. You should be used to her disappointing you by now, princess.*

I shook my head. I wouldn't let myself be brought down by those obsessive thoughts, by worry, by negativity. Whatever Mom's reasons for not coming were, it didn't have to be my problem.

"You okay?" Nikolai craned to speak into my ear so I could hear him. I shook my head yes and pasted on a smile.

"My mom can't make it," I yelled back to him, and for a moment, he almost looked relieved, which I found odd. But then he nodded sympathetically. I thought, then reached a decision. I wouldn't let anything bring me down, not tonight. I was seeing the Bloomer Demons play! Nothing was going to blight this evening. Nothing. "I'll be right back; I've just got to do something real quick."

I jumped up from my seat, made my way over to the barricade, and pushed myself over again, making a beeline for the short, black-haired girl with the devil horns. As I approached her, pushing my way through the unmoving crowd—there had to be at least fifty more people here than were there ten minutes ago—her amber-colored eyes widened and she stared at me. She knew who I was. Of course she recognized me! I had to remember that I was famous now too. Thanks, Phillip. Oh well, too late now. I was already standing in front of her.

I pushed past the giraffe guy and extended a hand to the girl. She took it reluctantly, her hand a little limp and sweaty as I shook it. "Hey. I'm Stormy."

"I know," she called back, then cleared her throat. "You're Phillip's girlfriend. I'm Beth."

"Hey, Beth," I said with a grin, noticing her crop top, recognizing the blond, curly-haired man with the violet eyes emblazoned on the front. "Is that the Vampire Lestat on your shirt?"

"Yup," she said with a grin. "I'm obsessed."

"Phillip would love that," I said, and her face lit up. I gestured toward the front row. "Look, one of our party just bailed, and I know you can't see jack shit with Lurch in front of you. Want to come watch from the front row?"

"Are you fucking serious?" the girl asked, and I looked down, realizing that she had a hula hoop—an actual hula hoop, one of those expensive, fancy light-up ones—hanging from her tiny shoulder. I nodded with a grin.

"I'm totally serious, but only if you promise to use that thing when they play 'The Death of Love.'" I grinned enthusiastically. "Whaddaya say? Will you join me?"

"Fuck yes, I will!" Beth's blue devil horns on her head seemed to glow under the venue's fluorescent lights. They were LED too, I noticed with amusement.

As we walked back to our seats, I thought, *The guys should hire her as their official band hooper.* I made a mental note to ask Phillip. After all, he owed me a favor.

The lights dimmed, then dimmed some more, eventually going so dark that only the occasional flash of neon bracelets under the strobe lights were visible, the old-fashioned kind that reminded me of being a kid. Someone had been handing them out for free at the entrance, and I wished I hadn't been in such a screaming hurry to get to the front row and snagged one. An electric blue circle shone off Roberta's wrist beside me, and I was jealous that I didn't have one. The gleam of her teeth as she smiled in excitement made my envy disappear, though. She was as giddy as I was.

Beside me was Beth, my newfound friend, who was smiling so big you almost couldn't see her unique amber eyes above her cheeks. On the other side of her, Jamie, who looked a little confused but perfectly fine with his sudden seatmate, and beside him, Lee, who was carrying a literal clipboard on his arm, looking like a giant nerd. I supposed he could have been backstage, but I was glad he'd chosen to sit here with us and enjoy the show. On the other side of Roberta was Nikolai, who had stood up and was clapping furiously as the first tones of Phillip's bass check reverberated through the venue. The crowd erupted in cheers, screams, and frenzied yelling as he began to play a few notes, warming up. Rows of goosebumps went up my back at the sound, and I almost had to sit down as a rush of pure elation went through me. Beth shrieked and began to jump up and down like a little wind-up toy, her glittery devil horns shimmering and seeming to dance in her flying hair.

"Where the fuck is Benny?" I asked Roberta, irritation creeping into my voice. She grinned and shook her head, raising her hands as if to say *I dunno*. I frowned, looking down at my phone. The band was set to play in less than two minutes and he still wasn't here! What, had he fallen in in the john?

My heart skipped a beat as the first few notes of Jason's guitar arced through the air. I craned my neck as I listened, trying to pick out which song they'd finally settled on playing first. The last I'd heard, Phillip and Jason hadn't been able to agree; it was a toss-up between "Devil May Care" and "Blood Covenant." This sounded like neither.

I didn't have a chance to figure it out because the lights flashed, and the stage was suddenly illuminated in an aura of bright turquoise, the Phillip's and Jason Langley's silhouettes standing front and center, Nate "Ollie" Green standing slightly behind Jason, his rhythm guitar at home in his hands as though it had never left. I heard the familiar clicking one, two, three, of the drumsticks and squinted to see the new drummer— Phillip had told me they'd hired a really great session musician and that I'd love the way he played—who definitely had his work cut out for him, replacing the great Kim Rzeznick. Then my mouth fell open in shock.

Benny, aka the Black Wolf, was sitting behind the drum kit. He held his drumsticks high for a split second, then launched into a ferocious, heavy beat.

"The *fuck!?*" I screamed to Roberta, not looking at her because I couldn't tear my eyes away from the stage.

"They wanted it to be a surprise!" she called back, her voice full of glee.

"You assholes! I didn't even know he was a drummer …" But the words died on my lips as the band launched into their first song, my entire being wrapped up in the melodic sound of Phillip's bass and the image of him standing at the front of the stage in shadow, nothing visible of him but a ghostly apparition of his long, white fingers as they stroked the bass, and the merest flash of his green eyes under the neon lights. As I watched, Phillip did his signature slide, and as his fingers seared down to the top of the bass, those eyes locked with mine and I could just barely make out the sexy smirk he shot me. My heart began to thump.

Jason and Ollie were strumming along with a beautiful melody I'd never heard before when Phillip stepped up to the mic and began to croon, his razor sharp, velvety voice carrying out over the club. I felt the hush of the crowd go through my entire body as I stood there watching him. His fingers plucked the bass effortlessly, as though he'd never put it down, Benny tapping out a slow, steady beat behind him.

Phillip had written a new song. Just for this occasion. I listened intently, trying to memorize every word, goosebumps breaking out on my arms.

> From the cradle to the grave
> I crawl back out again
> Baby you're as beautiful
> As good old homemade sin
>
> I'll crawl by my fingertips
> To be right by your side
> Bring you back to my resting place

A place for us to hide

You're my coffin girl
Oh, yeah
The hand that rocks the coffin
Rules the world

I screamed with laughter and joy, tears running down my cheeks as I swayed along to the music. Phillip had written a song for me! When had he written it, and how had he managed to keep it a secret? How had he managed to keep *Benny* a secret?

As Phillip hit the chorus, the lights came back on at full force, encasing the entire stage in fluorescent light. I gasped for the second time that night. Phillip Deville, my beautiful Phillip, was wearing his usual uniform of black jeans, a black tank top, and black combat boots; I'd seen him pulling that same outfit over his muscular, still-damp body fresh from the shower just hours earlier. But to my surprise, he'd slicked back his black hair, which was still growing out from the impromptu, impulsive haircut and was barely below his ears, into a 1950s greaser style. It highlighted his extreme widow's peak and gave him a dangerous, old-fashioned look that matched perfectly with the glossy leather jacket he wore. The jacket was covered with patches from bands they'd toured with, shows they'd played, and just things Phillip liked. I felt tears spring to my eyes again. I knew that jacket well, had seen it in many a picture over the years. Reporters had asked about it in the nineties dozens of times, asked what each individual patch stood for, and Phillip always demurred. "They're just for me," he'd said more than once. I'd assumed that jacket was lost forever, had been auctioned off, given away, or tucked into a box when he'd died.

Jason must've kept it. Kept it and given it back to Phillip for this show.

I wiped at my eyes, grinning. Phillip looked *so damn good* up there. They all did. But Phillip … I felt a wave of lust roll through my body, so strong it made my knees weak. Suddenly, I couldn't wait to get him home, upstairs to his old bedroom. It was all I could do not to rush the stage and grab him *right fucking now*.

As if on cue, Phillip did his signature slide *again*, running his huge hand up the neck of the black bass and sliding it down effortlessly, deliberately doing it slowly, eking it out, drawing out the effect for as long as possible, the alien screeching sound reverberating through the venue and making everyone scream with delight. He segued the slide into a slap 'n' pop rhythm, looking down at me again, quick as a flash, and giving me a sexy wink.

Roberta and Beth both elbowed me in the side at the same time, and I grinned, proud. "That's my man!" I screamed, and Roberta laughed.

"You *fan.*"

"Always!" I screamed, and then I was hopping up and down, putting tiny Beth to shame, bouncing with the music, letting it flow through my body. I was fourteen again. It was perfect.

As they segued straight from the new tune into "The Death of Love,"_I closed my eyes and let my body move along with the music as though it were taking me away on a breeze. I knew this song so well, could sing not only every lyric, but every single note from every single instrument. In the past, I'd joked that this song was like my lover. Now that the composer *was* my lover, I knew just how apt that comparison had been.

I was lost in the music, letting it carry me halfway to bliss, when Roberta's arm crashed into my side, hard. My eyes sprung open.

"Ow!" I rubbed at my ribcage and mock- glared at Roberta, figuring she'd jostled into me by accident. She'd had two gin and tonics to my one already. But Roberta was staring past the stage into the rafters, and she pointed to a shadowy figure standing among the speakers, one tanned hand holding onto the curtain as though he meant to bring it down around us all.

I couldn't hear Roberta's voice over the crowd and the loud, scorching music, but I could read her lips as she turned to me, her face white, her expression full of fury. "Stormy," her lips spelled out, "That's Shank."

Eleven

Time seemed to shrink, then to expand, and finally, to stand still. I stood there watching the man standing in the wings as he watched the band. From my far-off vantage point, with all the lights in my eyes, I couldn't tell who he was looking at, but I could imagine well enough that he was staring at Phillip.

For a moment—one that felt like hours—I stood there, unable to move my limbs, as though I was under one of Lydia's infamous locking spells. After drawing a ragged breath, I found my strength propelled myself forward, poking at Roberta with one hand and Nikolai with the other. "It's … him …" I managed to spit out, pointing toward the stage and nodding at Roberta, whose eyes were wild and frantic. I knew she'd fill him in. I turned to Jamie, who was happily bopping along to the music, his eyes closed, in a state of bliss I hated to interrupt. I grabbed his shoulder and gave it a shake.

"What is it, darlin'—" he started, and I interrupted him through clenched teeth.

"We have company." I pointed to the wings, and Jamie's

eyes widened. I could barely hear him over the music, but I could read his lips.

"Who is that?"

"Shank," I said, assuming the name would mean something to him. It did. His brows furrowed into an expression of fury and his shoulders tensed. He started toward the barrier that separated our seats from the stage, and I pulled him back.

"We can't cause a scene. Besides, security will try to stop us. We have to find another way around." I realized we were missing two people in our party. "Where's Lee?"

"I think he might've went for another drink," Jamie said. "Or maybe he was doing manager shit; I'm honestly not sure. I was watching the band."

"Come on." I looped my arm through Jamie's with one sad glance back at the stage—I hated to leave the *show of a lifetime*, but it couldn't be helped—and we did our best to carefully wind our way through the sardine-packed rows and into the main area where the crowd was packed even tighter. We had to find someone in security who would see my pass and let us backstage, and quick. I couldn't let Shank, whatever he was here to do, carry out his plans.

It felt like it took hours, but finally, we made it to the back of the venue. The bar was packed with young people all nursing their various cocktails and draft beer, but there was no sign of Lee. "Bathroom?" I asked, out of breath, and Jamie shook his head.

"Maybe." He swallowed. "Do you think he saw Shank and decided to take care of it himself?"

"It's possible, but I doubt it. Lee's in manager mode; he's not an impulsive hothead like us," I said with a joyless laugh. "Come on, let's head out to the back. Maybe we can find someone who will let us in through the side door." As I grabbed Jamie's arm, a flash of blonde hair caught my eye, over near the bar. It was hard to see through the ever-growing crowd, but I was sure I'd caught a glimpse of long blonde hair, a carefully made-up face, and an expression I knew very well …

I felt a tug on my purse and turned, irritated, expecting to find some drunken man hitting on me. Instead, it was Beth, her face flushed and her hula hoop still hanging off her shoulder.

"Why aren't you back watching the show?" I asked, confused. I glanced over at the bar again, looking for the blonde girl I thought I'd seen, but the only blond there now was a man with a braid down to his back. I shook my head; in my anxious state, I was seeing things.

"You looked upset," Beth said with a shrug. "I could feel it. I thought maybe you needed my help." She shrugged again, the little LED lights in her headband pulsing with her movement. "So what can I do to help?"

"You should go watch the show. You don't have to …" I began, then had another thought. "Actually," I said, looking to Jamie, "there *is* something you can do. If you don't mind performing for the general public, that is."

"Lucky for you, I'm an extrovert," Beth said with a grin.

I flashed my backstage pass at the beefy security guard standing by the outdoor entrance. "I'm Phillip Deville's girlfriend," I said, and took a brief nanosecond to let myself feel the powerful little thrill that went through me at those words. "He's onstage right now, and I really need to get in the back. It's an emergency." I waved the pass dangling from around my neck again. The guard seemed to hesitate, then nodded.

"I can let you back," he said, his face unmoving in the glare of the streetlamps. "But I can't let your friend back without a VIP or backstage pass."

I pasted on my most convincing, dazzling smile, the one I used on Phillip when I wanted him not to be annoyed with me. "He's one of our party, though. You can see from his ticket he's sitting in the front row with me."

The security guard shook his head, his arms crossed over his torso. "No dice. Sorry. Just you."

I turned to Jamie with a grimace. "I'm sorry. I guess I've got to go back there alone."

"I don't like that a bit, darlin'," Jamie said. His face looked more serious than I'd ever seen it, an odd contrast to the easy-going, sexy smile he usually displayed. He pulled me off to the side, out of earshot of the security guard. His eyes darted toward the door. "I'll be just as dead as your boyfriend in there if I let you go in guns blazing to confront that maniac by yourself."

"Well, somebody has to go back there," I whispered hotly. "Why is Shank backstage at Phillip's show? He's obviously got some terrible plan. I have to stop him before someone gets hurt. And I need to hurry; that girl Beth can't keep them all entertained forever. I'm surprised security hasn't stopped her yet." From inside the venue, we heard the voices of the crowd raise in excitement and then loud clapping as the band finished another song. My new friend Beth, bless her, was standing on top of my chair in the front row, hula hooping her little heart out, her flashing LED lights hopefully distracting the crowd and delighting them enough to keep them from noticing any potential scenes that might take place in the next few minutes. At least, that's what I'd asked her to do. I only hoped she was able to comply.

Jamie wore a pained expression. "Deville is gonna kill me." He sighed. "You got your cell phone on ya, darlin'?"

"Of course."

"Call me if *anything* goes wrong. I mean anything at all," Jamie said in a low voice, looking into my eyes. "I'll come runnin'. I'll pull the fire alarm if I have to. Hell, I'll leapfrog onto the stage and tackle Phillip's big ass if I have to. You feel me?"

"I got it," I said with a grateful smile. "I promise, I'll be careful. And I'll call if anything happens. You try and go back and fill in the others. Tell them to … to …" I honestly didn't know *what* to tell them. "Just tell them to be on high alert."

"I'll try to find Lee too," Jamie said with a nod, and then he scurried back around to the other side of the venue.

I took a few seconds to catch my breath and center myself, closing my eyes and leaning against the venue's brick siding and listening to the muffled sounds of the Bloomer Demons as they launched into another song. I couldn't make out much of the melody, just the heavy thrum of the bass and the steady beat of Benny's drums. Shank was *dead* for making me miss this, the motherfucker.

I moved toward the door, and the security guard opened it for me. I nodded in thanks and hurried inside, pulling the hood of my black jacket over my head as I went. If Shank was lurking around, I could use all the cover I could get. If he recognized me—and he definitely would—before I happened to see him, it would all be over.

As I walked flush against the wall, it occurred to me that I could have just told the security guard what was going on. There was still time … I could go back, sound the alarm. Let them handle it. That was their job, after all. But something instinctual told me they wouldn't take me seriously, and that even if they did, they'd bungle it somehow.

Instinct had taught me in a very short time that matters to do with Guthrie and Elvin and their magic, and the people it had left in its wake, were matters best handled internally.

My head throbbed in muscle memory as I recalled the last time I'd seen Shank. That encounter had landed him, Phillip, and me in the hospital. Phillip had been shot, and I'd had a nasty concussion. Shank had fared the worst of us, thanks to me. I'd basically cracked his head like an egg on the concrete floor of our motel room. The noise his head had made when it connected with the hard floor, which had been barely cushioned with cheap, thin old motel carpet, was a sound I still sometimes heard in my dreams. Or nightmares. I knew Shank had lived—Phillip and I had made sure of that before we'd hightailed it out of Dodge—but he must have had had a hard recovery. Phillip had laid a few heavy blows to him as well before I'd seriously put him out of commission. And with Lee, his former boss, having a sudden change of conscience, and Guthrie, his even bigger boss, dead and gone, I'd assumed, or at least hoped, that Shank was out of the game. That he wouldn't have any need to bother of us further. In fact, I hadn't even thought about him since I'd been back in Georgia. I'd never even thought to ask Lee about him, to make sure that he wouldn't come after us.

It was an oversight among so many other oversights. I had to get better at this, at anticipating threats before they showed up at my door. I *had* to.

Too many lives were being threatened; too many had already been destroyed. Now, with Phillip by my side, reuniting with his band and being in the public eye, my mom (and now my father) back in the picture and this beloved newfound family around, I had to be more careful than ever. I had people to protect, people other than myself. And they meant everything to me.

The hall was pretty dark and smelled awful. I briefly wondered what kind of musty, moldy sludge might be lurking on the ancient, ripped old carpet. I'd come in this way with Phillip when he'd been loading in instruments, but I'd been busy tapping away on my phone, checking social media and coordinating with my friends. I'd barely paid attention as I'd followed him around backstage.

The hall dead ended at a little room that had four separate doors—two straight ahead, and two to the right. From the loud thumps and muffled sounds of Phillip's screeching voice, I could make out that he had now moved onto one of my favorites from their second album, "Silver Bullets." I smiled despite my trepidation; I'd always wanted to hear that song live. It was a loud, heavy, thumping metal song that never failed to get my blood pumping, and it featured some of Phillip's highest vocals. From the sounds beyond the door, he still had it. Damn Shank to the very depths of hell for ruining this for me.

I wondered if Phillip had noticed I was missing from the front row. It wasn't like he could just throw off his bass and disappear to look for me, but wondering where I was and worrying about me was likely to throw him off his game. He needed no distractions. I hoped that, for once, he was not poking around in my head.

I stared at the doors ahead of me for a moment, then pulled one open, going with my ears. Jackpot. A small set of black, rickety looking steps led up to what I knew was the stage. I could hear Phillip's voice as I bounded up them, an unstoppable grin breaking out on my face just as he hit the high note I'd been waiting for.

"Phillip, you sexy motherfucking *beast*," I muttered under my breath, pulling the hood down further over my eyes. It was mainly deserted backstage, save for a couple of guitar techs who were bent over what looked like Jason Langley's second guitar. I recognized the familiar blue strap. I made my way past them, giving them a friendly nod and letting them see my face briefly, but they were too busy to look up to acknowledge me. I crossed over to the other side of the stage, my fingers lightly resting on the deep, solid black curtains, nervously trying to dissipate the odd tingling sensation that had begun in my knuckles, fanning them out subconsciously. The curtains were so heavythat they barely moved beneath my touch, but as I rounded the corner toward the side stage, I felt resistance give beneath my fingers. Something was pulling the curtain taut.

My eyes met Shank's, and before I could stop myself, I let out a shriek. Because there was someone else standing there with him too.

Shank's dark eyes, nearly hidden beneath his black baseball cap, glowed like embers as he stared at me, his face full of hatred. I could hardly blame him for the ill will he harbored toward me. I had tried to kill him, after all. Only thing was, he'd tried to kill me first, so I had just as much reason, if not more, to hate him right back. Plus, he *had* given me a concussion. That was *after* kidnapping me and holding me hostage at some abandoned house in Boston. He'd drugged me too. And had tried to talk Lee Courtenay into straight up killing me.

So as far as I was concerned, we were even.

Well, maybe not quite even. I still had a score to settle.

What I couldn't quite understand, though, was the burgundy-haired guy standing beside him. The worn Charles Manson T-shirt that hung on his skinny shoulders suited him better than the teal Hawaiian shirt I'd seen him in last time, and his facial piercings glinted in the dim light as he smiled, cold and calculating. His eyes were dark as coal.

"Why the fuck are you here?" I seethed, clutching the black curtain tightly in my right hand. I held onto it to brace myself because I was shaking with rage and nerves. "And who the fuck are *you?*"

"Hi, pretty lady," he replied, his face lighting up in a very sinister and very ugly grin. Beneath his cap, his head was bald as an egg. I had nothing against bald guys—in fact, I'd come into my sexuality watching *The Mummy* like every other adolescent girl my age, and had thought Imhotep was plenty fine— but something about Shank's hairlessness, combined with his heavy, dark eyebrows and even darker eyes, and his dark, slightly pointed goatee, made him look like an actual devil. And not the good, authority-defying, sexy modern-day devil, either, but a medieval, depraved, genuinely evil devil. "How have you been?"

"What the fuck are you doing here?" I repeated, but his grin only got wider in response. His free hand clutched at the curtains, which explained the tautness I'd felt as I'd rounded the corner to find him waiting in the wings. Beyond the curtains, I could hear Phillip play the starting notes of a searing bass solo that I'd only heard him play once or twice before. Fucking Shank, to make me miss that of all things. I glared, my fingers still tingling. I clenched them into a fist.

"Your husband is dead, I hear," he said, his smile fading, but he didn't look sad or even angry.

"I don't have a husband," I shot back.

"You know what I mean, pretty lady," he leered. "Your ex-husband. Good ol' Tessie. Whatever you want to call him don't change the fact that he's dead as a doornail." He snickered. "Dumb fucker."

"And is this his replacement?" I asked, disdain dripping from my voice. "Your latest lackey can't cut it, Shankie. He can't weigh more than a hundred pounds soaking wet." The man glowered at me, his own long fingers curling into fists by his side. My eyes widened. I recognized him! I knew who he was! "Oh my god—you're Colt Leather, aren't you?"

"Guilty." The cold, calculating smile was still on his face, but he was anything but happy. I could feel his resentment and bitterness from where I stood. I hadn't kept up with his story too much, but last I'd seen on Twitter, he'd been fired by his manager, kicked out of his band, and even his agent had jumped ship. Women were still posting Insta-stories detailing the many depraved things he'd done over the years, each more horrible than the next. From the looks of his ratty T-shirt, the rumors about his serial killer obsession must be true. Rather than fear, though, I just felt pity. Charles Manson, really? The man clearly had never had an original thought.

"Nice shirt," I said, casually inspecting my nails. "How'd you end up with this bald idiot?"

"How did *you* end up with that has-been hair metal pansy Deville?" he shot back, and I smiled.

"Big talk coming from the place where emo goes to die." Even as I spoke, my brain was clicking over, trying to figure out if Phillip had ever mentioned this dude. Did they have some long-ago beef?

"Nice way to treat the man who saw your ex take his last breath," Shank said, smirking at me. "Well, *try* to take his last breath, anyway, huh, Colt?"

I glared at Shank, trying to swallow down my rage. I felt pain deep in my stomach, grief and anger and sadness and fear mingling to make an explosive cocktail that threatened to double me over. Whatever Tess had been like—and he definitely had been no saint—he hadn't deserved such cruelty. My face must have shown my despair because Shank threw back his head and laughed.

Something came over me. I didn't think, I didn't stop to even breathe. Before I knew what I'd done, I reached forward with my left hand, unballed my fist, placed my palm against Shank's shoulder, and leveled every ounce of rage, power, and magic I had at him.

His eyes widened, and he staggered back with a jolt, the electric shock pulsing between us for a moment before he began to fall, clutching his right hand to his chest like someone having a heart attack, like a caricature of Fred Sanford of my dad's favorite show *Sanford and Son,* screaming for Elizabeth.

In any other moment, I might've laughed at the image—how ridiculous, how weak and pathetic he looked—but there was no time for that, because my eyes had fallen on something small and black clutched in the hand Shank now held to his chest. His eyes were fluttering, rolling back in his head, and he was not conscious as he fell, but I grabbed at him anyway, the magic still pooling in my fingers and seeming to sizzle as I touched him, trying to prevent him from hitting the floor.

Trying to prevent him from dropping the little black device clutched in his hand.

A second too late, I saw a pair of retreating black motorcycle boots and a flash of a ratty white T-shirt. A door flew open—an exit I hadn't known existed—and Colt Leather sprinted through and was gone without looking back.

"What are you holding—" I shouted at Shank, but before I could finish the words, before I had time to understand the magnitude of what I'd seen, Shank hit the floor, his fingers opened, and the explosion went off.

Twelve

The high-pitched squeal in my ears was so painful it was beyond pain, a pressure in my eardrums that was somehow heavy, tight, and sharp all at the same time. It felt like I was being stabbed repeatedly in the ear drums with the world's heaviest and thinnest knitting needle. My vision seemed to pulse with flashes of white, off-white, silvery-white, nothing but white, white, white. As far as I could see, *white*, seeming to expand and constrict in time with my heartbeat. As I raised a sweaty hand to my face, I realized that I was lying down. When had that happened?

I slow-blinked. The pulsing white had been the view from behind my eyelids apparently, because my eyes had been closed. I was having trouble opening them now; moisture had quick dried in my eyelashes, and they were sealed half-shut. I slow-blinked again, forcing them open, and gasping in horror at the sight above where I lay.

Papers were fluttering all around me. I wasn't sure where they'd come from; was it pieces of Phillip's set list for the show? Confetti? Why would there be confetti at a music venue …? My thoughts whirled, my ears still picking up that high-pitched frequency and nothing else. I struggled to move, to get up, to assess the situation, but I felt stuck to the floor. My limbs were so heavy, and there was a sharp pain in my head where I must have fallen. It seemed like a million years ago, but it had only been a couple weeks since I'd had a concussion, and I wondered if I'd reinjured myself. What did that mean? Could I slip into a coma and die? I slow-blinked again, willing myself to stay awake, even though my body was made of pure adrenaline and there was no chance of me falling asleep. My head was throbbing, the squeal in my ears unbearable, and my voice was hoarse, my throat scratchy and painful, as I tried to call for Phillip, who probably wouldn't hear me anyway.

Oh god, oh god, oh god.

What have I done?

I couldn't think about that now. I had to get up.

I still couldn't hear, and all I could see was a haze of smoke and the fluttering bits of paper, but I felt the thudding of footsteps on the stage. Or maybe it was just on the floor below the stage, likely a stampede of people trying to get out of the venue, and any second, people would be running around all around me. I'd get trampled if I didn't get up, practically invisible in my oversized black hoodie, which was still pulled down around my face.

I pulled myself up to a sitting position, wincing, and assessed my injuries. There was the thunk on the head I'd suffered, and my left hip felt a little tender; I'd likely landed on that. I bit down and ran my tongue over my teeth—nothing broken. My fingers wiggled fine, and so did my toes. It seemed I was largely uninjured. Wait. My right arm was wet just above the elbow. I felt with my left hand, and a smear of blood came back on my fingers. Fuck.

I groaned with pain as I pulled myself upright, forcing myself to stand, my feet slipping on the floor, and began to fall back again, grasping for the heavy black curtains and finding no purchase. Going down, I braced myself for the inevitable impact when a pair of arms caught me and held me in place.

"She's bleeding," I heard a voice say, frantic, small, and tinny beneath the wailing squeals in my ears. "Look, her arm!"

"I can see it," came another voice, this one closer, deeper. I felt hot breath on my face, quick and fast, and the rise and fall of a chest against my back. "Where can I take her?"

It was Phillip. I tried to smile at him but couldn't seem to move my facial muscles properly. Now that he was here, holding me safe and secure, I could stop struggling. He would take me somewhere safe. Somewhere I could rest and think. My thoughts weren't coming in order, and the flashing white in my head was growing stronger and stronger. Had my eyes closed again? I didn't even know.

What have I done, I thought again miserably, slumping into Phillip's warm body, my head nestling against his sweaty chest.

"What does she mean by that?" Lee's voice, scared and angry. I hadn't even realized I'd spoken aloud.

"There's a dressing room through that door." Benny. "There's a twin bed in there, and looks like a first aid kit. Let's put her in there for now, get her out of the way."

"I think we should leave the venue," Roberta was arguing. "I don't feel like we're safe here. We need to get her somewhere outside with fresh air. What if there's more explosions?"

There won't be any more because he's dead, dead, dead, dead ...

"What's she saying? Who's dead?"

"Maybe we ought not move her, darlin'." Sweet, blessed Jamie. So he was okay. I wondered about the pretty dark-haired girl, the one I'd brought to the front row. I couldn't remember her name now for some reason. Was it Betty? Bella?

Phillip's voice was close in my ear. "She's alright. She

jumped down from the seats and ran out just before the stampede."

Stampede? What on earth was he talking about? I couldn't make sense of anything. I couldn't even gather where I was. Some type of club or something, but why?

Another voice. Jason. "Everybody got out safely. Me and Ollie ran up to the front and led them all out single file. Everybody's outside and okay."

Thank goodness for that. My head swam. Wait; what was I thankful for? I couldn't remember.

"Let's just get her out of eyesight, out of the way," Benny urged. "Then … I can help her. I think."

I tried to move my hands, to grab at Phillip, but he was behind me, and I ended up flailing, my arms grasping at the air.

"Stop trying to move, hon." Roberta's voice was a low, comforting croon. "Just be still and let Phillip carry you."

"Phillip?"

"Yes, Phillip, honey," she said, her voice higher pitched now, concerned. "Phillip Deville. Your boyfriend."

I laughed, wishing my eyes would open properly so I could look at her and laugh right in her face. "Phillip Deville? Like he would ever be *my* boyfriend. Even if he was alive, he wouldn't know who the fuck I am." Imagine. "You're such a bitch, Sloan." My giggle quickly turned into a wince as strong arms hoisted me and began to jostle me. It hurt. "Put me down, Uncle El. I don't like it here."

"Oh, shit, guys." Her voice had given way to tears. Why was she crying?

"Right." His voice was in my ear, making its way over the squealing that still tore at my eardrums. I realized—or remembered, I wasn't sure which—why we were at a venue and why we were here. Phillip was playing a show. "Grab her legs, Benny, and let's try to get her in there, but we've got to go slow, and be gentle. She might have internal injuries."

He sounded so calm, his voice measured and even. But only I could read what he was feeling inside. His emotions were a swirl of many things: fury at his show being interrupted, confusion, impatience, but most of all, pure, unadulterated fear. I'd never felt him so scared, and the two of us had been through many things together. Phillip was terrified.

I must be more hurt than I'd thought.

But then, as soon as the thought appeared in my head, it was gone again, and the grasp I had on the situation began to slip ...

"B-B-Benny and the Jets," I whispered, though I wasn't sure why that song had appeared in my head.

I felt two strong arms hoisting up my legs, and a loud wail came from somewhere beyond ... Then, as the two of them carried me, gingerly, I realized the wail had come from me. I was in pain, but it was a weird, disjointed sort of agony; I could feel it, but I could only feel it outside of me, as though I were picking up a frequency that someone was putting down. It was me but it wasn't me. Inside me but outside of me.

I tried to cling to my awareness, my mind desperate to continue taking stock of my situation, to take inventory of my injuries, to keep alert for more danger, to be present for whatever Phillip and Benny were doing to help. To remember where I was and who these people were. But it was too much. I felt myself drifting, like a wayward float in the path of a rip current; powerless to stop the wave as it carried me out to sea. Drifting, drifting ... My chin slumped to my chest, and I passed out before they got me on the couch.

Daddy's calloused and rough hand enclosed over mine, but I happily left my fingers intertwined with his as he led me to the metal bleachers in the corner of the dusty lot. It was a hot day, and very dry, so dry you could see the faint outline of red Georgia clay-dust lingering in the air. On a windy day, it might swirl a little and seem to dance, but today it just hung there like a dirty, murky mirage.

I was used to this place; it was almost like a second home. Every Saturday and sometimes on Sundays, I would get up early with Mama in the summers, when it was warm and light before 6:30 a.m. I'd often complain at just how early she'd get me out of bed, but she'd always reward my good behavior with a slightly cold, cheese-stuffed biscuit and a Sprite, which I'd gobble hungrily as our old, rusty Buick traveled down the highway in a mad rush to get the best tables. Sometimes we sold, and always we shopped. Mama said the earlier you got to the flea market, the better deals you would find. We relied on the "fill up your bag for $2" tables, the exhausted mothers selling their kid's outgrown shorts and jeans for fifty cents apiece (Mama would haggle them down to a quarter every single time), and the produce tables, always tucked away at the end, where the Mexican families would sell the biggest, freshest watermelons you'd ever seen, hacked in half with a bread knife sticking out of the gooey, sweet flesh. Customers were expected to hack off their own piece and pay for it on the honor system, and once Mama had caught me trying to wiggle a piece free with my hand as she stuffed a bag with beefsteak tomatoes, distracted, and gave my hand a slap. To my delight, she'd asked the man behind the table, "How much?" "A dime," the man had said, his grin as wide as the moon. He grabbed a plastic shaker and sprinkled little red granules all over the fruit. Then he wrapped the piece of watermelon in wax paper and placed it in my little hands, along with a big wad of brown napkins The way that watermelon had tasted—

sweet, juicy, with a salty, spicy tang from the little shaker—still lingered on my tongue.

From that point on, Mama made it a point to stop there every weekend for tomatoes, potatoes, and sometimes, when she was feeling extravagant, a juicy peach or big wedge of sweet pineapple or juicy watermelon for me. From that day forward, I always asked for the "spicy red sprinkles."

Daddy loved the flea market too, but he came on Saturday nights rather than in the mornings. Often, Mama came with us, but there were plenty of times she didn't. Daddy had no use for shopping, and when Mama did show off her purchases to him, he'd wrinkle his nose in disdain and admonish her. "I might not have a pot to piss in, but damned if I want to wear somebody else's cast-off clothes," he'd say with a voice full of spite. Mama got to where she just didn't tell him where things came from. He knew, but as long as he didn't know out loud, it seemed like he was okay with it. It was one of many things about my daddy I didn't understand, but I'd learned to not ask questions.

The one thing Daddy liked about the flea market was the wrestling matches. Every weekend, sometimes twice if there was a double billing, we'd go. I had almost no memories of spending real, quality time with him other than the wrestling, which I loved. Often a live music show—bluegrass or country rock—would follow, and Daddy was friends with one of the bass players, so we usually got good seats. That's where my love of music, and a good live show, had begun.

Tonight's wrestling match was a double. We'd see two wrestling matches and then live music; the greasy flyer taped to a power pole said the band was "southern fried rock." Daddy had patted his pocket and told me we'd eat at the match, a prospect I was excited for because that meant corndogs or nachos thick with bright yellow cheese, a real rarity. Mama hadn't come with us today, so it was just the two of us. I followed Daddy up the metal bleachers to the very top, where he sat and patted beside him. I sat down, grinning ear to ear, and Daddy read over the flyer, then handed it to me.

I was getting pretty good at reading, so I was able to make out all the words with only a little difficulty. "Double Match Ex ... extrav ... aganza. Championship Match; Snake-Eyes Blake battles The Swamp Thing for the heavyweight championship belt. Junior Heavyweight Match; A.J. Floyd defends his junior heavyweight title against newcomer THE BLACK WOLF. Later: Music by Johnny Hollis and the Gators on the deck at Beau's Barbecue Shack! The best Southern Fried Rock in South Georgia!"

"Are we eating barbecue, Daddy?" My stomach rumbled excitedly.

Daddy laughed and shook his head. "I ain't got barbecue money, little bit, but I could go for a slaw dog. You want?"

"Just a plain one for me," I said, and stuck out my lower lip. "With extra ketchup. Nachos too, please?"

"Well, I reckon. But only if you say please, and I ain't springing for jalapenos." He laughed again, and I laughed too. "And we'll split us a co'cola."

"Okay," I said brightly, beaming. I could already taste the waxy, salty cheese sauce. We didn't eat out often, so when we did, it pretty much made my day.

"I'll go get 'em now before the match starts. You hold our seats," Daddy said, waggling a finger at me. "Don't talk to no strangers, and don't leave this spot. Anybody tries to bother you, you, uh ..." He scanned the bleachers in front of us and pointed at a lady with curly blue-gray hair sitting in front of us, chowing down on a chili cheeseburger. "Tap that lady on the shoulder and ask her to help you." He grinned and disappeared down the bleachers, pulling his wallet out of the back pocket of his tight blue jeans as he went. The lady with the cheeseburger craned her neck to look at him as he went.

Ladies always did that with Daddy. Sometimes men too. Mama teased him about it, and he pretended she was crazy. And then sometimes Mama didn't find it so funny. I didn't really understand men and women, and I almost hoped it stayed that way. It seemed like when they weren't fussing with each other, they were quietly fretting, and I wasn't sure which one was worse.

I hoped nobody would bother me because I sure didn't feel like tapping the lady on her shoulder. Her hair was such a weird color, and I bet her breath smelled like chili. I contented myself with reading the flyer again, focusing on the pictures of the wrestlers. The flyer was in black and white, but I found I could easily fill in the colors with my mind. Snake-Eye Blake I knew well—he was a tall, skinny man with blond-red hair that was always pulled back in a high ponytail atop his head. He had striking blue eyes, and his signature move was the piledriver. I liked him okay, but he'd been champion for such a long time, and he was a real big hit with the ladies. They always screamed and shrieked over him, something I found very annoying. The Swamp Thing was more interesting because he was big and hulking and wore a mask that obscured his entire face, except for his eyes, which were beady and so dark that I was certain they must actually be black. His long, stringy hair was always wet and falling over his eyes, and I found him more than a little bit scary; he really did look like he'd just come out of a swamp.

The junior wrestlers were my favorite, though, because they were young. Often, they were teens, but sometimes we'd get a really young wrestler, the odd thirteen- or fourteen-year-old. I'd seen A.J. Floyd wrestle once before, and he was a wiry, tough kid with a smattering of acne on his forehead and chocolate-brown eyes. I could tell already that when he got grown, he'd be another Snake-Eye Blake, preening for the ladies.

Then there was the Black Wolf, who I'd never seen before. I scanned over the picture, committing it to memory. He couldn't have been more than thirteen, but he stared at the camera straight on, holding his arms over his chest like someone in deep prayer, or perhaps lying in a coffin. It was a weird pose, but it suited him. His jet-black hair fell over one eye. His eyes were dark and hollow, with gray smudges under them that could have been natural or eyeshadow; it was hard to tell. His fingernails were painted black, and he had a nose ring, which I found shocking. People could get earrings in their noses? My eyes scanned the picture over and over, a weird feeling going through me. I'd never seen a kid like this before. But something about him called to me, and I felt myself fervently hoping he'd win this match tonight. This new kid, this brilliantly dark outsider.

"Who you bettin' on tonight, little bit?" Daddy was already back, sliding in beside me. He handed me a hot dog wrapped in aluminum foil and placed a plastic platter filled to the brim with chips beside us.

"Swamp Thing," I said, holding the warm hot dog, enjoying the toasty feel of the hot aluminum foil in my hand, "and for the second match ... this one." I pointed at the Black Wolf with my free hand.

"The new kid?" Daddy wrinkled his nose and took a giant bite of slaw dog, wiping the excess dressing from his chin with a napkin. "He looks like a punk ass to me."

"He is not!"

Daddy laughed and opened the little plastic container of cheese sauce, drizzling it all over the chips. "He's wearing nail polish. Of course he's a little punk."

Hot tears sprang to my eyes. "He IS NOT!"

"You like his little nose ring?"

"Stop!"

"Alright, alright. Eat your hot dog, little bit." Daddy laughed and took a long sip of Coke. He shook his head. "Ain't

*no daughter of mine gonna grow up and be no goth. I aint'
havin' it, see?" But he was smiling.*

*I was miffed, but I was also starving, and I knew better
than to argue with Daddy, especially if he was in a good mood
—those could turn sour on a dime. I grabbed a chip and
munched it, resolving to silently root for the Black Wolf as
much as I wanted. Daddy couldn't stop me.*

*The first match went pretty much as expected. The Swamp
Thing gave as good as he got and even surprised Snake-Eye
Blake with a steel chair to the noggin at one point, but not
even a carefully delivered suplex was enough to win the
match. Snake-Eye was simply too wily and beloved for all that.
At the very last second, he'd gotten Swamp Thing's giant body
into a figure-four headlock, and that was the end of that
match.*

*After a brief intermission and bathroom break, it was time
for the second match. I found myself almost vibrating with
excitement. I couldn't wait to see the Black Wolf.*

*Daddy, much to my surprise, had gone back to the conces-
sion stand during the break and emerged with a huge paper
plate of funnel cake, crispy and golden and topped with a
cloud of powdered sugar and cinnamon drizzle. I'd never
tasted funnel cake, and my eyes must have been like dinner
plates as I watched him approach, holding the paper plate
high above his head, where it bent and threatened to rain
powdered sugar down on his head. I'd asked for funnel cakes
plenty of times, but at every fair, every festival, Mama and
Daddy had always said they were too expensive. And Daddy
was so cheap he'd squeeze a nickel until the juice ran out.
How many times had I heard him say, "Dessert? What
dessert? What you need me to buy candy and shit for when
they's cereal at the house?" And yet here he was with funnel
cake. What had brought* this on, *I wondered.*

The ring announcer entered the arena, and my heart

clenched. Daddy sat the funnel cake down beside him and looked at me.

"Somebody's gonna join us for this next match, okay?" he said, seeming suddenly nervous. Which was weird, because Daddy never got nervous. I stared at him, wide-eyed. "Somebody I want you to meet."

"Okay." I sipped the dregs of the now-flat Coke, pretty much just ice now. I'd met plenty of my parents' friends before. I wasn't sure what the big deal was.

"This friend of mine," he said, wringing his hands together, "is a special friend. Not a friend of your mama's and mine, but just mine alone. You understand what I mean?"

"Yes," I answered, though I really didn't.

"She's a real nice lady. I think you'll like her. She has a son about your age. You'll like him too."

"Okay," I said again, my eyes flickering back and forth from the ring to the funnel cake that sat beside Daddy. I was equally exited for both. Who cared about Daddy's dumb friend?

A woman sat down then, her aura a blend of Aqua-net and Body Fantasies perfume, the kind in the little different colored plastic bottles I always begged for at Walmart. Her hair was curly and very blonde, almost white. Her orange-lipsticked mouth smiled very wide, so wide she reminded me of the Cheshire cat, but she didn't seem sinister. Rather, she seemed to be a little desperate in a way that made me feel sorry for her. I managed to look away from the funnel cake long enough to give her a welcoming smile, the best I could muster, wiping nacho cheese from the corner of my mouth. Then I noticed the boy who sat down beside her.

The boy was very tall, and very skinny. I guessed he was a couple of years older than me, or maybe he just appeared so because he was so tall and lanky. His hair was the same shade of light, almost white-blond as his mother's, though his was spiked on top and longer in the back, ending in a rat-tail that looked like it hadn't been brushed in a few days. He had blindingly bright blue eyes, and thin lips over a straight, white smile. He stared at me silently, solemnly, and did not smile back at me, even though I gave him the same welcoming grin I'd given his mother.

"This here is Stormy," Dad said, his own smile big and wider than I was used to. He suddenly looked like a used car salesman, his chest all puffed out in a semblance of pride, his hands big and gesturing. "She's a little bit shy, but she's a sweet girl. Ain't you, little bit?"

"Hi," I said, and the woman reached out and tousled my head, her long red nails glinting in the late afternoon sun. I didn't much like that, but I sat still and let her. I was used to older people making a fuss. They'd always say stuff like "ain't you pretty" and comment on my manners.

"Hey there, Stormy," the lady said in a smooth, soft voice, as though she were afraid to startle me or herself. "I'm so happy we finally got to do this. I've been wanting to meet you for a long, long time."

"You have?" I said, surprised. I didn't have the first inkling who this woman was.

"And this here is my son, Nikolai," she said, putting a hand on the boy's back and giving him a little caress. "He's shy too, like you."

"Am not." The boy's voice was such a low murmur I could barely hear him.

"There's something special about Nikolai, Stormy," Daddy said, his grin even wider. "Something that's also special about you—something the two of you share." He ripped off a giant hunk of funnel cake from the plate beside him, then ripped the hunk in half, and handed me a piece. He handed the other half to the boy.

Nikolai was still staring at me. Whatever this special thing was, he already seemed to know. I felt uncomfortable and put on the spot, so I popped a chip in my mouth and busied myself crunching as though I weren't bothered, leaving the piece of funnel cake on my plate (I'd go back to it later, when Daddy wasn't watching me so intently).

"Do you want to know what it is?"

"Okay," I said with a mouthful of delicious funnel cake, and the woman's smile dropped for a millisecond before she picked it back up again, bright and shiny as ever.

At that moment, the crowd began to cheer as A.J. Floyd emerged from the locker room and sauntered toward the ring. As he grabbed the ropes and launched himself into the ring, white fog poured from the locker room entrance, and a loud, throbbing sort of music started to play. I recognized it as Ozzy Osborne, who Daddy would sometimes play when he was deep in his cups. A silhouette appeared in the doorway and stepped through the fog, and out stepped a muscular young man dressed head to toe in black, and as he turned to survey the crowd, I saw a large black wolf on the back of his black jean jacket.

The Black Wolf! The sound was deafening, with the crowd evenly split between boos and cheers as the newest wrestler made his way to the ring. He took his time, playing to the crowd, smirking as people jeered him. I caught the blond boy's eyes and saw he was grinning with excitement too.

Daddy leaned over toward the woman and said, "I'll tell them after the match. I promise, darlin'."

"Sure you will," she said, and I could hear her bitterness loud and clear, even over the maddening crowd. Finally, I took a bite of funnel cake.

I woke up with the taste of sweet fried dough and salted watermelon in my mouth.

A hand was caressing my face. Wiping my forehead down with something cool and damp. It felt so good, and I was tempted to drift back off into the slumber I'd just returned from rather than deal with this latest catastrophe, the details of which were rushing back.

I opened my eyes slowly, carefully, since they were still partially sealed shut from my own tears. I didn't even remember crying, but obviously I had. Phillip loomed over me, wetting my face with his handkerchief, dampened with a glass of cool water that he held in his other hand. The water sloshed over the glass. Phillip's hand was trembling.

I smiled at him tenderly. "Phillip. I'm okay."

He leaned down and planted the gentlest of kisses on my forehead. "I know you are, love. Or very soon will be."

"You're shaking."

"Don't worry about me," he said. "I'm just rattled. You worry about yourself. How do you feel? Other than your head ... and your leg ... Do you have any other injuries? Anything else hurt?"

"My leg?"

"You got a pretty major gash on your left thigh," he said, and then I remembered the slick of blood that had come off on my hand.

"I think that's it," I said, my voice a croak. I cleared my throat and tried again. "I mean, I don't know, but I think so. My head really hurts. Bad. But other than that, I think I'm okay?"

"Benny's going to set you right," he said, gesturing to Benny, who stood behind him, a worried expression on his face. He brushed my cheeks with the cool cloth. "In just a minute." He peered at me. "Do you remember? Everything from earlier?"

"Yes," I said, staring back at him, wiping at my blurry eyes. "Why wouldn't I?"

"For a minute there ..." Phillip's lip trembled. "For a minute there, you forgot some stuff. You forgot me."

"I did?"

"Yeah." He wiped at his brow. "Worst two minutes of my life."

"What about Shank?" I asked, moving to sit up. Phillip's large hand held me down.

"Don't get up. Shank's laying out there in back of the stage, dead as a fucking doornail," he said matter-of-factly. "And good riddance to the fucker."

"For real this time?"

"For real," Phillip said. "Jamie checked the pulse. Nada."

"This is gonna sound weird, but ..." I took a shaky breath. "Does the name Colt Leather mean anything to you?"

A brief look of amusement passed across Phillip's face. "Well, yeah," he said. "He was in that shitty post-grunge band Necrofeelya back in the day. Well, till they kicked him out. I read recently he'd been getting up to some bad shit, not that I'm surprised. Why?"

"Did you two ever meet?"

Phillip thought. "Not that I recall. Though he did audition for the Bloomer Demons when I was gone." He laughed. "Scared them clean off auditioning anybody else. Jason ended up doing the vocals for that album." He looked at me strangely. "Why are you asking about that guy, Stormy?"

I started to move, but his hand was still pressed against my chest. "Don't even *think* about it, Spooner," he said, his eyes flashing fire.

I nodded reluctantly. "Your show ..." I said softly, and he lightly stroked my face . "It got ruined ..."

"It's okay," Phillip said, grazing my cheek with his fingers. "All that matters is that everyone got out okay, and that *you're* okay. That's all I care about." I exhaled a breath I hadn't realized I'd been holding. So everyone had gotten out alright. Everyone except Shank, that was. That was a good thing, so why did I feel so weirdly empty?

"He came here to hurt us," I said, my eyes filling with more tears. "To hurt everyone."

"I know."

"I can't understand *why.*" I moaned, a fresh throb hitting my temple. Phillip reached forward and gently closed my eyes for me, his hands warm on my face. I'd have to tell him about Colt Leather eventually, but I just didn't have the strength right now.

"Does it matter?" he asked softly. "At least we know he won't be chasing us ever again."

"Where's Beth?" I asked.

"Is Beth the girl with the black hair?" Benny asked. "She saved our fucking asses. I was wondering who the fuck the girl with the hula hoop was in the front row and why she was upstaging my show, then that bang went off, and half the people in the venue didn't even notice at first because they were so dazzled by her lights. Phillip dropped his guitar and shot backstage to find you. Then the next thing I know, the girl is rushing up onto the stage, dashing right under security's arms and grabbing the mic, telling everyone calmly to exit single file, slowly, that hula hoop still flashing like hell around her waist." Benny shook his head. "And they actually listened to her. Jason and Ollie helped organize the crowd, but it was her idea. Everybody got out safe because of her."

I closed my eyes again, grateful. Beth had come through. I made a mental note to thank her profusely later. It felt almost like divine fate had sent her to me at just the right time.

"If there's a silver lining to any of this"— a distinctly Southern voice spoke up beside me, Jamie — "It's that you'll get so much publicity out of this, Deville. Everyone will be talking about it."

"I don't think a bunch of media scrutiny is what Stormy needs right now, or any of us, for that matter." Phillip's voice was sharp. "And nobody will want to come to our shows now, probably. Not if they think it's a security threat." To my shock, Phillip's face crumpled and a lone tear ran down his cheek. He grabbed my hand and kissed my knuckles. "Oh Stormy, I'm so sorry. This was all such a bad idea. Can you forgive me?"

"There's nothing to forgive," I said, reaching forward to wipe away his tear. "You're just living your life. You shouldn't have to stop doing that just because of … of all this. I'd never ask you to."

Benny came forward, holding a small, cloth bag with a leather strap. He looked down at me with concern. "The cops will be here any minute, and I'm sure there will be paparazzi on their tails, so if I'm going to do this, I need to do it now."

"Do what?" I asked. I was having trouble remembering what was going on. My head felt woozy. "I didn't die, did I? You're not bringing me back?" I slow-blinked and laughed. "Wait, if I'm talking to you, then obviously I'm not dead … did I already get brought back? Am I undead now too?"

Phillip put his head in his hands. "She obviously has a head injury, Benny. I'm worried."

"It'll be alright, man." Benny put a hand on his shoulder. "I promise."

"So you're not going to bring me back?" I asked, head still throbbing.

Benny laughed. "That's your thing, not mine. You give life, I take it away, remember?"

"You're going to take my life away?"

"Not a chance." Benny grinned. "You just lay back, Stormy. I'm just going to say a protection spell over you. See if we can't put back a few of those marbles you seem to have lost and try to heal that leg."

"Can't we just put a bandage on it?" I sighed, trying to rise again, but Phillip and Jamie put hands on my shoulder to stop me. As I leaned back, I felt a wave of pain deep inside my torso, near my ribs. "I'm so tired of magic. No offense."

"None taken. I'm always sick of it," Benny agreed. "Though it's nice to have someone to share the burden with. However I feel about the magic, it's still a part of me. And yours is part of you. We can't get rid of it." He gave me a sympathetic look. "Besides, it's either this or the hospital. I'm assuming you don't want to visit the latter?"

I thought of all the reporters who might show up, the questions doctors might ask, having to sit in a cold, sterile, and uncomfortable bed with only bad daytime TV to keep me company, and nodded. "You got me. Fine. Do your magic, oh sage Black Wolf, and heal me by the light of the moon."

"I know you're being a sarcastic bitch, but I really liked the sound of that." Benny grinned and sat down at the stool Jamie had drug over for him and opened the little bag. "For real. I like it a real fucking lot. It sounds sexy and metal as fuck." He shook his head. "From now on, everyone can address me as the sage Black Wolf."

"Kiss my ass," I said, and Phillip laughed.

"She's already back to herself," he said with a smile, then looked at me with his blazing, dark eyes. "Is there anything you need? Anything I can get you?"

"Yes," I said, wincing as I leaned back on the flat little pillow, resting my aching head against the loveseat's armrest. "Nikolai, wherever he ran off to. I need to see Nikolai."

Thirteen

For once, no well-meaning yet overbearing man was making a move to stop me. I sat up on the loveseat. My head no longer hurt, nor did my ribs or leg. I splayed my arms out in front of me, inspecting them. All the soreness and disorientation I'd felt moments before was now gone, and I felt like myself again. Well, mostly. Benny had really fixed me up.

There was the small matter of the anxiety snaking through my stomach as Nikolai made his way into the room and sat on the stool Benny had just vacated. He stared at me silently, his piercing blue eyes meeting mine, cold and nearly devoid of feeling like always. I'd never been able to get a line on him. Was he *really* that cold and unfeeling, or was it a carefully constructed front? He'd given me a knife for my protection when I'd only known him a day or two. And he was *here*, wasn't he? All signs pointed to the fact that he *did* care.

And now I was pretty sure I knew why.

Phillip, Jamie, and Benny were in the corner of the room, talking. I could make out snippets of what they were whispering about—something to do with Shank and the location of his body, and the cops, whose sirens I could hear fast approaching—but it was hard to concentrate on that right now. The dream I'd had when knocked out was still at the very forefront of my consciousness, and I couldn't do a single thing until I confronted it.

Phillip was craving a cigarette, and badly. I could feel it, could feel his need, his weakness overtaking him. The magic was strong right now, probably because of what Benny had just done. "Phillip," I said, and all three men turned to me. "Don't cave and smoke. You've done so well; you can't give up now."

"I won't," he said, turning to look at me from across the room, his face equal parts embarrassed and annoyed. "Goddamit."

"Can you guys give Nikolai and I just a sec?" I asked. "Maybe go get Phillip some Nicorette?"

Phillip hesitated, then nodded. "I'm going to go out and greet the police. I'll … spin some kind of story. Figure something out to explain all this." He turned to Nikolai. "You guys make it quick, okay? Can you make sure Stormy gets out and meets me in the parking lot?" Nikolai nodded, and Phillip, Jamie, and Benny left the room, shutting the door behind them.

Nikolai chuckled as he turned back to me. "You sure know how to command a room. Give it another day or two and you'll be running the Wolfden. Benny doesn't know what's in store for him."

"God, that's the last thing I'd ever want. They're only being nice to me because I just got hurt," I said dismissively. "Benny will always be the one in charge." I shuddered. "I don't even want to know what it looks like out there."

"Not as bad as you'd think," he answered, running a hand through his long hair. "Shank's in the back—we all thought we'd better not move him—and there's a bunch of trash and debris back there too, but the front of the bar is fine. Everybody exited out pretty calmly after the explosion. It was very organized and really fast. I guess shit like this is par for the course these days and people know how to get themselves to safety efficiently."

"That's both depressing and a relief," I said, and he nodded.

"There's very minimal damage to the venue, from what I can tell," he went on. It occurred to me that he seemed nervous. His hand, still wound around his blond hair, was trembling a little. Phillip's had been too. Everyone was more rattled than they wanted me to know. "I don't think the venue will have to petition their insurance for too many repairs. We really lucked out."

"We?"

"Yeah, 'we,'" he answered, looking at me strangely. "Haven't you figured out that we're all in this together?"

"I guess I'm still getting used to that."

"You're one of us now," he said kindly.

"Thank you," I said, touched, then, unable to put it off any longer, "Nikolai, are you my brother?"

His cold blue eyes widened, and he looked away for a second. He swallowed hard, his Adam's apple bobbing in his pale throat, then looked back at me. His eyes, usually so emotionless, had softened. His shoulders softened too, as though he was losing a tension he'd held onto for a long time. With the slightest, almost imperceptible nod, he said in a very soft voice, "Yes."

"Why didn't you tell me?"

"I wanted to," he said, and cleared his throat. "I tried, but I lost my nerve."

"Back at the Wolfden? When you gave me the knife?"

Nikolai nodded. "Yes. That knife was—is—a family heirloom, passed down from my mother, and I wanted you to have it. I know you aren't blood related through her, but it felt … significant … to me that you have it now that she's gone. That knife has female energy; it's meant to be wielded by a woman." He sighed. "I wanted to tell you then, but you were in a hurry to get going with Roberta and Benny and I just … chickened out. I was afraid, I guess." He sighed again, more deeply this time. "I've been holding it in for so long, I just got used to the feeling."

"I'm sorry about your mother," I said softly.

"It's alright," he said. "Every day it gets a little easier."

I wondered what had happened to her, but now wasn't the time. "I had a dream," I said instead. "When I was knocked out. Daddy introduced us at the wrestling match, back at the flea market, when we were kids. The first time I ever saw Benny—the Black Wolf. His first ever match. It was the same day." I closed my eyes, remembering how vivid that dream had been. I could still taste the cloying sweetness of funnel cake and see the wedge of watermelon, dotted with Tajin. "He introduced us, and I think he was planning on telling me you were my brother, but he wussed out in the end."

"Runs in the family." Nikolai chuckled, but then his face turned serious. "That really did happen. Just like you described. I was about eight years old, I think. You would have been about five."

"What happened after that?" I asked. "I don't … I don't remember."

"He didn't tell you," Nikolai explained. "And Mama was pissed. That was the last straw for her; he'd let us down so many times. She was just done, I guess." He shook his head, apparently lost in memories. "For a long time, Mama and me lived a few doors down from you guys in the same trailer park. It was a total cluster fuck. As you can imagine, your mother wasn't exactly thrilled with our father moving his mistress and son in right under her nose. All three of them fought all the time." His mouth was downturned, his eyes sad. "You and I had a good time, though, for a couple years. We'd get out and ride bikes together, play catch, sneak down to the creek and catch frogs, ignoring our mothers screeching in the parking lot."

"I don't remember much of that at all," I said. "But I'm hoping it'll come back. It sounds nice."

"It was. Both Roberta and Jamie moved to the trailer park around the same time I did, and we'd all play together. We had a lot of fun … for a while," he said. "It was around then that Roberta's dad Elvin started tinkering with all us kids that my mom and your mom came to blows."

"They did?" I wasn't surprised to hear it.

"Yep. Mama gave as good as she got, and they both ended up with black eyes. The battle might've been a draw, but Laureen ended up winning the war. She told our father she was going to leave him if he didn't end things once and for all—with both of us."

"She told him not to see his own son?" I asked, incredulous.

"Yep." Nikolai nodded. "That she did."

My mother had done a lot of things in her day, but this made me feel far more ashamed than I'd ever felt of her before. "But you're older than me. Which means that you were born long before Daddy and my mom were even dating, much less married. What reason would she have to keep him from his own son?"

"Jealousy, probably," Nikolai answered. "I guess Laureen didn't believe his excuses that he'd only had us move to the trailer park so he could spend time with me. She wasn't stupid; she knew they were still carrying on. She was right not to trust him. He's garbage." Nikolai's face was red. "From what I understand, Laureen just finally got sick of pretending she didn't know what was going on. She issued an ultimatum, and well, I was collateral damage." He twirled his hair with a finger. "So we moved out. It sucked. I missed you, and I missed our father, too, even if he was a drugged-out bastard. But at the same time, I was kinda relieved to be away from Elvin and that scene. The things he was doing, messing with all our heads … It scared me."

I didn't know what to say. I was still getting all those memories back, and thinking about how Elvin had forced me to go along with his weird spells and hypnosis chilled my blood.

Nikolai continued. "I wanted to protect you so bad, but there was nothing I could do. I was just a little kid. Jamie and I used to hide from him all the time. And then he went and wiped your memories … I'll never forget the time Mama and I came back to the trailer park to get some of our stuff we'd left behind and I saw you on the front porch, swinging on the porch swing. I came over to see you, and you just stared blankly at me like you'd ever seen me before." To my horror, Nikolai's bright blue eyes filled with tears. "I never tried to see you again after that. It was too hard. All of it was too hard. Before, when you didn't know you were my sister, that hurt. But to have you not know me at all … that was too much."

"I'm so sorry." I got up from the loveseat and kneeled over him, pulling him into a clumsy hug. His blond hair was soft against my face. "I'm sorry about all of it. My mom, Daddy, Elvin … all of it. It must have been so hard for you."

"It was harder for you," Nikolai said, his voice muffled against my shoulder. His arms closed around me, warm and familiar. "I've been so worried about you for so long. You've always been my little sister, even if you didn't know it."

"You don't have to worry about me anymore," I said, cradling his head against my shoulder. "And you will always be my brother." We stayed there for a moment, just hugging, enjoying the familiar-yet-unfamiliar feel of each other, making up for lost time. I took a deep, long breath, relief washing over me, filling an empty spot inside me that I didn't know I had.

Then the door opened, and Roberta stepped inside, out of breath. If she thought anything weird about the two of us embracing, her face didn't show it. "Guys," she said breathlessly, gesturing toward the door. "You'd better get out there."

FOURTEEN

"You'd better not be asking me to revive Shank's dead ass," I grumbled, following Roberta out into the wings of the stage. "Because I refuse. I made that mistake once, and besides, Phillip would tan my hide if I even tried. As much as I might enjoy that, he's probably right—"

"It's not that," she interrupted. "Fuck Shank. I hope he's rotting in hell."

"Then what is it?" Nikolai asked, ambling behind me. The wings were dark; either Shank's homemade makeshift bomb had killed the lights or someone had turned them off, probably Colt. I could barely see in front of me, but the acrid, stale smell of smoke lingered in the air and burned my eyes.

"The cops are here," Roberta said, gesturing toward the EXIT sign that loomed in front of us. The lights weren't illuminating it, so I could only just make out the white block letters. "Phillip and Benny are out there talking to them, but we agreed you guys probably shouldn't be lingering inside when they come to investigate."

"Let me guess—they're leaving out the part about how I encountered Shank and provoked him to blow the place up."

"Stormy, you provoked him?" Nikolai's voice was quiet in the darkness, but I detected a hint of disappointment—or judgement.

"I mean, I didn't like, poke him in the stomach and say 'I dare you,' but I wasn't exactly nice to him," I said guiltily. Why had I antagonized him? Why hadn't I noticed what he was holding in his hand sooner? Maybe because I'd been too busy trading barbs with some washed-up, fake goth boy to pay attention to the very real threat in front of me. "I, um, I gave him a shove. Just to get him away from me. I didn't realize he had a bomb. I'm sorry. I should have diffused the situation."

"Ha ha. Diffused," Roberta said in a dry voice, then pushed the exit open and held the door as Nikolai and I stepped outside onto the side ramp. "Even in times of crisis, you've got the puns."

"It was an accident."

"Sure." She grinned at me and cuffed me on the ear. "Benny said he fixed you up. That right? My best girl okay now?"

"Since when was I your best girl?"

"Since you rescued me from my dad a week ago," she said, and for a moment, her expression was sad. Then she perked up again. "And since I realized you're as petty as I am. I need more girlfriends to gossip with, and I suspect you'll talk shit with the best of them."

"You would be correct on that score," I said. "So where are we going?"

"Phillip said not to wait for him; he and the band are likely to be here a while. He's got all sorts of shit to deal with—insurance, the cops, all of that. To say nothing of the crowd of fucking fans and reporters and Instagram influencers all currently hanging out in the front of the venue, waiting to descend on him like a mob. He said to drive you back to the motel or to your dad's, wherever you want to go." She grinned.

"My marching orders were simply 'get her the fuck away from here.'"

"That's quite a vote of confidence from my lover," I said.

"I'm pretty sure it is," Nikolai said, giving me a brotherly nudge in the ribs, one of what I hoped would be many. He smiled at me. "He's trying to protect you from all that, you knucklehead."

"Where should we go, then?" I asked, winking at him. "You have seniority, after all."

"Wherever you want to go," he said affably, shoving his hands in the pocket of his JNCOs.

"I'm not deciding."

"Me, either."

"Fuck y'all," Roberta said, reaching into her pocket and producing a Tootsie Roll pop. "I've still got a buzz from the show, and I have a cherry sucker, and I've got *all day*. I can wait y'all out. Don't test me." She unwrapped the lollipop and stuck it in her mouth, her expression pert. "So fess up. What's going on with you two fools?"

I sighed. I raised my eyebrows in a silent question, and Nikolai's mouth slacked a little bit. We could trust Roberta. We both knew it. I smiled shyly at Nikolai and turned to Roberta.

"Burt … I'd like to introduce you to someone. This is … my brother. Nikolai."

"Shut the fuck up." Her eyes went wide. The lollipop hung forgotten from her bottom lip, threatening to fall on the asphalt.

"It's true," I said. "You don't remember from the trailer park?"

"I mean, of course I remember us all hanging out, and I remember you guys playing together some, but nothing unusual …" Her eyes widened even further and she shoved Nikolai in the shoulder. "You mean your mom … and *Chad* …"

He nodded slowly, his face the picture of shame. "Yeah,

they were a thing. For years. Until she finally wised up and moved us the fuck out of that place."

"Just in time," I said softly, and Nikolai put an arm around my shoulder.

"Jesus Christ. Did we live in a soap opera or fucking *what?*" Roberta laughed.

"It isn't funny. It's sad, is what it is," Nikolai said, but his mouth was turning up at the corners.

"It's a Greek tragedy." I nodded, smirking. "Except we ain't Greek. We're redneck orthodox."

"I hate you," Roberta said primly. She crunched down on her lollipop and stared at us, chewing. "So where the fuck are we going, siblings? I'm game for anywhere, as long as it's not an attic."

As Roberta's SUV ran down the ramp and out of the parking deck, I could hear people shouting and chanting in the parking lot before we'd even rounded the corner. As we took a sharp turn toward the right and neared the venue, my eyes widened as I saw just *how many* people were milling around. There were so many they'd bled into the street and had all but stopped traffic completely.

A couple of traffic cops were doing their best to direct the flow of traffic, but it wasn't doing much good. The people gathered outside were paying them very little attention, walking in front of cars, clogging up the road, seemingly oblivious that there were actual vehicles trying to move past.

As Roberta inched forward, they chanted, "PHI-LIP! PHI-LIP!"

"Holy shit," I gasped, suddenly very grateful that Roberta's windows were tinted and nobody could see me. Nikolai put a protective arm around my shoulders.

"See why he wanted you out of here?" he said.

"God, what are they even doing? Just like, waiting to see him?"

Roberta nodded. "A lot of these kids who were at the show. Some of them showed up after they heard about the explosion, and then you've got your usual vultures, the media, who all showed up as well. They're all hoping to catch a glimpse of Phillip and see if he makes a statement or whatever." She looked at me from the rearview mirror. "I doubt many of them know about Shank—that there's a dead body backstage. They probably think it was a prank, or just some right-wing troll causing trouble."

"It's all my fault," I said, squeezing my eyes shut, pressing a finger to my temple. My head was starting to hurt again. "If I'd just told security that I'd seen him instead of rushing in to confront him myself—"

"Never mind that now," Nikolai said. "There's no sense crying over spilled …"—he smiled at me and cuffed my chin —"almond milk."

"Take me to Phillip's house," I said, wrapping my arms around myself, unable to laugh at Nikolai's joke. I felt sick with guilt, grief, and anxiety. "I just want to curl up in his bed and wait for him to get home."

"Well, I'll try, but it's going to be a while before we get there," Roberta said, tapping on the horn, though it would do no good. At least ten people stood directly in front of us, not moving at all. "And Phillip? Well, if you're lucky, he might roll in sometime tomorrow afternoon. This is one hella clusterfuck."

FIFTEEN

"I need to tell you something." Roberta was crunching on a Tootsie Roll pop again—this time grape—and I now realized this was something she did when she was nervous, a fact I found kind of endearing. We sat together at the kitchen table at Jason's house, a table that had once belonged to Phillip's parents. Phillip had told me it was the first piece of furniture they'd ever bought together. We sat with two mugs of steaming tea in front of us, a third mug on the counter waiting for boiling water should Phillip come in any time soon.

"Shoot."

"You're not the only one with a long-lost brother," Roberta said, and I took a sip of tea, bracing myself. This wasn't a topic Roberta mentioned often.

"I know about your brother," I reminded her gently, sitting my cup back down. "You mentioned him, remember?" Roberta had told me about her brother Jorge, who was in jail on drug-related charges. Not only had she barely mentioned him in the time I'd known her, but when she did, her entire body became like a coil of nerves, tensed and ready to strike.

"Yeah, I told you that he's in jail, right?" I nodded, and she went on. "But what I didn't tell you was how and why."

"I'm listening now," I said. I pushed her mug toward her and smiled. "Let's hear it."

She didn't drink but wrapped her fingers around the mug, as if enjoying the warmth. "Well, you might've guessed, you might've not but … Jorge got into drugs because of my dad and Guthrie." Roberta's voice was full of bitterness. "He was always a good, well-behaved kid until they started on him."

"What happened?" I asked. "What did they do?"

"To tell you that story I've got to tell you everybody's story," she said. "You know some of it already, that Guthrie and my father were into the drug game. That it wasn't just the magic that kept them afloat, that they were dealing. Well, it was a much larger operation than you might imagine. Much, much larger." She looked at me. "And it has carried on, all this time. Those who were in back then—well, the ones who aren't dead or in jail like Jorge—are still very much in."

"I see." Roberta was warning me, giving me a chance to protest, to decline, to keep pleading ignorance. But we were too far into it now. "Tell me."

"Guthrie started out just dealing pot back in the nineties," she said, running a hand through her damp curls. "Him and literally everybody else, right? Everybody in town, including the cops, I assume, knew he was dealing weed, but he was a middle-aged white hippie guy so nobody gave him any trouble, so long as he stayed out of the big time. But eventually he wanted to start dealing harder stuff, like cocaine, heroin, stuff like that." She sighed. "He had a good gig going, was making all kinds of money, but he got greedy. That's when he enlisted my dad."

"Your dad was a heavy drug user?" I thought back to my gapped-up memory. Had I ever seen Elvin with anything other than baggies of weed and the odd pill? I didn't think I had, but nothing would surprise me.

"Not really. Not for himself, anyway," Roberta answered. "But he was never one to miss an opportunity to enrich himself or exploit someone. As soon as Guthrie decided to expand his business, so to speak, my dad wanted in."

"Ugh."

"That's an understatement," Roberta said, her face pinched. "I don't know the particulars of how they got their supply or whatever since I was too young and then when I got older, I didn't *want* to know … But at some point, they started dealing heavy shit. Pills, then heroin and coke, and some other stuff too. They had a pretty lucrative business going for a number of years. And as time went on and they got a reputation and a list of 'clients,' they also found themselves a few worker bees to help them run drugs and recruit more clients. It's only grown over the years, and before Dad and Guthrie died, it was a full-on operation." She grimaced. "That was one of the main reasons Lydia left Guthrie, you know … a lot of it had to do with the magic and her discomfort with his exploitation of it, and a lot of it had to do with the way he treated Lee … but the main part, the part that scared her, was the drugs. She was so afraid there would be a raid any day and that Guthrie would go to prison." She smiled grimly. "If only that had happened; it might've saved us all a lot of heartbreak."

"So your brother was one of their, um, their employees?"

"Yes," Roberta answered. "Him and quite a few others. Can you guess who else?"

"Tess," I said automatically, then frowned. "Sloan."

"Yep." She clucked sympathetically. "And me and my brother for a while, until he went to jail and I decided to get out of it. And Shank, of course. Lee, from time to time, when he wasn't having a crisis of conscience. And …"

I finished for her. "… And my dad, right?"

She slowly nodded.

I stared at her, my stomach rolling over with unease. I'd already assumed as much, but hearing her say it so casually still made my stomach churn. "Is he a former employee or current?" I asked, dreading the answer.

"I don't know," Roberta admitted. "That's what I'm hoping to find out. But I'd guess current, or at least up until the house fire." She finally took a sip of her tea. "I don't know who burned his place down, but it reeks of some kind of 'warning,' some kind of message they were trying to send him."

"He says he's clean," I said stupidly, looking down at my lap. "He's been saying it for a long time."

"He may very well be," Roberta said in a soft voice. "He might have just been helping them without actually using. Maybe he decided he wanted out, after everything that's happened recently. Maybe it had to do with you—trying to keep you safe. And somebody retaliated against him."

I gulped. "Now I need to tell *you* something." I quickly relayed what I knew about Colt Leather and how he'd been backstage with Shank before running off into the night like a coward. "Shank said he"—I swallowed again—"insinuated that Colt was the one who started the fire that killed Tess. He *laughed* about it."

"What motive would this Colt dude have to run with Shank and the rest of that bunch?" Roberta asked, her face pinched in confusion. "How does he tie in?"

"He doesn't, really," I admitted. "Except Phillip said he'd auditioned for the Bloomer Demons once. He didn't get the gig. Sour grapes, maybe?" I shrugged. It was a long shot, though, and I knew it.

"Maybe," Roberta said thoughtfully with a long sigh. "But Shank could have been lying. It could've been anyone who started that fire. It could've been my brother." As she said the words, her voice barely a whisper, her face turned drawn, and she almost looked haggard with sadness.

I stared at her for a moment. "But how?" I asked, my eyebrows furrowing in confusion. "You said Jorge is in jail."

"I said he *was* in jail," Roberta answered, her soft brown eyes full of distress. "He got out a month ago, Stormy. He hasn't called or shown up at the house. I've been wondering all this time where he was, why he didn't come to see me. I can't help but think maybe … what if … what if he's behind all this? Some kind of revenge plot …? I can't bear the thought." Roberta put her head in her hands, face down on the table, her dark curls bobbing as she cried.

"Hold on … slow down." I came over to her side of the table and put an arm around my friend. "Let's not jump to conclusions. What reason do you have to suspect your brother of such a thing?"

"I don't have one, really," Roberta said, raising her head and wiping at her cheeks furiously. "But he should have called me, he should have come home. We talked about the day of his release for months; we were looking forward to it. He was so excited to get out. He had all these plans … He wanted to fix up Uncle Albert's land." She gulped, and I suppressed an involuntary shudder. That land was the patch of swampy wilderness and outbuildings we'd pinned Elvin to, where he'd almost managed to kill Benny and Roberta. "And he wanted to go back to school. He's always been interested in becoming an electrician. He was going to go to tech school. He'd already started applying for loans and grants. He wouldn't have just … disappeared!"

"There's got to be some logical explanation," I said hopefully.

"Like what?" she demanded. She pushed the mug of tea away. "I wasn't able to meet Jorge there the day he got out, and he said it was fine, that he'd just take the bus and come to the house. He never showed, and for a couple days, I just assumed he was sowing some wild oats, that maybe he'd hooked up with a girl or was meeting up with old friends. But after a few days, I started to worry." She bit her lip. "If he isn't behind what happened at your dad's, then that means something even worse has happened. That somebody has taken him, like they took Lee! He could be in danger, or he could be—"

"I'm sure that's not the case," I said, but my voice didn't carry any real certainty in it. What if she was right?

"I thought for a while there—" Roberta's voice choked up and she cleared her throat, swallowed, and continued. "I thought Jorge might be the body in your dad's house. I … I feel bad, but I was relieved it was Tess. Relieved because it wasn't my brother."

"Oh, Roberta," I said softly, and she shook her head. "Why didn't you tell me any of this?"

"A lot of reasons," she confessed, looking down. "I already had so much other shit to tell you, and I had no idea how to start. It's just one more thing to add to the pile, and I guess I was feeling embarrassed, and ashamed, and protective of my brother. I didn't want you to assume he's just like my dad and my uncle."

"I wouldn't do that," I said. "Does everyone else know, at least? At the Wolfden?"

She shook her head, surprising me. "No," she said, guilt crossing her pretty features. "I haven't told anyone, Stormy. Nobody knows that Jorge is out of jail, much less that he's been a no-show."

"Roberta!" I was shocked. "You tell them everything! For all that talk you do about how we're a family, how—"

"I know!" Roberta interrupted, spots of color appearing on her cheeks. "I know, okay! I should have told everybody. I *will* tell everybody." She squared her shoulders, a gesture that seemed both defiant and delicate. "It's just that he's my *brother.* The only family I have left at this point, the only one I've ever been able to trust fully. I love Lee, but I can't even say that about him, Stormy. I feel protective over Jorge in a way that I can't explain. He's my blood!"

"I get it," I said, and I did. I might not have grown up with my baby sister Shably or my newfound brother Nikolai, but there was an instinctive, built-in unconditional love that came with having a sibling, especially one vulnerable or younger than you, that I understood already. I could see—and feel—that Nikolai saw me that way too. And I was grateful for it. "You don't have to feel guilty for loving your brother, Burt."

"I keep thinking I should go home," she said. "Coming to Boston with you guys was a mistake. I wanted to see the show so bad, and I thought maybe a distraction would do me some good, but I can't stop thinking about him." Roberta sighed. "I feel like I should go back home to Brunswick and wait. What if he shows up and I'm not there? What if he's wondering where I am?"

"Then you should go," I said firmly, and she looked at me in surprise.

"Seriously?" she asked. "I figured you'd want me to stay. At least until you guys are ready to go home."

"I'll even go with you," I said, making up my mind on the spot. "We'll make a little road trip out of it, just you and me."

"I can't ask you to do that," Roberta said, her eyes welling up. "I know how much you've been looking forward to these shows. And after what happened earlier, you deserve to see one good set that hasn't been ruined by some idiot with a bomb."

"You're more important," I said with a shrug, putting my arms around her shoulders and giving her a little squeeze. "And who knows if the second show will even happen. I mean, the venue was bombed. It might be cancelled. Phillip will understand," I argued. "He'd want me to be there for you."

"I do appreciate it, Stormy, but I can't ask you to do that," Roberta said with finality. "I want you to be here with Phillip. You deserve to be." She faced me with a smile. "I feel bad that I'm flaking on you right now after what just happened."

I mock-glared at her. "No ma'am. I won't hear that shit from you, Burt. It's not your job to pick up the pieces. I can take care of myself. You have to put your needs and your family first. And I can guarantee you that Benny and Jamie and Lee and Nikolai and Clara would all say the exact same thing."

"Thank you," she said with a genuine smile. "I think I just needed to hear somebody say that out loud. You know?"

"I do," I said. "Sometimes it just takes someone else giving you permission to put yourself first."

Exhausted, I pushed my way back inside the house, kicking off my combat boots the moment I stepped through the doorway. I picked them up and padded up the stairs toward Phillip's room, doing my best to be quiet.

It had taken Roberta a few hours to get her ducks in a row, her bags re-packed, and the necessary motivation to get in her SUV and begin the arduous drive back home. I was relieved that Clara had offered to go with her, even if Clara wasn't my favorite person, because I didn't relish the thought of Roberta driving back home by herself. I'd tried to talk her into letting me come with her, but she'd refused me no less than ten times, insisting that I stay in Boston and enjoy my time with Phillip. She'd barely allowed me to walk outside and see her off, but I'd put my foot down.

Now she was headed back to Georgia. Upon her return, I

hoped she'd find that Jorge had turned up and all was well. But worry lingered in my belly.

Ollie was sitting on the bottom stair, thumbing at one of Jason's acoustic guitars. His impossibly clean black Vans were tapping on the floor, keeping perfect time as he played. "I didn't know you played guitar," I said. It was still a marvel to me when I found out new things about the band I'd loved since I was a teen.

He chuckled and picked out a casual rendition of "Blackbird," his low, smoky voice crooning out the words. Then he rested his hands on the guitar and smiled. "You know how many drummers start out wishing they were the front man? Just about every drummer knows how to play two or three other instruments. Just in case they end up the lead singer."

"You have a great voice. Why didn't you consider fronting the band after …" I trailed off, not wanting to finish the question. Now was the time to bring up that I'd seen Colt. But Phillip should be here for that conversation too.

Ollie was watching me. He stood up and placed the guitar back on its stand in the corner of the foyer. "You know, Stormy," he said, even though I hadn't spoken. "There's no replacing Phillip Deville. We're going to have a hard enough time replacing Kim." Then, to my surprise, Ollie stepped forward and gave me a hug.

He was warm and smelled good, and I found myself resting my head on his shoulder, comfortable and easy, as though I'd known him for years. When he pulled away, his eyes were kind. "You looked like you needed that," he said, and I realized he was right.

"Thank you, Ollie," I said, my hand on the banister, moving to go upstairs. Then I turned back, giving him a grateful look. "I'm so glad you guys are back together. I really am."

"Me, too, girl," he said, and disappeared into the kitchen. I walked up the stairs to Phillip's room, touched.

I pushed Phillip's door open to find the room empty; he must be in the bathroom. It was late and I was tired, so I decided to change into my pajamas and get the bed ready for us. Phillip was no doubt far more tired than I was. It had been well into the afternoon before he'd finally made it home; he'd pulled an all-nighter. He hadn't wanted to talk about the ordeal, but I knew that having to talk to all those cops, reporters, and fans, combined with the endorphins from playing his first show in over twenty years and worrying about me after the explosion, likely had him feeling totally insane. It had been less than twenty-four hours since the show and the explosion that had cut it short, but it somehow felt like years had passed, and I was dog tired.

Whatever it took to make him feel all better, I would do. I smiled to myself, turning down the covers and patting Phillip's pillow. Whatever he asked for, it was his.

I stripped off my gauzy blouse and reached for the suitcase at the foot of the bed, pulling out my favorite cozy 7 Year Bitch T-shirt, so old and worn and beloved that it had holes in the collar and the armpits, but it was soft as a baby blanket. I pulled on a pair of fleecey boxer shorts with black roses and skulls on them that I'd bought at Hot Topic a million years ago and grinned at my stupid reflection in the mirror. I looked about twelve years old; the only tell that I wasn't an angsty adolescent and in fact a thirtysomething nerd were the dark, tired circles under my eyes. If I wasn't so tired, I'd go for something sexy, like a black, lacy teddy or my candy corn thong that Phillip loved, but tonight was all about comfort.

Pulling my hair up into a messy bun, I called for Phillip. The light was on in the adjoining bathroom, the door ajar. "You taking a shower, honey?"

He didn't answer. I noticed a Dos Equis on the night table that he'd opened and left, still beading with condensation. I grabbed it and took a long swig, sighing with pleasure as the cold liquid went down my throat. I sat on the edge of the bed, relief hitting my shoulders as the tension started to slowly leave my body. I took another long sip of Phillip's beer, savoring the icy coldness. I'd have to go get him another one if he didn't hurry up and come out.

Beyond thirst, I realized I was ravenous. I hadn't had a real meal all day. Phillip likely hadn't either. I wondered if there were any local barbecue joints that had vegan options where we could grab takeout. Not likely—this was Boston, after all, where there was likely no barbecue, much less the vegan variety—but I was craving the comforts of home, which meant Brunswick stew, tangy barbecue, and mountains of mac n cheese and squash casserole. Banana pudding for dessert, the whole nine. If Dee, who hadn't known how to do anything but burn Pop-Tarts when she'd married my dad, could whip up a full Southern vegan meal, surely there was a restaurant around here with a decent facsimile of a veggie burger.

"Phillip, you hungry?" I called. He still didn't answer. Weird. Oh well, I'd find something myself; do a food delivery service. I picked up the phone, and as I opened Google, the phone immediately went dead. I groaned. I didn't feel like digging out my charger, which always seemed to be lost, so I dragged myself from the bed and over to the little table where the landline phone was and the phone book, leftover relics from Phillip's teen years that Jason had never gotten rid of. I made a mental note to tease him about that, this weird time capsule he called a house. It was downright creepy. Fuck it, I'd open up the yellow pages and find some food the old-school way.

I frowned; the phone wasn't on the table. I noticed the cord was reaching from the wall and into the bathroom. Phillip was on the phone, and for some reason, he'd taken the call in there. *Weird*, I thought again.

Curiosity piqued, I dropped the yellow pages and ventured over to the bathroom, pushing the door open ever so slightly.

Phillip was sitting on the edge of the bathtub, his legs actually in the tub, with his back to me, one long finger winding the cord around and around like a teenage girl. I smiled; he was so damned cute without even trying. I could imagine this was how he'd sat romancing girls on the phone when he was in high school.

Phillip nodded, listening to whoever was on the other end of the line. I opened my mouth to admonish him for dirtying up the bathtub with his crusty shoes and to let him know I was home when he said something that made me stop cold.

"Yeah, so I'm thinking just a twelve-stop tour will be the best bet; we don't want to overwhelm ourselves with any more than that. I don't want to be gone all year. Let's just do one season, mid-size venues at first, see how ticket sales go, and decide from there?" He was silent for a moment, listening to the response, still nodding. "Yeah, and I figure if we release like, one single before the tour, and then drop the entire album about mid-way through? That seems to be how bands are doing it these days ... lots of promotion via social media. Maybe we can hire someone for that because we're all too old for that shit, and Lee's got enough on his plate ..." He laughed. "I might not look it, but inside, I'm just as old as you, you fucker ... Oh, shut up about the magic. Are you going to throw that in my face every day?"

My face burned. Phillip was planning not only a tour but an entire *album* and social media blitz, and I hadn't heard so much as a word. When was he planning on telling me? Hadn't we spent the first portion of our relationship arguing about how I never kept him in the loop? After everything that had happened the night before, he hadn't even considered running all this by me first? Didn't we have more important things to talk about before he began planning the next year—or more—of our lives?

His life. Not mine. The thought occurred to me as I quietly shut the door. The fact that he hadn't mentioned it to me first just illustrated that point. I might be Phillip's girlfriend, but he was a one-man show, and all I could do was hope to trail behind him as his career took back off and he left me in the dust.

I turned and went back to bed, pulling on my running shoes and grabbing my phone, blinking back tears. I knew I should just talk to him outright, but for the moment, I just wanted—needed—to be alone. Suddenly, barbecue was the last thing on my mind. I needed to go for a run to clear my head and keep myself from crying.

I hadn't intended on ending up at Lydia's, but my feet found their way there, and the next thing I knew, I was standing on her porch for the first time since I'd been literally stuck there in a binding spell.

I stared up at the cobwebby trellis, my heart pounding in my chest. I stepped onto the first step, then the second, wondering what in the hell I was playing at. Why had I come here?

By the third step, the door had opened and a familiar white, curly head poked out.

"Well, if it isn't Fee," Lydia said with a smile—well, what counted as a smile for Lydia, which was little more than the expression you make when you eat something sour—gesturing for me to come forward. "Come on in; I was expecting you."

"You were?"

"Why yes, of course," Lydia said in her thick Boston accent, taking her time to settle down in the chair across from me. She seemed a little more sprightly than usual, but she was still pretty worse for wear. I wondered how far her cancer had progressed; the last time we'd spoken, she'd told me she was stage four. In fact, most of her involvement in trying to subdue my magic was because she had plans to revive herself when her inevitable demise came.

"Thank you for your concern, Fee, but I'm a good deal better," she said, crossing one leg over the other with some difficulty. She was wearing jelly shoes, like the kind all us kids wore in the eighties, over taupe pantyhose, and smiled with bemusement. "I don't think my imminent demise is as imminent as it once was."

"How is that possible?" I asked. Cancer was cancer, after all, and Lydia had even had an oxygen tank the last time I'd seen her.

"Oh, I suppose it helps that my son is dating someone with certain ... talents," Lydia said, winking at me, and my eyes widened. Benny. It made perfect sense. Of course he'd be willing to heal Lee's mother; he'd do anything for Lee.

"Oh, he hasn't healed me; his powers don't extend quite that far," Lydia said with a dry cackle that might have been a cough. "I'm not completely restored, but I think he might have prolonged these old bones for a couple years longer."

"That gives you plenty of time to wield a spell for immortality," I said with a smirk, and she rapped her walking cane on the floor and laughed.

"From your lips to the goddess' ears, Fee!" Her cheeks scrunched with merriment. "To write such a spell, can you imagine?" She leaned back and reached for a pack of her long, gross cigarettes. I'd have thought that she'd have quit smoking by now, after what Benny had done for her, but I supposed old habits died hard.

"They do indeed, Fee, and you just mind your own business. I'm a grown woman, after all." She smiled, and I felt my own cheeks flush with embarrassment. "Now. Why are you here?"

"I … I don't exactly know," I admitted.

"Are you … recovered … after your ordeal?" she asked with as much kindness as I imagined she could muster.

"Oh … yeah. Benny healed me too. I'm okay," I said. "A little shaken up still about Shank. But I hated him, so I don't know why I'm worried about it."

"Shank's dead? Well, good riddance to him. He was a grade-A piece of trash," Lydia said primly, lighting her mile-long cigarette. She took a long drag and smiled. "With any luck, he's rotting in hell with my husband. But that's not what I meant. I meant the ordeal at Elvin's."

"Oh." Of course that's what she meant. Lydia probably had no idea about the explosion at Phillip's show. "Yeah. I guess I'm okay with that too. I'm mainly just glad all of *you* are okay. Benny, and Roberta, and Lee … and you and Renee too."

"And that blonde bimbo you call a best friend?" Lydia asked, ashing her cigarette with a repugnant expression.

"Sloan? She's not my best friend anymore," I said.

"I imagine you're smarting from that too," she said. "When you lose friendships in your thirties, for some reason, you feel them so much stronger than when you were younger. And it's so much harder to replace those friendships when you're an adult too. Why we don't place as much importance on friendships as we do romantic relationships is a travesty. All types of love are important to have a healthy, spiritual relationship with one's own self."

I looked at her, surprised. I'd been having similar thoughts recently. It was a comfort to hear someone else say them.

"I'm occasionally wise," Lydia said with another dry cough-laugh. "So stop dodging my question, Fee. Why did you come here?"

"I told you I don't know," I said, throwing up my hands. "I went for a run, and I just ... found myself here."

"We didn't get a chance to speak much after you all rescued Renee and me," she said, drawing on her cigarette. "I imagine you'd like some things cleared up?"

"Yes and no," I said honestly. "Some things I'd rather just forget at this point, move on. But I wonder ... I wonder ..."

"What is it?"

"I know I got my powers from you," I said, wringing my hands in front of me. "I know what happened when I was a kid. That my mother OD'd and you were trying to save her, and I came in and pooled my magic with yours and that's when everyone found out I was special. When Elvin decided to start, I dunno, playing with my head. Using me as his little magical conduit or whatever. And I know Guthrie was part of that too, at least to some extent. It's what led to everything happening these past few weeks. Me and my stupid magic."

Lydia frowned, but she didn't interrupt.

"So I know the magic started with you and somehow came to me. And I know Guthrie and Elvin are the main two who were behind all the bad stuff that's happened, from then to now. I thought when they were both gone, it'd be over. But stuff keeps happening. My father's house burned down, Shank tried to blow us all up, I find out that Nikolai is my friggin' *brother* ..." I swallowed. "And a lot of this stuff seems to lead back to my father. Up until a few days ago, I'd seen him maybe twice my entire adult life. But now I find that he's as knee-deep in all of this as anyone." I looked at her. "You remember my dad, right?"

"Of course," Lydia said quietly, stubbing her cigarette out in a thick green glass ashtray. "I remember everything."

"So then you know ..." I trailed off, not sure how to phrase my question or certain I even wanted to ask it.

"What is it you're wanting to find out?" Lydia asked calmly.

"Was my father ... *is* my father ... one of them?" I spat out. "Working with, for, however you want to phrase it, Guthrie and Elvin? I know he did at one point when I was a kid, but has he always been a part of this?" I shook my head. "Because the former I can digest, but if I find out he was still working for them when they were sending spies after me, having me kidnapped, trying to harm me, and Phillip and everyone close to me ... if I find out he had a hand—even indirectly—in Tess' death ..."

"It's unforgiveable," Lydia finished for me.

"Yes," I said. "I would never forgive him."

Lydia seemed to consider this for a moment, then reached for another cigarette, lighting it with a trembling hand as the smoke from her previous cigarette lingered around her. The cherry flickered bright orange as she inhaled, then she regarded me with a soft look. "You know, when things started to get *real,* as you young kids call it, I was the one who suggested that Guthrie and I move to Boston." She smiled, appearing lost in her memories. "We'd both lived in Georgia for so long, and it really felt like home. I loved it there. South Georgia has such a dry, eerie feel to it ... something lurking there in those swamp waters, near the sea; it called to my spirit and still does. I was sad to leave it, but I wanted to get Guthrie away from Elvin. I knew his brother would only drag him down into the evil. That even though Guthrie might want to pull free at some point, it would be near impossible. I knew once he was fully enmeshed in his brother's world, he'd be lost."

"He'd be powerless against Elvin's powers," I mused.

Lydia snorted. "Fee, you know as well as I do that Elvin had no powers of his own. What little he possessed were simple parlor tricks I taught him in the hopes of mollifying him, and what he was able to glean through exploiting you and others." She shook her head. "I'm not speaking of magic here, or any other type of otherworldly power. I'm speaking of good old-fashioned malignant narcissism. Elvin was good at manipulating people, especially those who loved him. Guthrie loved his brother and would have done anything for him." She smiled sadly. "When my husband was young, he was quite a different person than the Guthrie you knew. He was sweet. A bit naïve, even. Gullible. In the beginning of our marriage, when Lee was very little, we were happy. But then Elvin moved to be near us and started sinking his hooks into Guthrie, and that was the beginning of the end.

"So I talked Guthrie into moving here. He agreed pretty readily; I think deep down he knew he needed to get away from Elvin, from the drugs and everything that was going on. He knew Elvin had been doing exploitative things with the kids in his old trailer park—you and the others—and it made him uncomfortable. We moved here and got away from all that, and for a couple blissful years, I thought everything would go back to normal. It very nearly did." Lydia sniffed. "He was still selling marijuana here and there, and probably harder stuff too, though he kept all that from me. The only time we really fought was when he sold Phillip Deville that spell. He laughed at the time and said I was being paranoid, that nobody would ever know how to use that spell, even if they were dumb enough to try. I guess we showed him, huh?"

"And how," I said, and she laughed.

"You speak like an elderly person for such a young woman," she said with a dry laugh. "I like that about you, Fee. You're very old world. I think that might be down to your powers. Anyway, it was around the time he sold that spell to Phillip that he began talking to Elvin more and more. Phone calls, the odd trip down to visit for the weekend, things like that. And then one weekend, he went down for one of his trips, took Lee with him, and come Sunday evening, they just … didn't come back."

"He took Lee?"

She nodded. "When they still hadn't turned up by Wednesday morning and Guthrie wasn't returning my calls, I was forced to call the police and file a missing persons report. It was only after the cops showed up down in Brunswick that Guthrie finally called and told me he wanted a divorce. He thought he'd keep Lee; didn't even *ask* or wonder whether I might want custody of my only son, just announced it like it was an already made decision." She shook her head angrily. "I told him I'd bring his whole operation down around his ears and Elvin's, too, if he didn't bring back my son. We worked out a 40/60 arrangement, and that continued all the way into Lee's adulthood.

"But after that, Guthrie was a lost cause. He fell right back into all the illegal drug dealings with Elvin, hanging out with and employing some very shady characters. He got heavily invested into the magic side of things too. Elvin convinced him that he if tapped into the power like he had, he could be very powerful. Of course, it didn't work, but they were both convinced." She put out her cigarette. "He was the one who asked for a divorce, but he never did sign the papers. Years went by, and he never did sign." She smiled grimly. "I suppose I get the last laugh because I've inherited his house on Jekyll Island, the house where he died. Not that I want it; I've already signed it over to Lee."

I shuddered involuntarily. I was responsible for that death.

"Guthrie is responsible for that death," she said, reading

my mind. "What's that they say—play dumb games, win dumb prizes?"

"So what does this have to do with my dad?" I asked, confused.

"I meandered on the point, I suppose." She laughed. "I wanted to illustrate to you that Guthrie wasn't always bad, or all bad. At one point in time, he was a sweet, gentle husband and father. We had some good memories. But he was manipulated by someone stronger and more malicious than him. In some ways, I don't think he could even comprehend that his brother might not have his best interests at heart. He trusted him implicitly."

"Are you saying that my dad …"

"I'm saying that your father, along with many others, was duped, manipulated, and coerced by Elvin for a very long time. We do not have to forgive them for that. But I think understanding how it happened is important for our own healing." She sat up in her chair, crossing her legs in the other direction. I could tell it was uncomfortable for her, sitting up so long. "What you choose to do with the information you have is up to you and you alone. Only you can decide who to forgive and when, and what forgiveness means."

"So my father is still involved," I said bitterly.

"Still? As you say, everyone is gone now," she said kindly. "Perhaps 'up until very recently' is a more apt way of looking at it."

"Either way, he had an active hand in hurting me," I said. "Hurting Phillip. And literally everyone else I care about. How am I supposed to live with that?"

"When you discover the answer to that puzzle," Lydia said, shifting again in her seat, "do let me know. Now, I think, Fee, you ought to go on home to your handsome man and let him explain himself."

I grimaced. Of course she'd read in my thoughts that I was

upset with Phillip. I didn't feel like talking to him right now, but I could see that she was tired, so I stood reluctantly. "I'll let you get your rest. It was nice talking to you, Lydia." The truth was, I felt worse than I had before, but I supposed it had been good to see her.

"Liar." She chuckled and accepted my extended arm, pulling herself to her feet, her other hand clutching her cane. "One more thing, Fee; You said that you 'got your powers from' me that night your mother was ailing?"

"Yeah," I said, puzzled. "What about it?"

"That's incorrect," Lydia said. "You already had the power. I believe that's why you were drawn to me; in your subconscious, even at such a young age, you recognized I was like you. You saw me doing a spell, and in a way, it activated your own powers. You started pooling yours with mine on instinct, through no intent of your own. It was all your magical self, your spirit self, tapping into your powers." She smiled. "I gave you nothing."

"Then where did it come from?" I asked. "Where does *your* magic come from? Why do some of us have powers and others, like Elvin, never do? Where did it all begin? Why is it I can bring someone back from the dead and someone like Benny can do the opposite?" I didn't want to say "kill someone" out loud, for some reason. Maybe it felt too real. "Is there any rhyme or reason to any of it?"

Lydia's laughter carried through the room. "That's an awful lot of questions, Fee, and I don't blame you for asking them, but I really am very tired." She gripped her cane and turned to the doorway. "I suggest you ask Benny. I'm sure he'll have some answers for you. I don't know him well, but I believe he's made a fairly extensive study of his own powers, and I'm sure he'll be glad to enlighten you."

"I will," I said, a little disappointed.

"I do hope Lee marries him," Lydia said, her haggard face

taking on a hopeful look. "Though I don't know how Lee will cope with a witch for a mother, a failed warlock for a father, and the most powerful one of all as his husband."

"He'll just have to learn to deal," I said. "Because Benny is perfect for him."

"I agree," Lydia said, and she gave me a little shove with her cane. "And Phillip Deville is perfect for you. Now get out of my house and go find him, Fee. Conflict is so very boring."

Sixteen

"Your phone's ringing," I said, unable to keep the sullen tone from my voice. Phillip looked at me for a moment, about to say something, then put it on silent.

He speared a piece of smoked cauliflower on his fork. He held it out to me, and I took it reluctantly. How did he instinctively know those were my favorite? Little things like that normally made me fall in love with him more, but I was so upset from the phone call I'd overheard earlier that it was hard to smile. "We're having dinner; I can call them back."

I leaned forward and let him feed me another bite of cauliflower. It was damn delicious, I had to begrudgingly admit. To my surprise, there had been bags of takeout on the kitchen table from a soul food and barbecue restaurant that boasted "alternative faire with a southern flair" right on the bags, waiting for me when I'd walked in from Lydia's. Phillip had ordered us dinner.

I dug into my vegan taco mac and brooded. As touched as I was, I was still mad at him.

"Something wrong?" Phillip asked finally, peering at me. Before I could shake my head no, his phone rang again.

I pushed it toward him. "They won't stop calling until you answer."

Phillip looked at me apologetically and hit the green button, holding the phone up to his ear. Even after all this time, he still held it slightly away from his head, as though he were one of those folks afraid of dangerous radiation or nanobots infiltrating his brain through his ears or something. "Phillip Deville here."

His face brightened at the voice on the other end of the line. "Oh, yes! Lee told me you were going to call. Sure, I can talk." I shook my head and shoveled in another bite of mac n cheese, then moved on to my tomato pie. Lee was really picking up steam as the Bloomer Demons agent. I wasn't surprised, and deep down, I was pleased that he was helping Phillip, but I hated how this train seemed to be barreling down the track so fast without me. I hadn't even brought that up to Lydia, though she probably would have told me to stop bitching and just be glad he had a job. For all her faults, one thing Lydia definitely was, was proud of her son.

"Well, I'm currently in Boston and I have another show tomorrow. But we could arrange for a shoot sometime … next week, maybe?" Phillip said. "I don't have a calendar in front of me; what would next Wednesday be? Would that be enough time to hit the Goth rock issue? You said you go to print in early May?" He nodded. "Do you do clothes and makeup, or do we need to bring our own provisions? You know what, scratch that—just give Lee a call and he'll sort all that out for us. He's got a better idea of everything we have going on, anyway. He's the one to handle it."

I put my container of food down on the table and scooted my chair back quietly, Phillip seeming not to notice as I left the room. I left most of my food uneaten and trudged back up the stairs to his bedroom. I sat on the bed for a few moments, hoping he'd immediately come up after me so we could hash this out—I hadn't told him about Colt Leather, after all—but he was still downstairs on the phone.

I pulled myself to the shower and turned on the water. As it was warming up, I decided if he wasn't upstairs by the time I was finished with my shower, I was leaving and driving back home to Brunswick. I wouldn't take off like a thief in the night this time, but I certainly wasn't going to stick around while he made all these huge life plans without even talking to me first. Sure, I could go to him, but … shouldn't he be coming to *me?* After all the lectures he'd given me about letting him in and keeping him in the loop. All those lectures about honesty.

Phillip Deville and the Bloomer Demons were in full fame mode again, well on their way to their big comeback, and I just knew he was going to leave me behind. And he didn't even have the decency to talk to me about it.

I stripped down and stepped into the shower, letting the too-hot spray run down my back, scalding me a little, feeling my muscles loosen their tension. I'd read once that women with anxiety tended to be more thrill-seeking when it came to pain—they liked scalding hot showers, tattoos, spicy foods—anything to give them a slight amount of pain and release endorphins to mimic that panic-mode they were so used to living in. I sighed. It was a generalizing, sexist stereotype, but it was probably true. I liked my showers hotter than the sun.

Still salty as hell at Phillip. I reached a little too aggressively for the shampoo bottle, knocking the shampoo, conditioner, and face wash off the ledge and onto the shower floor. "Goddamit!" I reached down to grab at the shampoo, trying not to slip and fall and break my neck in the process.

"Let me get that for you," a voice said behind me, and I jumped and almost slipped again. Strong arms caught me, wrapping around my waist and pulling me close. Phillip.

I started to ease myself back into him, to melt into his wet skin, then stopped. I was mad at him. I wasn't going to let him disarm me by being hot and sexy in the shower.

"I know you're mad at me," he said.

"Shouldn't take poking around in my head to figure that out," I said crossly.

He grabbed at my shoulders and turned me around to face him, reaching up to push my wet hair out of my eyes, caressing the droplets of water from my face. "I'm sorry," he said. "I don't have a bunch of stupid excuses to make or any dumb reasons to give you. I should have been checking with you about every single plan I've made, and I didn't, and I'm sorry."

I stared at him. "That's it?"

He nodded. "I know it's not good enough. It's just that ... well, I didn't expect Lee to go off and running quite so fast. He booked all these shows and promotional things so quickly that me, Jason, and Ollie were totally caught off guard. Hell, Benny's his boyfriend, and I don't think even he knew half the wheeling and dealing Lee managed to do until after the fact. But it's hard to turn it down. The money is really good and ..." He looked down for a moment, embarrassed. "None of us are spring chickens. It might be our last chance as a band."

"I'm sure that's not true," I said. He handed me the shampoo bottle, and I began to lather up my hair, still looking at him.

"It is, though," Phillip said. "You know what Lee said to me? He said, 'These days, thanks to social media, everyone's attention span is so short that all our fifteen minutes of fame are more like fifteen seconds.' He told me we should get while the getting's good because as soon as they get bored of my resurrection, everything will dry up."

I sighed, rinsing the lather out of my hair. Sometimes Lee annoyed me with how pragmatic and logical he was.

"Still," I said. "It would have been nice if you'd run all these plans by me before you'd just said yes. Because it does affect me, you know. If you're going to be gone touring all the time … and me just sitting back home …"

"No," Phillip said, taking my hands in his wet ones, holding them to his chest. "I have a plan for that. That is, if you're agreeable."

"What's that?"

"You're going to come with me on tour. You said the other day that you wanted to write. Why not start with a tour diary or blog or some type of column about being on the road with a touring band? It'll be a working trip for both of us, but the best part is, we'll be together." He pulled me close to him, pressing his wet mouth to my neck. "You'll be the groupie I take to my bed every single night." He placed another kiss near my collarbone. "What do you say? Will you come?"

"Yes, I will," I said, relaxing and letting him encircle me in his arms. I bit at his chest, enjoying the low moan that came from him, taking his hand and moving it downward. "Right now. You owe me, Deville. As for the tour, I'll let you know my answer later."

His eyes widened as realization dawned. "You dirty girl." He began to chuckle and grabbed at me roughly, pressing down on my mouth with his own. "I am 100 percent at your service."

Somewhere around the fifth or sixth ring, my phone woke me up from the deep sleep I'd finally been enjoying. I groaned, rolling over and feeling around under the pillow, producing the phone and almost dropping it before holding it up to my ear. I glanced at the time—4:50 in the morning. Someone had better be dead. Actually, scratch that; I hoped nobody was this time. I'd seen enough death.

"Hello?" I said into the phone, my voice little more than a croak. It had only been about an hour and a half since I'd managed to drift off into sleep. I was beginning to understand why they said that sleep deprivation is a form of torture.

"Stormy, it's Daddy."

I sat up in bed, leaning over to jostle Phillip awake. "What is it? What's happened? Is everyone okay? Shably or—"

"Calm down, calm down," he said on the other end of the line, his voice slurred. I sighed, though it wasn't in relief. My father was drunk. Drunk and calling me at five in the morning. So much for being on the straight and narrow. "Everyone's fine here. Well, relatively." The word "relatively" came out 'ruhltivey.'

"What is it, then?" I asked, trying to keep the anger from my voice and failing.

"You ran outta here the other night before I could tell you," he slurred, his voice pained. He sounded so far away. "And I can't stand it, Stormy. I can't stand no more secrets, you see? All the secrets is how we got into this mess. All the secrets is how come things have been bad for you."

"No shit," I said angrily. Phillip had switched on the bedside light and was looking at me curiously. "So what is it you need to tell me? Because it's five in the morning, and we're trying to sleep over here."

"Sorry, sorry," Daddy said. "I don't sleep much these days. Insomniac an' all. Sometimes I forget not everybody's up, pacing the halls."

So I came by that trait honestly, it seemed. "What is it?" I asked again.

"Tess," Daddy said, and my heart skipped a beat. "I know why he died. Why he was in the house."

"You do?" I asked. "I just assumed it was because of drugs; same shit, different day."

"It was because of drugs, sweet pea," Daddy said slowly. "But Tess wasn't the one with the problem."

"I don't get it."

He took a large, audible breath, and when he spoke, his words came out in a flood. "When I left your mama and moved down to Florida, I got clean. I stopped doing all that shit, stopped working with that asshole Elvin, got clean. On the straight and narrow. Stayed that way for years too," Daddy said, his Southern drawl thick with drink. "I stayed clean for a long-ass time. I wish you woulda come around more then, Stormy. You woulda been proud of me."

"Yeah, well." I sighed, the hand that held the phone up to my ear trembling a little.

"It was a good ten years at least that I stayed out of trouble. Made a good life down here. Put a little by, bought a house, turned the corner. So I thought. Till Elvin came calling again. He kept offering me more and more money. I kept sayin' no. He'd offer more, I'd still say no. Then he caught me on a bad day. Dee had overspent on some furniture, and I'd gambled a little too much that weekend, and we was a few hundred short on the mortgage. And Elvin just happened to call, and the job seemed pretty easy, so I took it."

"When was this?" I asked.

"Month or two ago," Daddy said. I heard the sound of a beer tab popping open. "And once I got back in, I couldn't get out. One day, I'm just mowing my lawn and be-bopping around my house, sober as a judge, and the next thing I know, I'm selling drugs out of the goddamn boot of my car and then Elvin starts asking questions. Questions I don't want to answer." He paused. "Questions about my daughter. About you."

"Like what?"

"Like when's the last time I seen you. How often do you come around. Who do you hang with. What kind of stuff are you into these days, where you work, where you hang out, stuff like that," Daddy answered. "I didn't like to answer him, so I dodged the questions, but he was getting real aggressive about it. Starting to scare me. I tried to call you, to warn you, but I couldn't never catch you at home. I tried Tess too, and he told me he hadn't talked to you in months. And then I found out he was working for Elvin and Guthrie too, and I regretted calling him."

"He went back to Elvin and snitched?" I guessed.

"No, but he would have, I reckon. If Guthrie hadn't up and died and then Elvin right after him," Daddy said. "Tess was so wrapped up in all that, more than I was, even. He was working with that joker Shank, who was downright *evil.*" He paused. "Shank's the one that burned down my house."

"How do you know?" I asked, though I'd guessed as much.

"Because Tess told me." I drew in my breath with a gasp, and Phillip stared at me from his side of the bed. I hadn't expected *that.* "He left me a voicemail. I didn't get it because I was on that fishing trip, and when I checked it later … well, it was there. I didn't tell the police."

"Why not?" I asked.

"Because it would have implicated him more, and I didn't want to do that. Not after what he sacrificed for me."

"What did he sacrifice?"

"Stormy, he tried calling me and left that voicemail and couldn't get through, so I reckon that's why he showed up here. He wanted to make sure me and Dee and the gal got out before the fire started. With Guthrie and Elvin gone, Shank had designs on trying to 'take over' what little of their business was left. He strong-armed Tess into joining him—Tess always was kinda weak, huh—and the first order of business was to shut up anybody that knew about the shit they were doing … and since I was on the payroll *and* connected to you, that made me enemy number one."

"So what you're saying, so I'm clear, is that Tess came to warn you? And that's why he died?"

Daddy's voice was full of tears. "I think so, sweet pea. I really do. I believe Tess was here to warn me, and either Shank happened on him or followed him or something, and he started that fire when Tess was still inside the house. I think he was like a sitting duck, and Shank disposed of him like he wasn't nothing. And then he went up to Boston to try and do the same to you." He gave a ragged sigh. "I dunno what happened to make y'alls marriage go bust, but Tess loved you, Stormy. He wasn't too good at showing it, but he did."

I swallowed the lump in my throat. "Daddy, does the name Colt Leather mean anything to you?"

To my shock, he replied, "That greasy-haired singer? Yeah, I met him once or twice."

"When?"

"He was part of that group. Elvin and Shank and Tess and all of 'em. Caught up in the same shit as the rest of us." He hiccupped. "Stay away from that fella; he's bad news. He ain't like Phillip, Stormy."

"Preachin' to the choir, Daddy."

"He's trouble," he said as though he hadn't heard me.

I was silent. So it *was* likely that Colt Leather had been there the night Tess died. Shank had been telling the truth.

Daddy went on. "I was so glad when your mama called me and told me y'all were okay after that concert. I been following Bloomer Demons on the computer a little—Dee showed me how—and when I heard about that bomb, I knew it was Shank. I just knew. I was so worried." He dissolved into sobs.

It was eerie, hearing my father cry. But I found I could shed no tears of my own. I was all dry, at least for now. What he said tracked, though. I could believe that Tess would do that for my father. He had been a coward, and a little bit simple on occasion, but Tess had not truly been an evil person. He was just another kid who'd grown up on the wrong side of the tracks with hurts to nurse, easily led by those who intended to exploit his pain and ignorance for their own purposes. And it had caused not only our divorce but his death.

I sighed, not sure what to say. Phillip was a silent but comforting presence beside me. "Daddy," I said quietly, swallowing hard. "Why didn't you ever tell me I had a brother? Why didn't you ever tell me about Nikolai?"

"I did," he said, his voice still logged with tears, so slurred I almost couldn't understand him. "Didn't I? Surely I did at some point or 'nother."

"No," I said evenly, gripping the phone. "Never once, in my entire life, did you tell me that you had a son. That I had a brother. Why?"

"Aw, shoot, sweet pea," Daddy said, his voice almost a whine. "I guess I meant to. I just … didn't get around to it. It was weird times back then. Your mama didn't like me to mention it, you understand. Anyhow, it don't matter now, does it? You're both grown. Call him up if you want. I ain't gonna stop you."

"No," I said, surprisingly calm. "I don't suppose you will." I started to hang up the phone, then thought better of it. "There's something you can do for me now, if you care to. It won't make up for everything, but it would … it would mean something to me."

"What is it?" he asked, his voice a little wary.

"Send me that voicemail from Tess," I said, my voice cracking. "I'd like to hear it."

"Hey, Chad … long time no talk. I hope you doin' okay. Listen, uh, I don't quite know how to say this, and you're gonna think

I'm crazy but ... I thought about callin' Stormy, but she and I ain't exactly on speaking terms and I can't say I blame her. But look. Listen, Chad...whatever dealings you had with Guthrie and Elvin, you might want to clean it up. Just in case. Shank's talking about getting the business back up and running. And he ain't looking to put you on the payroll, if you catch my drift. So just, uh ... just watch your back. I always liked you and Laureen. I know Stormy has her differences with y'all, but you're still her folks, and I care about what happens to you. If Shank turns up in Florida, you run as far as you can. I'm keeping my eye on him, but he's wily as all get out. Right when you think the bad guys are gone, another one takes their place out here in the real world. Just be careful, Chad, okay? Anyway, talk to you later, bye."

SEVENTEEN

"Talk to me about the magic."

Benny cocked an eyebrow and sat his can of Jack and Coke down on the table. I'd brought a four pack of the pre-made cocktails to his motel room in the hopes of bribing him. Lee and Phillip were back at Jason's house, having a meeting to discuss the tour, so it was the perfect time to get Benny alone. "That's a tall order. What do you want to know?"

"Everything," I said. "I asked Lydia, but she was, as usual, cagey as all get out. I know nothing, Benny. Can you please tell me like, the basics? Anything?"

"Witchcraft for Dummies?" He laughed.

"You're joking, but yes. That. Anything." I swallowed. "I'm desperate. I can't have this power in me, feeling it bubble up in my hands, knowing it's running through my blood, without understanding it. Without knowing how to use it or why I have it. What my limits are. I don't know *anything*, Benny."

He cocked an eyebrow.

"What I did to Shank … okay, I know he deserved it, but … I didn't *mean* to do what I did. Someone is *dead* because I couldn't control my magic, Benny. I need to know how to control it. Before someone else dies," I pleaded, my desperation evident in my voice.

"Okay, okay," Benny replied. "I don't know everything myself, though. My own knowledge is limited so all I can do is tell you what I've learned."

"Lydia said you'd done research."

Benny laughed. "That part is true. I checked out actual books from the library. I took notes. What a nerd, huh?"

"Tell me what you knooooooooooow," I said in a silly voice, slapping my hands on the table. "Fuck, read me the notes verbatim, I don't care. Just talk magic to me, Benny and the Jets."

"Where do you want me to start?" Benny asked with a grin.

"At the beginning," I said, "When you first got *your* powers."

"Well, that's difficult to say," Benny said, taking a guzzle of his Jack and Coke. "Because I've had them as far back as I remember. I wish could tell you I know how it happened or why, but I don't. I do have theories, but." He looked thoughtfully at his can, turning it over and over in his hands. "I guess I first noticed there was something about me that was different when I was five or so. I don't remember much before that age, so maybe I'd noticed things before, but that's when I really remember starting to think, 'hey, something's not right.' That's when things started to happen."

"Like what?"

"Well, the first thing I remember was realizing that not everyone could hear thoughts like I could." He frowned. "I just automatically knew when someone was sad, for instance, or I knew what my mama was going to cook for dinner that night without her having to say. I knew when my folks were fighting, even if they went in the other room and shut the door so I couldn't hear them. I just assumed everyone had that power, and when I realized they didn't, it kind of freaked me out. I thought there was something wrong with me." He took another small sip. "And then I realized something else. Not only could I hear, or read, however you want to say it, people's thoughts, but ... I could suggest things to them and they'd think they thought of it."

"What? Are you serious?"

"Yes." He looked at me. "Can't you do that?"

"I don't think so. Have you ... ever done that with any of us?" I asked. "With me?"

Benny shook his head. "No. I resolved years ago—after causing plenty of trouble for myself and others, believe me—that I wouldn't do that sort of thing anymore."

"So what kind of things could you make people do then?"

"I couldn't really *make* people do things ... just ... plant a suggestion. The person would assume they'd thought of it themselves, but often people talk themselves out of things, or don't even give conscious attention to their thoughts. So even if I planted an idea, there was no guarantee the person would put the idea into action." He sat back. "I did have some success though."

"Examples?"

Benny grinned. "Let's just say back in my younger days when I was first starting out as a pro-wrestler, I may have talked a few of my opponents into giving less than their best."

"Oh my god, you cheater." I laughed. "Is that how you managed to beat guys three times your size when you were like twelve years old? Is that how you beat A.J. Floyd that time?"

Benny grinned at me, eyes widening in surprise. "How do you know about that match?"

"I was there," I said proudly, beaming. "My dad took me to a lot of matches at the flea market when I was a kid, and I saw you wrestle quite a few times. That night was particularly memorable because …" I paused, then went on. "Because that was the night I met Nikolai. He's my brother, you know." I looked at him to gauge his reaction.

"I know," he said, to my shock. "He told me a while back, around the first time I met you."

"He did?

"Your dad has been on our radar at the Wolfden for a while because of his associations with Elvin and Guthrie," Benny answered. "When you turned up with Roberta, Nikolai thought I should know who you were, just in case."

"I guess that makes sense," I said, a little deflated that he hadn't told me first, but I understood why he'd sat on that info. How on earth would I have reacted if he'd told me that first night out by the bonfire when I was already so freaked that he was my long-lost brother? I probably would have run screaming for the hills, or punched him in the face.

"I can totally see it," Benny said, looking at me. "That you two are siblings. You both have the same strong, quiet way of just getting on with things, of handling business, but it also gets you in trouble. You're so used to being self-sufficient and let down by people that you end up pushing people away."

"Thank you, Dr. Freud," I said with a giggle, but inside, I felt hurt. Though he was right, of course.

"You also have the same cheekbones," he said with a chuckle of his own, and I instinctively raised a hand to my cheek. "I'm glad you know now," he said softly, reaching across the little table to pat me on the shoulder. "Now you two can build a relationship." He sighed, then gestured for the whiskey. "I wish I had siblings—or any other kind of family— to fall back on."

"Are they all …" I trailed off.

"My mom is dead, Dad is in jail," Benny said matter-of-factly, twirling his can. "He went in when I was thirteen, right around the time I started wrestling, on a trumped-up, bullshit charge, and right around the time I started realizing I could use my powers for certain things." Benny smiled grimily. "My mom never let me visit him or write too many letters to him before he died. She knew Dad was framed, but her culture is very conservative, and she didn't want to be, I don't know, tainted by association." He frowned. "Then she died when I was fifteen."

"Oh," I said, curious. "I'm sorry about your mom. And you don't have any siblings or grandparents or anything?"

"None to speak of," he answered. "My grandfather in New Mexico lives on the reservation. I've never even been there, never met the man. With my father being in jail, I guess that'll never happen now unless I reach out. My maternal grand-mother moved back to China after my grandfather—he was American—died. This was in the late seventies, before I was even born. My mother told me stories about them both, but I've never met them." He drained the Jack and Coke and set it back on the table. "I've pretty much been raising myself since I was an adolescent, and I got used to being alone. But don't feel sorry for me … I have a family. The Wolfden is my family."

"I didn't know you were Native," I said, surprised. "Or Chinese, for that matter."

Benny smiled. "You can't tell by looking at me?"

"I can now," I admitted, giving his dark brown eyes and sharp features an appraising glance. I'd always thought Benny made a handsome and imposing figure, but he did even more so now that he'd opened up to me and I knew him better.

"I hope you don't mind …" I said, smiling shyly. "I'm kind of starting to see the Wolfden as my family too. Well, except for Clara."

"The Wolfden *is* your family. In every sense of the word." Then he grinned. "And just ignore Clara. She'll come around eventually."

I wasn't so sure about that. Not to mention, I wasn't sure I wanted to be close with her. "Far be it for me to give you advice, but ..." I said tentatively. "You should consider reaching out to your remaining grandparents. Especially the one here in the States. What if you inherited your magic from one of them? What if they can help you learn to navigate it?"

"I've thought of that," Benny said. "I've also thought of the alternative, that he'll know the kinds of powers I have, the things I can do, and tell me to take my evil ass away from there."

"But it's your family," I pressed. "Aren't you curious?"

"Maybe one day," Benny said in a voice that made it clear he was finished talking about that subject.

"So tell me more about the magic," I said, content to let it drop, even though I was dying to hear more about Benny's childhood, his dad's arrest, and his grandparents. I hated when people pried in my life too. Family shit was so complicated.

"I just started ... I don't know ... figuring out how to use it," Benny said. "To wield it? Is that the word? I don't know how to explain it. All I know is that I always sort of felt like I was different, like I had different experiences than others. Part of that was growing up as a mixed-race kid in the South, but it was more than that. And as things started to go sour at home, I felt that power rushing through me more and more. It's like ... when I was stressed or upset about my dad, or when my mom started to get sick, I could feel it, just running through my fingers, like it was just lying there dormant, waiting for me."

"I've felt that too," I said softly.

He nodded. "And as I got older, I started to kinda ... push it forward. One day, it occurred to me that I could splay out my hands, and I just sort of ... pushed ... and it was like, zap! Next thing I knew, I'd pushed my friend Jeremy into the wall without ever touching him. I practiced, and I figured out other things I could do. I realized I could do that 'zap' thing and knock somebody out cold. I'm not saying I'm proud of it, but I did that more than once. It came in handy when I was being bullied in sixth grade."

"And then you used it in wrestling matches?"

"Yes, but more subtly. I mainly stuck to the power of suggestion with the matches; I didn't out and out cheat. I never knocked anybody out in the ring, but I do confess to using a little light zapping to shove someone off me when they had me in a headlock." He grinned. "I'm not ashamed to admit that I used my powers to my advantage. Being that young, on my own, trying to make my way doing the amateur wrestling circuit in South Georgia ... Well, let's just say the odds were stacked against me and then some. My powers enabled me to make a living when I needed a roof over my head and food to eat. I don't regret it."

"I wouldn't, either."

"So yeah, that's pretty much it ... for a while. I wrestled all through my teen years. Crashed on a few couches at first, then saved up enough to rent a trailer of my own and buy a car when I was sixteen. I met Clara around that time, and she and I teamed up and did a few co-ed tag team matches." He looked at me with an embarrassed smile. "You said you saw me wrestle a bunch. Did you ever see us together?"

"No," I admitted. "Though I wish I had. That sounds awesome."

"It was." He grinned. "I had an unfair advantage, but Clara was just a badass. When I met her, she was already all muscle, just stacked. All that blonde hair, and she wore it in this messy bun on top of her head, and she wore purple glittery eyeliner that matched the purple lipstick she always wore. It sounds tacky, but she made it work. She was sexy, tough as shit, and it was perfect. The crowd always ate her up. She was pretending to be twenty years old when she was only seventeen, so half the guys screaming for her didn't realize they were lusting after jailbait." He laughed. "She and I were already an item then, though, so I wouldn't have let anything happen to her. Not that I would've needed to intervene. She could kick asses better than I could."

"So what happened between the two of you?"

"Well," he said, shifting uncomfortably in his chair. "Two things happened, actually. One of them has to do with the magic, and the other …as you might've guessed, has to do with Lee." He gestured at me. "Get up."

I got up from the table, and Benny stood up too, coming to stand directly facing me, only about a yard away in the small motel room. He held out his arms and gestured for me to do the same. "Zap me," he said.

"No," I said automatically, clenching my fingers into involuntary fists, holding them to my chest. "I don't want to do that."

"You won't hurt me, I promise," Benny said with a smile. "Scout's honor. Just a small zap."

"But …"

"Go ahead." He grinned. "You know you want to flex the old muscles."

I sighed, fully aware that it was somewhat theatrical, because he was right—suddenly I *did* want to. I splayed out my fingers, stretching them, enjoying the buzzing feeling as I moved my hands. I was still getting used to that odd electric sensation that always happened when I moved my fingers; it was a pleasant thrum, not unlike how I imagined electricity running through wires might feel like, if one were the wire. It was hard to explain, but Benny knew what I was feeling, which explained the wide smile on his face as he watched me prepare and stall for time. I shook my hands once, twice, then bent my arms at the elbow and back out again, extending my fingers to their full length as I did, and before I had a chance to rethink and stop myself, I shot out as much power from them as I could, directly in Benny's direction.

I could also *see* it in my mind's eye. I could visualize a glowing, blue-green ball of light hurl through the air directly toward Benny's chest. Time seemed to stop for a moment as I watched it barrel forward, heading right for his heart, and my breath caught in my throat. My fingers were stretched out still, my arms cast forward, and I desperately scratched at the air, as if I could take back what I'd already unleashed.

The air seemed to crackle between us, the atoms floating there seeming to pop and jump.

Then, in less than seconds, Benny reached out and grabbed at the air, his fist closing around nothing, and with a mischievous look, he hurled his hand forward, unfurling his fist, and shot it back toward me.

I had only a split second to think before I reached out and grabbed, somehow knowing on instinct what to do, where to grasp. My eyes widened as my hand curled around what felt like pure light —the same feeling I so often felt in my fingers and other limbs, concentrated and in my palm. I opened my hand and saw nothing. My hand seemed a little illuminated, as though I were standing in a beam of sunshine, but that was all. And yet the feeling of fullness, of light, of *pure power* was undeniable. I stared down at my hand, shocked.

"Didn't know you could do that, did you?"

"How did you … how did I … did we just play a game of catch with a ball of electricity?" I asked.

"Close your hand," Benny said, ignoring my question. "Just … close your fingers and sort of hold it there."

I did what I was told, closing my fingers slowly, one by one, into a gentle fist. As my hand came to settle, I felt the odd sensation of electricity seeping into my skin through my palm, tickling, buzzing, like touching the world's gentlest electric fence. And then the sensation was gone.

"What the fuck."

"That skill will come in handy," Benny said. "To protect you from others and to protect others from *you.*"

"What do you mean?"

His soft brown eyes met mine. "Sometimes you'll find yourself unable to control the power. It wants to come through you, to use you as a conduit. It seeks its target. But if you learn to master it, you can tame those urges into submission." He reached forward and thumped my hand. "And you can use it to thwart attacks from others too, like I just did."

"You're teaching me magical self-defense," I said, rolling my eyes. "This is too much." Deep down, though, my stomach was rolling. I wished I'd known this when I'd zapped Shank and got Phillip's entire show blown up. Someone was dead because of me.

"He was also a total asshole who was determined to blow that place up long before you ever zapped him," Benny said quietly.

"Hey!" I looked at him in surprise. "Did you—"

"Sorry," he said with a sheepish smile. "Sometimes when I get to playing around with the magic, it's like … the veil slips and I forget to stop listening." He cuffed my shoulder. "You should know by now that people—well, the ones like us—can read your thoughts. And you can read ours, if you want to." I didn't have time to digest that before he continued. "But honestly, Stormy, I already figured. We all did, actually. And nobody judges you; we're all grateful that you were there, trying to protect us."

"I'm not sure Phillip will see it that way," I said sullenly. I hadn't had a chance to really talk to Phillip about what had happened at the show, or Colt's death specifically. We'd been too busy focusing on the next show and the tour. Though that was only partially true, if I admitted it to myself. I'd been avoiding the topic, and Phillip had been letting me.

"Of course he will," Benny said. "He already does. Like I said, we can't help but see some of what's in your head. Phillip already knows what happened in that venue, Stormy. Why do you think he was so quick to talk to the cops and get everything cleared up? To protect you." He squeezed my shoulder. "You should have seen him when you were out. He was running around, frantic, desperate for me to make you better. He didn't give two shits about his show, or Shank, or anything other than making sure you were safe and okay."

"I have a habit of ruining things for him," I said dejectedly. "For both of us."

"I don't like this on you," Benny said, his voice turning a bit sassy. "It's not a good look, simpering wimp feeling sorry for herself. Bitch, you're a badass witch. You're the girlfriend of a legit fuckin' rock star. And most importantly, you're the newest member of the Wolfden, which means you're my family, and I don't let nobody talk shit about my family. Got it?"

I couldn't help but grin. "Got it."

"Daps." He reached out his fist. When I bumped it with my own, a spark of electricity jolted me, and I jumped backward, watching as a bright blue spark fell from Benny's hand to the ground.

"I have a few more tricks that you don't," Benny said with a laugh. "But that's only because you haven't practiced. You can do anything I can ... if you just hone in on your abilities."

"I can't kill people," I said pointedly, and he cocked his eyebrow again.

"Yes, you can," he said. "If you want to."

I looked at him in horror. "No, I can't. At least not on purpose. You kill people ... I bring them back."

Benny shrugged. "If you say so. Let's just say our talents ... and our desires ... are different."

"Okay," I said, not ready to pull at that thread any longer.

"But it's driving me nuts, Benny, not knowing the origin of this magic, what it means, why I have it. I need answers. I hear you have notes too. I'd love to see them."

"I'll happily show you the notes, but … I think you'll find it has a lot more questions than answers."

"Lydia said you'd done all this research."

"I did," he answered. "And pretty much all I found is that there's no real rhyme or reason to any of it." He sighed. "One thing that seems to be a common denominator in the people like us that I've met —and there aren't as many as you think— is that we all suffered some form of neglect or trauma as children. Most of us are just the smart, hurt kids who learned how to dissociate. You know, I really believe that all humans have the powers we have, it's just that the majority of them never learned, or maybe they knew as babies but forgot as they grew up, how to harness that power. It's like toning a muscle you're not used to using. Somehow, some of us kids learned how to tap into those powers as a way to self-protect."

"I can sort of see that with the 'parlor tricks,' as Lydia calls them," I said thoughtfully, taking a sip of my own drink. "But raising the fucking dead? Having the power to kill someone with your bare hands? Being able to prolong someone's life? Benny, that's serious magic. That's not easy magic like moving a pencil across the room or reading someone's thoughts. There has to be something more behind those abilities." I met his dark brown eyes and shook my head. "For god's sake, I recited a spell on the back of an album and reanimated someone who had been dead for over two decades, summoned him to my house, and now he's alive and can read my mind. You can't say that's just some self-care basic witch shit that I created to cope with my trauma. I can't believe that."

"Well, but in your case," Benny argued, "you were influenced by Lydia at a very young age. You witnessed her, a very powerful witch, using her power to bring your mother back.

You joined in, so to speak, and I think that activated something dormant in you. And then, when Elvin started putting you under hypnosis, having you try out different types of small magic ... I think it flexed your powers, gave you a workout, so to speak. Your powers grew and grew, out of both necessity and practice. So by the time you recited that spell, you were primed." He looked at me with sadness. "And he indoctrinated all the kids at the trailer park—Burt, Jamie, Nikolai—with the same powers. They gained their abilities because of their proximity to *you.*"

I frowned. "I'm not sure I like the sound of that. I'm their witch mother, basically? And Lydia and Elvin are their witchy grandparents?"

Benny laughed. "In a nutshell, yes."

"And you? How did you get 'primed'? I'd argue that you're far more powerful than me. This isn't Harry Potter; most people can't wave a wand and kill somebody with their mind."

"I flexed my muscles too," Benny said quietly. "I told you my home life was pretty bad when I was a kid. I've spared you details, but let's just say that I was stuck by myself a lot with nothing but time on my hands to figure out my powers. And remember, I met Elvin as a kid too." He grimaced. "I was a bit older than you, but he was every bit as predatory, believe me."

I wanted to ask further, but something in his expression shut me down. "But ... necromancy?"

"I seem to remember the phrase 'it's all about intention' swirling around that noggin of yours a lot when we first met," Benny said with a small smile. "As Lydia will no doubt have told you, a huge portion of your magic really *is* about how you intend to use it. There are limits, of course, but you're the weaver, the wielder. If you write the spell—whether that's literally with quill and ink, or just in your own mind—you can make that spell a reality. You were able to bring Phillip back because you *wanted to.*"

"Lee is … like Phillip," I said, and he nodded.

"I know. He doesn't like to talk about it a lot. It bothers him," Benny said. "I think it's a reminder that his parents were always trying to fix something they'd already broken rather than not breaking it in the first place."

I nodded. I could understand that. The truth was, I'd been dying to hear the details of Lee being brought back ever since Lydia had first told me, but I was afraid to ask. Something in Lee seemed so delicate, so afraid of the truth. And part of me was afraid too. Whatever I learned about Lee might also apply to Phillip. It was a power so big I was afraid to confront it. "Do you think it was easy for me to bring Phillip back because I'd already interacted with someone who had that ability?" I asked, and Benny nodded.

"There's some type of, I don't know, string of fate, that ties the four of you. You had this connection with Lydia, and years later, Guthrie had one with Phillip. Roberta thinks Guthrie and Elvin orchestrated a lot of that, that it wasn't coincidence. I wasn't there so I can't say, but whatever tether you have to this group of people, it's very strong."

"Don't I know it," I said glumly. "Still … I'm not satisfied with this. It's too much of a coincidence for all of us, who just so happen to have grown up within a few miles of each other in South Georgia, to have these powers. That we'd all find each other again as adults. I know what you're going to say— that we all seek each other out subconsciously or something — but no. There's more to it than that."

"I don't disagree. But I've never been able to find out what that link is," Benny admitted, his face regretful.

"So that's it, then? There's no history or lore I can pour over to learn about who I am? No more information? Just … nothing?"

Benny reached into his suitcase and pulled out a spiral bound notebook. "Take it with you. I've written things down over the years, stuff I've studied about magic, about witchcraft and the occult. You might find it helpful. But yeah, that's it, as far as I know. We're just blessed, or cursed, however you want to look at it, with these powers. We've cultivated them with our own minds, and now we are who we are."

We sat in silence for a few moments, me holding the notebook, my hands lingering over the pages, wanting to look. I'd wait until I was alone when I could really delve into it. I was hopeful that, despite what Benny said, I'd get some answers. Something I could hold onto, even if it was a flimsy explanation. I decided to change the subject.

"So … I can't help but notice that you dodged my question earlier. What happened with you and Clara?"

"I didn't dodge it," Benny answered. "I showed you how to manage your magic to illustrate a point. There was one time when I didn't know I could do that. Well, to be honest, I knew I could, but I chose not to put it in practice. I liked winning matches, you see. I really liked it. I make good money as a wrestler, and being the heavyweight champion or whatever, it was a boost to the ego that I had a hard time letting go of." He sighed. "The ironic thing is, I know now that I could have beaten any of those guys on my own steam without using magic at all, and I have. But back then, just a couple years ago even, I was scared of letting go of control. Scared not to use my power."

"What happened?"

"Clara and I had a tag-team match with this husband-and-wife duo—you ever heard of the Brunswick Bulldawg and Lady Tela?"

"I can't say I have." I suppressed a snort. "That's quite a … quite a pair of names."

"Yeah, it's bad," Benny said, but his face was dark. "I

hated that guy. His real name was Lance, and I'd been seeing him on the circuit for years. You make a living in a small town in a niche like wrestling and you get to know guys. Y'all are sharing a dressing room, or sometimes just a small, dirty-ass bathroom with these guys. Working small venues like clubs, flea markets, outdoor festivals … you get to know a person. And I knew Lance. More than I cared to." His face bore a grim expression. "He was a bully. Racist as fuck. Mean as a snake. Not just in the ring, either."

"Oh," I said quietly, understanding. "That sucks."

"You can imagine I was gunning for him, solely based on that," Benny said. "One night a couple years ago, we were all at a cookout after one of the weekly matches, and we'd all been drinking a lot. Bathroom was occupied, so I walked around back of my buddy's house to take a whiz, and I happened upon Lance and Tela fighting. I rounded the corner just in time to see him clock her right in the nose. I ran up on him, ready to tear the bastard limb from limb, but a couple of my buddies pulled me back. They kicked Lance out of the cookout, but they didn't do anything to him, and of course Tela got right in the car with him. I was so fucking pissed. Nobody held him accountable, nobody did anything. They held *me* back so I wouldn't do anything." He shook his head. "I came so close to zapping them all that night. Anyway, I'd been seeing him bully younger and smaller wrestlers for years, so when he punched Tela, that was it for me. I decided I was going to whoop his ass into next week. Fuck the match, I didn't even care if I won. I just wanted to get my hands on that son of a bitch."

"I can imagine."

"I didn't tell Clara that I was planning to go all in on Lance. For all she knew, I'd let the whole thing go and this was just a normal match. We had everything scripted out, planned —you know how wrestling goes. The moves are somewhat choreographed, and while there's a little room to improvise here and there, it's largely drafted ahead of time."

"Including the outcome of the match?" I asked.

"Sometimes," he replied. "Depends on the venue, on the event. That particular match, there was no clear-cut winner. We had a timeframe, a general script to follow, and a few moves we were expected to do, but the end moves were ours. I planned to win that night," Benny said. "Not just win, I wanted to *kill* the motherfucker."

"I can imagine what happened," I said. "You went in there and zapped him, didn't you?"

"Yes ... and no," Benny said. He paused, sighing. "This part doesn't really put me in a good light. Just so you know."

"Noted," I said, but I was excited to hear the rest. Benny was good as gold in my eyes, and I welcomed anything that made him seem human, warts and all, like the rest of us.

"I didn't zap him in the ring. The truth is, we didn't even get to the ring. The match never even happened. Turns out, I couldn't keep my anger in check long enough to get to the match ... It all went down before that. In the dressing room."

"What happened?"

"We were due to shoot one of those promos, you know, where one wrestler is giving an 'interview' in the locker room, and the next thing you know, the heel runs in and interrupts to talk shit? A fight breaks out?" He grinned. "Surely you've seen those."

"Yeah, like a little teaser to get you pumped for the match," I said, remembering back to my childhood and the countless locker room brawls I'd seen between "The Nature Boy" Ric Flair and Macho Man Randy Savage or Bret the Hitman Hart. "Those were always the best parts. These two beefcakes yelling at each other and pointing fingers and some nerdy looking interviewer standing in the background sweating."

"Fun to film too," Benny said, grinning wider. "I always

wanted to sign with one of the big dogs like WWF or WCW and get a chance to do that on a larger scale. That'd be a blast. But I've never left the amateurs." He shook his head. "Anyway. So we were set to film one of those promos, and I was running late because I'd had car trouble. Clara and Lance were already there, and I was rushing to get to them so they wouldn't have to wait. I'm throwing on my makeup as I'm running down the hall of this—well, basically it was a glorified gym, nothing fancy—and I can hear them talking in the locker room. I round the corner and go in, expecting to find the camera crew all set up and them waiting for me, pissed. But instead, I find the camera crew is nowhere to be seen, and Lance has taken the moment alone with Clara as an opportunity to pin her to the corner and grope her."

"Oh no."

"Clara can handle herself just fine with most everybody; she's tough as nails and she can win matches with guys three times her size. But I guess Lance caught her at a bad moment or something, or maybe it was the way he had her pinned, with one of his legs in between hers, kind of skewering her back into the corner … She was trapped. She was pleading with him to just let her go, that people would be here any minute, that she'd get him fired. But he didn't care. As I'm rushing over, I hear him go, 'Nobody would believe you since you've slept with half the crew anyway.'" He grimaced. "You can imagine what happened next. I pulled him off her and wailed on him. Something just came over me, and I was dealing punches— Clara got a few in herself too—and by the time we were done with him, Lance was in a heap on the floor, curled in the fetal position, trying to shield his head. Blood pouring out of his nose, just a really bad scene."

"Can hardly blame you for it," I said. "I mean, he was about to assault her. He *did* assault her."

"If I'd left it at that, yes. But I didn't leave it at that." He shrugged. "I felt that surge, like I just showed you. I could feel it building in my hands, growing and growing and becoming this, like … this *thing*. Like my anger and rage was all transferring to this power that I held in my hands, this tangible thing I could touch and feel and *use*. I knew it was wrong, even as I felt it. Looking down, I could see that Lance was barely conscious at it was; I'd already hurt him pretty damn bad. He'd likely get fired for assaulting Clara, and he was fucked in more ways than one. There was no reason or need to do anything else, but … I was still angry. And even though I knew by then that I could control the power I held in my hands … I … I didn't want to." His voice had gone quiet as he looked at me, his dark eyes glowing with fire. "The thought just went through my head, very briefly, almost casually—'I could kill you.' I didn't even say it out loud. It was so fleeting. And I just … without even thinking, I looked down at Lance, crumpled in that ball by my feet, and I aimed and shot everything I had in my hands—all that anger and rage and power—into him."

"And what happened?"

"You know the answer already, don't you?" Benny asked, then didn't wait for my answer. "What happened next is that Lance died."

He went on, ignoring my wide-eyes and gaping mouth. "His arms that had been guarding his head sort of went lax, and he was very still. Clara was staring at me in shock, and I asked her if she was okay. She didn't answer or nod or anything; she just kept staring at me like she'd never seen me before. So I reached down and put a hand under Lance's nose to feel for breath. My hand was shaking so bad that I accidentally brushed his face and got blood all over my hands. There was no breath. He was dead. I'd killed him." As his fingers resumed nervously brushing the rim of his can, I could see that they were trembling. "I don't know how … or why, even … I did it, but I did. I'd killed him instantly with nothing but my magic, and I hadn't even been really *directing* it. All I had thought, absently, was, 'I could kill you,' and that's all it took."

"How did Clara react?"

"I had to shake her a little to get her to help me to um ... to hide the body," Benny said. "In hindsight, I wish I hadn't involved her because it really took a toll on her. It fucked up our relationship, our friendship, all of it. It's never been the same. But at the time, I was so panicked, and I didn't want anyone to find Lance there. It wasn't like I could explain that I'd accidentally zapped him to death. People would see his bloody nose and assume we'd beaten him to death, and that meant we'd both go to jail. I had to get rid of the body, and quick."

"Oh, Benny." My shoulders tensed. This was heavy. "What did you guys, um ... what did you do?"

"We found a spot," he said quietly. It appeared he still wanted to keep a secret or two, and I couldn't blame him. "We made quick work of it, and when it was done, Clara was crying silently. She still hadn't said anything, but the tears on her cheeks said it all." His face was dark. "She knew I'd done it for her, but the fact that I'd killed someone, and the shock of seeing my powers without knowing about them ... I guess she'd maybe suspected that something was weird at the matches, why I was so much more powerful, but she didn't know outright, and I think seeing it scared the shit out of her. It was all too much. When she finally spoke, it was to break up with me.

"We had a big fight. She accused me of keeping secrets from her, said that she couldn't trust me now or even feel safe around me because I'd concealed who I really was from her, the powers that I had. She wasn't wrong; it wasn't something I could argue with. But I was desperate not to lose her. And truth be told, I was a little afraid she was going to turn on me and go to the cops, which is really unfair because she's always been loyal. So I said a few things I'm not proud of. I accused her of cheating on me, of leaving me to be with someone else. I threw what I'd heard Lance say about sleeping with half the crew in her face." He looked ashamed. "But she was able to easily counter that accusation. Since I'd been unfaithful to her too. An affair I thought I'd been discreet about, but it turns out she'd known about it for months."

"Lee?"

Benny nodded. "Yes. Lee." I couldn't help but smile, seeing how Benny's face began to glow at the mention of Lee, even when talking about such a difficult subject. "We'd met a few months before, and one thing had just led to another ... I was already head over heels in love with him, and we were stealing away to see each other every second we could. Lee wasn't out yet, and it didn't bother me that much back then because I had Clara. I was having my cake and eating it too. Stupidly—arrogantly—I thought Clara had no idea, that I was getting away with it. But she knew. She knew, and she was really torn up about it. She'd started taking pills to cope with her depression. Truth was she'd just been waiting for the right time to confront me and give me an ultimatum. Before Lance's death, she'd been planning on forgiving me, giving me another chance, if I'd finally agree to marry her and leave Lee for good. But after she saw me kill somebody with my bare hands, I guess she realized that wasn't what she wanted. And she just sunk deeper and deeper." Benny smiled sadly. "The ironic thing is that I would have agreed to leave Lee and marry her, just for the security of knowing she'd be loyal to me, that she wouldn't turn me in. I was so shellshocked, so ashamed of what I'd done. But Clara was finished with me by then. It turned out to be a blessing in disguise, in that regard, though I still feel responsible for her addiction."

"God, that's a lot to happen at one time," I mused. "Your

girlfriend is assaulted, you accidentally kill the perpetrator, and then you both admit to cheating on the other and break up. *Damn*, Benny. I don't even know what to say."

"My life has always been one drama after another." He grinned, picking up his empty can and raising it in a gesture of salute. "A feeling that I think you might unfortunately be all too familiar with. You got another one of these bad boys?"

"If that isn't the fucking truth," I agreed, passing him a cold can.

"Things are okay with Clara and me now," Benny said, popping open the tab. "But only okay. We have a begrudging kind of peace between us. And she says she's clean now. We stay out of each other's way. I like having her at the Wolfden. She's strong and tough, and yes, loyal. But she hates Lee. I don't think that will ever change. And she doesn't trust me anymore, not like she did. She loves me, I guess, or the idea of me, but sometimes she looks at me like … like she expects me to sprout horns and a barbed tail."

"She accused me of working for the people who kidnapped you," I said.

"She did?" Benny looked surprised.

"Yeah. After Elvin and Sloan kidnapped you off the porch after you got shot," I explained. "Phillip and I jumped in the car to follow and get you back. But before I left, she stopped me. She accused me of being a plant, of working with them to try and hurt you. I assured her that I only wanted what was best for all of us, but I don't think she really believed me. I'm surprised she came to Boston for the show, honestly. Whatever her reasons, it wasn't for Phillip and me."

"No," Benny agreed, nodding. "But that doesn't mean she's a bad person, Stormy. I hope she'll come around, and you'll see that for yourself. Clara's tough, and a good ally to have on your side. But I've caused her a lot of pain, and that takes some time to get over. You know?"

"I do," I said. I'd felt the same way about Tess ever since our divorce. Tess … who was now gone forever. I'd never see him again. I shouldn't be surprised at how acute the pain was at that thought, how much I was actually grieving him, but I was. Tears well up in my eyes and I looked down, not wanting Benny to see. I felt for him, even though I didn't agree that Clara had good intentions. I didn't trust her.

"It's hard, losing people we once loved," Benny said, noticing despite my efforts to conceal my pain. "Even if we think we don't love them anymore, we grieve who they were, what we had with them. We grieve the chance to make things right. We grieve so many things." He stared at the floor. "I still miss my mother so much it wakes me up at night ten years later. Now that I know I have some powers of healing, that I can stop, or at least slow down sickness … I never stop thinking about how I could've helped her. How I might have kept her here, at least a little longer. I never even tried because I didn't know I could."

"You didn't know," I said. "It's not your fault."

"I know that logically," Benny said. "But that's grief."

"That's true," I said. "I just wonder when the grieving will finally stop. For all of us. I wish it would, you know?"

"You and me both," Benny said, standing up and coming over to give me a warm hug. His huge, muscular arms were strong and tight around my shoulders. I hugged him back, grateful. "You and me both, sister."

Eighteen

Another night, another front row. Not that I was complaining. I stood in front of my chair, nerves coursing through me, this time without the benefit of having Roberta or Jamie or any of my other friends there. My mother had even hitched a ride back with Nikolai, which I found very weird, but I was grateful that he had been able to help. Everyone was gone back to Georgia, save for Benny and Lee, but both of them were back-stage, readying for the show. We planned to head back ourselves first thing in the morning, but I wished I had someone here to hang out with, to help keep me calm.

Phillip and Lee had arranged for beefed-up security all over the venue, and with Shank and Colt gone, there was nobody left who had the potential to harm us in any major way. But I still felt very exposed and very anxious for the show.

In the truck on the way to the venue, I'd peeked at Phillip's profile as he drove, noting his mouth was set in a serious line, knowing he felt the same way. Not only did he also have reason to be nervous about security, but I knew he was nervous about the show too. Several big music outlets planned to attend tonight, and the band's performance would be written about and reviewed. The success of tonight's show would determine just how well the *big* tour would go. They were planning to announce it tonight, after the encore.

As I'd peeked at Phillip, seeing how tensely he was gripping the steering wheel, a song from my teen years had come on the radio. "Huh," I'd said, turning up the dial as the familiar guitar of Live's "Lightning Crashes" came through the speakers. "I haven't heard this in years."

"I don't remember this song," Phillip had said, glancing over at me. "I recognize the band, though. When did this come out?"

"Um …'94?" I said. "Maybe early '95? It was a huge hit. Everybody got so sick of it that summer." I realized, not wanting to say it out loud, that the song had been released only a few short months after Phillip's death. I remembered seeing the video on MTV around the same time we were still getting updates on the band and how they were doing in Phillip's absence.

"It's pretty," Phillip said, listening. "Sad. But hopeful at the same time."

"It's not even one of their best, really," I'd countered, then listened in silence for a few moments as Ed Kowalczyk's searing vocals became louder and more insistent. Then, to my horror, I realized I was crying. I furiously wiped at the tears on my cheeks, hoping Phillip hadn't noticed.

"What's wrong?" Phillip asked in alarm, looking over at me. "Do I need to pull over?"

"No, no," I'd insisted, still wiping away the flood of tears that had started so unexpectedly. "I think I must be about to get my period or something. I don't know what came over me. It was like … I was listening to the song and just remembering what it was like back then, realizing that like … what feels like a couple of years ago was actually twenty years ago. And I just … I don't know. The song just hit me in my feels, I guess," I said, horribly embarrassed.

"Nostalgia?" Phillip said, putting a hand on my knee. "It hits you funny sometimes, huh."

"I guess so," I'd answered, still embarrassed that he'd seen me react that way. "It isn't like I loved this song or anything. I don't know what came over me."

"It's okay, Stormy," Phillip said, his hand still on my knee, his voice soft and full of understanding. "It's okay."

I shook my head, taking a long sip of my Sprite. I hadn't felt like drinking tonight; I was too keyed up. What had caused me to break into tears like that? Phillip must have thought I was losing my marbles.

Now, I felt a tap on my shoulder and turned around, brightening as I saw the petite, black-haired girl standing there behind the barrier, hula hoop balanced over her shoulder. "Beth!" I leaned forward to give her a hug, realizing the barrier made that impossible, then gestured for her to jump over. "Join me!"

"I can't stay," she said, returning my hug with a beaming smile. "The guys asked me to hoop for part of their set; can you believe that?"

I smiled back at her. After introducing her to everyone the night of the last show, Benny had suggested they have Beth hoop during some of the band's more energetic songs. I'd been pleased when Phillip, Jason, and Ollie had agreed readily. We owed her a debt of gratitude, after all. Her hooping to distract everyone while I'd confronted Shank and Colt had likely saved a lot of lives and kept a stampede from happening when everything went down. Besides, she just looked damn cool up there, and not many sludge metal bands could say they had their own hooper. "I can't wait to see you! Do you want to come sit with me when your part is over?"

"Sure!" She pushed her black bob behind her ears. "They asked me to go on tour. Isn't that wild?"

"I'll be there too!" I said, grinning. "I'm going to do a working blog about the tour. I can't wait to see what you've got and write all about it!"

"Is Nikolai coming with you guys?" Beth asked innocently, and I grinned. I hadn't realized she'd even said two words to him when they'd met the other night, but evidently, an impression had been made.

"No, he went back to Georgia yesterday," I said, her face falling. I added, "But you know, Nikolai is actually my brother."

"I didn't know that," Beth said, brightening. "So he'll be at more shows in the future, I assume."

"I'll make sure of it." I winked at her. I could tell she and I were going to become fast friends. She had a very open, airy energy, despite her all-black ensemble and heavy dark makeup, that I liked very much.

"I like your energy too," she said, and my eyes widened.

"Did you …"

"I tried to hint at it the other night," Beth said, leaning forward conspiratorially, her hoop pulsing with bright purple light. "But there was a lot going on. I don't think you picked up on it."

"Picked up on …"

"I can tell you have powers," she said casually, pushing her hair behind her ears again. "I do too."

I gaped at her for a moment, her hula hoop pulsing, then in a flash, she was blowing me a kiss and scrambling over the barricade toward the backstage. "See you after! Wish me luck!"

"Good luck!" I managed to squeak, but I was dumbfounded. How many of *us* were there? And how was it they seemed to find me so easily? I was still standing there, shellshocked, trying to figure it all out as the familiar, razor-edge tone of Phillip's bass came crashing around my ears. I was so lost in thought I almost missed him swagger out onto the stage, decked out in a slim-fitting black suit and crimson-colored tie, his shiny black shoes glinting under the heavy stage lights.

He slid his hand down the bass, looking straight at the front row through heavily-lined eyes, his mouth pursing into that familiar, sexy smile that I knew so well. Jason began to strum his guitar, and I stopped, surprised, as Phillip's deep, melodic voice began singing the opening lines of "Lightning Crashes." I met his eyes, and he blew me a kiss between verses. And then I forgot everything else.

Sweat ran down Phillip's face in rivulets, his black hair soaked and sticking straight up, his forehead and cheeks red and clammy with exertion. He looked like he'd just run a marathon or possibly a leg of the Tour de France. Every single string had been ripped out of his bass, and having played that thing and felt how strong and thick those strings were, I knew that was no small feat. His heavy black eyeliner was pooled under his eyes, giving him an accidental smoky-eye that made me want to rip his face off, in a good way.

The entire concert had gone off without a hitch. No hidden bad guys intent on doing us harm, no interruptions, the guy's entire set had been incredible, Beth's hooping performance had gone over well —somebody had already shared a clip of her in action on social media, and it was going viral—and they'd announced their big comeback tour right at the end to loud, raucous applause. There had been three encores, and the crowd was demanding a fourth when Phillip said goodnight for a final time. There were *still* people milling about in the front of the venue, hoping to catch a glimpse of the band and get an autograph.

"Good show?" I asked with a wink. He picked me up and twirled me in the air, his bass heavy and clunky between us, jamming me in the ribs, his soaking-wet shirt transferring half his sweat onto my gauzy black blouse. But I didn't care. I laughed, throwing my arms around his neck, happily receiving the sloppy, passionate kiss that landed somewhere near the vicinity of my mouth.

"Hell of a good show," he said with a huge grin, sitting me down, wiping at his sweaty brow. "Shit. I got sweat all over you."

"Like you haven't before," I said, and he raised an eyebrow.

"Well, that was different. And now that you put me in mind, I'll be doing that later," Phillip purred, giving me a onceover, eyebrows still slightly raised, the wild, lustful look in his eyes setting me on fire from my toes to the top of my head. Warmth coursed through my body, and my cheeks got hot. "So did we sound good?"

"You sounded amazing," I said, remembering myself and the dozen or so other people backstage with us. Our animal lusts would have to wait until later. "The cover of 'Lightning Crashes' … that was a surprise … I loved it. It was all just so good, you guys. You brought down the house. Did you hear the way they screamed for you?"

"Three encores," Jason said with a grin, pulling his red guitar from his neck and placing it gently in the case. "And I think they would have happily gone for four if Phillip hadn't torn all the strings out of his bass. I swear, you haven't changed a bit. But those things are fucking expensive, dude."

"I won't do it every show," Phillip said, his eyes still bright and excited. "I couldn't resist."

"It was so good to be back here, playing on our home

turf," Ollie said, popping the tab on a can of lemon La Croix. I suppressed a giggle; it was so weird to see these guys who, all through the nineties, had been known for doing as many drugs and drinking as heavily as possible, finish up a show with seltzer waters and fruit platters. "I never thought that could happen again. I never thought it would be possible."

I turned to Beth, who was wiping sweat from her brow, a good deal of her heavy makeup coming off on the cloth. I was surprised to see that beneath all the white pancake makeup and thick black eyeliner and lipstick, she was fair and freckled, her skin delicate against her pretty amber eyes. "You looked amazing up there," I said, gesturing at her hoop. "How do you get that thing's colors to change like that? It was purple at first, then green, and then I swear at one point it was flashing all the colors of the rainbow!"

"It's connected to me," she said, and I paused, not understanding until she winked at me, reminding me of our conversation before the show. "Like a mood ring, but … it's my aura."

"Whoa," Phillip said, putting an arm around me. "We got more than we bargained for with you, Beth!"

She smiled mysteriously and continued wiping off her makeup. I had a feeling Beth was not without drama of her own.

Phillip ripped off a black grape and held it to my lips. I dutifully let him feed me, enjoying the sweet, juicy burst as I bit into it. He popped a grape into his own mouth, his full lips closing over it just a little too slowly to be anything but deliberate. His dark eyes met mine, burning fire, and I wondered where the hell the dressing room was in this place. We were going to have to sneak away, and soon, or I might end up ripping his clothes off right here backstage in front of everyone.

"Ooooh, are those grapes?" Jason exclaimed behind me. "Can I have one?"

"Help yourself," Phillip said, his eyes never leaving my face. We stared at each other, our gazes locked in a battle to see who could break first. The usual electricity between us was thrumming hard, and I could feel it in the air, crackling and intense.

"Oh, get a room, you two," Benny said, popping open a Coke. "Roberta's right; you can't take those two anywhere. They're always eye-fucking each other like they just met."

"I know." Jason laughed with a mouthful of grapes. "Phillip always did have the most success with girls. Groupies hanging off him, fighting over who got to sit in his lap, while the rest of us were just sitting backstage playing solitaire like a bunch of chumps."

"That's not exactly how I remember it," Ollie argued. "I seem to recall *all* of you would partake in uh, groupie activities, from time to time. Except me, of course; I'm a saint."

"Don't believe a word of it," Phillip said in a mock whisper, his eyes still locked on mine. "Not a word. It's all lies and fabrications."

"You seem to forget I was alive back then and read a magazine or two," I retorted, a smirk crossing my face. "I've seen photographic evidence that what they say is true."

"Is it true?" he asked, a devious expression on his full lips. "I can't seem to recall."

"No?"

"I can't seem to recall anything before you."

Then he was pulling me into him, his mouth crushing mine, his arms holding me so tightly around the waist that I could scarcely breathe. He was still damp with sweat, and his lips were salty as I kissed him back, not caring who saw. My man had just played the most amazing hardcore goth-metal set I'd ever heard, looking like a bona fide sex god on that stage, to hundreds of screaming fans, and then he'd come back here and grabbed me up like a wolf hungry for its prey. And I was *all about it.* Everyone could eat their hearts out.

"You guys are so fucking gross."

I didn't bother to pull away from Phillip's embrace as I gave Jason the finger from behind my back.

"I think it's romantic," Beth said, and the guys laughed.

I put a hand on Phillip's forearm, giving it a tight squeeze, pulling back slightly to look up into his eyes. His lips were still inches from mine, curling into a devious, delicious grin that I knew all too well. I gave him a look. *Shall we find somewhere to be alone?* I didn't need to speak the words out loud; he knew my meaning plain.

I expected him to grab me by the shoulders and lead me down some dark corridor, and I was more than willing. My irritation at him from before the show had all but dissipated, and my plans to hash things out were gone. All I wanted was Phillip, right here, right now. But to my surprise, Phillip took a step back and pulled his arm away. He slipped his right hand into the pocket of his dark jeans and looked at me with a solemn expression, the playfulness from moments before melting away. His eyes were imploring, almost reverential.

"Stormy," he said, his voice suddenly high pitched, wavering with something like nerves. I looked at him curiously. Phillip never got nervous. "I have something to ask you. Something I've been wanting to ask you …"

Suddenly, the entirety of the backstage was silent. Benny and Jason had stopped gabbing, and Ollie and Beth were clustered by the dressing room doors as if they wanted to moonwalk backward into them. Lee had been on the phone almost the entire time we'd been backstage, but then he, too, had stopped what he was doing and stood there staring at us. I felt pinpricks of goosebumps on my arms, and closed them over my chest nervously.

I stared at Phillip, waiting, watching as he pulled a small, shining object from his pocket. He slipped it onto the end of his finger and held it out toward me, the pink in his cheeks deepening into a flush, another rarity. I realized that him wearing a suit and tie to the show was about more than just aesthetics. He'd dressed up for *me*.

"I had a million ways I planned to do this, a million different plans ..." Phillip swallowed. "I thought about doing it onstage in front of everyone, but that didn't seem right ... I thought about going to Driftwood Beach, but that place holds so many others' memories, and I wanted something that was just *ours* ... I thought about waiting until we got back to your place, or maybe to the Wolfden, but ... again, everybody else's memories, and besides, it'll be a while before we get there, and I can't wait." Phillip swallowed again and took a step forward, taking my hand in his. His skin was warm to the touch, except for the cool bit of metal that rubbed against my fingers as he turned my hand over, palm up, as though he were positioning me for prayer.

"Stormy," Phillip Deville said, his eyes huge and luminous. His hand trembled a little in mine. "Will you marry me?"

Jason's gasp reverberated through the backstage area, and though I was completely silent, standing there gaping at Phillip, the sounds inside my head conveyed a similar shock. For a moment, I just stood there, unsteady on my feet, staring. His hand was a warm weight in mine, the coolness of the bauble on his finger a punctuation mark on the question he'd just asked me. I knew it was a ring, but I was afraid to look down, afraid I'd realize I was hallucinating, that this wasn't really happening ... afraid to look anywhere but in Phillip's eyes.

I found my voice, and, clearing my throat, took a deep breath. "I ... I ... of course I will, Phillip."

A cheer erupted behind me, but I scarcely heard it. I was

too busy rushing into Phillip's outstretched arms, burying my face in his neck, the happy tears already beginning to course down my face. After a moment, Phillip pulled back and gave me a soft, lingering kiss on the lips, this one full of tenderness and reverence but with an undercurrent of the passionate moment we'd shared before. We needed to be alone. *Right now.*

"Do you like it?" he asked in a soft, sensual voice, and I realized he meant the ring. I hadn't even looked at it!

I took his hand and looked at the ring on his index finger, just above the knuckle. It was silver with a thin band, and had a small, bright turquoise stone in the middle. It was no frills—no diamonds or gems—but absolutely exquisite, and I could tell it was very, very old.

"Yes," he said, though I hadn't spoken. His eyes were shining. "It was my sister Claire's." I looked up at him, my own eyes bright. I'd never heard him mention his sister before outside of interviews. "I recently found out that she uh, that she'd passed away ..." He cleared his throat, his voice husky. "And Jason was kind enough to give me a few of her things, things that had been left in the house. This was among them." He wiped an eye. "When I was a kid, I loved that ring. I'd always steal it from her jewelry box and wear it on my pinky when I was playing rock star. I think in my childhood brain it reminded me of something Axl Rose or Sebastian Bach would wear. Anyway, I hope you like it. If you don't, we'll get you something else—whatever you want." He stared down at me, his eyes glistening. "I just want you to be happy. I just want you to be my wife."

"Are you sure?" I asked, my voice a whisper. We'd both been through this before, and Phillip had already taken on so much in his newfound life. Add to that a brand-new marriage ... Phillip was a brave one.

"I've never been more sure of anything in my life," he

answered seriously, taking the ring from his finger and slipping it onto mine. "All the future holds, whether it involves magic, or music, or family, or all of the above, I want to spend it with you. I want you by my side for all of it, forever, better or worse, till death do us part."

"And if death does us part, I'll just bring you back," I said, laughing through my tears. "Again."

"I'd expect nothing less," Phillip said, leaning down to kiss me again. "The old ball and chain, tied to my ankle for infinity."

I chuckled, bit his lip, and then leaned to whisper in his ear. "If I don't get you alone in the next thirty seconds, I'm changing my mind."

"As you wish, my betrothed," he whispered back, and scooped me up into his arms, carrying me out the backstage exit toward his dressing room without so much as a word to anyone.

Nineteen

I snuggled down into the covers, enjoying the feel of the cool, stiff sheets on my bare skin. The sheets on Phillip's childhood bed were the old kind that were full of starch and held a crease when you folded them. Most people preferred their sheets the softer the better, but I liked something crisp and cool. Phillip had told me these same sheets had been on his bed since he was a kid; they were a legit relic from at least the eighties, if not earlier. They were cream colored with a dusky-rose colored floral print. Hardly the thing you'd imagine a hardcore rocker to have on his bed, which made it all the more quaint.

I leaned into Phillip's shoulder, sneaking a glance up at his profile as he lightly slumbered. I'd worn him slap out, apparently. We'd only stopped our marathon session to pack up the dressing room and make the short drive back to Jason's house before resuming our steamy session.

I grinned and poked a finger gently into his shoulder. He didn't move but let out a little sigh and turned his face further into the pillow. Once upon a time, scores of black hair would have fallen over that face, but now it just framed his defined cheekbones and fell behind his ears. God, he was handsome. It was like he was chiseled from stone by a sculptor commissioned by God himself.

"Never say—or think—anything like that ever again," Phillip groaned, turning toward me and cracking one eye open. "That was the cheesiest thing I've ever heard."

"I thought you were asleep," I said, propping myself up on his shoulder, my chin on my hands. "And you *didn't* hear me."

"I hear your thoughts, pretty woman," he said, one eye still cracked open, peering at me. "How many times do I have to remind you of that?"

"Well, you've been told to stop poking around in my noggin," I said pertly, shutting one of my own eyes, mocking him.

"It's hard to do that when you think so *loud.*" He propped himself up on his elbow and brushed my hair back from my face. "You should take a nap yourself while I pack up. You haven't been sleeping well lately, and we've got to go in just a couple hours."

"What makes you think that?" He was right, of course, but I thought I'd done a decent job of hiding the insomnia that had kept me walking the halls of Phillip's family home the past couple nights. I'd tiptoed out of the room after Phillip fell asleep, not wanting to worry him. After all, there was nothing he could really do. My nerves and anxiety were just getting the best of me, like always.

"I'm not blind, Stormy. I do notice when you get out of bed in the middle of the night, when I roll over and your side of the bed is cold."

"I'm sorry."

"Don't be sorry. Just tell me what's giving you sleepless nights." He looked at me seriously, his face softening. "Unless you're just … needing some time away from me?"

"No, no, not that," I said, leaning forward to plant a kiss on his lips. My cheeks still felt tender from where his stubble had rubbed me raw. "Never that. I just … I have a lot on my mind, I guess."

"Like?" He reached out and caressed my shoulder, his hands warm. "Tell me."

"Just … well, there's a lot of things. Things with my dad, for one. Nikolai. What happened at your show with Shank. What's going on with Roberta. Worrying about what Sloan is up to—because she's always up to *something*."

Phillip sighed. "You're taking on everyone's problems again; no wonder you're exhausted."

"I can't help but worry about those I love," I countered. "And, well …" I looked down at my lap. "I keep thinking about Tess too. All these memories rushing back, blindsiding me. I guess … I guess I miss him. Is that terrible?"

"Of course not, Stormy." Phillip pulled me into his arms. "He was your husband. You loved him. Of course you're grieving him. I wouldn't expect anything less."

"But he—we—"

"As usual, you're entirely too hard on yourself," Phillip said sweetly into my ear. He placed a gentle kiss on my temple. "It's going to take time. You're still in shock; it's only been a few days. The past few weeks have been a lot for anyone, but especially for you with all these new things you've got going on. Stormy, please, give yourself a break."

"Thanks." I felt tears spring to my eyes. I nuzzled my face in Phillip's warm neck. He always knew just what to say to make me feel better, his unique mix of tough love and complete understanding that seemed to right every wrong, untie every knot.

"You do that for me too," he said softly.

"Are we really going to do this?" I asked, turning and raising my left hand toward the lamp on the nightstand, admiring the ring on my finger. It felt strange there, but in a good way. Like something new that would soon become a part of me. "Are we really going to get married?"

"Yes," he answered, raising his own hand and lacing his long, thin fingers through mine. "I want you to be mine, body and soul. And I want to be yours. I've been wanting to ask you since we were in Savannah. I kept waiting for the right time, for the right moment, and I realized … any moment is the right moment. As long as I have you."

I kissed him on the nose. "So do we like … plan a whole wedding? Elope? How do we do this?" I laughed, enjoying the way his fingers felt intertwined with mine. "Nothing about you and I has ever been traditional, or easy, for that matter. I have no idea where to even start."

"I'm happy with a big, gaudy wedding or dashing to the courthouse some boring afternoon," Phillip said, his voice tender. He kissed me on the cheek this time. "Whatever makes you happy. And I mean that; I honestly don't care one way or the other, so long as I get to marry you."

"You'd wear a tux and cut a big, goofy cake and dance to Frank Sinatra with me in some hideous, tacky banquet hall?" I giggled.

"In a heartbeat." Phillip grinned. "I'd throw the garter and let people pelt me with birdseed and even smile for the overly staged photos. I'd dance to The Police's 'Every Breath You Take' and let you decorate the entire reception with nothing but burlap and lace and mason jars, far as the eye could see. I'd do anything for you, Stormy Spooner."

"Be careful what you wish for," I teased, my heart bursting with love. "You haven't seen my Pinterest board."

"What's Pinterest?"

"Again," I said with a laugh. "Careful what you wish for." If he saw the wedding boards I'd already started, he might run screaming from me.

"What I wish for right now is for you to give me those

lips." Phillip growled, turning my head to face him and pressing his mouth to mine.

The sun was already shining bright through the windows, and we needed to get up, get packed, and get moving, but I couldn't resist the way he tasted, how incredible his warm, strong arms felt around me. I nuzzled closer to him, pushing a hand under the covers and caressing his chest, letting my fingers trail down his ribs to his stomach, giggling against his lips as he gave an involuntary shudder. Phillip Deville was ticklish.

The last time I'd packed up in this room, it had been in a hurry when Phillip was in the shower. I'd left in the night, without telling him, to go back and clean up a mess I thought I'd made. While it might be true that I had made it, I hadn't made it alone. What had resulted in that midnight solo trip had turned my entire world upside down. I'd almost lost Phillip as a result. It was hard to believe I was back here now, in the same bedroom that had so enchanted me when Phillip and I had been falling in love. It was even harder to believe it had only been a few weeks since those events had happened. It felt like I'd already lived a lifetime between then and now.

"Stop thinking." Phillip said gruffly s he pulled back and stared at me fiercely. "Stop fretting." His hand on the back of my neck was firm. He gripped me as though I were a baby kitten and pushed my face toward his, his mouth inches from mine. "You're not going anywhere this time. You understand?"

I stared at him, my eyes wide, his rough kisses still burning on my lips. I ached for him to kiss me again, and at that moment, I would have done anything he told me, agreed to anything at all. His hand holding the back of my neck was gripping me hard enough to hurt. His eyes were glinting with steel, and his jaw was clenched tight. "Do you understand?" he said again, his voice full of cold fury.

I nodded, momentarily without words. My skin felt hot and

clammy, my chest and arms pinned against Phillip as he held my head, forcing me to look at him. For a brief moment, a ghost of a smile passed across his face. "Is this okay?" he said in a whisper, as though he didn't want anyone to hear. "Do you like this?"

"Yes," I whispered back, and then the smile was gone, replaced with another expression of absolute fury.

"You will never leave me again," he directed, his eyes staring holes in me, his mouth inches from mine. Oh, how I ached for him to kiss me. Instead, he pulled back a little, leaving me breathless and panting. "Will you?"

"No," I said, my own voice moving from a whisper to a croak. "I won't. Ever."

"Good," he said firmly, his fingers clenching the skin of my neck. Pretty soon, I was going to start purring. "If I make you my wife, that means forever, Stormy Spooner. No running off in the night to get away from me. No breaking up with me. No running after other hotter and younger rock stars. Capiche?"

I laughed then, but a quick shake of my head made me stop. "Capiche," I said, but I couldn't stop the grin from breaking out on my cheeks. "The same goes for you, Deville."

"We're not talking about me right now," he growled furiously, but it was too late. I'd gotten the upper hand. I pushed him back on the bed, and with a quick movement, straddled him, coming to sit on his hips and pinning his arms against the bed. He could have easily overpowered me, but he didn't try. Instead, he gazed up at me with wonder.

"You won't leave me, either," I said, matching his cold tone. "You won't shake me over for some younger, prettier woman. You won't abandon me if things get too weird or too crazy. And they fucking will, because … well, because that's what happens. If I marry you, you're stuck with me, Deville. Right?"

"Right," he agreed easily, his lips curling into a sexy smile. "So now that we've established some boundaries, are you going to finally fuck me, Stormy Spooner?"

I grinned down at him and shook my head slowly, wagging a finger in his face. "No."

"Why not?" His voice was almost a whine, and I shimmied against him a little, enjoying watching him squirm. As satisfying as that was, though, a shiver went through me at remembering how forceful he'd been just moments before.

"Because I just changed my mind," I said playfully, letting my own voice drag out into a pouty sigh. "I think I *do* want to leave you, after all. I'm bored … greener pastures, yadda yadda."

"Is that right?" Phillip's voice had gone dangerously cold and quiet.

"I'm afraid so." My voice was a squeak.

The next thing I knew, I'd been flipped over onto my back, and Phillip's entire tall, muscular frame was hovering over me, his spiky black hair tickling my face, his arms holding mine down onto the bed. I didn't try to resist but bucked my hips against him once, twice, and on the third time, he pinned them down with his knee.

"Tell me you want to leave me again," he said in my ear, then started placing kisses slowly on my neck, agonizingly slow, down to my collarbone. His stubble tickled my skin.

"I'm going to … leave …"

"Say it."

"… leave …"

"Or would you rather stay and let me fuck you?"

"… leave …" I panted, determined to win this round. But his lips felt so good on my collarbone, and now they were traveling down further, his warm, large hand cupping my breast. "… stay."

"That's what I thought."

Twenty

"I can't believe you turned down a huge wedding," Roberta said, her arm linked in mine as we walked toward the concrete steps, my vintage black shoes making pleasing clack-clack sounds on the pavement. I'd picked out a very understated, but very classy, 1920s-style day outfit to wear, and I was grateful that the normally chokingly-humid September sun was milder than usual. The black sack-style dress came down to my shins, and I had on opaque black stockings beneath, and leather mary janes that reminded me of the ladies you saw dancing the Charleston in Harlem. Around my neck was a choker on a velvet chain—a pre-wedding gift from Phillip—that held a turquoise cameo to match my ring. He'd had it custom made; I was afraid to ask him what it had cost. We'd only been back home in Brunswick for a week, so whoever he'd hired had worked at lightning speed. My hair was pulled into a low, loose bun, and atop my head sat a black bowler hat with a sleek, fine feather sticking out of it. Roberta had helped me with my makeup; we'd decided to go with the theme and do a rosebud lip in a shade of rose-red, big eyes rimmed with black kohl and feathery, jet-black lashes. Roberta had been a bit miffed to not be present for our engagement, but she'd quickly fallen into wedding planning with me, and I wasglad for it. She'd pretty much handled it all so I could sit back and look forward to the day.

"I know … he offered, but …" I licked my lips, mindful of my lipstick. "Honestly? Tess and I had a big wedding—my dream wedding, in fact—and the marriage turned out to be shit." A fresh pang of hurt hit me in my lower belly. Despite the epic failure that had been our marriage, our wedding had indeed been lovely. Now that Tess was gone, remembering how I had laid my head on his shoulder as the salty spray from the tide had splashed over us was sweeter than ever. We'd danced in the sand, Tess' pant legs rolled up and his bow tie discarded on a beach blanket. We'd drank sangria and laughed and frolicked until dawn. It had been one of the last times I could remember when we'd been truly happy.

I swallowed, banishing the memory. Today was not about my memories with a man who I would never see again in this lifetime. Today was about Phillip.

"Besides," I continued, "who has the time for all that planning? Phillip's got more shows, and I want to focus on my writing. I can't believe GOTHzine just accepted my pitch without making me do a trial run or a writing sample or anything."

"I can," Roberta stated, turning to me with a smile, snapping gum. She was dressed in her own homage to the 1920s, but her flaming-red flapper dress was a lot more casual and looked absolutely fantastic with her dark hair and skin. "You can do anything you decide on, Stormy. It's one of your gifts. You're really off and running with this thing, and I'm proud of you. You just decide to switch careers and that's it; you're in!"

"I'm sure Phillip had something to do with it," I admitted. "I hope people won't think it's nepotism since we're in a relationship. I'd like people to judge me on my writing talent, if I have any, and not my husband." As I said the words, a thrill went through me. *My husband.* It was weird to say that again and weirder still to feel the excited current that ran through my blood as I said it.

"I'm sure a few people will have something to say—they always do these days—but fuck them," Roberta said as we made our way up the steps to the heavy wooden door. "Once they read your work, they'll realize you're the real deal."

"I hope so."

"I *know* so." Roberta looked at me confidently. "I may have only known you a short time, but I can see crystal clear how great you are. I'm so proud of you and so happy to have you as my friend."

"Thank you. I feel the same way about you, Burt." Tears pricked at my eyelids as we stopped at the door, facing each other, Roberta rushing forward to give me a clumsy hug. I pulled back after a moment, nerves fluttering in my stomach. "Well, here goes nothing. How do I look?"

"Absolutely beautiful," Roberta said, dabbing at her own eyes. She adjusted her red pillbox hat over her dark curls and gave me a wink. "But Stormy … black? At your own wedding?"

I laughed and took up her arm again. "Have you met my future husband? Did you really think we'd have a white wedding?"

"I guess not." She grinned, and we made our way inside. "But I thought you might go the Blanche Devereaux route and wear red or something."

"Nope. Black. Black as my heart." I giggled. "Besides, *you're* in red."

Just as we turned to go inside, we heard a shout behind us. I turned to see Beth running toward us, her face flushed and sweaty. She was wearing a beautiful little black dress and black platform Doc Martens, and in her arms, she held a slightly wilted bouquet of dark red roses, so red they were almost black. She handed them to me, her face apologetic.

"I saw these and thought you might want to add them to your bouquet," she said, out of breath, her eyes falling to the wilted petals. "I'm so sorry I'm late. I um, I got sick on the way."

"Sick? What's wrong?" I asked her, alarmed. She looked pretty worse for wear.

"Don't tell Nikolai, it's embarrassing, but … I was up half the night with some stomach thing. I feel like I lost twenty pounds overnight. I even had to stop halfway here and puke on the side of the road," Beth confessed, putting a pale hand to her sweaty brow. "I was dry heaving air by the time I was done, and I *still* feel queasy."

"Do you need a doctor?" Burt asked, looking Beth's pale face over.

"Oh no, I'll be okay. It's likely just food poisoning. That'll teach me to order French toast at eleven p.m. from room service. It had probably been sitting out for hours." I grimaced. Beth was staying at a local hotel despite our urgings to for her to stay with one of us. She didn't want to put anyone out. The idea that any of the hotels in the area, which were basically just *motels,* all in equal states of disrepair, would even offer room service was a surprise to me. That they'd have French toast and Beth was brave enough to eat it made me feel kind of queasy myself.

"Are you sure you want to come in? I'll understand if you want to go back and lie down," I said, reaching into my bag for a tissue, which I handed to her. "Your eyeliner is running just a little bit there, at the corner of your left eye."

"Oh, damn." Beth dabbed at her watery eye. It looked red and irritated, her undereye puffy. "It's a new one; I should have known not to use unfamiliar products on a day like this. I got such a good deal on it though, and it's all local. I'm just batting a thousand today, huh?" Before either of us could answer, her face turned a little green, and Beth ran around the building to be sick again.

"Consider it good luck?" Burt said, looking at me with a hopeful smile.

"How on earth is that good luck?" I asked with a laugh.

"I have no idea," she confessed, laughing too. "I just didn't know what else to say."

It was quiet inside the courthouse as I dutifully went through the metal detector, accepting the elderly security officer's congratulations with a proud smile. As I waited for Roberta to get scanned, he turned to me with a kind smile and said, "I bet I know who your groom is. He's dressed all in black, just like you. Tall fella, with black hair?"

"That's him," I said, my heart thumping. "That's Phillip."

"He's already in there getting your license. Down the hall and second door on the left," the man said, reaching out to shake my hand. "Good luck to you both and congratulations."

"Thank you." I wiped at my eyes. Jesus H, I hadn't even seen Phillip yet and I was already crying. I hoped my eyeliner wasn't running. So much for choosing a courthouse wedding to avoid any heavy emotional scenes.

We made our way down the corridor, following the security guard's directions. As we approached the door, I could see Lee leaning against the counter, his head propped on his hands. He turned, sensing us, and gave me a bright smile. His light hair was slicked back, making his freckles stand out and turning his boyish face a good five years younger. I marveled at his chestnut-colored suit. I'd never seen him wearing anything but jeans and a T-shirt, and his signature, custom UGA cap. He looked so dapper.

"Well, ain't you a sight for sore eyes," he said suggestively, his Southern accent turned up to eleven. "Goodness gracious."

I leaned forward and gave him a big hug. "It's not too late to make it a double wedding," I pointed out, batting the tears away. I couldn't ruin my eyeliner at zero hour. "Then we'd both be married to rock stars."

"It's tempting," Lee said, reaching forward to push a tendril of my hair back under my hat. "But I have to work up the nerve. I've put that man through a lot. He might tell me to fuck off."

"I'm positive he won't," I said, smiling.

"Maybe you're right," Lee said, his voice turning formal. "We'll see. As of right now, though, this is your day." He extended an arm. "He's right in there; shall I take you to him?"

I looped my arm in his. "Please." I batted my eyes again, willing back the tears, realizing this was as close to someone giving me away as it would get, and it was Lee who was doing it. Lee Courtenay, after all we'd been through. It felt as though everything was coming full circle.

"Your bride is here," Lee said as we entered the little administrative room where Phillip had his back turned to me, filling out paperwork. Lee nudged him in the shoulder, and when Phillip turned around, I gasped audibly.

He wore dark black fitted slacks with a blazer that was tight on his arms and chest, fitted perfectly. His dress shirt and tie were black too, and the buttoned collar against his pale throat made me swallow instinctively. The ensemble was similar to the sleek suit he'd worn onstage at his last show, but a classier version, all crisp, pressed lines. Phillip's dark, spiky hair was slicked back behind his ears, and I could see that it was beginning to grow back, to get a little length to it. It was almost shaggy, and the black hair against the nape of his neck made my mouth water. He had on his usual black Doc Martens, but somehow, they looked absolutely perfect with his new suit. His green eyes gleamed as he looked me up and down, his expression full of the same awe and tender love that was undoubtedly staring back at him.

"My lady," Phillip said, holding out his hand to take mine. When I placed it in his, he lifted my hand and kissed the tops of my fingers. "My bride. My god, you look fucking beautiful, Stormy."

"So do you," I said honestly, reaching in my purse with my spare hand for the black hankie tucked inside. I just couldn't stop crying, eye makeup be damned.

"Let me," Phillip said, and produced his own handkerchief from the pocket of his black pants. "You've got eyeliner on your face." He dabbed at his own eyes first, an endearing and adorable movement that only made me cry harder. Then he reached forward and dabbed at the corner of my left eye, followed by the right. He wiped at the smudge of errant makeup on my upper cheek, then leaned down and placed a kiss there. His lips curled into the most beautiful smile as he moved to kiss me on the mouth.

"Are you ready?" he said in a whisper, his face only inches away from mine. Suddenly unable to speak, I nodded. He nodded back, our eyes locking, all the words we wanted to say flying through the air from my brain to his, from his heart to mine, without either of us having to utter a syllable out loud.

Then I was gliding back down the corridor on Phillip's arm with Lee and Roberta trailing behind us to the makeshift chapel area, a non-denominational room with a small corner devoted to ceremony, surprised momentarily to find it wasn't a chapel. Briefly, my brain had stopped firing, and I'd forgotten this was a government building, and those things didn't happen in real life. And then we were standing before a guy in a slightly linty gray suit who was holding a book loosely in his hands and asking us to repeat after him. Benny stood up beside him, resplendent in his own black suit that barely covered his large shoulders and arms. I barely registered the words; I was too busy floating on air, as if I was outside my body, but my soul came crashing back into my chest as Phillip turned to me, his green eyes flashing, his face full of loving purpose, and began to recite words he'd no doubt memorized that morning.

"Stormy Spooner, I promise to love you my whole life, to honor and cherish you, to never part from you, in sickness and health, and"— his eyes twinkled and a ghost of a grin appeared on his lips—"not even death will do us part."

My eyes filled with tears that I wiped quickly away as the officiant asked me to say my own vows. God, wasn't I supposed to be a writer? I had prepared nothing. I'd been too nervous, too full of excited anticipation to even think of anything. I decided to just go from the gut.

"Phillip Deville, you are my miracle. I still don't know what exactly brought you to me, or how, but I will cherish you for my whole life, honor and love you, in sickness and in health, through everything life throws our way, both chosen and unchosen adventures ..." I swallowed a flood of tears, mirroring the last part of his vows. "And nothing, not even death, will part us."

"Good," the officiant said, nodding. "I now pronounce you husband and wife. You may kiss the bride, if you wish."

I handed Roberta the makeshift silk bouquet, noticing she was full on sobbing into the sleeve of her red dress, bless her. I turned to Phillip with a triumphant smile, tears drying on my cheeks, ruining my carefully applied foundation, but I didn't care. He pulled me to him, planting a sweet, feathery kiss on my temple, catching me by surprise. Then his mouth was on mine, his kiss passionate but reserved, full of reverence and romance. It was a wedding kiss; of course it was. Everything

Phillip Deville did was undeniably perfect, and this was no different.

When he pulled away, his own cheeks were a little damp. His eyes were bright as he whispered, "We did it!"

"We did!" I giggled, our noses touching. "We're married!"

"Holy shit," he said seriously, then kissed me again, his lips brushing mine tenderly. "You're my wife."

"And you're my husband," I said, my eyes wide. "Wow."

"Congratulations, you two!" Roberta's voice cut into our reverie, and we both turned, smiling, to see Roberta, Lee and Benny beaming back at us.

"What now?" Phillip asked in a laughing voice after we'd signed the necessary papers and thankfully accepted congratulations from the courthouse staff. "We can't just go home. We have to celebrate."

"Dinner and drinks are on me," Benny said, clapping Phillip on the back as we walked out into the parking lot. "Pick your favorite vegan joint, and I'll call ahead. Then later, if you guys are down, back to the Wolfden to celebrate. I've already got champagne, beer, and rumor has it that someone might've whipped up a wedding cake to smash in Phillip's face." He winked at me, and I could feel my cheeks flush with happiness as he threw his arm around Lee and gave him a sloppy, celebratory kiss. "Weddings make me happy, so fucking sue me."

"Maybe we'll have one of our own one day," Lee said tentatively, and to my delight, Benny's face brightened and he pulled Lee close, one hand on the back of his neck.

"Maybe we will. But first thing's first." They turned back to us, both their faces aglow. "So what do you say, newlyweds? We down to party?"

"What do *you* say?" I asked Phillip happily, my arm in his. He looked down at me, his face flushed with happiness, and my heart soared.

"That sounds absolutely perfect," he said with his best

wolfish grin. Then he leaned down and whispered to me conspiratorially, "Just so long as I can go home later and ravish my wife into oblivion."

"They're waiting for us out at the bonfire!" I screeched as Phillip picked me up and threw me over his shoulder, carrying me through the trailer's hallway. He had to crouch down to avoid hitting his head on the low doorframe as I kicked and flailed against him, but we both knew I was full of it.

I wanted him as much as he wanted me. More, probably. I'd been aching for him ever since I'd stood in front of him at the courthouse and we'd said our vows. As he carried me into the bedroom, which Jamie had kindly offered up to us for the second time this week so we had somewhere to change, I looked down at my hand and admired the turquoise ring there. Smiling to myself, I playfully hit Phillip in the lower back. "The party is for *us,* you goon! We're the guests of honor; we can't keep everybody waiting!"

"If you think for one second that they aren't expecting me to absolutely *smash* my wife the first chance I get—"

"Did you just say 'smash'?" I snorted as Phillip entered the bedroom and deposited me on the bed. "Jesus, have you been on TikTok or something?"

Phillip looked down at me, miffed. "I'd never fucking go on that website."

"It's not a website, it's an app." I leered at him, pleased. There was something about him being a sexy rock god with a secret fuddy-duddy attitude toward modern times that really got me going. It was the best of both worlds.

"I don't know what that means."

"Come here, you." I gestured to him, and he leaned down

on the bed, his face inches from mine, close enough to plant a gentle kiss on my lips that left me wanting. "That's not good enough, Deville."

He grinned at me and stuck out his tongue, licking the tip of my nose. "I thought you said we had a party waiting for us. I'm ready to get out there; are you?"

"Well, since you brought me all the way in here …"

"No, we really should get out there to our reception …"

"You asshole." I grabbed him by his black necktie and pulled him toward me. "If you don't take off your pants right now, I'm going to divorce you."

"You can't divorce me." He smiled. "You'd never."

"I'll get it annulled. After all, we haven't consummated it."

"Touché." Phillip loosened his necktie and pulled it downward, letting it hang down the collar of his shirt; the top two buttons were already undone, and I could see the tiniest bit of black hair on his muscled chest. Christ, my mouth was actually watering. This was no good at all. Here we were just hours into our marriage and already I was totally losing the upper hand. If he didn't make love to me *right now,* I was going to literally explode.

Before I knew what had happened, Phillip had pushed me down on the bed and was lying on top of me, his arms pinning mine over my head. "Keep your pants on," he said in a low, sexy voice as he trailed his lips from my collarbone to my ear. "Or rather, take them off, I should say."

"Get out of my head," I protested weakly, but all the fight had gone out of me. I was too distracted by Phillip's glorious weight on top of me and how right it felt … how soft and fine his black hair was as it tickled my face, how good his lips felt grazing my skin.

I wanted to run my hands down his arms, his hips, then back up to unbutton all the delicate little buttons on his black dress shirt, to rip it off him, and feel the hard flesh of his chest under my fingers, to play with the hair there, to tickle him the way he was tickling me before reaching down to unbuckle his belt, unbutton his pants … but he was pinning my arms down, preventing me from doing anything but receiving his kisses, kisses that were getting rougher and more intense as they trailed back down. I could do nothing but squirm beneath him and do my best to send him the X-rated thoughts that were running through my head—thoughts he was no doubt receiving, if the fervor with which he'd started kissing me and caressing me through my dress were any indication.

He moved to kiss my mouth roughly, and I moaned against him, squirming harder to free my arms. He finally let me go and laughed against my mouth as I ripped at his shirt, not bothering to unbutton it, hearing it tear. Too late, I thought, *Oh no, that's his wedding shirt,* but it was done now. My hands free to roam, I ran my fingers through the dark hair on his chest and down to his taut stomach, which was tense but soft beneath my hands.

We'd done this dozens of times before, but somehow, it now felt finally, truly real. It was right and perfect and everything I'd ever wanted.

Phillip let out a low moan, then whispered in my ear, "I love you, Stormy Spooner."

"Do you want me to take your name?" I asked, laughing a little as he turned me onto my side and unzipped my dress agonizingly slowly. "Stormy Deville?"

He pushed the dress off my shoulders and pulled me toward him again, his eyes taking in the black lace lingerie I'd worn special for the occasion. His lips curled in a smile, and he leaned down to plant a kiss on my décolletage. "Never. You're Stormy Spooner, and that you'll always be."

"Good," I said with a grin, lifting my hips to shimmy out of my dress. "I was secretly hoping you'd say that."

Phillip rose to his knees, unbuckling his black belt and

unzipping his sleek black pants, moving out of them in no time at all, with almost no effort. It never ceased to amaze me how easily he moved, how quickly … Whether he was cat-like or wolf-like, I wasn't sure, but whatever it was, the animal magnetism and grace by which he occupied space never stopped awing me. I lay there for a moment, just staring at him, admiring his naked body by the moonlight, the faintest bits of orange light from the bonfire outside flicking their way into the windows occasionally, lighting Phillip's chest with tiny flashes. He glowed. I smiled up at him, filled with wonder, lust, and so much love.

"I love you too," Phillip said in a loud, clear voice, full of purpose and naked honesty, and my eyes filled with tears. Because I knew it was true.

Then his weight was on top of me again, his hands winding in my hair, his mouth against my neck, as he plunged into me, both of us gasping, eyes full of tears and hearts full of love.

"I guess we should get out there, huh." Phillip's voice was loud in the darkness, and my eyes flew open.

"Shit. I fell asleep." I sat up quickly, blinking. In the pitch-black dark room, I could still see the faint flicks of orange light coming from the window, and I could hear the faraway strains of Tom Petty playing from the stereo. The sound of laughter drifted in too, and I smiled. It was our wedding night, and our friends—our family—were having a party. A party that we were missing. "How did I manage to do that? I never sleep!"

"Our hot lovin' put you out, darlin'," Phillip said in a mock Southern accent, pulling me onto his lap and enveloping me in his arms. He leaned down and gave me a passionate kiss, our breaths mingling as his tongue explored my mouth, and when he pulled away, I could feel his smile in the darkness. "I'm glad you got a little rest, though, even if it was only ten minutes. You needed it."

"I guess that's true," I said, nuzzling into his neck. I wanted to stay here forever and never leave. I would have been content to do so; forget the party. I didn't need anything like that when I had Phillip. My husband, my husband. But the party was in our honor, and my beloved family at the Wolfden had done so much for me …

"We have to at least show our faces," I said, reaching out to run my fingers through Phillip's hair. It had grown just long enough to pull into the tiniest ponytail. I couldn't see his face fully in the dark, but I could make out his strong jaw. I leaned down and planted a kiss there. "They're doing all this for us. I heard they even got us a wedding cake."

"Well, I guess we'd better get out there then," Phillip sighed reluctantly, burying his face in my chest and groaning.

"Hey, no motorboating on our wedding night!" I exclaimed, and he answered by furiously wiggling his face back and forth, making the most obnoxious noise into my bare skin. I cackled. "Stop it!"

"Never! These breasts belong to me now!"

"Gross. Come on, you pervert, let's get outside." I jumped up and flicked on the overhead light, squinting at the brightness that flooded the room, and grabbed the gauzy black sundress I'd brought for the occasion, slipping it over my head. As I fastened the tie in the back, I looked down at Phillip, who was lying naked on the bed with a pillow pulled over his face to block the light. He was beautiful, and he was all mine. I smiled and nudged at him with my foot. "Get up, you big lug. I have a wedding cake to smash."

"I thought you had enough smashing for one day." He rolled over with a wink and blew me a kiss as I pulled on my motorcycle boots, not bothering with tights or leggings. It was always humid at the Wolfden, and I'd just about sweat them off if I tried. Phillip threw on his usual uniform of black jeans and black T-shirt, brushed back his dark hair with a damp comb, and took just enough time to plant another passionate kiss on me in the doorway before we ventured outside to join the merriment, hand in hand.

The bonfire was bigger than I'd ever seen it before, the flames high enough to lick the roof of Jamie and Nikolai's trailer from the looks of it, and all our friends—including my mother—were crowded around, holding beverages and swaying along to the stereo, which had been propped up on Jamie's old S-10 and hooked up to huge speakers. Apparently, nobody around here had gotten with the twenty-first century and bought a Bluetooth, I thought to myself with a laugh, swaying along as I walked toward the fire, losing myself in the music. It was an old song, one I remembered Mama playing a bunch when I was a kid, a dance-techno song that went, "I wanna know, what you're thinking ... Somebody must have let her play DJ, because this old eighties dance relic wasn't something I imagined anyone at the Wolfden would pick.

And yet, as I grabbed an ice-cold hard seltzer from the cooler, I could see Lee and Benny over by the truck, arms around each other, bodies pressed together, swaying along with the music as though they were the only two people alive. I loved watching them. Their love was every bit as strong as passionate as Phillip's and mine, and I genuinely hoped they'd always be together, whatever obstacles were thrown their way. And now, not only were the two of them my Wolfden family, but they were part of the band as well. The four of us would be forever joined—forever friends, forever family.

Lee must have felt my gaze on him, or felt my thoughts, because he turned and met my eye. I raised my can to him in silent salute, and he raised his own Solo cup to me, and we gave each other a silent toast. Then he turned back to Benny, resting his head on Benny's shoulder.

We had come so far. All of us. I felt a lump of happiness in my throat. It was almost too much.

"Didn't you want something?" I asked Phillip, gesturing to the cooler.

"Yes, but I don't drink those weird things," he replied, wrinkling his nose in a gesture that was undeniably adorable. "I have a bottle of something nice stashed in your car. Let me go get it."

"Already got it," Roberta called from over by the bonfire. "Come here, you two, and let's see the happy couple!"

As we stepped into the light, everyone cheered. I flushed and looked down, embarrassed, but forced myself to raise my head and grin. This was a moment of celebration. I scanned each face around the fire, taking a moment to silently thank them for being here with Phillip and me, for sharing in our love. Roberta, Jamie, Nikolai, my mother, Lee and Benny, the newest addition to our group, Beth, who had followed us back from Boston, something that might've seemed weird to me once but now made perfect sense, and Clara, whose smile didn't quite reach her eyes. I gave her an extra little nod of appreciation and was pleased to see her nod back at me, a silent agreement that we'd bury the hatchet—for now. Then I saw a face I didn't recognize—a tall, dark-haired man with full lips and a beard. I stared at him for a moment, curious, then Roberta came forward and grabbed my arm.

"Stormy," she said with a wide smile. "I'd like you to meet my brother. Jorge." The relief and pride on her face was a beautiful thing to see. I stepped forward and shook Jorge's hand. "Jorge, this is Stormy. Pretty much my best friend these days, god help her."

"Why didn't you tell me he was home?" I asked Roberta accusingly.

"It was your wedding!" she exclaimed, looking at me like I was stupid. "I wasn't going to take away from that!"

"It's nice to meet you, Stormy," Jorge said with a sweet smile. "Thanks for taking such good care of my sister."

I was so relieved for Roberta that he'd finally turned up, and that she now knew, without a doubt, that he'd had no involvement in the house fire or any of the other events that had taken place over the past month. As I'd find out later, Jorge had simply been trying to put his best foot forward and better himself before coming back home, working a temporary job to get some money saved and staying at a halfway house until he had a little nest egg. That was something I could respect.

"Thank you all for being here," I said sincerely, putting a hand over my heart, meeting the eyes of everyone in turn. "Or I guess I should say, thanks for letting *us* be here. It's been so great getting to know you all—well, again"—everyone laughed—"over the last little while, and I'm so touched and honored to be able to call you family." I caught Nikolai's eye and my voice wavered a little with emotion. "Some of you quite literally. You guys mean so much to me. I love you all, I really do."

"I do too," Phillip echoed behind me, his hand warm on my lower back. "How much you all have helped us ... supported us ... It means a lot to me. Thank you."

It was silent for a moment, all of us lost in thought, in the memories of everything we'd all been through lately. God, it had been a lot. I swallowed hard. People going missing, long-lost connections, memories being recovered, break ups, make ups, drug busts, and so many deaths ... It would take time for all of us to acclimate to what normal meant for us now. If normal, whatever that was, was even possible.

Roberta's voice cut into the silence. "Come on, we can get

all weepy and shit later. This is a celebration! It's time to cut your cake! Before the damn thing melts!"

I shook my head, clearing my dark thoughts, and grabbed Phillip's arm, excitedly leading him to the little makeshift table set up by the porch. It held a three-tiered cake that was decadently iced in thick, dark chocolate frosting with little burgundy roses. "Please tell me someone took a picture of this," I said, my mouth watering. "Because I'm going to need photographic evidence of its beauty before I cut into it."

"Of course I took pictures," Roberta said, rolling her eyes. "We all did. You're just lucky Instagram didn't see them before you did."

"I appreciate your restraint!" I said with a giggle.

"It's your favorite—devil's food cake with raspberry filling, and dark chocolate ganache," Mama said, sidling in on the other side of me. Her eyes were a little bright, and I was touched. "The roses are edible too."

"It's gorgeous," I said, touching a finger to the bride and groom that sat atop the cake. Someone had outdone themselves because they were perfect renditions of Phillip and me—the bride short with mousy, flyaway hair, and a vintage black dress and shoes, and the groom a tall, muscular figure with jet-black hair and piercing green eyes. "Who did you hire to make it?"

"We didn't hire anyone," Roberta said proudly. "We made it. Me, your mom, and Beth. Who knew she was a pro cake decorator?"

"I certainly didn't," I said, turning to the bonfire where Beth was dodging requests to do some hooping for everyone; someone had turned off the eighties dance tunes and switched it over to Alice in Chains. While they were one of my faves, I agreed with Beth that it wasn't exactly hooping music. "When did she even have time?" I thought back to Beth's pale, sweaty face and the sounds of her retching behind the courthouse and hoped whatever she had was indeed food poisoning and not contagious.

"She put the finishing touches on it yesterday, thankfully," Roberta said, nudging me with her elbow. "I think she's better today. So do you like it? And more importantly, are you two going to cut into the damned thing so we can all have a piece?"

"Yes," I said, my eyes meeting Phillip's, both of us grinning. I couldn't wait to smash the biggest piece of cake right into his gorgeous face, right into that angular jaw ... and then lick it off ...

But I was getting ahead of myself again. "Got a knife, anybody?" I asked, and Roberta frowned, rummaging among the cutlery and napkins on the table.

"Oh damn, I forgot to—"

"Wait, never mind," I cut in, reaching down to my thigh. "I've got one right here." I pulled out the knife Nikolai had given me, raising it for a moment to admire the intricate and beautiful handle, and the sharp silver blade. "This will do nicely, I think."

"Where on earth did you get that?" Mama asked, her voice equal parts awe and worry. "That's a weapon!"

"It's a ceremonial knife," I said, running a hand across the carvings and aiming it at Phillip's chest, pointing the tip right at his heart. He smiled, putting a hand over the blade, pushing it in a little further so the point almost pierced his skin. He knew I'd never hurt him, but just a little push further and I could cut open his shirt, draw a little blood ... I shook my head again. God, was he bewitching me on *purpose?* "Nikolai ..." I paused, then continued. "My brother gave it to me."

Nikolai still stood over by the bonfire by Beth, keeping a careful distance, but I could see him watching us. I gestured for him to come closer, and when he did, I put an arm around my brother, giving him a sisterly hug. I met Mama's eyes. "It's one of my most treasured possessions now. And so is he. And so are you. I hope that … that after everything that's happened, now that Phillip and I are married and we're all safe and sound, that we can put everything behind us and move forward as a family." Another lump welled up in my throat. "Family, both blood and chosen. That's what I've always wanted. I really hope we can do that."

Mama looked at Nikolai. He was staring down at the ground, and to my surprise, she reached out and gave him a motherly touch on the arm, making him look up in surprise. "Yes. Of course we can do that. I'd like nothing better." Nikolai smiled.

"Now let's cut that cake before Roberta passes out from starvation," Phillip cut in, and I laughed, bringing the knife forward. It glided into the shiny ganache like butter, and I cut a triangular chunk, bigger than it needed to be, taking a moment to lick frosting from my fingers as I held the slice up to Phillip.

His eyes were wide. "That's way too big. I can't eat all that."

"It's for us to share, lover," I said with a giggle, licking more frosting from my hand. "Go for it."

He gave me a saucy look and leaned in. He knew what I was going to do; bless him for being a good sport. He opened his mouth to take a bite, and I smashed the cake with all my might into his face.

Frosting fell with a plop from his chin, and he gave me a look of mock anger, his lips covered in raspberry filling, dark chocolate streaks on his chin. "You bitch." His frosting-smeared mouth turned up into a grin as he reached for the knife. Still licking cake off his lips, he cut an even bigger sliver.

"Save some for the rest of us," Roberta whined, and everybody laughed.

"Thank god I'm not wearing white," I said, and Lee snorted behind me. I shot him a look.

Phillip didn't even give me a chance to pretend to take a bite. The moment the cake was cut, he shot his arm forward and smeared it into my face, taking special care to rub it in. His index finger found its way into my mouth, and I sucked the frosting off it. His eyes widened, then he grinned and wiped a little ganache off my chin and popped the same finger in his own mouth, giving me a sultry look.

"You guys are so disgusting," Roberta said happily, grabbing the knife from me and cutting the bottom tier into smaller pieces. "But I love you both so much."

"We love you too," Phillip said, pulling me close and pressing his lips to mine. Our faces were smeared with cake and frosting, but neither of us cared. His lips tasted sweet, like raspberries and vanilla and dark chocolate and everything good in the world. His arms encircled my waist, and he picked me up off the ground, our lips never leaving each other as he held me there. I felt like I was flying, and I never wanted to come down. I opened my eyes and smiled at him as he beamed back at me.

Roberta took a bite of her own slice and closed her eyes in pleasure. "This is delicious, if I do say so myself," she said in a dreamy voice.

I was surprised as Jamie sidled up to her and put his arm around her waist. "Let me taste, darlin'," he said, and before any of us knew what had happened, he pulled her face to his and kissed her. Roberta's arms went around his neck as she kissed him back, and a cheer went through the group. I beamed at Phillip. Roberta had been carrying a torch for Jamie *forever.* It appeared the feeling was mutual.

For a moment, I just stood there, leaning on Phillip's arm and watching everyone. I felt so happy, just genuinely happy. Everyone I loved, right here with me, celebrating my wedding to the love of my life, the man I'd been besotted with since I was a teenager. Everything was perfect. I had everything I ever wanted. Nothing—nothing at all in the world—could bring me down on this day.

"Any cake left for me?" a voice said from behind me.

I went cold in Phillip's arms, my limbs going completely stiff. He instinctively grabbed onto my shoulder, holding me back. I knew that voice. I knew it well. "Let me go," I whispered in Phillip's ear, and he let go of my arm immediately, dutifully handing me a napkin, his eyes blazing. I wiped the cake from my face and turned around, full of dread.

Sloan stood there, regarding me with a bemused expression.

"You make a beautiful bride, Stormy," she said. "But you have some cake on your nose."

I wiped at my face some more, momentarily speechless, and Phillip thundered, "What the hell are you doing here, Sloan?"

"I came to congratulate Stormy," she answered with a smile, looking only at me. "I wouldn't have missed your wedding for the world. You're my best friend."

"You *did* miss the wedding," I said, wadding the napkin up, my fingers clenching around it. "Everybody did, by design. And you weren't invited to the reception, last I checked." *And you're not my best friend,* I thought. *You never were.*

"You made a beautiful bride," Sloan said again, ignoring me. "I saw you walking into the courthouse. I knew you'd wear something vintage. It really looked amazing; and whoever did your makeup, well, bravo. I couldn't have done better myself." She grinned. "I mean, I could have probably, but they managed quite well."

"Yes, well, thanks very much and all," I said, reaching for my abandoned can of hard seltzer on the table, suddenly very much in need of a drink. "But this is a closed party, for family and close friends only, so ..." Sloan was definitely not either, not anymore. I found that the thought no longer caused me pain. Perhaps I'd lost too much by this point, or maybe I was ready to finally move on. "Especially considering you tried to poison my fucking friend Beth with your shitty makeup."

Sloan didn't have the decency to flinch or blanch or show any sign of regret or guilt. She just shrugged. "It was meant for you. I didn't know she was going to put it on. Who does that?"

"Who poisons makeup like a fucking weirdo?" I countered.

"Don't you remember me talking about Aqua Tofana?" she asked, and I rolled my eyes. "The techniques she used in Sicily centuries ago are pretty interesting; the stuff she was able to do with just a few plants and herbs. You can straight up kill a person with the right combination! Just a drop and they're dead as a doornail."

"You were trying to kill me by fangirling over some shit you heard about on a podcast?" I asked incredulously, and she finally did flinch. Evidently, that was enough to offend her, an irony that wasn't lost on me.

"It wasn't on a podcast," she said petulantly. "I've been doing a lot of studying. Makeup and hair have *always* been my thing, or didn't you notice? Always too busy thinking of yourself." She smirked. "And anyway, I wasn't going to actually *kill* you. I just wanted to … teach you a lesson, I guess. Put a damper on your big day."

"Why?"

"Why not?" Sloan shrugged. "After all you've put me through lately, do you really think you deserve your big HEA?"

I swallowed. Phillip's strong arm was a welcome presence around my shoulders. "Why don't you just get out of here, Sloan. You've made your point."

"Fine, I'll go. I don't want to cause any trouble; I only wanted to congratulate you both." Were Sloan's eyes actually a little misty or was it just a trick of the dim light? "I've missed you, and I feel like … I just wish we could fix things. I wonder if we could try to, one day."

I stared at her. What the *hell*. "You literally just said you were going to poison me to teach me a lesson and put a damper on my big day … that I don't deserve a happy ending. And in the same breath, you say you want to congratulate me and fix things? Are you high?"

Her smile was equal parts sad and triumphant as she stared back at me. "What can I say—I contain multitudes."

"So you *are* high." I rubbed at my head, exhausted.

She moved to go, turning back toward the bonfire as though she meant to say goodbye to everyone and realized that nobody here was her friend. Her face really *was* a little sad.

My pity for her was short-lived because Sloan turned around once more, a sly little smile on her face, reared her head back, and spit right on my beautiful chocolate cake.

Rage blew up inside me. I moved toward Sloan, but before I had a chance to act, Roberta stepped forward, threw back her arm, and clocked her right in the face. Sloan stumbled and fell backward, breaking her fall with an elbow.

"Jesus!"

"Consider that your wedding present, guys," Roberta said to me with a tight-lipped smile, and walked back over to the table, where she picked up her paper plate and resumed eating cake. Just behind her left shoulder, Jamie stood with wide eyes, amazement and lust plain on his handsome face.

Twenty-One

Phillip generously poured from the expensive bottle of Shiraz , into my Solo cup and clinked his cup against mine. "To us," he said, his eyes shining. "To our marriage."

"To us," I agreed, taking a sip of the wine, which I had to admit, despite being a cheapskate who never bought anything outside a grocery store, tasted like heaven. I took another sip, letting it slide smoothly down my throat, trying to ignore the pangs of sadness and anger doing battle in my gut.

After Burt's masterful—and badass—punch, we'd all watched as Sloan had slowly risen up from the ground, cradling her jaw with her hand, and given the best rendition of a dignified walk back to her vehicle that she could muster. To her credit, she'd managed not to limp or even look back at us and had gotten in her car and driven away without another word. I had to give it to her; I knew Sloan, and it must have been hard as hell not to swing back, not to try and gain the upper hand.

Had she really wanted to wish me well? No, not likely. More likely, she wanted to ruin my evening and realized she was outmatched a little too late. Well, whatever. Let her be.

Hopefully, she'd gotten the message and wouldn't be back to cause more trouble. Deep down in my belly, though, I worried she would.

But now, the moment wasn't about *her*. It was about my wedding reception. Nothing, not even Sloan, was going to take me away from this beautiful moment my wonderful friends had planned for Phillip and I. I took another long sip and savored the rich taste of the wine, letting my body sway a little to the warbling, dulcet tones of T. Rex's "Debora," another favorite song from my childhood, an a capella almost-love song that my parents danced to in the kitchen when I was a kid.

As if on cue, my mother appeared. "Who let you DJ?" I asked her. I was glad to see she was holding a can of Coca-Cola, and even gladder to see a box of Nicorette peeking out from the pocket of her jean jacket.

"Hey, my music's killer!" Mama protested, laughing. "Are you having fun?"

"I am," I said, scanning over the scene. The bonfire had died down a little, but my friends' energy had not. Almost everyone was dancing, and the scene, to an outsider, would have looked ridiculous: Phillip, Benny, Lee, and Roberta in a sort of conga line, dancing around the fire like demented spirits, hollering and giggling, Roberta's brother Jorge watching and snapping pictures on his phone. Phillip was a picture in his all-black ensemble, a head taller than all of them, his black hair flashing in the firelight. He was adorably drunk; he'd had three Solo cups of wine to my one so far. Beth was hooping again, having finally acquiesced to everyone's requests, just a few paces from the dancing fools. The LED lights in her hoop were pulsing bright red and pink, and I could only assume those were happy colors. I smiled, thinking how awesome it had been of the Bloomer Demons to ask her on tour. Jason and Ollie rose from the lawn chairs they'd been sitting in and joined in the fray. To my surprise, Jason pulled out a solid rendition of a moonwalk, and Ollie was screaming at him to stop, that he was embarrassing. I grinned. They'd arrived just after Sloan's dramatic entrance, much to Phillip's and my surprise. We'd had no idea that they'd planned to drive down to help us celebrate.

Jamie and Clara were over on the porch, and though neither he nor Roberta had said, I was pretty sure he was guarding her, though he was taking great care to not make it obvious. At some point in the last two weeks, Jamie had put a miniature pool table right on the front porch, and he was currently squaring up, getting ready to make his first shot. Clara was leaned up against the porch railing, a full bottle of PBR in her hand, staring off into the distance. Jamie kept sneaking glances at Roberta, who was dancing with Phillip and Benny, and I could tell he wanted to drag her off into the bushes, since his own bedroom was currently occupied. My heart soared with elation for Burt. Between her brother coming home and finally getting the moves from Jamie, I knew her happiness must be dialed up to eleven.

"You just enjoy it," Mama said, clinking her can to mine. My little Solo cup had been toasted so much I was surprised it wasn't bent by now. "Don't worry about … the other. Her."

"Oh, I'm not worried." But I frowned. I was disturbed by what I'd learned, and I definitely planned to find out just what the hell she was playing at. How had she known I'd gotten married and where we'd be after? Why had she shown up bearing well wishes only to turn around and spit on my cake?

I looked down at my motorcycle boots, streaked with mud from prancing around in the dirt, dancing and celebrating, and looked back over to the bonfire where Phillip and my friends were having fun. I might just have some idea of how Sloan always knew where to be, and it sure as hell wasn't clairvoyance. I turned up my wine, guzzling the rest of its contents, threw the cup into the metal trash can, and walked over to the porch.

Our reception was more important, that was true. And I'd come back to it in short order.

But I had to take care of this business first. Right now.

As I marched up the steps, I could feel Phillip watching me. I gestured at him, a little 10-4 salute, and he gestured back at me with an understanding smile. He knew what I had to do. *If you need me, I'll come.* His voice flowed seamlessly into my head, and I blew him a kiss.

Jamie put down the pool cue and looked at me in surprise as I bounded up the steps. "Now darlin', you just enjoy your reception—"

"I am enjoying it," I said, looking down at the little gift bag. "But I'll enjoy it a hell of a lot more after I clear the air."

"I hear that," he said with a grin, and reached for his beer. Jamie was always reaching for his beer and it made me giggle. "Can you believe Roberta clocked her like that? I was like, 'damn'!"

"So I saw," I said with a grin, cuffing him on the shoulder. "You treat Burt right, you hear me?" And with that, I turned to Clara, who stood there in the corner, still as stone.

"It was you, wasn't it." It was more of a statement than a question. She looked at me warily, as if considering my words.

"It was me who what?" She held the pool cue between her hands as though she might lash out and strike me with it, but I wasn't worried. She didn't need a weapon; Clara was bigger than me both in stature and height, to say nothing of her muscular, athletic build, and could break me in half easily. Her purple hair was pulled back in a tight bun, giving her face a further pinched, angry sort of look. But I knew she wouldn't do anything to me, not here in front of everyone. Not with Phillip, one person who actually *was* stronger than her, waiting in the wings.

Phillip aside, I wasn't scared of Clara, though. Not now, not ever. Having heard Benny's story, I felt like I knew her, understood her a little better, even if I still didn't like her. And boy, I did *not* like her. So much for what I'd thought was a silent agreement between us earlier to bury the hatchet. No, Clara was a snake. I couldn't trust her any more than she trusted me.

I felt a familiar buzzing in my fingers. "It was you who told Sloan where we'd be. Where we were getting married and where the reception was. I think you might've even brought her to Phillip's show," I said in a low, calm tone. "I'm right, aren't I?"

Clara shrugged moodily, then gave a small, frustrated sigh and fixed a steely glare on me. She ran one hand through her purple hair, upsetting her bun. "So? I didn't know she was planning anything sinister. She just said she wanted to see you get married."

"Right," I said. That didn't seem bloody likely. The old Sloan might've been hurt by being excluded from my wedding, but now that I knew all the details of how she'd been carrying on for years, I wasn't sure about that. "I didn't know you two even knew each other, but it makes sense. You make a good pair." If I'd been a betting woman, I'd wager that Benny was wrong, that Clara hadn't gotten clean at all. Pills, he'd said, that she'd started taking after their relationship went sour.

It always seemed to lead back to drugs in these parts, and drugs always led back to the same dastardly group of people.

If Clara got the insult, she didn't let on. "I mean, you two are best friends. It seems reasonable to me that she'd be there for things." Clara's tone was sullen, defiant. "Unless of course you're the type of person who loses friends quickly—or rather, throws them away."

"Only the ones worth throwing," I spat back, and went inside the trailer, slamming the screen door behind me. "Benny and I have that in common." I turned to look at her through the screen. "You and I are not finished, Clara. Not by a long shot."

She opened her mouth to retort, but I didn't hear her reply. My legs buckled beneath me and I fell to the porch floor, my vision suddenly going black.

Twenty-Two

I panted heavily as I slowly pushed open the screen door with a creak, which took some effort, because it suddenly felt as heavy as lead. I'd exhausted myself completely, and it was all I could do to put one foot in front of me.

Somehow, I'd managed to get up off the porch after coming to—I was pretty sure it had only been a few seconds, but it had felt like an age—and grab onto the railing, assuring my friends, my mother, and Phillip, who had all come running, that I was okay. But I'd felt the rising sense of panic in my chest, the tingling in my face, the numbness of my lips, and knew that a panic attack was coming; a doozy. I'd held onto Jamie's outstretched arm for balance, ignoring Clara's smirking smile as she still stood in the corner, and assured everyone that I was fine, that I just needed a quick minute.

Phillip had insisted he should join me in the trailer, but I'd shaken my head and stopped him with a small smile. "No. You enjoy the party. I just want to splash some water on my face, and I'll be right back out. I'm okay, I promise."

He'd reluctantly let me go in alone, but he'd stayed on the porch, standing beside Clara, his face a thundercloud. I'd excused myself to the bathroom, where I splashed cool water on my cheeks and stared at my reflection, noting that my dark, dramatic wedding makeup was smeared around my eyes and mouth.

Then I'd thrown up.

Gripping the sides of the sink, I'd taken deep, gulping breaths and sobbed my way through the next few minutes. It was too much, and it had all come rushing back at once—and now, on what should be the happiest day of my life, Sloan back to wreak havoc. How much more could I take? How much more would I be forced to endure before Phillip and I could just have a normal life?

Your lives will never be normal, a small, unidentified voice said in my head, and I shuddered.

I'd managed to collect myself enough to head back outside, to reassure everyone that I was okay. Phillip, still on the porch, immediately rushed to my side, cradling me in his arms, his flashing green eyes suggesting he didn't believe a word I was saying. But thankfully, he was quiet. The last thing I wanted to do was ruin our wedding reception. We deserved this one good thing. I resolved to put my panic behind me and just *enjoy.*

"You sure you're okay?" Phillip asked in a low voice, holding tight to my arm.

"Yes," I said and took a step forward. Then I passed out again.

I woke up in a hospital bed, and I was *pissed.*

"Who brought me here?" I demanded before I'd even fully gained consciousness.

Benny, sitting across from me, looked at me calmly, a book

in his lap, one leg propped over the other. "Well, good morning to you, princess," he said with a grin.

"Why am I here?" I repeated, irritated at the term of endearment. Sloan had called me that too, and too recently. "What happened?"

"You passed out," Benny answered, reaching forward to pat my knee. "You just like … took a step forward and sunk to the ground. Hit your head pretty hard. Phillip was terrified; I thought he was going to rip the trailer apart with his bare hands trying to find a phone to call 911."

"Why am I here, though?" I asked again, glaring at him. My mouth tasted terrible, my tongue fuzzy and thick. "You could have just fixed me, couldn't you? You've done it before! I thought we didn't involve … people … when we didn't have to!"

"I can't bring people back from the dead; that's your thing," Benny said calmly, putting his book down on my bedside table and sitting up to his full posture. He had put his one white contact in for the first time in a long while, and his eyes almost seemed to dance. "This is the second time you've had a bad head injury in a few days; it's not the kind of thing you leave to chance. You could be concussed, Stormy. Again." His voice had taken on the tone of an exasperated teacher, and I resented it. "Plus … well, we wanted to get you away from the Wolfden for a bit. Just to make sure."

"Make sure of what?" Was my pounding head making me confused, or did he not make a lick of sense? "What the fuck is going on?"

"If you'll stop bitching at me for a second, I'll tell you." Benny laughed. He leaned forward and lowered his voice. "Stormy … Clara is gone. She got away." He sighed. "Not that we were like, holding her, exactly, but … we were just keeping eyes on her. You know. Because … because …"

"Because she's working with Sloan," I finished for him. "Whatever that means."

"Yeah," he said. "Up to no good, basically. She left during all the confusion when Phillip was calling 911. Just got in her car and drove off without a word to anybody."

"How did you guys let that happen?" I demanded, and he winced. No doubt he'd been asking himself the same question.

"I thought I could trust her," he said simply, and the sadness was evident on his face. My heart went out to him.

"I should have dealt with her when I had the chance," I said fiercely, and Benny shook his head.

"Your magic is strong, but Clara is stronger," he said, and I vowed then and there to prove him wrong one day. "You couldn't have fought her off. Besides, she hasn't technically done anything to you. We don't know if she's involved in … in anything."

"How did they get away?" I asked. "Jamie was watching her! And I couldn't have been out for more than a couple minutes! What the hell happened?"

"It was my fault," a voice said miserably from the corner, and I turned, realizing that Roberta had been in the room the whole time. She came over to the bed and took my hand in her own clammy one. "When you went inside, I called Jamie over to dance. We got to making out, and … well, I distracted him. I'm so sorry."

Despite my fury, I couldn't help but smile a little at that. Jamie and Roberta. A pairing I wholeheartedly approved of. "You guys were off boning and Clara got away? Is that what you're trying to tell me?"

Her face flushed crimson, and she bit her lip, her eyes pleading with mine for forgiveness. "We weren't boning! Just dancing … and well, kissing. It was such a festive, fun night … I drank a bunch of that punch. I guess I let it go to my head. I'm sorry, Stormy!"

I winked, giving her hand a squeeze. I couldn't be angry at her. Not at Roberta. Besides, it wasn't anyone's fault. Clara was a free agent, and we couldn't exactly hold her hostage just because she was a bitch with shitty taste in friends. Benny was right; she hadn't exactly done anything *to* me, had she?

"So how do we find her?" I asked just as Phillip entered the room clutching potted flowers. He held them out to me and I smiled, pressing the delicate black petals to my nose to discover their scent. Only Phillip Deville would find me a live plant—black pansies, to boot—to bring me in the hospital.

He leaned down and gave me a tender kiss on the forehead, taking the plant and placing it on my bedside table. His long fingers brushed a tendril of hair from my face. "You're not finding anyone," he said firmly, his mouth closed in a tight-lipped expression. "Your only job right now is to get better." "But Sloan could be—" I began, and he silenced me with a look. "Clara …"

"We'll worry about her later," he said, his eyes boring into mine, quieting me. He meant business. "Your one and only job is to recover, get well, and go on our honeymoon." Then he grinned. "Well, I guess that's three jobs."

"What honeymoon?" I asked him, surprised. Phillip and I hadn't talked about a honeymoon. I'd just assumed we'd plan one later, if at all. Neither of us really stood much on cere-mony, and we'd done so much traveling lately, it just hadn't seemed important.

He busied himself fluffing the pillows behind me, then bent over me, a sly smile on his lips. "Get yourself better and you might just find out, Spooner," was all he would say.

Twenty-Three

I rolled over in bed, fully awake but completely unable to get up. I was in a state of bliss; the sheets were crisp and somehow cottony-soft at the same time, the light streaming through the windows soft and delicate, and there was a pleasant smell in the room, no doubt coming from the bubbling jacuzzi I heard whirring in the bathroom.

I could just barely make out Phillip's voice over the jacuzzi; it sounded like maybe he was talking to Lee. Reluctantly, I sat up in bed, languidly stretching my arms over my head, unable to stop the smile from spreading across my face as I yawned contentedly. I stood and walked over to the sliding glass window, easing it open and poking my head out to enjoy the gentle morning breeze as I looked out over the Atlanta skyline. Sunlight glinted off the gold-capped top of the capitol building, shiny and bright.

"Hey, dirty girl," a sultry voice said behind me, and Phillip's arms wrapped around me, tight, pulling him into his warm, shirtless chest. He placed a wet kiss behind my ear, and his breath fluttered my hair, making my entire body erupt in gooseflesh. It was a little chilly in the room, especially since I was clad in only a silky black teddy with tiny, embroidered skulls on the bodice (my honeymoon present to Phillip, who had made no promises not to rip it to shreds before our stay was over) that didn't cover much of my flesh. Phillip had already tested the jacuzzi from the feel of it, his skin so warm it was almost hot. I sunk into him, enjoying the feeling of his hot skin against my cool skin. He crooned against my ear, making my knees go weak. "Want to get clean with me?"

"If there's a choice between getting clean or getting dirty," I said, whirling to face him in the early morning light, "I'd rather get dirty."

"Touché." Phillip's lips met mine in a crushing kiss, his arms wrapping around my waist, picking me up off the floor. When he finally set me down, my entire brain was whirling.

"Is that delicious smell coming from the jacuzzi?" I asked, my mouth still against his, my voice coming out a dreamy murmur.

"Yes," he answered, stepping back to take a look at me. "I used all the fancy bath products that were in there. Gardenia or something." He smiled, his eyes flashing. "You sure are pretty in the mornings with your hair all rumpled and your eyes half-asleep. I hope I never get used to that."

I blushed. "Stop. I haven't even used any mouthwash. I probably stink. My hair's in a knot—"

"With all due respect, Mrs. Deville, please do shut up." Without another word, Phillip picked me up and carried me across the suite, using his bare foot to kick open the double doors that led into the expansive bathroom. The smell of gardenia was strong and sweet as he deposited me on the edge of the jacuzzi. "Now take that thing off before I tear it off with my teeth," he ordered, his eyes dancing. Without argument, my heart pounding, I slid the strap down my shoulder, unable to tear my eyes away from him.

We'd been here for a whole day already, but I still couldn't believe Phillip had booked the Ritz Carlton—and a suite, no less—for our honeymoon. By most celebrity standards, the Ritz Carlton wasn't the crème de la crème or anything, but for a girl who had grown up dirt poor and still lived in a singlewide trailer, it was beyond my wildest dreams. I was still marveling at all of it—the view, the amenities, the crisp, gorgeous sheets on the California king bed, the room service, the jacuzzi … it was too much.

And I intended to enjoy every moment of it.

Most especially, I intended to enjoy every moment with—and every inch of—my handsome, sexy husband. I slid the other strap of my teddy down, giving Phillip a playful, defiant look.

He bent down onto one knee, his arm resting beside mine on the edge of the jacuzzi, and leaned close to my face. Then he growled, showing me his straight, white teeth. Despite myself, I began to tremble and pushed the teddy down faster. It now lay at my hips. I moved to stand up and take it the rest of the way off, and Phillip stopped me, holding me down fast.

"Let me," he said, his voice still a growl, making me shiver. He placed his hands on either side of me, his warm hands tugging the silk over my hips, the sensation of the silky fabric and his warm hands running over my skin, invoking a sigh of pleasure. He gently lifted my feet, pulling the teddy out from under me and carefully folding it, placing it on the shelf so it wouldn't get wet. *He's so thoughtful,* I thought to myself almost bashfully, but Phillip silenced that thought with one glowering look. His eyes burned as he stared up at me, his face set in determination, burning with a glow that almost seemed to come from within.

"Open your legs," he commanded, and my eyes widened, but I did as he asked. His soft black hair fell over his forehead and tickled my knees as he buried his face in my thighs. I clamped a hand over my mouth, sensations washing over me.

Phillip's kisses started near my knees, gentle and playful, but became more insistent and rough as he neared my inner thighs. I cried out as he nibbled at the delicate skin there, then moaned loudly when he bit me for real, his teeth sharp and pointed against his soft, wet lips.

"Too much?" Phillip raised up and looked at me inquisitively, a ghost of a smile on his face.

I panted, pushing his head down. "Not enough."

His lips felt so good against me that I soon forgot how to think at all.

Sometime later, I did actually bathe—and I was still sitting in the crook of Phillip's arm as I languidly washed at our intertwined legs with a soapy loofah, legs that felt like jelly from the heights of passion he'd taken me to. I sighed against him, moaning softly as his hand came up to gently graze my thigh.

"Is this it?" I asked, raising the loofah up and ringing it out, the warm suds feeling wonderful against my skin.

"What?" he asked, watching the soap as it dripped down my arms and onto my chest. "Good lord, that's sexy."

"Surely you must be spent by now." I giggled, turning to face him, the hot, bubbling water lapping against our shoulders.

"With you? Never." He laughed, unable to tear his eyes away from my soapy body. "You'll fuck me back into the grave, I'm sure of it." Then he wrenched his eyes upward. "What do you mean, is this it?"

"This. The Ritz Carlton, the jacuzzi ... all of this." I gestured, flinging water droplets into the air. "Is this the big honeymoon surprise, or is there more?" He chuckled, and I rushed to say, "I mean, if this *is* it, this is totally perfect. I've never stayed anywhere so nice. It's like a dream. I wouldn't want or expect anything more. I didn't mean to imply that … like …"

"Oh my god, Stormy, shut the hell up." Phillip kissed me passionately, his arm wrapping around me and pulling me onto his lap, where I could feel that he was, indeed, ready again. His other arm grazed at my soapy breast as I opened my legs to him, gasping a little as he entered me.

I wrapped my arms around his neck as I straddled him, the pulsing of the jets sending bubbles as high as our shoulders. Phillip's hips bucked against me, and I cried out against his neck.

"No, this isn't it," he growled in my ear, his sharp teeth grazing me again. "There's more, my dirty witch. There's always more."

This time, I bit him back.

I could feel beads of sweat traveling beneath my shirt, down my back, making a damp spot. I grimaced as I ran toward the souvenir shop, one of at least a dozen in my general vicinity, hoping to get a moment's respite from the sweltering sun. I leaned up against the building's faux-wood façade, grateful for the momentary shade, and smiled as Phillip sauntered up after me.

He leaned in close, pressing on the building with one long arm, and went for a kiss. I met his mouth eagerly, despite being sweaty and overheated. I'd never turn down my lover for a kiss, especially not after the night and morning we'd shared back at the hotel. Even now, standing in the blistering sun in ninety-five-degree Georgia midday sun with the humidity as thick as a wet thermal blanket, my thighs burned in anticipation, imagining what might transpire when we got back to the hotel for the evening. I planned to step into the huge, luxurious shower with its fancy rain spout and wash all the sweat off me, and then … well, maybe I'd just pull Phillip into the shower *with* me.

"Are you having fun?" Phillip asked, pulling back from my kiss reluctantly, reaching into the pocket of his black jean shorts for a hair tie. He pulled his hair back—it was really starting to get long again, and I couldn't *stand it,* he looked so sexy—into a short ponytail.

"I am," I said, beaming up at him, wiping a sheen of sweat from my brow.

"I feel bad," he confessed, his brows furrowing in sympathy. "I didn't know you don't ride rollercoasters. And I didn't know it was going to be quite so hot today when I planned this."

"Oh, honey," I said, touching his arm. "Please. Don't feel bad. I'm having a great time. And like I said, it's just the upside-down coasters I don't like. I'll totally get on the Scream Machine with you."

"Promise?" Phillip's eyes danced.

"I promise. It's the least I can do after you planned this whole thing for me, and since you've graced my eyes with the view of you wearing shorts." I fanned myself with a hand and Phillip laughed.

"Shut up. It's hot out."

"No kidding." I shielded my eyes from the sun and scanned the crowd. It was surprisingly crowded at Six Flags for a Tuesday, but I supposed that in the summer, theme parks were busy pretty much around the clock. There was certainly no shortage of people today. "Where did our folks go?"

Phillip was still digging in his pocket. He fished out another hair tie triumphantly and gestured for me to turn around. I did, smiling as Phillip wrapped my hair in his hands and put it in a high ponytail. He'd been taking care of me like that the entire day—our entire honeymoon, in fact. If he wasn't careful, I was going to end up seriously spoiled. And I didn't mind it one bit.

"Nikolai and Beth, and Roberta and Jamie all went to ride the Ninja," he said, naming one of the rollercoasters I definitely would *not* be riding. I smiled. Nikolai and my new friend Beth, hooper extraordinaire, seemed to enjoy spending time together. I loved to see whatever was blooming between them taking form. "Benny, Lee, Jason, and Ollie went over to Monster Plantation. They said they'd hold the line for us."

"Monster Plantation!" I exclaimed, whirling around with childish glee. "I'd forgotten all about that!"

"I take it it's some kind of like … kid's ride?" Phillip chuckled as I looped my arm in his and dragged him forward, forgetting about the heat in my excitement. "Lee said it's like a haunted house but with Muppets or something."

"Even better," I assured him as he walked along. How could I have forgotten Monster Plantation? As a child, it had been my favorite ride at Six Flags. I could still hear Daddy complaining. Every year it'd be the same—"I didn't pay fifty daggum dollars to see you ignore all the coasters and just ride that dumb boat over and over," and Mama would tell him to shush up, that he hadn't had to pay for my ticket anyway and to just let me enjoy myself. It was true; I'd earned my ticket every year through the reading program at school, and I knew that Mama had afforded her and Daddy's tickets by hoarding Coca Cola wrappers from the two-liter bottles and cashing them in. I wondered if those sorts of rewards programs existed now so poor folks could come out and enjoy themselves. Then I began to wonder just how much Phillip had paid for all this— the hotel, tickets to Six Flags for us and our friends, and who knew what else he had in store … and began to feel guilty.

"It's our honeymoon, baby," Phillip said, his hand

caressing the back of my neck and moving up into my pony-tail. "You're not to feel guilty about one single thing. The first part of our relationship was spent dodging bullets and god knows what else. I never got a chance to spoil you, and I'm making up for it now. You got a problem with that?"

"No," I confessed happily as we walked along. I could see the outline of Monster Plantation off in the distance.

"So tell me more about this ride, then," Phillip said with a satisfied grin, having won the argument.

"It's … as weird as it sounds. It's a kid's ride, like you said. You get in this little rickety boat, and it leads you through this old plantation house—"

"As in, a Southern plantation? Like the pre-Civil War kind?" Phillip grimaced.

"Yeah, I know. Not great, huh. But inside, there's monsters. And that's all I'm going to tell you. The rest you'll have to see for yourself." I gestured at the line forming outside the old fake plantation, and Phillip looked up at it, bemused.

"About time you two lovebirds got here," Lee said, gesturing for us to join them. I hesitated, but the couple behind them ushered us forward. He clapped me on the shoulder. "You're literally damp, Stormy."

"Well, *someone* didn't tell me we were coming to Six Flags, so I stupidly wore a black polyester shirt!" I said, rolling eyes at Phillip, but I wasn't really angry. Besides, it'd be air conditioned inside. I'd get a momentary break from the sweltering sun.

"I could always run to one of the thousands of overpriced gift shops and get you a Looney Tunes themed T-shirt," Phillip offered with a grin. "One with your favorite, Pepe Le Pew?"

"If you call me '*mon petit bebe,*' I'll kill you," I said, and he burst out laughing.

"I wasn't going to," he lied.

"Then you were going to say something about me liking problematic men; just remember, that's a self-own."

Jason and Ollie, standing just a few yards ahead of us in line, were busy chatting up a couple of women who looked to be about our age. They saw us and returned our waves, but then quickly went back to talking, Ollie confident as usual, his always-impeccable Vans (seriously, did he buy a new pair every month?) decked out with flames. Jason hung back, a little shyly, I thought, but the twinkle in his eyes was more than a bit flirty. I wondered if the girls were fans. Likely not, because they would have noticed Phillip immediately. That was something I was still getting used to— Phillip being recognized everywhere. He'd signed two autographs in the first hour at Six Flags alone, to say nothing of the chaos he'd caused in downtown Atlanta the night before when we'd briefly crept out of our room for a romantic dinner. I found I didn't hate it, though—I was very proud to be on Phillip's arm, and not just because he was handsome and beloved by fans everywhere, but because he was mine, and I knew just how special he was. How lucky I was.

"I'm the lucky one," Phillip murmured in my ear, and kissed me on the cheek.

"Hey, Stormy!" I turned to see Roberta running up to join the line, flanked by Jamie, who had his arm draped around her shoulder, and Beth and Nikolai, who hung back a little, lost in conversation. "I can't miss the Monster Plantation!"

"Best ride at Six Flags!" I called back, and she nodded. Jamie groaned, laughing.

"Seriously?" he whined, but Roberta shut him up by planting a big, sloppy kiss on his grinning mouth. He responded by wrapping an arm around her waist and pulling her close, not caring that people were watching. I smiled while watching them, so happy that Roberta had finally found happiness, then looked at Nikolai. He met my eyes for a moment, sharing a private look, then put his attention back on Beth, who was talking animatedly about something. She hadn't dulled her look for Six Flags. If anything, the opposite—she was clad in black bike shorts, a skull T-shirt cinched at the waist, black platform sandals with metal studs, and her thick, dark hair was pulled back in a bun and wound with a scrunchie that appeared to be made out of bones. She looked adorable, and from the looks of it, my brother agreed.

For what felt like the millionth time, a wave of love swelled in my chest for this group of people, my chosen family. My *pack*. These chuckleheads who'd driven all the way to Atlanta on a week day to come to Six Flags and ride some dumb kid's ride with me just because it was my honeymoon and they loved me. Loved Phillip.

And I loved them every bit as much.

"Come on, guys, we're up." Benny gestured at the boats rolling up onto the entrance ramp, and I stepped forward, surprised. That was the fastest I'd ever gotten through a line at Six Flags, on any ride. It must be my lucky day. The attendant, a skinny guy with a high ponytail and thick black eyeliner, gestured me forward impatiently. I stepped into the boat in front of me, grabbing Phillip's arm and pulling him down beside me. He was so tall that his knees were forced uncomfortably into the seat in front of us, where Benny and Lee sat. Jason, Ollie, and their two female companions were in the boat just ahead of us, and as they rolled off the metal beam into the water, rickety and squeaking, Jason turned around and gave us a "hang ten" sign, grinning all the while. Phillip gave him one back, promptly followed by his middle finger.

Just as we were pushing off, the boat jostled. Two women, one skinny and petite in baggy gym clothes, and the other muscular, had skipped the line and were trying to jump into the back of our boat, where there was a spare seat. They were wearing cheap masks from the gift shop—Tweety Bird and

Wonder Woman—the plastic kind that I remembered from childhood Halloweens. I giggled at the sight. The attendant hadn't noticed the line-jumpers, busy helping someone get into another boat, so I shrugged and ignored them. It wasn't like they were bothering us.

Roberta, Jamie, Beth, and Nikolai were still standing at the turnstiles. I gave them a sad shrug. "Catch the next one!" I called to Roberta. "We'll wait for you guys at the exit!" She nodded and gave me a thumbs up.

"Do you want to put your legs in my lap?" I asked Phillip, noting how uncomfortable he must be, squished into the middle seat of a fake boat made for children.

"I'd like to put something in your lap, but not my legs," he whispered back to me, and my face flushed. His lit up in a grin.

"You just stop that, Deville," I whispered back, but my hand had already wound its way into his lap. We couldn't keep our hands off each other, couldn't keep our minds out of the gutter. Oh well, we were on our honeymoon. Let everyone eat their hearts out.

The little boat inched its way through the water, and the two old wooden doors I remembered from my childhood opened, the boat floating inside to the plantation's entryway. Immediately, we began to hear hillbilly style country music, and the first "monster"—basically a huge, glorified Muppet— greeted us warmly in an overexaggerated accent. Phillip laughed uproariously, and I grinned. He was going to love this. It was just the type of spooky kitsch he lived for.

In the boat behind us, people giggled and talked excitedly. I sighed happily and leaned into Phillip's shoulder. The boat meandered down the pre-set watery track, rounding corners and visiting every monster resident of the plantation, each cheesier and funnier than the next. I watched Phillip more than

I watched the show, laughing every time he laughed, relishing how much he was enjoying himself.

As we neared the end of the first part of the tour, the boat inching toward the second set of double doors, I felt a tap on the shoulder. I turned to face the teenager in the Tweety Bird mask, who was holding out a little trinket to me. I was surprised they were still wearing it. People wore masks and capes all over the park, but the Monster Plantation ride was already so dark, how could they see? "Yeah?" I asked.

"This rolled into the back of the boat just now," the voice said. It was muffled but sounded like a young woman, her voice high pitched. "I think you may've dropped it."

I took the little trinket and inspected it. It was my pot of lip gloss, the one I usually carried in my pocket. It must have fallen out when I was climbing onto the boat. "Thanks!" I said.

The girl nodded, her thick plastic mask unmoving. "No prob."

With another smile, I turned back to the front of the boat, twisting off the lid of the lip gloss and running my index over the waxy, smooth surface. The familiar blueberry smell was sweet and cloying, and for a moment, I had the oddest sense of déjà vu. A chill crept up my back, then was gone. I swiped the gloss over my lips and pushed the pot back into my pocket.

I nudged Phillip. "Here we go!" He glanced at me, his eyes twinkling with bemusement as the sheriff monster yelled after us in a terrified voice, "Wait! Don't go into the marsh!"

The little boat drifted through the double doors and into the second portion of the plantation, where it was dark and ominous, the music desolate and eerie. Neon green lights twinkled in the gnarled trees, the only source of light in the pitch black. I grabbed Phillip's hand as we floated down the path, the first of the scary monsters leaping out at us from the darkness.

I could feel Phillip's shoulders moving with his laughter and I grinned. I knew he'd love this.

We rounded another corner and were confronted with another scary monster, this one with a gaping maw for a mouth that emitted a painful, mournful howl. Behind us, a boisterous woman catcalled the monster, and I laughed, ignoring the increasing anxiety that was swirling around in my chest.

The boat continued to drift, and I cast my eyes to each of my friends, noting where they were in the expanse of dark, hearing their laughter, and I smiled. I tilted my head back a little, my eyes glancing back just for a split second, and nodded. It was time. Now or never.

As if on cue, what little eerie light there was flickered out, and we were suddenly pitched into complete and total – actual – darkness. The boat stopped. A collection of tittering laughter and groans came from the suspended boats, but they soon died as people realized this wasn't part of the attraction. "Hey! We're stuck!" Ollie complained from up front. "Somebody fix the boats!"

"Stormy?" Phillip asked again. "Are you okay?" His hand was on my arm, but I couldn't see him. I couldn't see *anything*.

"I'm fine," I said, reaching for him in the dark, giving him what I hoped was a reassuring pat. I could just barely make out his profile. "Everything's fine. Or soon will be."

"What's going on?" he asked, his voice full of fury.

A voice I knew as well as my own spoke up, clear as a bell, from the seat behind me. No longer high pitched, it was low and calm. "Stormy and I have some business to attend to," she said from behind the Tweety Bird mask.

"Indeed we do," I answered, running my fingers over my lips, still wet from the gloss I'd applied. "Hi, Sloan."

"Hey, Stormy," she said, and pulled off her mask.

Twenty-Four

Phillip was tense with rage beside me in the little boat. He had recognized Sloan's voice too. I, on the other hand, found myself oddly calm. My hand, which had been grasping for him, found his leg and gave it a squeeze. *No,* I thought, forcing myself to calm down and hoping that calm translated into my thoughts. *Don't do anything. Stay right there.*

Somehow, I'd known it would come to this. That Sloan would sniff me out, hunt me down, and force me into a confrontation. That's just who Sloan was. She wouldn't let me go without some final showdown.

But I was fine with that, I realized as I sat there in the darkness, the little boat rocking beneath me.

I felt okay.

I was okay.

I looked down at the little pot of gloss, repressing the urge to laugh. Oh, she'd tampered with it somehow. I should have known the moment I'd seen her dumb Tweety mask (who had always been her favorite), or at the least when she'd pressed that lip gloss into my hand. She'd tried to warn me, after all, at my own wedding.] How stupid was I to believe that it had fallen out of my pocket and rolled into the back of the boat?

But would Sloan actually stoop so low to poison *me?*

I cleared my throat and tried to speak. My voice was a bit squeaky, but at least it came out. "So," I managed to sputter. "Crashing the party again, I see."

"Are you having a good honeymoon, Storm?" she asked me, her voice still calm and cool as a cucumber.

My hand closed into a fist, a feeling of buzzing numbness filling my fingers. A feeling that was quickly becoming familiar. The tingling, buzzing feeling of my power, pooling into my hands, at the ready should I need it. I opened my fingers and closed them again, taking another gulp of air into my lungs. The darkness freaked me out a little, but I vowed to remain calm.

"What's going on?" a voice cried from another one of the boats. "Is something wrong? Is somebody hurt?"

"Are you okay, Stormy? For real?" Benny's voice was close to my ear, and I reached out and found his arm, giving him a reassuring squeeze. He called out, "Everything's fine, guys!" Then, his voice lower, near my ear again, "Do you want me to handle her?"

"I've got this, Ben," I said, then reached for Lee, fumbling until I found his wiry shoulder. "I suspect Clara's here somewhere. I think she jumped from the boat right before the lights went out."

"She put the lights out," Sloan said from behind me, her voice easy, as though this were the most natural thing in the world.

"How in the hell did none of us notice the two of them in our boat?" Lee said incredulously, his voice full of rage.

"Masks," I said. "They were wearing masks." I turned back to Sloan. I couldn't see her well, but from what I could make out, she was just sitting there in the back of the boat, her hands folded in her lap, pretty as you please. The same way she'd been back at the trailer on my wedding night. The same calm, cool, unbothered stance she'd been taking for the past year while secretly, covertly trying to undo every facet of my life behind the scenes. If I had been paying better attention, I would have known her figure, her posture, anywhere, even in the baggy shirt and oversized gym shorts she was wearing. Clara, too; after all, she was a literal wrestler with the muscles to go with it. But I'd been too busy flirting and lusting after Phillip to pay attention to anyone else. I'd had my head in the clouds for days, and it was making me stupid. "And she disguised her voice. But I figured it out. Eventually."

Time and again, I'd fought against her, railed against her, but she kept slipping away. Only to return again, with that same cool smile on her face, and she'd keep trying until she finally succeeded.

I couldn't let that happen.

I was finally ready to do what needed to be done.

"Stormy," Phillip said uncertainly beside me. His hand on my leg gripped me like a vise.

"Go with Benny and Lee; get everybody off the boats and to the exit. Then try to find Clara," I said. I thought for a moment. "And look for the attendant with the ponytail and the eyeliner. Don't let him get away."

"I don't want to leave you alone with her," he seethed.

"I can handle it," I said. "I promise. Really."

Reluctantly, he stood up, the tiny boat wobbling beneath his weight. It swayed in the water as he stepped off the ledge onto the fake grass of the attraction, off into the darkness. After a moment, a little square of light lit up from his phone as he turned on the flashlight app. He turned back to me, illuminating Sloan and me in the boat—she was sitting exactly as I had imagined—and then walked off toward the fake monsters, all of whom seemed a lot less creepy and whimsical without their mechanical operations. Behind them were a set of signs, including one that said EXIT and another that said LIGHTS. Off to the side, Benny and Lee were helping a young couple off the first boat and onto the fake grass.

I turned back to Sloan, who was once again shrouded in darkness.

"It's getting kind of sad," I said, rubbing absently at my still-tingling hand. "You following me around like this. I never pegged you for one of those types."

Sloan didn't answer.

My lips had started to burn a little, but I kept smiling.

"I know you didn't poison me," I went on. "The effects are already starting to fade. It just burns some. What did you use, cayenne? Ghost pepper? I don't believe for a second it's poison." I pressed my lips, which felt slightly swollen and tender, but nothing too serious. "You must've been pretty sly to get it out of my pocket, I'll give you that, but what are you trying to do here, Sloan? We both know you aren't going to kill *me*. You don't have it in you.

Sloan snorted but still said nothing.

"Besides, you couldn't hurt me even if you did really want to. I'm too powerful. I think you know that. Is that why you keep showing up, trying to test me? Are you trying to force my hand? Is that it?"

Silence.

"And now you've dragged Clara into it. What reason could she possibly have to help you? Why get mixed up into all this?"

"Clara hates you." There. That had done it; I'd finally goaded Sloan into talking. Her voice was sullen in the darkness. "As if you didn't know."

"Yeah, I knew," I replied. "And I couldn't give less of a shit."

"You don't want to know *why* she hates you?"

I shrugged. "Not really. It has to do with Benny, and him and Lee, I guess. Maybe she just doesn't like outsiders. Maybe it's an alpha female thing. Honestly? It's none of my business, and I just don't care. I don't like her, either." I realized as I said the words that it was true. Clara disliking me was none of my business. The feeling was mutual. We didn't have to all sing kumbaya and be besties just because we had mutual people in common. Knowing you weren't liked and being okay with it was a very freeing feeling.

"That's your problem," Sloan said. "You don't care. You don't care about the hurt you've caused. The people who have suffered because of you. The people who have died because of you." Sloan grabbed my shoulders, her fingers icy cold. My own hand tensed into a tighter fist. "Shank. Tess. Guthrie and Elvin. All of them are gone because of *you.*"

"No, all of them are gone because of *them,*" I said coolly, breathing through the tension as I carefully, calmly extracted Sloan's hand from my shoulder. "Just because I learned what they were doing and decided to defend myself doesn't make me to blame for what happened to them. Every single one of those people is dead due to the consequences of their own actions." I swallowed, feeling tears spring to my eyes. "Even Tess. Though I suppose your friend Colt Leather helped him along, didn't he?" I hadn't recognized him right off—he'd dyed his greasy burgundy hair black and was wearing it different now, and the heavy eyeliner had disguised those piercing, wild eyes of his, but the attendant who had waved us forward was him, all right. I should have guessed he was running with Sloan all along. He was just her type.

"It's just so *easy* for you to deny all responsibility, isn't it?" Sloan sneered, poking me in the shoulder with another icy finger. "Poor, precious, sweet little Stormy. She's never to blame for anything. She's so fragile, we all have to protect her, even though she can read minds and raise the dead and knock people out cold with her hands, but oh, she's such a delicate little flower, she needs all the big bad men to come to her aid!"

"That's rich, coming from somebody who spikes makeup to hurt people, like a weirdo fucking coward." I sneered. "You've got so much talent, a whole business doing hair and makeup, and you're squandering it, to what? Cosplay as some kind of medieval-style poisoner? Bum around with bitter, jealous drug addicts and plan revenge plots? Do you think you can really just play at being a witch by stirring some shit into a bottle of foundation?"

Sloan's hand, still resting on my shoulder, curled, her fingernails poking into my skin.

"Touch me again and you'll regret it," I warned, pushing her off me, feeling the light pulsing into my fingers. I glanced up, seeing shadows in the darkness heading toward the exit. Benny and Lee had gotten most of the people off the boats, though I could barely make out Ollie and Jason over by one of the monster figures, hovering, watching. I smiled, touched. They wouldn't leave me. I wondered if Phillip had found Clara yet.

"You want to know why I'm here?" Sloan asked, her voice low and cold in the darkness. "Why I followed you?"

"Sure," I said. "I'm all ears."

"I hacked Phillip's phone. Really early on, before you guys ever went to Boston. He's damn stupid when it comes to technology; he didn't even notice. I've been tailing you everywhere." So that explained it. How she always knew where we'd be. It hadn't been all Clara, after all. "I was honestly starting to get bored," she went on. "You and that lump of crap you call a boyfriend are the most boring people on the planet. Colt was right—he's a washed-up has-been. He's supposed to be a legit rock star, and all you two ever do is lay around doing nothing.

"I guess you've never had a good sex life, Sloan," I said

with a laugh. "Especially if your latest guy is Colt 'sex scan-dal' Leather. My condolences."

I could feel her indignant huff of breath. I'd wounded her; since we were teens, she'd been bragging on her healthy sex life and how attractive men found her. She'd always been more blessed than me, a perpetual wallflower, in that regard. There were plenty of proms and homecomings I spent holed up at home with no date while Sloan had to fight off suitors. How far she'd fallen—going for men like Guthrie and Colt—and so quickly, and what was worse, she *knew* I knew it. It must be killing her. Still, she went on. "After your wedding, I thought about laying low for a while, just letting shit go. I'd made my point, anyway. And I have a business to run. But then I saw Phillip was planning a little honeymoon for you, with a stop off in Atlanta for a Six Flags' day. Well, I couldn't resist that. For old times' sake, you know?" I sighed. Sloan and I had come to Six Flags together more than once when we'd been teenagers. Day trips with friends, field trips … We had plenty of memories together at this place, in these very boats at Monster Plantation, in fact. It had been both of our favorites. It was oddly flattering that Sloan would follow me here. Flattering in a completely unhinged, maniacal sort of way, but flattering all the same.

I sighed again, massaging my fist with my other hand. The burning in my lips had almost completely subsided, and I found that my voice had returned to normal. "So now what? You've stalled out the boats and cut the lights and we're here. You've got me alone. So what's next?"

"Next," Sloan said, her voice suddenly inches from my ear, "is that I kill you."

For a moment, I couldn't catch my breath, unable to form words, to think of what to say next. My heart thudded dully in my chest. Then I forced a shaking breath into my lungs and burst out laughing.

"Oh, Sloan," I said through my laughter. "You can't kill me. That ship has sailed, girl. Pun very much intended."

"Wanna bet?' Her voice was like ice in the darkness. She was angry. Furious. I knew that tone.

"Oh, absolutely I do."

The rickety little boat shook as Sloan stood up. I could make out her outline, standing over me. I stood up too, trying to get my bearings as the boat swayed on the tiny beam of metal that acted as the track. The water was surprisingly high; it sloshed over the boat and soaked my shoes.

"You think I don't have the power?" Sloan demanded, her voice deep with fury. "You think just because I wasn't born with it, because I wasn't one of Elvin's golden children, that I don't have any power?"

"That's exactly what I think," I said, my voice matching hers in intensity, staring her down, meeting her eyes in the dark. "And I think you're so mad about it—you've been so mad about it for *years*—that it's made you lose your mind. You're jealous, Sloan. So jealous that it's made you bonkers. You've created this whole persona to try and fight it, but at the end of the day, you're still just a little girl with no powers, out of her element and out of her mind."

Sloan let out a fierce, mad howl, and propelled herself forward, throwing the entirety of her weight at me, crashing into me hard, throwing us both off the small boat.

We hit the water, Sloan still clutching at me, trying to tear at my hair, my face—and sank.

I'd thought the water was surprisingly deep. Really only a couple feet were necessary since the boats were actually operated by the little metal track, but I thought, as I sank into the depths, that the water was at least four feet deep, if not more. My feet kicked and flailed in the water, trying to get to the floor, but found no purchase. I struggled to wrench myself free from Sloan's grasp, her hands tangled in my hair, still pulling and trying to cause me pain even as we sunk.

Finally, with one quick jerk, I wrenched myself free from her grasp, sending her floating off into the depths. Kicking my feet, I found the floor and tried to stand up, cracking my head on something hard as I moved to stand. Stars appeared before my eyes, and I waved wildly with my arms, trying to find a way out of the water. I sputtered, forcing my mouth to stay closed, lest I swallow a mouthful of nasty, stale water.

My hand reached above me and found a blank, empty space. I tried to stand again, doing so easily this time. On shaky legs, I pulled myself up, the water coming up to my chest, and surveyed the scene. The little ledge with the fake grass was right beside me; that's where I'd hit my head. All the boats were empty. Jason and Ollie were no longer crouched by the monsters; off in the distance, near the EXIT sign, I could hear yelling. They must have found Clara, I assumed. The monsters seemed to leer at me in the darkness, the twinkling green lights in the fake trees casting the entire space in an eerie glow. It was little more than a room, but it felt like I was lost on some deserted desert island, only Sloan, still flailing beneath me in the water, here to keep me company.

I sighed, watching the ripples just a few yards away, Sloan struggling to find purchase with the slick floor, the water closing over her head again and again. I shuffled through the waist-deep water and grabbed her arms, pulling her up and onto the ledge, both of us drenched. Sloan sputtered for a moment, spitting out a mouthful of water, and stared at me, her eyes dark and black as coals.

I stared back, saying nothing, just watching her. She suddenly looked very small, and very sad.

"You're right," she said finally, wiping at her wet cheeks. "I couldn't hurt you—not really—even if I wanted to. And I don't really want to."

"Then why all this?" I asked, gesturing in the darkness. I could still hear yelling off in the distance.

Sloan took a ragged breath. "I got tired of being the guest star, the best friend character, I guess. You're so powerful and … and … sought after. And for years, you didn't even know it. Tess, Phillip, Elvin … all those weirdos at the Wolfden … they'd all die for you, and you didn't even know. I just wanted to feel like, even a third as powerful. As desired. As respected." She looked down at her drenched shoes. "I was tired of standing in your shadow, Stormy."

"You've never been in my shadow," I argued, but she silenced me with a hand.

"Yes, I have," Sloan insisted. "I guess it was just easier to blame you for it than to step out of it and move on with my life."

"I never did anything to hurt you on purpose, Sloan," I said solemnly. "I had no idea you felt this way. I had no idea … about so much. For so long."

"I know that," Sloan said. "But your ignorance was one of the reasons I hated you so much. The world falling down around you, and you were just … oblivious."

"I can see how that would be hard," I said. I had no intention of apologizing, but I could give her that. Make her think I empathized. Which I did, in a weird, fucked-up way. My own trauma, I supposed.

"I loved Tess too," she said in a whisper, wiping at her eyes. Then she looked at me. "And …Guthrie too. It was fucked up, what we had but … I did love him. In a way." She shook her head. "I haven't handled anything well. I shouldn't have brought Clara and Colt into it, but …but I just … I'm just so *angry.*"

"So am I." On impulse, I grabbed Sloan's hand and squeezed it. To my surprise, she squeezed it back.

"I guess this is the end of our friendship," she said simply, her hand hanging in my mine, both of them damp. "Unless you can find a way to forgive me."

"I don't know," I said honestly, tears prickling at my own eyes. "I really don't. Sloan, people have *died* because of you."

"I never meant to truly hurt anyone." Her voice was small, and for a moment, sounded sincere.

"You've got to be kidding me," a voice said behind us, and we both turned, startled, to see Clara standing there, hands on her hips. "I hijacked a boat and climbed into the rafters to cut the lights just so the two of you could sit there and hold hands like two lovers on a picnic?"

"Clara, we're just talking—" Sloan began, her voice a little unsure.

"You might be too much of a coward to follow through, but I'm not," Clara said in a tight voice, her hands curling into fists.

I let go of Sloan's hand and stood, my damp shorts trickling water down my legs. "I don't know what beef you think you have with me, Clara, but I should warn you—"

"What beef *I* have with *you?*" Clara laughed, her voice low and tight with anger. "I wouldn't know where to start! You got Tess killed, didn't you? You broke up any chance Benny and I had of getting back together. And you inserted yourself into my family like Queen Shit and just took over, breaking up the whole group! Then there's Sloan here and all you've put her through. I have every reason to hate you, Stormy Spooner. And I do. Believe me, I do."

"I had nothing to do with Benny—" I started, but Clara wasn't stopping to listen. She lunged at me, grabbing me by the hair before I had a chance to finish the sentence, the two of us stumbling on the ledge and tumbling into the shallow water.

I could hear Sloan's muffled shouting from somewhere above us as I fought to untangle my limbs from Clara's vice-like grip. She really was strong. I kicked and tried to wrench myself free, but she held my arms tight, locked in front of me, and as I tried to kick at her, my right leg hit something mechanical and my entire body erupted in bright-hot pain.

My chest was beginning to tighten; I needed to find the surface and breathe. I was rapidly running out of oxygen, my head light and woozy, my uninjured leg still kicking but finding nothing. Her strong arms pinned mine down against my chest, a pressure that made it even harder not to open my mouth and scream, letting the dark water in and drowning me. I flailed uselessly, sparkles of white light appearing behind my eyelids. I was going to lose consciousness soon.

Then, suddenly, hands grabbed me and pulled me upward. Clara's grip tightened even more, then abruptly gave way. A loud grunt sounded in my ears as I hit the water's surface, gasping for air, my eyes flying open just in time to see Clara stagger backward and hit one of the boats with her lower back.

I was pulled back onto the ledge, this time falling into the fetal position, taking a few moments to catch my breath and squeeze the water from my eyes and nose. I turned, expecting to see Phillip, or perhaps Lee or Benny, but Sloan sat there before me, her eyes wide and clear. "Are you okay?" she asked.

I nodded, surprised. "Are you?"

"Yes," she said. "I'm sorry. That I started this." Then her eyes cast upward. My gaze followed hers, unsurprised to see Clara advancing on me again, stepping out of the water onto the ledge, completely undeterred. Jesus, she was strong.

"Clara, please," Sloan said in a pleading voice. "I … I don't want to do this anymore. Let's just sit and talk, okay? We don't need to fight."

"Don't you dare touch me again," I warned, not believing her for a second. I was still panting. "Or you'll regret it."

"Do you think after all this I'm just going to let it go?"

Clara demanded, her face red with anger. "Do you think I'll just let her walk out of here?"

"Please," Sloan said again, but Clara didn't seem to hear her. She reached forward, her hand curled into a claw, her intention clear. She was going to drag me by my hair back into the water. Drown me, most likely. A cold rope of fear wrapped around my heart, but I stared at her head on, raising my cold, wet right hand.

"Benny taught me this," I murmured, saying a silent thank you to my friend as the ball of light made its way down my arm and into my curled hand, hovering there in a little orb, glowing and illuminating the room with the fake monsters. "See? For a long time, I couldn't control it. It just came out whenever it wanted to, whenever I was in danger. But now? Now I know how to use it. When to use it. It's totally within my control. He was right."

Clara smiled. "So you can choose not to use it." Her hand was close enough to touch me. She grabbed a tendril of my hair, wrapping it around her finger, a shudder going through me.

"Yes, I can," I said, holding the tiny glowing orb there in my hands. "But the thing is, Clara, I told you not to touch me again or you'd regret it. You heard me, clear as day. And then you fucking did it anyway."

"Clara," Sloan pleaded again. "Please."

Clara took a step back, her eyes wide, the water sloshing against her as she backed into one of the boats. She grabbed ahold of it, trying to clamber in, but she couldn't get enough leverage. She landed back in the water with a splash. It was as though she'd suddenly realized the magnitude of the situation, that she had no power. "You can't. You wouldn't."

"The old me wouldn't have," I said calmly, twisting my wrist to move my hand round and round the little ball. "But

I'm not that girl anymore. And you've messed with the wrong bitch."

And with that, I threw the ball of light directly into Clara's chest.

She sunk into the water without another word, her body slipping under the water silently, like a ghost. Like she'd never been there at all. Then, after a moment, she resurfaced, face-down, bobbing in the water, her light-purple hair trailing behind her.

I stared at Clara's lifeless body for a moment, watching her faded purple hair flowing in a halo around her head in the murky water. Benny had been right. I could kill too. And now I had.

I turned to Sloan, tears in both our eyes, and shrugged piti-fully. "I'm sorry," I said to my former best friend, watching as one single tear rolled down her cheek. "I did what I had to do. And I'd do it again." I stood up and squared my shoulders. "I forgive you, Sloan."

I swallowed the sob in my throat , and climbed up onto the grass ledge and trudged toward the exit sign to find my chosen family.

The lights came back on right as I hit the exit, the music resuming and the monsters animated, robotic dancing all around me. I found myself face to face with an animatronic spider that loomed down from a phony web and was suddenly laughing. I almost felt giddy as I pushed open the door and stepped out into the sweltering sun.

Outside, it was so bright I had to squint, temporarily blinded after being in the dark for so long. My hair dripped onto my clothes as I looked around. I was in the back of the building, the area where normally only employees were allowed. It was deserted back there, and I made my way down a pathway toward a storage building, hoping to find my way back around front to people.

But first I needed a minute. A minute to collect myself. I sat down right on the grass, looking down at my hands. I had left Clara inside, face down in the water. She was dead; I knew she was. And I'd just ... left her there with Sloan. I had killed her.

What—and who—was I now?

"Stormy!"

I turned, surprised to see Roberta in the doorway of the exit I'd just come out of. She ran over to me, pulling me into a hug. "Fuck, you're dripping wet! What happened?"

"A lot," I said, gulping, watching as Jamie, Nikolai, Beth and several strangers came milling out of the door. Everyone but my friends walked past single file, headed back toward the front.

As one woman passed by, she muttered, "Stupid old equipment. They ought to do regular maintenance on these rides so you wouldn't have them quitting right in the middle."

"We were stopped in the first part of the ride for the longest time," Roberta explained, looking down at my wet clothes, her brows furrowed. "It seemed like an eternity before the boats began to move again, and then when they did, once we got into the second part of the plantation, the lights came on. Then it stopped again, and the employees made us get off the boats and leave through the emergency exit!" Her eyes were wild with excitement. "Security arrested one of the attendants right in front of everybody. It was wild."

"Let me guess—the guy with the ponytail and the thick eyeliner," I said, and she nodded. My shoulders relaxed with something like relief. Phillip had moved fast. Colt Leather was in police custody, and I couldn't be happier.

"They didn't say anything about it, but I'm pretty sure I saw someone floating in the water," Nikolai said in his quiet voice, his eyes meeting mine. "We got worried for a second, worried that it was you."

"Well, I'm fine," I said. "But I know who it is in the water."

"Who?" Beth asked.

It's Clara."

Roberta stared at me, her eyes wide. "You didn't."

"I did."

"Fuck." The words lay unspoken between us, but we just stared at each other, the weight of what I'd done hanging between us in the air.

I opened my mouth to speak, but Roberta knew what I was going to say before I had the chance. "You want to go back in, don't you," she said, and it wasn't really a question. "You want to go in and bring her back."

"Do I have any choice?"

Roberta stared at me for a long moment, then finally shook her head, her curls, damp from the humidity, bobbing against her cheek. "I don't suppose you do. Not if you want to be able to live with yourself."

"Let's go then," I said, grabbing hold of her arm. "Before I change my mind."

As we walked back toward the exit, we heard yelling from inside the plantation. "Hurry!" I shouted, still holding Roberta's arm with one hand and Beth's with the other. I had to get in there and undo what I'd done before Clara's body was discovered, before calls to 911 were made, before people found out—before I lost my chance.

The three of us ran back into the plantation, past the creepy singing monsters and over to the water, where the boats were still suspended, and gaped.

Jamie stood on the little ledge, looking down into the murky water. His face was drawn tight. He looked up at us as we approached. "Did you do this? he asked me, pointing to Clara, who lay floating face down, her purple hair floating listlessly, and I nodded. Nobody had noticed Sloan, who was still sitting on the fake-grass ledge, her head tucked between her knees, rocking back and forth.

"Damn," he said, shaking his head. "Well, we'd better get her out of there and hide her, fast. What should we do with her, y'all?"

It was a little sick, but I couldn't help the flutter in my stomach and the warm feeling that spread through my limbs as I realized that Jamie—and all my other friends at the Wolfden, most likely—were more than willing to just accept that I'd killed someone, someone who had been one of their own, and help me hide the body. No questions asked.

Instead, I shook my head and balled my hand into a fist, a gesture Jamie understood immediately. He stood up and took a step back, his face clouding over. "Are you sure you wanna—"

"She has to, hon," Roberta said, stepping over to him and putting a hand on his shoulder. She pulled him back another few steps to give me space. "She can't leave it like this. She can't leave Clara's death on Sloan's conscience, for one." So she had seen Sloan. I looked at my best friend and gave her a tight, grateful smile.

"I guess you're right," Jamie said reluctantly. "But I kinda hate it for you, Stormy. That girl is a fuckin' bitch."

"She sure fuckin' is," Beth agreed, undoubtedly thinking about the poisoned makeup that had almost done her in.

"Alright," I said, jumping back into the lukewarm water. "Better get it over with." I approached Clara's body with something like reverence, almost afraid to touch her, to look at her. With a gentle hand, I moved to turn her face up so I could see what I was doing. I stopped. "Wait. I can't do this without … I need Phillip. Can somebody find Phillip for me?"

"Phillip's right there, darlin'," Jamie said, pointing.

I looked over at the animatronic ghouls, leering with their monstrous teeth dripping with fake blood, and began to laugh. Standing there amongst the singing monsters, huge and hulking, soaking wet and looking like a demented, furious Frankenstein's monster himself, was Phillip Deville, his hands on his hips, his eyes blazing like fire as he watched me clutching Clara's body.

"You're going to do it again," he said, his tone somewhere between accusatory and awestruck.

I leaned down and pressed my face to Clara's chest, her T-shirt waterlogged, and felt no movement or heartbeat. "I didn't want to kill her, Phillip," I said, my voice starting to crack. The weight of what I'd done began to wash over me. Clara and I had never liked each other. We'd been enemies from the very beginning. And yes, she'd been a total bitch. But she'd been roped into this by Sloan, overcome with jealousy and heartbreak over Benny. She might've been a shitty person, but no matter what she'd done to me, she hadn't deserved to die.

I might be a lot of things—a novice witch, a nosy busybody, sometimes a judgy, indecisive, and co-dependent friend—but I was *not* a cold-blooded killer.

"I know," Phillip said softly, so softly that I couldn't hear him against the loud sloshing of the suspended boats, but I could *feel* his words. I could feel them in my head and all around me, enveloping me like a warm blanket. He was standing yards away, but I could feel his arms around me, tight. "You don't have much time. Do it now. We'll try to keep everyone out."

Thank you, I thought, smiling sadly at Phillip in the low light of the room. I bent back down to Clara's lifeless body, her face serene and peaceful. I could see the heartbreak and pain in her face, and it made me sad. "I don't even know her last name, y'all …"

"It's Jennings," Burt said quietly, putting a hand on my shoulder, then stepping back to give me space. I noticed absently, gratefully, that she stepped over to Sloan, sitting down beside her as she still rocked back and forth. Burt was such a good friend.

I put my hands under the water, on Clara's lower back, and allowed her to float upward as I cradled her, mimicking how one would hold a baby being baptized. When she was suspended in front of me, I removed one hand from her back and made a fist, feeling the power pool in my fingers. I released the fist and let the ball of light linger there in my palm for a moment, becoming rounder and pulsing with a glowing gold light. I closed my eyes, allowing the power course through my veins and into my hands, imagining a magical, invisible tether transporting that power from me into Sloan.

I thought back to the night in my little trailer when I'd melted cinnamon-scented wax, burned sage, and recited a few odd lyrics. I remembered it like it was yesterday. The room almost devoid of air, humid and sultry, the only sound in my ears the odd crackle of lightning and thud of thunder from the impending storm outside, the only light I could see the small, blinking red light of a phone recording. I had recited the spell with intent and purpose, and everything that had happened sense was because of those few lines, spoken by a drunken witch who didn't know she had powers.

I recited the words soundlessly, knowing that everyone in the room could hear me. They could hear me in their heads. A gift from the departed Guthrie that none of us minded anymore.

With salt in air and water in veins

I call the pale rider to loosen his reins
I call for death to loosen his chains
I call for air to return to the breast
I call for fire to ignite the rest
Let what was earthside return once more
Restart the clock, and settle the score
Reanimate the dead flesh of woman
Render **Clara Jennings** alive again.

The lights, which had just come back on moments before, flickered, then went out. Roberta screamed.

"You're soaking wet," Phillip said as he clutched my arm, leading me out of the Monster Plantation. "You said you hit your head? Do you need the paramedics to check you out?"

"I'm fine," I insisted, giving him a look. "It's nothing Benny can't fix. Stop fussing over me, Deville."

"You scared the shit out of me," he said, not ready to be over his anger yet. "I came back in and you were gone, and that bitch was lying face down in the water—" He swallowed, his eyes bright with tears. "I thought you had—"

"I'm fine," I promised. I stopped as we reached the walkway and stood up on tiptoe to kiss his lips. "Phillip, I swear. Stop fretting. I'm okay."

"Alright." He put his hands up in mock surrender, but his eyes betrayed the worry he felt. "I'll stop fussing over you. I'm just so fucking pissed that they ruined our honeymoon. I wanted this day—everything—to be absolutely perfect."

"It is absolutely perfect," I declared, reaching up to brush a lock of his damp hair from his eyes. "They didn't ruin a damn thing. Sloan doesn't have that kind of power. She doesn't have *any* power."

"I love you," Phillip said, his eyes blazing as he looked down at me.

"I love you too." We kissed again, and I was happy to see Phillip smiling for real when he pulled away. I would never forget the splash he'd made, jumping into the water to come and rescue me when the lights had flickered out. When the lights came back on, he was standing beside me, clutching me in his arms, our eyes wide as we realized Clara was staring back at us.

I had still been holding her in the water, suspended, and she'd turned her head to the side, spit out a stream of murky water, and turned back to me, her eyes blazing with anger. "You bitch," she'd said, then wrestled herself from my grasp, standing up in the water and screaming bloody murder.

We hadn't needed to subdue her. Moments later, the paramedics had shown up. Evidently, the employees had seen her body floating in the water and had already called 911. Thankfully, now there was no dead body to greet them. But Clara had done enough yelling and screaming to convince them she wasn't well. Even though she was very much alive, Clara had still been carried out of Six Flags on a stretcher. I hoped she would make a full recovery, but beyond that, I also hoped I'd never see her again.

"The guys found someone who wants to talk to you," Phillip said as we walked, his arm looped through mine.

Down the walkway in front of the carousel were Jason and Ollie, each perched on either side of the park bench. Between them, clutching a wet Wonder Woman mask in her hand and looking like she'd rather be anywhere but here, was Sloan.

"Got something you've been looking for," Ollie called to me gaily as we approached. I noticed that his brand-new Vans were scuffed and dirty; he and Jason must have chased her all around the park.

As we neared the bench, my eyes locked on Sloan, who looked back at me, her eyes clear and wet with tears. "Are you alright?" she asked as I neared her, and I nodded.

"Yes. You?"

"No," Sloan said, her voice choked with tears. Her fingers clutched at the wet mask. "I'm sorry," she said. "About Clara. And Colt. And about … everything else."

"I know."

If there was anything else she wanted to say, it would have to wait. I wasn't hanging around to hear more. I had a honeymoon to finish.

As we walked right past the bench, Phillip's arm still hooked in mine, I turned to him with a grin. "Ready to ride the Scream Machine?" I asked, and he grinned back at me.

"I thought you'd never ask."

"I think it's time we call it a night, guys," Benny said, raising his glass for another toast and downing the last dregs of his whiskey. "Leave these two honeymooners to do what comes naturally." We had invited everyone—Benny, Lee, Jason, Ollie, Roberta, Beth, Nikolai, Jason, and Ollie—up to our suite for a drink. After the events at Monster Plantation, to say nothing of riding coasters all day in the sweltering heat, we'd all been ready to get good and toasted.

Lee groaned, tipping back his beer. "How is it that you're not even thirty and you talk like an old timer in the 1950s."

Benny grinned and poked him in the chest. "Keep it up and you won't get any tonight yourself."

"I'm sorry, lover." Lee leaned in for a kiss that Benny returned readily.

Phillip's arm grew tighter around my waist. I could feel his thoughts, and they were none too innocent. Benny was right. It was time for everyone to go. I put a hand to my mouth and gave a theatrical yawn. "I am pretty tired," I said regretfully.

"You're the worst fucking actress on the planet, Stormy," Roberta said, standing up and taking her glass to the kitchenette, where she rinsed it out and sat it on the counter. "But I'll forgive it since you're on your honeymoon. Come on, y'all. Let's leave the old witch bitch to her man."

"Thanks, Burt," I said, putting my hand to my heart. "You really know what to say to make me feel so warm and fuzzy inside."

"I love you, beyotch," she said in response, grabbing Jamie's arm and tugging him to the door. "Bye."

"Love you too," I said after her, then turned to the rest of my friends. "I love you all too. I hope you know that."

"We do," Nikolai said, coming over to give me a hug. "We're heading out too."

"Call me when you get there," I said, smiling down at Beth, happy they were together. "It's a long drive back."

"We're flying back to Boston tomorrow," Jason said after getting his own hug. "But we'll all be back together soon enough. We've got a tour to plan!" His voice lowered and he looked at me. "But first ... Would you mind, Stormy, if I ... if I visited that girl Clara in the hospital before I left?"

I looked at him in surprise. "No, I wouldn't mind. Why do you ask?"

"I just thought ... Well, I feel like I understand her in some weird way," Jason said, shrugging. He looked embarrassed. "Other than Phillip, she's the only other person who ... who knows what it's like. To come back. I keep thinking about her, alone in the hospital ... Is that wrong?"

We had all been saddened, but not surprised, to find that Clara was in the hospital. Not because of any physical injuries —she'd easily overtaken me at Monster Plantation, and I'd never stood a chance in that regard—but because she was clearly unwell. I wasn't at all surprised when Benny told me she'd checked herself into an outpatient program to address some mental health issues. I sincerely wished her well but still hoped I never saw her again.

The name Colt Leather had been trending on social media for hours now. A crude cellphone video of his arrest outside of the Monster Plantation attraction had cropped up and immediately gone viral, circulating across news outlets. It was just another in a long list of scandals and fuck ups the former Necrofeelya singer had brought on himself in the past year or so, and from the looks of it, his goose was well and truly cooked. I didn't know how long he'd be in jail, but he'd have plenty of time to read his serial killer books and mull over the death of his music career — and to come up with more shitty band names — that was for sure.

As for Sloan, she'd also checked herself in to rehab. Looking back, I should have seen the signs that she had a drinking problem—and one with drugs as well, thanks to Tess —but I'd been so caught up in my own bullshit I'd never really thought about it. I hoped she was getting much needed therapy too, something I myself planned to seek out as soon as I had a chance to breathe. Thinking all of it through, I'd reached a decision. "Only if you don't judge me for visiting Sloan when I get back to Brunswick."

"You're a good one, Spooner," he said, pulling me in for a hug.

"So are you, Langley." I grinned, grabbing Ollie to envelop him in a hug too. "Did you get those girls' numbers from Six Flags? Maybe you can invite them to the show."

"On it," Ollie said with a laugh.

Soon it was just me, Phillip, Benny, and Lee. Phillip opened the sliding glass window to let in the night breeze, stepping out onto the balcony for a moment to take in the stars. I'd join him there soon, but first, I needed to say something to my friend.

Lee was tidying the suite, picking up the candy wrappers and beer bottles that had been scattered around the little table. "Leave it, Lee," I said, looking at him gratefully. "I'll take care of it later."

"No, you won't, because I'm doing it now."

I walked over and put an arm around him, pulling him close for a clumsy hug. "I love you best, you know," I said softly in his ear as he clutched the empty beer bottles to his chest. "After Phillip, I mean. You're my favorite. Even if you did kidnap me that one time."

"I love you too, girl," he said, his eyes bright. "You're my best friend. Even though you zapped my dad with your magic hands."

"I guess we're even," I said with a laugh, giving him a sloppy kiss on the cheek.

"Even Stevens," Lee said with a grin.

"At least it's all over now," I said hopefully as Lee deposited the bottles in the recycling bin. I smiled. "Well and truly over. Though I have to say, if Elvin wasn't dead, I'd bring him back to life and kill him all over again just for putting all of us through so much."

"I mean, I'm just sayin', between the two of us, we actually have the power to do that." Benny was grinning as he leaned against the doorway, his eyes flashing mischievously. "We really could."

"Now *that's* an idea," I said, raising my eyebrows.

"Bring him back from the dead just to kill his ass again," Benny said, throwing back his head with a hearty laugh. "Just as a treat."

A jet-black head poked in through the window from the balcony, the eyes blazing with fire, the face a picture of annoyance. "Don't you even *think* about it, Spooner."

I looked at my husband, my very own dead rock star, Phillip Deville, with doe-eyed innocence. "Who, me?" I said, and he glowered.

Epilogue

"Can I interest you in some chicory coffee and beignets?" I pushed my sunglasses up and opened my eyes, staring up at Phillip, who loomed over me holding a grease-covered bag and two paper cups. I sat up on the beach towel, pulling my cover-up over my shoulders, and took the cup gratefully.

"That smells heavenly," I said, taking a sip of the dark, rich coffee. Phillip sat down beside me, directly in the sand, and reached into the crumbled bag, pulling out a huge beignet glistening with sugar. My mouth began to water.

"It's vegan," he said, holding the delectable pastry up to my mouth as I took a huge bite, closing my eyes in sheer bliss. "I bought every last one they had. Reinforcements for today."

"Good call," I said, my mouth full. I smiled as he sat back and picked up his dog-eared copy of *Prince Lestat*. He had borrowed the entire series from Beth, who had been only too happy to talk all things vampire with him every chance they got, which it turned out was often, since she was now on tour with the band. Beth, the Bloomer Demons hooper, now famous in her own right, even had her own line of merch.

"Have you heard from anyone? Jason or the guys? Lee?

Benny?" I knew vaguely that Jason had visited Clara, who hadn't really been interested in getting to know him, something that didn't surprise me. Between her hangup over Benny, and her burgeoning, not-a-little-bit toxic relationship with Sloan, she likely didn't have the bandwidth for anyone new. Jason had gone back to Boston, licking his wounds, but I knew he'd be okay.

"Not a soul," Phillip said, laying back onto the sand, propping himself up with one arm, opening his book. I marveled how he just made himself comfortable anywhere. "They know not to contact us under threat of death."

I sat my coffee down and lay back with him, though thankfully, I had a beach towel under me. Phillip might like roughing it, but I didn't feel like digging sand out of my bikini bottoms for the next two weeks. I glanced over at him as he began to read, plonked in the sand as if he'd sprung out of it fully formed, skin pale white against his black swimming trunks, his hair pulled back in a messy half-bun, and began to laugh. He certainly made a picture, lying there devouring The Vampire Chronicles—he'd managed to catch up on the entire series over the past two weeks and only had one book left, with plans to binge the TV series next—without a care in the world. Being a man of leisure suited him.

Every day since we'd arrived home after our wedding, Phillip and I had gone to the beach. The beauty of living in Brunswick meant we were close to Jekyll, but Tybee Island and St. Simons Island were reasonably close too, so we'd decided to alternate between all three, waking up every morning and just heading wherever the wind—or our own whims—decided to take us. We'd surfed on Tybee (well, Phillip had; I'd mainly taken pictures of him and jeered when he'd fallen off his surfboard), sketched the horizon out on St. Simons, and laid around the cool, muted beaches of Jekyll. When we weren't on the beach, we'd gone bird watching, had taken a helicopter ride *and* a boat tour, and we'd even managed to spend one sizzling night in the jacuzzi at a local motel (and left to go back home later that evening because the both of us were genuinely sick of motels for the foreseeable future). It wasn't a real honeymoon, but it'd been the perfect thing for us. After all, Phillip and I had spent the first several weeks of our relationship traveling all over, dodging threats, chasing others, and doing everything *but* the normal stuff new couples do. We hadn't gotten to date, spend days together in bed, or have long talks where we got to know each other. We'd never gotten to grill out together, go flea marketing, or see a movie.

More than any expensive trip or cruise or the like, we just wanted that. Normalcy.

I glanced down at my phone, blissfully happy to see that I had no new notifications, missed calls or texts. Everything was quiet on this front. That was down to our wonderful friends at the Wolfden, who knew how badly we craved privacy and alone time, and were making damn sure we got it. I knew, though, that once we were ready to be "back in the world" again, they'd be there for me. For us.

Lee hadn't called once with news about the upcoming tour, though tickets were already sold out and that the press was dying for Phillip to do publicity. So far, Nate, Ollie, and Benny were handling things, but soon enough, Phillip would have to re-emerge.

The tour would begin next month, and so, too, I hoped, would my writing career. I had the blog planned out, the pitch already accepted, and I also planned to start writing a memoir of sorts, just to see what panned out. I might turn it into fiction to protect the innocent (and not so innocent) or I might cast off the shackles and speak my truth. I wasn't sure yet, but I was sure that I wanted to write.

At my feet was a notebook full of Benny's loopy scrawl, all the research he'd done on the "lore," what little there was, that our magic was comprised of. I'd read it a bit here and there, but I'd yet to really dive in to discover what made us *us*, where our magic originated from, and how it was best used. From what I'd seen from skimming through the notebook, Benny was right—there was no real rhyme or reason to the abilities that I possessed. It seemed that people like me (and Benny and Lydia and Beth) simply manifested our own abilities through coping mechanisms we'd used, little self-made recipes that we'd developed for ourselves when we'd been vulnerable and in need of protection. Basically, our own anxieties, our fight or flight, had manifested itself into a kind of real power—magic. We had adapted, or maybe evolved, depending on how you looked at it, to tap into an alternate, magical reality to defend ourselves when it was needed. And perhaps that meant that in the future, more people would have the same kind of ability. It was a thought that brought me some comfort. I kept thinking of a phrase I'd heard once, *the mind is kind,* and it seemed the body, when it worked in tandem with the mind, was too. Somehow, I'd managed to manifest powers into myself that ensured I'd always be protected, would always be safe, and that I wouldn't be alone. And maybe one day, others would have that same power of protection.

I had brought Phillip into my life; had manifested him. And I would never, ever let him go.

I grabbed the rest of the beignet from the bag and stuffed it into my mouth, savoring the fried, doughy sweetness, gulping it down with coffee. Sloan popped into my mind suddenly, as she often did when I was enjoying a delicious meal or beverage, especially coffee. She and I had shared our favorite coffee spot and those late-morning brunches and early boozy dinners for so many years that it was hard to banish her from my mind, even more so when something wonderful was on the table. She was doing an inpatient rehab program at a local facility, and she was allowed visitors, the nurse had told me over the phone.

I hadn't visited her yet—I was taking my time to decide what I really wanted to do, not to mention enjoying my little local-honeymoon—but I planned to eventually. What I'd say to her, I had no idea. When I told her I forgave her, I'd meant that. But I hadn't *forgotten*. I never could. Still … I knew, deep in my heart, that my story with Sloan was not over. I could not give up on her; my heart wouldn't allow me to.

There was more to talk about. Much, much more. To work on. To work through.

Just not yet.

I banished thoughts of Sloan and the past from my brain and leaned back on an elbow, staring out at the water. It was choppy today, the wind picking up a little blue-haired boy's kite and throwing it high into the air.

The sky near the horizon was a splotch of dark in the otherwise sunny sky. There was a rumor of storms tomorrow. Oh well, that meant Phillip and I would just have to spend the whole day in bed. My lower belly throbbed at the thought of all I planned to do to him.

Phillip chuckled, licking his finger, and then turning the page, not noticing me crinkle my nose up in disgust. I wasn't sure if he was chuckling at the book or the illicit thoughts I'd just been having.

"You old man," I teased, reaching out to poke him in the chest. "Don't lick your finger then touch the book; that's nasty."

"Shhh," he said in a mock whisper, pursing his lips. "I'm at the good part." He chuckled again, then looked at me. "That Lestat sure does think highly of himself, doesn't he?"

"Well, they don't call him 'the Brat Prince' for nothing," I said. "But why do you say that?"

"He thinks he can have his cake and eat it too," Phillip said, pausing to look at me. "Not only is he devilishly hand-some, but he's managed to cheat death, everyone wants to be his lover, he's got a coven of loyal friends who'd die for him, he's been a rock star, seen Heaven and Hell, and that's not enough for him; no, he has to become the literal prince of the vampires." He threw back his head and laughed, his green eyes flashing under the midday sun, his black hair damp from the ocean. "He intends to have it all, and anyone who stands in his way, well, Devil be damned."

"Sounds like someone else I know," I said, and waited to kiss the inevitable smirk right off Phillip Deville's face.

ACKNOWLEDGMENTS

As ever, my deepest thanks go to Elizabeth Tankard, Dead Rockstar's "biggest fan" and inspiration for Beth the Hooper, the Bloomer Demons newest hype girl! Thanks for always believing in this story and for loving Phillip Deville, Stormy Spooner, Benny the Black Wolf, and the rest of the motley crew as much, if not more, as I do. Holding you to that tattoo!

"It's me again, Margaret"—thanks to Jessica Johnson for always being the best cheerleader, the best "sister from another mister" I'll ever have, the Blanche to my Dorothy, the Samantha Jones to my Miranda Hobbes, and the Ray Stevens to my Judy Blume ("Are you there, god? It's me again, Margaret"). And thanks for giving me a godson, who I named a certain pesky reporter after!

To Jennia Herold D'Lima, editor extraordinaire: I can't believe (yes I can because it was a choice!) you've edited all my books but one. You've been such a great help and support over the years, and I'm glad we've been able to work on all these books together. I feel like our love of Type O, Pepe le Pew and all things spooky and grunge have bonded us and I couldn't be happier for it! Thanks for loving this little trilogy and for being a champion for me when the imposter syndrome is kicking in!

To Lauren Emily Whalen, my friend of over 15 years, fellow black cat owner, and co-author extraordinaire! I can't wait for us to be in the writing trenches together again, with all the iced coffee, lengthy voice note sagas and goth-pop hybrid music we can stand to get us through!

My deepest, most sincere thanks also go to:

Amanda Wright, who originally took a chance on this odd little story about an (un)dead rockstar, then later drew him to life; Elle Beaumont, Lou Wilham and the team at Midnight Tide Press; Laura Ellen Burke, Amelia Ross, Rae Standridge, Daryn Cash, for all the sexy gay pirate and sexy gay vampire memes (and for 20+ years of friendship which is almost as an important), Kelley Lawson, Bailey Nix, Dylan Britton, Brat (I mean Bart) Johnson, Jordan Rothacker, Tracy Adkins, Emily Edwards, Cate Short, Micah and Tanya Hudson, Megan's Bookish Life, Madison County and Oconee County Libraries, and the many people who have supported my writing over the years by buying books and attending events! Your support means more than you know.

As always, thanks to my parents, John and Teresa, my Nonna Anita, my brothers Chris and Jonathan, and to my son and future rockstar, Callum: I couldn't do any of this without you.

In honor of the dearly departed Nicolae Lisowski and Jesse Lynn Campbell.

And, finally, in honor of Peter Steele, former frontman of Type O Negative and the inspiration for Phillip Deville.

About the Author

Lillah Lawson is the author of novels Monarchs Under the Sassafras Tree (2019; nominated for Georgia Author of the Year 2020); So Long, Bobby (February 2023); The Dead Rockstar Trilogy ('20-'24); and Tomorrow & Tomorrow with Lauren Emily Whalen (October 2023).

Lillah enjoys writing across genres, specializing in historical fiction, southern gothic, and horror. She also writes a monthly column for her local newspaper. In addition to writing, Lillah works at a non-profit, is a genealogist pursuing her BA in History and English Literature, and proudly serves as secretary on her local library's Board of Trustees. An avid music lover, she's happiest at metal shows. She lives just outside of Athens, Georgia, with her husband, teenager, and two fur friends.

Also by Lillah Lawson

The Dead Rockstar Trilogy

Dead Rockstar

The Wolfden

Driftwood Dreary

Standalones

Monarchs Under the Sassafras Tree

So Long, Bobby

Tomorrow and Tomorrow

Doomed Girls of Jefferson (January '25)

The Vamp (September '25)

More Books You'll Love

If you enjoyed this story, please consider leaving a review!

Then check out more books from Midnight Tide Publishing!

The Hex Next Door by Lou William

What's a little necromancy between family?

For the Crow Witch, Icarus "Rus" Ashthorne, Moondale seemed the perfect hiding place. But like they always say, you can't go home again, and Rus finds out quickly that nothing is how she remembered, while at the same time very little has changed. Then she comes face to face with the only woman she's ever loved, Az Elwood, and... well, things get messier than she thought they ever could.

The Elwoods are a staple of Moondale, respected, feared, powerful, and Azure Elwood was always happy with her place amongst them. Happy to play the part of the good little witch, until Rus Ashthorne. Eleven years ago, Rus got on a bus and left Azure behind, but she's back, with two little girls trailing her like ducklings, and enough unspoken things between them to drown the town.

Now witch hunters are knocking at their proverbial door, the council of magic is being a real pain in the ass, and Rus wonders how much magic it'll take to protect the people she loves from herself and the danger following her.

Available Now